The firing stopped.

The only sounds inside the Toyota were the panting of Megan's breath, and her frantic tugging. From outside in the darkness came the clicks of car doors opening and softly chunking closed. She gave up pulling on what she thought was the seat lever and squirmed in the small cramped space, desperately working a hand underneath her into the backpack, looking for the gun.

She had just gotten her fingertip on something cold and hard when she sensed them just outside, six shadows standing on the grass beyond the curb and looking down on her, blotting out the stars. Heard them muttering amongst themselves.

Then, the passenger door scraped loudly across the curb and dug a wide trench into the grass and the dirt, and Megan lifted her head to look up at the pants and shoes of the men who would kill her.

She felt an urge to swallow, that for some reason, she fought hard to resist.

"Stiff upper lip, kiddo," she heard her father say.

"Don't ever let them see you cry," Mom added.

She rolled her eyes to look up at the indiscernible faces above her, seeing only an arm extending into the circle of light, with a fist at the end of it and a gun in that fist, aimed at her eye, inches away.

Also by the Author

Thy Neighbor's Wife

Alexander Ferrar

This is a work of fiction. All of the characters portrayed in this book are fictitious, and any resemblance to real people or events is purely coincidental. Should any resemblance seem apparent between characters or events in this book and you or your own life, a long hard look in the mirror and subsequent therapy is highly recommended. Freak.

THY NEIGHBOR'S WIFE

ISBN: 1718624182

Published by Bunbury

First edition: June 2012
Second Edition: March 2014
Third Edition: January 2017

Cover art and design by Alexander Ferrar

A Note on the Text

The words herein were set in Palangana Retroscript, a font first devised by the early Christians in their efforts to distance themselves from the Jews, committing subtle acts of subliminal sedition using curliques and suchlike, usually accenting letters like the lowercase G. It was later used as an ironic homage by the Illuminati against the very Church that originated it, and then by the French Resistance during World War 2. The practice of using Palangana for seditious means has fallen by the wayside, for 60-some-odd years, until now. Together we stand. Death to the (fill in the blank) !

www.alexferrar.com

This novel is dedicated to the ghost of the unidentified woman whose life ended under similar circumstances, causing the blackout in Tampa, circa 1997. May she find peace.

Prologue

Rabbit came bopping out of a store in a shopping center, packing his cigarettes against his palm, and Blue Tick looked down at him and asked "Are you ready?" The little man with the snazzy suit and the moviestar hair grinned. He was nervous and trying not to show it, and anybody else would've been fooled, but Tick had been his henchman for years, and knew better. "When'd you start smoking again?"

"I'm not. I'm just going to have a few because she smokes, and I can't stand the smell or the taste of a smoker if I'm not smoking too."

"Good thinking," the muscle-bound skinhead said, nodding, hoping his sarcasm wasn't too subtle.

Rabbit lit the first cigarette and took a long drag to get into character. His expression grew thoughtful.

"Yunno what I heard someone say a minute ago? It was a bit disturbing. 'The children of single mothers grow up knowing what'll get them laid.' I had to think about that for a bit. But yeah, if Mom's coming home with some new guy all the time, the girls see how she acts and, when they come of age, follow her example, and the boys watch the jackass she comes home with and start to imitate him. The cycle continues—"

He jerked forward suddenly as if elbowed in the gut, his eyes going wide behind his sunglasses.

"What is it?" Tick asked, but then he remembered.

Rabbit felt a horrible sudden coldness inside of him, and gasped out a quick Excuse me. Dropping the cigarette, he turned and hurried toward the long corridor that led to the restrooms. Tick shook his head slowly, thinking If they *always* upset his stomach, why does he always start up again? *Always?*

He nodded slightly to the piped-in muzak he didn't consciously notice was playing, and thought about the sweeping generalization Rabbit had just made, and how it didn't apply to everybody. He made a note to tell him that when he got out.

A moment passed and his cell phone rang. There was only one person it could be, since hardly anyone had these fancy new things yet, except for people like him. He rolled his eyes, expecting to be asked to run go get Imodium.

"Yello?"

"Tick! There's a big guy coming out with a green shirt and a baseball cap on backwards. The shirt says STP. Grab him!"

"What? What do you mean 'grab him'?"

"Grab him and put him in the van and take him to the house in the woods! I'll meet you there!"

"Are you serious? We have a lot to do today."

Blue Tick saw a guy that matched the description coming out of the corridor, and sizing him up quickly, he saw the guy could fight to some extent, but not with any real skill, and he was a bit arrogant. He sighed, thinking Not again. Not now.

Rabbit had already hung up, so Tick followed the guy out to where the cars were parked.

Maybe an hour later, that guy was tied to a chair and telling Tick what would happen if he wasn't let go *this minute*, and the little man with the moviestar hair came in. The guy stared.

"You!"

"Yeah," Rabbit said. "Me."

"What the hell's going on here? You got—"

"Shut up until I'm finished talking, asshole. Since you are officially a captive audience, you're going to listen hard to my question and give me an honest-to-God answer or I'm going to kill you, right now."

"You can't be serious."

"I've got you tied to a chair."

The guy swallowed hard.

"Now, in that bathroom, there were five urinals. Five. And one stall. Why in God's name if there were five urinals did you have to piss, standing up, all over the toilet instead?"

"Is *that* what this is about?"

"Yeah, it is. Because I had to wait for you, I almost made a mess all over myself, and you didn't even need to be there. And when you came out, the entire seat was wet. You couldn't lift the lid? You couldn't clean it off? You left your piss all over the place for me to clean up before I could sit down, and you gave me that little smirk of Go fuck yourself as you were walking out because you knew I was temporarily handicapped and couldn't whup your ass until I got out of that stall. So what is it? Are you a dog marking your territory?"

"Oh my God. I can't believe—"

Rabbit reached behind him up under his jacket and pulled out a James Bond-style Walther PPK with obligatory silencer, and put it to the man's forehead.

"Can you believe it now?"

The man shut up, his eyes crossed looking up at the barrel.

"So think very hard. Why did you do it?"

"I…I don't know."

"That's a child's answer to an angry parent. Act like a man and take responsibility. Act like your life depends on it."

"I…I don't like to go in the urinal. I don't want faggots to see my dick."

Rabbit and Blue Tick both rolled their eyes, and the smaller man backed off with the gun.

"If that's the best you can do, then we'll give you a taste of your own medicine. Tick, pee on him."

"…What?" Blue Tick asked.

"You heard me. Right in his ugly face. And get some in his hair, too. And on his shirt."

"*You* pee on him."

"I already went, remember? I got nothing left."

"Oh, come on."

"I'm serious."

"But why?"

"Because he has to learn, and if I let him off easy, he'll just go and do it again. You know what they say: lessons not learnt in blood are soon forgotten. He has to know that his actions affect other people, and think about how he might just ruin somebody else's day with something as careless as this."

"But we're going to kill him either way."

The captive's eyes went even wider.

"Yeah, but I've been reading this philosopher lately who says that if reincarnation is real, and we die under especially unpleasant circumstances, we will carry that memory into our next life. By that rationale, this guy will enter his next life with an emphatic surety that pissing on toilet seats is not just wrong, but a really bad idea, without a conscious memory of why, and maybe he will teach his children not to do it, and the world will be a slightly better place."

"Don't we have to be somewhere?"

"Quit trying to change the subject."

The giant man heaved a sigh, making a big production of obeying reluctantly, which was comical considering his size in comparison to Rabbit's. Gnashing his teeth, he unzipped his pants. The captive tensed up and held his breath, scrunching his eyes and mouth shut, and braced himself.

The leaves of trees outside rattled against the house, and the ticking of the second hand on Rabbit's watch was suddenly very loud, five ticks going by before the man in the chair's eyes cracked open ever so slightly.

"Well?" Rabbit asked.

"I can't," Tick said quietly.

"What do you mean, you *can't?*"

"What do you think I mean? I can't."

"Why the hell not?"

"He's…he's looking at it."

"Oh, for Christ's sake."

"You can stop looking at it, too, yunno."

"You're three hundred twenty pounds of muscle and you can't pee on a guy because he's looking at you. That's rich."

"I ain't doing this," the big man said, tucking himself hurriedly back in and sulking while Rabbit shook his head.

The guy strapped to the chair was starting to chuckle, until Rabbit put his gun to the sweaty forehead and muttered "This is your lucky day, after all."

And pulled the trigger.

The sound of the exit wound was louder than the *ping!* of the suppressed gunshot, but both were drowned out by the collective gasp from all the other people tied-up in the room.

"I gotta be somewhere," Rabbit said, turning to face the five young men whose eyes bulged over gags that held their mouths shut. "But I'll be back before too long, so don't get too comfortable."

I

"The essential American character
is hard, isolate, stoic, and a killer."
—DH Lawrence

"Motherfucker," she said, pushing up her glasses.

Phil and Emmy blinked at her. There were two customers in the store at the time, flipping through stacks of vinyl, and they both turned to look at her, and then at each other.

"It's too vague," she continued. "*Used* to mean something, but now I hear it in comparison to everything. And *anything*. I'll hear a guy say that the test he took in class today was hard as a motherfucker, and then go onto some other topic, such as dating, picking up some chick at a keg party, and then he'll say she's as easy as a motherfucker. Well, what the hell *is* a motherfucker, then?"

Phil and his wife, Emily, both pursed their lips and blinked some more, suffering the girl. This was not unusual.

"And what brings this up," she went on. "While you two were at lunch, there were these three guys in here earlier, and when they found this bootleg CD of Mike Patton they were talking excitedly about how that motherfucker was badder'n a motherfucker. So, now that you're back, could you please explain to me the logic in that? By the look on both your faces, you are as lost as I am, so here's my way of remedying the problem. I'm going to write to our congressman, asking him to motion a bill to propose an internationally agreed-upon, set-in-stone, standard unit of measurement that will be concrete and unwavering, known as Motherfucker."

The two owners of the store, Big Beat Records, and both of the customers, stared at the one and only employee. She had gotten used to these long silences, and was no longer offended when her solutions went unappreciated. She gave her catchphrase sigh of exasperation and went to sit on her stool behind the cash register, underneath the picture she'd taken of herself and mounted on a card marked "Employee of the Month." Her audience raised their eyebrows and shook their heads. The customers returned to their browsing and her bosses went to the office in the back that overlooked the music store, neither of them saying a word.

She picked up a pen and tapped a beat with it against her counter, wondering if she was the only sane one in the world.

Her name was officially Bonnie Ophelia Delaune, but she called herself Megan because it suited her better. She was not beautiful, but she wasn't plain or ugly, either. She had the kind of face that could not ever be called sensual, enticing, delicate, or even cute, but she was attractive. She was not petite, but she was short and slim. Her face wasn't necessarily aquiline, aristocratic, or even patrician, whatever the hell that is, but it was dignified and intelligent and of the type that would continue to be whatever else it was even when she'd grown old.

In short, she looked like a Megan. How she'd been named Bonnie made no sense to her at all, and it was the only exception to the rule that she was convinced governed looks; regardless of genes and hereditary physical traits, people grew up looking like their names. There were no dashing and devilishly handsome womanizers named Marvin. There were no dentists or accountants or insurance salesmen named Val. And try as you might, you will never ever ever meet a graffiti artist wigger named Irving or an amateur bullfighter named Clive.

All little girls named Lisa or Heather would grow up to be heartbreakers, and all girls named Peggy, well, wouldn't. There were absolutely no librarians named Trixie, no strippers named Beatrice, and *definitely* no crack whores named Eleanor Lynn Barrington, and no big-time gangsters named Barnaby Snodgrass.

Megan secretly wished she could have been named Ashley McLachlin but her dad had told her to wish in one and shit in the other and see which hand filled up first.

Thanks, Dad.

A jingling came from the front door swinging open. She glanced up as a man walked in who just had to be named Jack or Tom. He *had* to be. She didn't have the breath to greet him and welcome him into the store and ask to be of any assistance. She just stared as he wandered in past her.

Tom or Jack was on the short side of medium height and, while not a hunk, was definitely gorgeous in her eyes. He wore a beige suit with a silver shirt that had the top three buttons open, and she could see the hints of a very nice chest through the V. His skin was tan, his hair and goatee dark gold and sun bleached with streaks that looked like he worked all day in the sun, but not before he'd combed lemon juice through it.

Not like she'd know anything about that, of course. This time around, her own hair was black. Her eyes were blue or gray or hazel, depending on what she wore or what mood she was in. Right now they were quickly turning blue.

He didn't notice her, which wasn't really a surprise, she thought. He was scanning the shelves for something in particular. Her spirits fell when she saw the wedding band, and she figured it was just as well. While she watched him, she wondered if she should start wearing her hair differently or put on makeup or stop dressing so conservatively. Or maybe start wearing dresses instead of her tight jeans and men's shirts and sweaters. Maybe wear nicer glasses too.

Tom or Jack, or maybe Brad, didn't find what he was looking for, picked up something else instead and brought it over, reading the back of it while he approached. When he got to her little station he looked up to ask her something and froze. His eyes were wide and green, and he stared at her as if he recognized her from somewhere.

What the—? She'd definitely have known if she'd seen him before, but he was suddenly embarrassed and at a loss for words. His lips had parted when their eyes met, and he remembered to close them when he tried to recover himself. He looked away and cleared his throat. Looked back at her, opened his mouth, and closed it again. Swallowed.

"Hi," he said.

"Um...hello. Can I help you find something?"

She didn't know what the hell all of this was about, and she was starting to think she had Tommy here pegged wrong.

He blushed, looked down at the CD jewel case in his hand. He *blushed*. His tanned face flamed scarlet. Then he scowled and twisted his mouth in disgust. Nodded as if agreeing with some voice in his head.

"Figures," he muttered. "Finally happens and I've gotta screw it up." He dropped the jewel case on the counter and it clattered loudly as he went to the glass door, pushed on it and walked out, the two big jingle bells that swung on a red braided rope from the handle ringing in mockery.

Megan went about the rest of her day, selling CDs and records and taking her cigarette breaks outside every fifteen, twenty minutes. Every now and then she'd remember the guy and wonder. Probably a nutcase. You can't judge a book, she thought, 'specially these days.

During a lull, she read a scientific study about the surprising discovery some folks had made with the chimps they were studying. Apparently, there is a grape-flavored drink that they love so much that they are willing to use it as money. They will trade certain amounts of it for something they want, and the kicker is that they will trade all of it for an opportunity to look at photos of the other chimps that rank higher in their tribe, or family, or whatever it was called. Hmm, she thought. Kind of like us with celebrity magazines.

When five o'clock rolled around, Phil came out from the office where Megan hadn't seen either his or Emmy's faces in the window for at least two hours. The skin around his mouth was pink and irritated. Megan suppressed a laugh. Not bad for an old-timer, she thought.

"Are you still here?" he asked good naturedly, feigning contempt.

"Someone had to watch the place."

"Anybody buy anything?"

"Eh, a few."

"Well why don't you punch your card and get lost? Surely you have better things to do."

"Oh yeah. Rent a movie and get take-out. Do my laundry. Maybe dye my hair again. Fun fun fun."

"You want to come over for dinner later?"

"No thanks."

"Emily's making lasagna."

"Appreciate it, but I can only be the third wheel so many times."

"Suit yourself. Go on and scram; we'll close up."

"Night, Phil." She got her bag and headed for the door. "Try not to sprain anything, you old goat."

She went out onto the sidewalk and stopped dead.

Whatshisname stood a little ways down the sidewalk, draping his jacket over the spindle back of a chair next to a café's outdoor table, one of those black iron "ice-cream" sets, gesturing to someone inside. She started toward him as he sat with his back against the plate glass front wall, lighting a cigarette. Before she got to him, a waiter appeared and took his order, and when she arrived at his table he looked up and jumped a little in surprise.

"Make that two," she said, and plopped down in a chair.

The waiter vanished back inside, and Whatshisname reached over with a long kitchen match to light Megan's cigarette, striking it with his thumbnail and looking oh so cool.

"Mm, thank you," she said, puffing it to life.

"It'd be best if you left," he said.

"I'm in no hurry to get anywhere. What's your name?"

"I'm Nick." Not Jack. Oh well. "What's yours?"

"Megan."

"Hi, Megan. Nice to meet you."

"Pleasure's mine," she said, blowing smoke at him.

"I'm married, Megan."

"Congratulations."

"Thanks. It'd be best if you'd leave."

"What, do you think I'm here to throw myself at you, or something?"

"No."

"Are you so sure of yourself that you think I *must* have you?"

"Not at all."

"Good. So why all the drama earlier?"

"I thought I'd seen you somewhere before."

"Ah. Is the confusion over now?"

"No," he let out a perfect smoke ring, and another.

"What do you mean? We don't know each other."

"No. But I've seen you. Look, don't waste your time—"

The waiter came out with four lowball Cuba Libres on a tray and set two in front of each of them. Megan was surprised.

"I didn't know that's what you ordered," she said when the waiter had gone again. Nick shrugged, picking up one of the glasses and draining it one long go. She was even more surprised. "Whoa, hold your horses there. It's only five o'clock."

"Time is relative," he said. "It's midnight somewhere."

"Are you an alcoholic? None of my business, I know, but—"

"No, I'm not. I'm just drinking until I can make a rational decision."

Oh really? "Oh, well, shit. That's the way to do it, I guess."

"It'd be best if you'd leave."

"That's the third time you've said that. I have to know why."

"You'll think I'm nuts."

"I already do. Tell me."

"It's stupid."

"Come on. You'll never see me again, so why worry about it?"

He looked at her a moment. "That's exactly why I'm worried."

"Oh, come *on*."

"Look! It's stupid and it's crazy and it doesn't make any sense…screw it, I'll tell you. It's creepy as hell, but…I've been seeing you in my dreams."

He didn't give her a chance to think about it, let it sink it. He kept on, running his words together, but she was automatically wondering whether or not she *wanted* to believe him. The way she always half-wanted to believe in ghosts, telepathy, or anything fantastic.

"—for the past couple of years, no matter what I'm doing in my dream, I come across you. You're always in bed, resting, tired and irritable, sick with something, but I don't know what. I've wondered about it and figured you must be always sick because you won't get out of the bed. You're always lying there, waiting to get better, and you never do."

"You're not a major figure in my dreams, but you're always in them. Well, for the past couple of months, I've been nervous around you. I feel like I did when I was a boy and there was a pretty girl who'd always be screwing with me, starting unnecessary arguments. Do you know what I mean? Well, my mom told me it was because she liked me, and that made no sense at all, but that's the thing I'd be wondering after that, always arguing with her, thinking *Does she like me?* And if she does, what am I supposed to do? Just lunge and grab her and kiss her? And that's what I've been wondering lately in my dreams. Do you like me? Should I make a move, and if I should, how? And what if I'm wrong?"

"And, well, the night before last, I threw caution to the wind and just reached down—you were on a futon cluttered with stuff in the middle of a cramped hallway—and I grabbed you and pressed my lips against yours, cutting you off in mid-sentence. For one split second you were surprised, but I could hear your thoughts as if they were on the air, as if you were broadcasting them, and you were like *It's about goddamned time!* And we were kissing so passionately. I haven't felt anything so hot as your kisses, even with my own wife. Not in years."

She was listening with her eyes wide and her lips parted.

"I was tingling all over, all my short hairs standing on end. It felt like your lips were water after I'd crawled through a desert, the way I'd suck the lower and the upper, from one to the other and back again, and when your tongue would dart out to tease mine, I'd get a jolt of this deliciously electrifying...God, I can't describe it! But it was so hot, so incredibly passionate, and then I opened my eyes—not my dream eyes, but my real eyes—and I was making out with my pillow."

Megan burst out laughing, and Nick shook his head with a little smile of embarrassment, a face that read yes, it's funny now, but it sure wasn't then. He changed the tone of the story to follow her change in mood.

"Yeah, I tried to close my eyes and slip back into the dream, but I knew it was my pillow I was mashing my lips against, my tongue coming out to lick, and that kind of ruined it. And then, of course, I looked to my right and saw my wife watching me, trying not to laugh and disturb me."

"Oh God, that must've been embarrassing!"

"You have no idea."

"So, did she take over? How could she not?"

"Well she's...frigid."

"What?"

"She's never in the mood. Ever. She was until she trapped me into marriage, and after that, nothing. Honeymoon was very disappointing, and the years after...But I have never cheated on her, not once. Not even in my thoughts until two nights ago. And all of yesterday, I've been consumed with these fantasies of what I'd do to this dream-girl. The things that I'm imagining when I'm waiting at a red light, or standing in line at the grocery store, they are things I've never done to a girl before. Things I didn't know I wanted to do."

"Like what?" Now she was more than just mildly interested.

"Well, I don't want to just go down on her. I want to flip her over and lick her behind, bury my face into the two beautiful halves of her ass, feel them cushioning soft and warm against my face, and lap madly at her...her...a rimjob. I've heard of them but never done it. And I want to suck on her cute little toes, and—and—"

"And what?"

"...then, last night, I went to bed praying I'd get to do all of those things. I was hoping so desperately for it that I'd convinced myself it was going to happen, and then..."

"What?"

"It was like Christmas Eve when I was a kid, you know what I mean? Lying awake thinking about how wonderful it will be and being frustrated that I can't get to sleep because I'm so *consumed* with anticipation. That was last night. And then, I finally fell..."

"*And?*"

"Nothing, I fell asleep and I woke up. I dreamed nothing at all. It was such a letdown, and all morning I was thinking about the same things I was yesterday, but it was bittersweet knowing that it was all just a dream and even if I could find you at night, seize the few moments I could have with you and taste as much of you as I can, you'd still evaporate like smoke when morning comes. But then, today…"

His eyes met hers, bright and fiercely green, and hers very, very blue.

"Today I came face-to-face with you. My heart stopped. I couldn't ever prepare for that moment, never. No matter how much time I had and warning that it would happen, if I had the chance to do it over again, I would freeze up just like I did today. I'll be honest with you, Megan. I have been wandering around, playing it back in my head and thinking about how I would've said this or that, how I could have maybe impressed you and convinced you to go out with me for drinks and we'd connect, and then I daydream about the thousand different things that would follow. But I'll never have it to do over again. I can't re-wind my life and have a second chance at making a first impression, maybe sweeping you off your feet. I had to stand there stammering like a nervous teenager…and Christ, now I've told you the whole embarrassing story. Well, that's it, Megan."

He looked down at his cigarette, noticing it had gone out, and relit it. Took a sip of his second drink. Hers remained untouched. She kept staring, eyes wide, lips parted.

She found that she'd been breathing heavily, leaning forward in her seat. Her heart was hammering so hard that her vision pulsed and blurred at the edges.

I could walk away from this man, she thought. He's married. I could just walk away, like I'm probably going to, and go home to the apartment I share with my roommate, and listen to her talk about her boyfriend until it's time to go to bed. And I could lie there awake until have to touch myself, masturbate myself to sleep. Just like last night. And the night before. Only tonight I'll touch myself thinking about this man. Thinking about what could've been. How somebody told me I was his dream girl and I walked away because he's married. And I might spend the rest of my life masturbating myself to sleep to the memory of this man and the fantasies of what could've been *real* memories. But then I'll cry. Or I could marry somebody and close my eyes when we're in bed and pretend it's this man instead of my husband so that I'll come quicker and we can be done.

Or I can throw caution to the wind…

Megan said *fuck it*.

Stood up and came around the small table, seizing his face between her hands and bending down to plant her lips on his, feeling them burning hot, feeling the tiny white peach fuzz on the back of her neck and her forearms prickle and stand on end. Her toes curled tightly inside her black leather shoes. Her heart sang, every fiber of her body, every atom, bursting into flame.

He kissed her like he'd described he would, kissing her lower lip first and then her upper, one after the other, quickly, one at a time, his tongue coming into her mouth to writhe against hers and leave again, tasting of cigarette smoke and Bacardi and Coca-Cola, but still tasting *good*. Tasting so good. And she felt herself hot and moist between her legs and—

He stopped, broke away, upset.

"I'm sorry."

Fuck!

"I'm sorry. I can't. I'm married. I can't do this."

No! Don't do this to me!

"I told you it'd be best if you left." He tried to maintain a calm expression, but it was plain to see anguish boiling just underneath the surface. She sank down slowly into the chair his jacket was draped over the back of, her heart racing. He reached over for his second drink, and she snatched one of hers.

"I was hoping this would calm me," he said, gesturing with the glass before he lifted it to his lips and drained it. He sighed deeply when he swallowed. "Thought it would take the edge off."

She took a long draught. It wasn't bad. Somehow, it tasted better when it was called a Cuba Libre instead of Bacardi and Coke.

"It didn't," he said after a moment.

"You son of a bitch," she whispered.

"I'm so sorry."

"No you're not."

"Oh god, I am. I want you so badly. I—" He broke off and looked around nervously, as if suddenly afraid his wife would have seen. And she understood.

"Come with me," she said quietly.

He looked at her in surprise.

"I would never do this. Ever. I can't believe I *am* doing this. But come with me, to my place. You can walk to my apartment from here. We can cut through these two alleys between the restaurant up here and the furniture rental/lease place. You know the one I'm talking about? It's a shortcut I always take. No one'll see you, so don't be afraid. Come with me. Come with me, please, Nick. No one will ever know."

He stared at her the way she had been staring at him.

"Tell you what," she continued hurriedly. "We won't leave together. Just in case someone you know can see you right now. I'll get up and go to the alley. The mouth of the alley is right over there, right between Allegra's and the furniture store. I'll go in there and wait a minute. I'll wait for you. Please don't leave me standing in there. Please don't. You'll break my heart. Don't sit here long enough to have second thoughts. Christ, I can't believe I'm saying this, but drink your drink, and drink mine, too. Just...I don't mean get drunk, you know, like guys are always trying to get chicks drunk so they'll come home with them. But, well, I guess I do mean that. Shit, I sound so desperate. I'm rambling, aren't I? Damn. God damn. I'm sorry. I'll shut up."

She twisted her mouth in disgust at herself, the way he had earlier, and she tried to drown it in the drink she held. She found relief at the bottom of the glass, but knew it was fleeting.

She looked over the rim of the glass as she swallowed the last of it, and saw the worry vanish in his eyes. They hardened with sudden conviction, determination. He reached for the fourth glass and drank deeply, as if it would cement his decision. As if his decision was already set in stone and this was the first coat of paint over it. He drank half of the glass and set it down. Turned in his chair and looked through the glass of the café, catching the eye of the waiter, signaling to him.

Turning back around, he reached toward her. No, past her, grabbing his jacket and pulling it to him. He fished his hand be-

15

tween the folds of it to find the inside pocket and pull out a twenty. Laid it on the table and stood.

Without a word, he turned and walked down the sidewalk. Away from her.

She stared after him.

Please.

The waiter came out and she grabbed the last drink, pouring what was left of hers into it and setting the empty one down within his reach. Turned the glass to the side Nick had drunk from, putting her lips where he had put his. Drank hurriedly. Watching over the rim as he walked away. The waiter stood patiently. As soon as she'd emptied it she handed it to the man, nodding thanks to him with her mouth full. He tried not to raise his eyebrow at her, and left.

Nick was passing the big blue mailbox now. The mailbox that stood outside the small jeweler's store. His jacket slung over his shoulder as he walked.

Please.

He passed the jeweler's, passed where she knew the furniture place to be. Slowed. Slowed to a stop. She held her breath.

He turned, hesitated. Looked over his shoulder behind him at the street, as if to assure himself one last time that Mrs. Nick or whatever her name was couldn't see him. And he walked into the alley.

She let out her breath and shut her eyes, sagging against the back of her chair. Opened her eyes and looked at the ash-tray. The waiter had not emptied it. Her cigarette had sat burning in one of the crevices in its rim, burned to an inch long ash, but his had gone out again, still half-long. In a strange, manic impulse, most likely brought on by the rum, she took his cigarette and put it between her lips, feeling his lips upon it as she had his glass. Lit it with her Zippo and took a long drag before she mashed it out in the ashtray. The faint vibration shook her own cigarette butt and the inch long ash crumbled and fell. Like my heart, she thought in a rum-born moment of poetic romance. Delicate as ash. My heart's as delicate as ash when it's held in your hands. But squeeze my body, though. Don't be scared to squeeze me tightly.

She grabbed her bag and dug through it, finding her cinnamon gum and hastily pulling out a stick of it, her hand shaking so that she tore the foil wrapped around it. Shaking so bad her fingers fumbled trying to tear the rest of it off and finally thinking *fuck it,* popping it into her mouth, foil and all. Chewing quickly to flavor her breath enough, trying to hurry.

She stood, took out the wad of it and dropped it in the ashtray. The sidewalk wavered a little beneath her feet as she walked. She wasn't much of a drinker. She fought to calm herself, to walk normally, suddenly fearing she'd do something stupid. Oh God, maybe even throw up in front of him. She kept combing her fingers through her hair, brushing it out of her face, but it kept falling forward again. She couldn't stop smiling.

She got to the alley with her heart in her mouth, turned into it and found him standing there. She went to him. He turned with her and joined her so she didn't break stride, his hand reaching and his fingers curling into hers, a jolt of electricity passing between them.

They walked down the alley in silence, came out of it behind the store and the restaurant, next to Allegra's two Dumpsters and she led him to the left, in between the restaurant and another building whose function or identity she didn't know. Past a large black homeless guy wrapped in a blanket. Past the rear of the book store, past Heartstrings, the knick-knack shop. Past the pizza place and the coffee bar to the other alley, having bypassed the corner of the two streets by walking the angle's hypotenuse. They came out of the alley, Nick looking cautiously both ways but not letting go of her hand, and they turned to the right.

Passing the Christian book shop and the thrift store, she turned him into a tall apartment building's door, led him up the stairs, to the third floor, went into the hall and to her door. Silent, the entire time. She looked at him as she dug in her bag for her keys. They both had a glow of anticipation, nervous smiles. When she found her keys, her hand was trembling so hard the apartment's keys rattled against the lock. She managed a short, uneasy laugh, but stopped when his hand closed around hers, steadying it, and together they slid the key into the lock and

17

turned it. She almost melted, but got a grip on herself and twisted the knob, shoving the door open and ushering him inside.

"Do you want something to—"

He took her by the shoulders and pulled her to him, planting his lips on hers. Her knees got weak, her bag falling from nerveless fingers to land with a thump on the hardwood floor, her hands going up to hold his face, to run them through his hair, and when her lips opened to take his tongue into her mouth and suck it her arms went up to hook over his shoulders and pull his head down closer to her. She ground her waist against his and felt a hardness there much larger than she'd expected. He slid his hands off her shoulders and under her arms, slid them down her side, feeling the hint of ribs, his thumbs grazing the slopes of small, firm breasts to grab her hips and pull them to him, and press her harder against him.

He was strong, she felt. Stronger than his size. She felt he could hold her up if she just let go of the floor with her feet, and that feeling made her squirm even more. He kissed well. Very well. He kissed her fiercely, and she wanted his tongue down her throat, but couldn't stop trying to put hers down his. Then his hands started moving.

They slid gently over the back pockets of her jeans, gently over the soft swell of her small ass. She pushed herself harder against the bulge of his trousers, and his hands tightened, rose up to the small of her back, under her gray sweater and the white men's button-down shirt she wore underneath to touch her soft skin, feel the two muscles that made a valley of her spine. Fingers pressed her skin and slid slowly down, pressing harder to lift her skin away from her belt and jeans, fingertips very slowly delving down, under the tight line of her panties.

Her jeans were too tight for him to go any further, and she hesitated, though still kissing him fiercely. Normally, she would never let it go so far, so early. She wasn't a prude, but she was far from a slut. Right now, though, she knew it could stop at any time. A single pang of guilt might stop him, even though her father had shared with her another pearl of wisdom: a stiff dick has no conscience. And even if it happened, she may never see him again, ever, unless she made this memorable.

Then again...even if she never saw him again, she deserved her money's worth.

She let his hair go, pulled her hand down between them and worked her belt buckle loose, tugged the top button of her jeans through its slit, and put her hand back up against the angle of his jaw. Let him do the rest of the work.

His hands now pushed their way further into her jeans, under her panties and over the smooth warm skin. Not kneading her like most would, just working his fingers in farther, the distance he went straining the denim and pulling her zipper slowly open.

She didn't know how long she kissed him, standing there in the hallway, but it seemed like forever and she wished it would go on forever, not caring if it never progressed any further.

Just as long as it didn't end.

Eventually though, one of his hands slid up her back underneath her clothes, up to the clasp of her bra. One finger, the middle one, slipped underneath and his index and ring fingers pressed firmly on the other side, expertly undoing the bra. None of that nervous fumbling. Just a swift unclasping and his hand came around her, lifting the cup of the bra away from her skin, and he was rolling her erect nipple between his forefinger and thumb.

She broke away from him, stepped back, his hand coming out, and she grabbed a hold of that hand with both of hers, dragged him with heavy steps down the hall.

The unframed art prints on the walls were held there with small bits of adhesive putty, because there was part of her lease forbidding the driving of nails through the walls. Three of those prints—Dalís—fell down and slid along the floor when her bedroom door slammed shut.

She lay staring at the ceiling, watching the fan blades slowly revolving. The shower was on in the bathroom, Nick washing away the evidence of his sin. She'd lost count of how many times she'd come, at least three times just during foreplay. There was not a single wet spot on the sheets. Every time he had come, right before, he'd reached over to the box of Kleenex on her nightstand and tugged out a handful of tissues to catch every drop, then wad it up and toss it across the bedroom into the wastebasket beside her desk, and then keep going. She squirmed under the sheets, rolling onto her side, wishing the pillow beside her was him, cuddling with it.

I've just had an affair, she thought idly.

The shower went off. *He's leaving soon.*

Loneliness was clawing its way up, trying to drag down her happiness, and she fought it. Please don't go home, Nick. Please don't go home to your wife. Your *wife*.

The threat of her impending sadness was quickly supplanted by a far more primal emotion, and far stronger. She threw off the sheet and padded across the room to the bath that joined her room to Neve's, her roommate's. She opened the door, startling him, finding him toweling off his well-muscled body—muscular, but not big, looking kind of like Bruce Lee with every fiber standing out—dripping and making wet footprints on the floor mat.

"Now what?" she asked, standing naked in the doorway.

He stood up straight to face her.

"You tell me," he said.

"No. You're the one with the wife. *You* tell *me*."

He was silent.

"Nick, we…we don't know each other. I've never done this before. Ever. I haven't ever slept with a man I didn't know, and didn't know *well*. We have no idea what kind of people we are, whether we'd click together or not, but I think we could. I think we'd get along. I think if we went out and had dinner somewhere together, we'd talk and laugh and have a great time. I might be wrong, but there's only one way to find out. I don't know, you might turn out to be someone I wouldn't like, but I can guarantee you right now that you would find me funny, intelligent, interesting, and loyal. If we could do that, and we click…look, you gave me a chance. We went to bed, and it was fantastic. Now, give me a chance at a dinner table. If we click…I don't know. We can have an affair. I can be your mistress. You can divorce your bitch wife who won't put out and go out with me. Whatever. Just give it a chance. Once wasn't enough. It can't be. I'm not a one-time girl."

They stood there looking at each other for a long time. She felt the steam from the shower and heard the second hand ticking on his watch.

"What do you say?" she asked, trying to be brave.

He looked at his watch on the toilet tank, next to his wedding ring. It was twenty past eight.

"My wife has been waiting for me to get home. I still haven't come up with a lie for where I've been."

She took a deep, shuddering breath, trying not to cry.

"Come here," he said gently.

She went taking small, tentative steps. He dropped the towel onto the edge of the sink, and took her in his arms. She put her head against his chest, held him tightly, her warm skin against his, feeling droplets of water smearing between them.

"It's one thing to be in love with somebody, and another thing entirely to love them. Do you know what I mean?"

She didn't, but she nodded her head against him.

"My wife says she loves me, but she's not *in love* anymore."

He held her more tightly.

"You might fall in love with me, but you wouldn't love me, because you don't know me."

They held on to each other for a long time.

"You could give me a chance," she mumbled.

"I could."

"Just take it one day at a time, see how it works out."

"Uh-huh."

"Are you in love with your wife?" she asked, looking at the ring next to the watch on her toilet tank. "Or do you just love her?"

His arms loosened their grip on her, only slightly, but enough to hurt. Her eyes closed.

"Honestly?" he asked.

She nodded again. "Honestly."

"I don't even like the bitch."

Her eyes popped open.

21

II

Neve was a gorgeous young woman, half black and half Vietnamese, who could tell first-hand the kind of problems that come with such a bloodline. Her black eyes were exotically slanted, her skin amaretto, hair long and black and curly, lips full and sensual. But there the benefits ended.

Her Vietnamese father had slept with a black woman, and his family would have banished him and stripped him of his name if hadn't severed all ties with her.

Her appeals to him, especially after she found she was pregnant, fell on deaf ears. Her own family turned their backs on her, saying that she'd disgraced them by "lying down with a yellow-assed slope." She would not kill her child, but she could not keep her, so she gave the baby up for adoption once she was born. But not before naming her Naviance.

Naviance Anquamette Moné Jamario Jackson. It sounded all French and fancy, she'd explained.

Gee, thanks, Mom.

She went by Neve, and she agreed whole-heartedly with her roommate, Bonnie Ophelia Delaune, that parents don't know what the hell they're doing.

When Megan's friends found out she was rooming with "Naviance Jackson," they looked at her askance and asked, Is she black? To which she smiled sweetly and said, No, she's a real pretty brown color.

There was a quote in Rudyard Kipling's *Kim* that she paraphrased because some of the terminology didn't jibe with that of Florida. The way she said it, there's no hatred like that of a half-breed for his cousin.

Her adopted father, Mr. Ramsey, read her one of Aesop's fables when she was little, apparently to prepare her for a hard life growing up. Maybe if he had left well enough alone, she wouldn't have grown up with that chip on her shoulder about being a bat.

The way the story went, the Birds and the Beasts were going to war, and both sides asked the Bat if he was coming out to fight for them, and since he didn't want to get involved, he told the Birds, "I'm a Beast," and he told the Beasts, "I'm a Bird."

When peacetime came about, neither side would have anything to do with him, and so he was left to live alone and come out only at night.

Mr. Ramsey told her she would have to pick a side eventually, but since both sides had rejected her, she opted to always side with other rejects. Her fondness for underdogs made her gravitate toward people like Megan, and become roommates with them in college.

Speaking of which, she came home from the study hall at the nearby university at a quarter to nine, about to call out *Honey, I'm home!* when she heard the savage pounding of a headboard against a wall, and saw a mist of plaster dust falling away from the crown molding by Megan's room. She stared, wide-eyed.

A muffled cry escaped into the hall, and another.

"Oh. My. God." Neve muttered.

She looked at the floor, saw Megan's bag.

And grinned.

"It's about goddamned time," she said, turning around and slamming the door behind her.

When she came back a second time, around ten o'clock, Neve found her roommate in the hallway making out with a gorgeous man in a suit, herself naked in his arms. Megan gave a little gasp and pulled the man in front of her. He grinned over his shoulder.

"You must be Neve," he said. "I've heard a lot about you."

She feigned stern disapproval. "Look here, mister. You may think you're hot shit, but that right there is my homegirl. You hurt her, or even make her think you've hurt her, and I'll make you wish you'd never been born. You hear me?"

"Yes'm," he answered, pretending to take her seriously.

"Now, I'm going to close my eyes for ten seconds. If she's not dressed and you're not gone, you can guess what I'm gonna do." She folded her arms under her ample breasts.

"Um, no. No, I can't."

"Well, I'll tell you. I'm going to leave again and let you two fuck some more. And don't you think I won't!"

They laughed, Nick still holding her tightly.

"Close your eyes so she can run get dressed," he said.

She did, and she heard him kiss her loudly and spank her on the ass to get her going. She yelped playfully, and he mumbled something to her that Neve couldn't hear. She opened her eyes again, saw him standing there alone.

"Be good to her," she said quietly. "She's the sweetest girl in the world. Be good to her. Treat her like a queen."

"I'll do my best," he said solemnly, walking past her to get to the door. "Cross my heart."

When he'd gone, she went into the living room and plopped down on one of the rattan wicker chairs, propped her feet on its matching ottoman.

"Well, come on, Meg!"

She came skipping out of her room in a bathrobe, grinning from ear to ear, and Neve laughed. Megan pranced about, bouncing on her toes in circles with her arms outstretched, singing a joyful song that had no words while Neve clapped her hands and cheered. When she came to a stop, she just stood there grinning, her face aglow.

"Tell me everything," Neve said.

Megan sat down on the floor and folded one leg, tucking that foot underneath her, and told her.

Everything.

The next morning was the most beautiful day Megan had ever woken up to see. The coffee she had for breakfast tasted better, the sun shone brighter, and the glow of her skin and her radiant smile made every man who passed by on her way to work stop and look again. Big Beat Records came to life when she swept in through the door, her mood coming off of her somehow like perfume, and the two bosses and early bird customers all brightened up.

"Morning!" she called, and they all looked up to see her contagious smile and succumb to it.

"Meg," Phil said, waving. "Why the long face?"

She grinned, dropped her bag on the stool behind the counter.

"You started wearing blush?" Emmy asked.

"No. Why?"

"Oh, you look...*oh.*" She understood, and was happy for her.

"I'm feeling ambitious today! Do you want all of the albums in the store reorganized alphabetically or by color?"

"You ever think of switching to decaf?" Phil asked.

At ten o'clock, they found themselves very busy, and at the peak of it, there came an interruption. A delivery man came in with a clipboard and asked if there was a Megan around. Emmy was running the cash register, which she insisted on calling a till, and called out to Megan, who was explaining the finer points of Mojo Nixon and the Skid Roper to a couple of acidheads.

"Excuse me," she chirped at them and hurried with a bounce in her step to the front. Emmy gestured to the delivery man, who smiled.

"Can you sign here, please?"

"What for?"

"Flowers."

Her mouth fell open, as girls' do, and she emitted that mewling sound girls make that cannot be described or duplicated. "For me?"

"Yes, ma'am—er, miss."

"Where are they?"

"They're in the van. I'll be back with them, after you sign."

She took the clipboard and signed *Bonnie Delaune (Megan)*, handed it back and smiled brightly at her bosses. The delivery man came back and made a gesture with his head behind a huge bouquet of roses that translated into Please get the door for me.

Nobody moved. They all stared, dumbstruck. There had to be four, five dozen of them. What was that? Fifty? Sixty? Good God! Megan's smile faded, her jaw gaping wider than before, her eyes bulging. Everyone was now staring at her, and the delivery man was still standing outside, getting irritated.

Phil combed his fingers through his bushy gray hair, coughed into his fist, and went to open the door. Standing outside to hold it for him, he had to reach and push some of the roses to keep them from rubbing the glass and falling away as the man carefully made his way into the store.

"The gentleman who sent these said he didn't know what color you liked best, so he got a dozen of each to be on the safe side." There were red, pink, white, coral, yellow, and a few artificially variegated. A dozen of each, Megan thought, seventy-two roses in all...gee, I wonder if he wants to see me again.

"Gosh," Emmy finally said, "Good Heavens!" She was the only person Megan ever heard say Good Heavens.

"Where the hell are we going to put them?" Phil asked, not wanting to ask in front of all these people what he really wanted to know. He knew where they were going to put them, right out here in front where everyone could see them and know whose they were.

"Is there a card?" Emmy asked for Megan, who was still gaping, speechless. The man was doing his best to be patient.

"Yes, ma'am, it's in here somewhere. Where should I set them?"

"Oh, right there on the floor in everyone's way is fine."

"No," Phil said. "How about here in the window?" he pointed to an empty spot on the display shelf, under the drum set painted on the glass. The delivery man carried his burden over, half-expecting them to change their minds and say No, better yet, how 'bout way over here in back, right past all that shit for you to trip over?

But they didn't. He set the huge display down, assured himself that it was a safe spot, and tipped the bill of his baseball cap, cowboy-like, at Megan as he left. Phil found the card near the base and handed it to his sole employee, who was trying to pick up what exactly all of the murmurers were saying around her. She took the tiny envelope and pulled the card out of it, trying to hold her hands steady.

"I must see you again," it read. "You have revived something in me I thought long dead" —oh, how poetic— "I have to catch a plane to Austin this evening for a long, boring convention, and am to be gone for three days. May I miss my flight and be with you instead? You'll find me at the Heather's. Ask for Mr. Coniglio at the desk. Please come. *Nick.*"

She clasped the note to her breast, and the murmurers kept on murmuring.

She only had a few dresses, and none of them seemed suitable, so Neve went through her closet and found her a lovely décolletage peach moiré "goddess gown" she'd grown out of. They sat down together and talked hair and makeup, and came up with the right shades and a way for Megan to wear her hair pinned up with tortoise shell combs, a few strategically chosen strands hanging loose in front of her face.

When she was finally ready, Neve looked at her and beamed. Her feet were encased in borrowed heels that gave her an extra three inches, and would bring her to eye level with Nick Coniglio. She wore costume jewelry, cubic zirconia set in silver, to flash at her throat and wrist and ears, and she was radiant. Neve wished that her roommate was going somewhere to be seen by many, because people just had to know how beautiful Megan Delaune could be. She took more than a few fashion show snapshots of the laughing vixen to be recorded for posterity.

At eight-fifteen, record time considering she'd gotten off work at five, she got in her blue Toyota and drove over the Gandy Bridge to the Heather-Leigh in St. Petersburg.

The posh hotel rose a good twenty stories into the evening sky. MacDill Air Force Base wasn't too far away, so the purpling blue was streaked and cross-hatched with red and orange contrails that the day's heavy winds had smeared into what looked like palm fronds. On such a beautiful evening, and looking as she did, Megan felt a little silly pulling up before the entrance to have her rinky-dink little car valet parked, but when she strode through the door a man in a lavender suit with braided golden ropes and tassels held for her, she felt only Wonderful.

As she was making her way across the lobby, she felt many eyes upon her, but sensed somehow a pair that made her glance to her left, and there was Nick in the entrance to the bar with piano music trickling out from behind him. Staring at her with something akin to awe.

She smiled, turned and went to him. He stood with a glass, a brandy snifter hanging from his fingertips clasping the rim, an amber liquor swirling around the bottom, his other hand reaching to unbutton his suit jacket. His suit was dark blue, almost black, and pinstriped, his purple shirt open at the collar. He turned with her as he had yesterday in the alley, raising his bent arm like a gentleman, and she slipped her own arm into it like a lady.

All eyes followed them as they found a table in the darkened lounge, most eyes envying the man. He kissed her cheek and pulled out her chair. She sat, and he excused himself, went to the bar and asked for the Arts & Lifestyle section of the local newspaper, and a bottle of chianti, if they had any lying around.

"Er, we definitely have the wine, sir…"

"Thank you, but I also need the listings of what's happening in town, and I don't mean what cinemas are showing what."

"Well, sir, we do have a concierge who'd be happy to help you," was the condescending reply.

"…Oh. Yes, I forgot about those wacky concierge types. Well done, Concord, keep up the good work. Now, chop chop with the grape juice, my good man." He rapped the bar with his open hand imperiously, covering up feeling stupid by acting even more stupid, as was his wont. The bartender stared at him for a moment.

Nouveau riche, he thought, as if being a bartender in the lobby of a hotel gave him the right to judge. *Concord?* Sheesh.

Nick Coniglio went back to the table where Megan was still smiling, still unexpectedly lovely. He sat and took out his cigarettes, offering her one. She took it and he pulled a kitchen match out of thin air, again striking it with his thumbnail, being a show-off. It was cute though, the way he did it, she thought. He scooted his chair closer to hers.

"I didn't know if you'd come," he said over the piano music. "I certainly wasn't expecting *this*."

"I wanted to look pretty for you. Neve helped me."

He leaned in to kiss her gently, careful not to smear her lipstick. A man was coming over with the wine and two glasses.

"Sir," he said. "The concierge is upstairs, but he can come down to speak with you if you'd prefer."

Megan looked a question at Nick.

"You look too wonderful for a simple night," he explained to her. "We must go out to some kind of event, maybe crash the party at some gala and have you photographed by paparazzi."

She blushed. "No, thank you, but we can't." She nodded to the sommelier. "We won't need to speak to anyone. Thank you."

The man bowed with affected dignity and left.

"We can't go anywhere," Megan told Nick. "Your wife…"

He hesitated, then nodded, as if he'd forgotten he had one.

"Besides," she said, scooting her own chair closer to his and laying her head against his shoulder. "I'm so happy here. It's enough of an event just to sit here and talk with Mr. Perfect."

"Ha! I am far from perfect."

"You're close enough."

"Care for some wine?"

"I'd love some."

They sat and drank, and talked, getting to know each other. They laughed. It occurred to Nick that she may not have eaten, and escorted her to the hotel's restaurant. They laughed more over lamb and duck a l'orange, finding that they did more than just click.

"I'm big on names," she said. "'A rose by any other name will smell as sweet' is pure bullshit, in my opinion, because, well, take gemstones. I don't much care for jasper and feldspar because their looks don't appeal to me much, but they *look* like their names. But there was one I really did like until I found out what it was called, and I can't even look at it anymore. It was pretty, but once it stopped being an anonymous gem and became a *carbuncle*, I couldn't have anything to do with it!"

"Carbuncle. Christ, you're right. 'Wow, Megan, that's a lovely necklace you have there! What is it?'" He mimicked her voice then, surprisingly well. "'Oh, this old thing? Why, it's a carbuncle!' You're right. It sounds like either something that grows on the bottom of a boat, or something you come down with. 'Doctor, I've got these horrible blistering sores all over my foot! Is it ringworm?' 'Oh, no, sonny, you've got yerself a case of the carbuncles. Worst case I've ever seen. You'll have to get that whole leg amputated. Them dad-burned carbuncles will rot the flesh off yer bones!'"

"Damn skippy, boo. But then we have to go the other way and soften our language because some schmuck thinks a word that matches what it means is too harsh. Like cripples. They're *cripples*, for God's sake! They're not disabled, differently-abled, or handicapable. They're fucking crippled! The kids on the short bus, while I may feel sorry for them, are not developmentally-delayed. They are retarded. I'm not vertically-challenged, or diminutive, I'm short; a plane crash in the ocean isn't a water landing; drugs aren't controlled substances; and when we finish our dining experience in this dining establishment, we're not going to leave a gratuity for our server—we're going to tip the waitress!"

"I feel ya, boo. Tha's real."

"I have to use their stupidass lingo to call it what it is. I call it euphemistic syllable augmentation."

"Ha! That's a good one!"

"Thank you. All it is, this euphemistic syllable augmentation, is somebody's sick and sad way to promote the ordinary and tint unpleasantness. By the way—I'm going to interrupt myself here to make a quick point—when you lighten something, that's tinting. There aren't any shades of white. Shading is when you *darken*. Now, before I was so rudely interrupted, when you elevate yourself by being pompous with words, trying to affect some kind of social significance—say, being Ethnic instead of foreign, or an Information Delivery System instead of a News Reporter—your intent is to *deceive*!"

"Ooh, well-spoken," he said.

"Yeah, I know. I mean, thank you."

"But our entire culture revolves around deception. Look at what we consider important. The proudest section of a city is the part that panders the most to the lazy. Snazzy clothing stores that sell what you cannot be active in without destroying. Penthouses designed for an easy life where other people do all your chores. Entertainments where your imagination atrophies. And cosmetic surgery clinics and salons where we can be "beautified", or rather, disguised. Face lifts, hair dyes, tummy tucks, nose jobs, breast implants, all this bullshit to defy aging, and on top of it all, cryogenics. Only in this era can you find cities where death is optional."

"Here's another example," she said. "You know forms that have colored carbons attached, so they can be automatically copied in triplicate? Usually they are a yellow and a pink one?"

"Sure. I deal with those things all the time. Twenty-seven-B-stroke-sixes."

"Well, read the fine print at the bottom, where it informs you of what color copy goes to whom. White copy is yours, yellow copy is theirs, pink one goes in the records file. That's what it *used* to be. But now they've added another color. Orangey, and it looks like yellow ochre. But they're not going to say it's ochre. They have to go and call it Goldenrod. *Golden-rod?* And even that's not good enough. They have to change yellow to Canary, to make sure there's no confusion and keep us, I guess, from getting into semantic arguments over what yellow really is. But if they're going to do that, why keep white and pink? I feel gypped with white and pink. I'm thinking of mounting a class-action lawsuit for damages caused by the mental anguish of having white and pink remain white and pink! *Reductio ad absurdum*, this is called, in case you didn't know. I want monetary compensation and a recalling of all quadruplicate forms issued so that they can be reprinted either as white, yellow, pink, and orangey—ochre, whatever—or vanilla, canary, goldenrod, and salmon. Or shrimp. Or nipple, even. Yeah, nipple copy for the records file."

"Nipple might be extreme," he said.

"*Extreme?* There's no such thing anymore! We have 'extreme' everything nowadays! Extreme *soft-drinks* for Christ's sake!"

A few of the nearby diners glared at her, and she put her hand over her mouth, ducking her head in, turtle-like, wide-eyed and embarrassed. Nick made a gesture that was maybe conciliatory, maybe just acknowledging, but it appeased the offended diners. They went back to their mundane conversations, reciting the same topics they do always, with maybe only subtle variation.

Megan went back to meekly eating the crispy skin that was left of her duck, making occasional faces of Whoops, sorry, while she chewed. Nick shrugged.

"Can I ask you something now?" she asked eventually.

"Honey, we've had our tongues up each others' asses. I think any time for shyness is over."

She laughed, her face going red.

"Don't ask if you can ask me. Just ask."

When she finally could, she spoke. "Who are you?"

"Who am I? I am Nick."

"Well, I already know *that*, but what do you do? Where have you been? What do you want?"

"Okay…I'm an antiques dealer, who also forges replicas, half as a business and half as a hobby. I've been to the Bahamas on my honeymoon, and nowhere else. And what do I want? Um…well, it looks like I have everything I can want right now. The only thing I want is for that to last."

"We'll come to that later, then. What do you mean you *forge*?"

"Just what it sounds like, I'm a bit of an artist, but I can't come up with anything extraordinary of my own. What I can do, though, is make a perfect duplicate of almost anything else. I can copy a sculpture, a lamp, a portrait, or a signature. The business is selling two of the same thing, and the hobby, the part that I actually have fun with, is convincing everybody that the copy is the original."

"So, you're a crook."

"Yes. I'm sorry, but I am."

"Is that how you made your money? I can't help but notice you seem to be well-off."

"Well no. It's my wife who has all of the money. She's from a wealthy family, and that's pretty much the only thing that doesn't suck about our marriage. The money doesn't hold me to her, though. I'm not that kind of guy. I'm not still with her because she's rich."

"…Then, if you don't mind me asking, why *are* you still with her? You told me you didn't even like her, so…"

"Because we're married," he said, as if that was still answer enough in this day and age.

"Um, I *know* that, silly. Why not get a divorce?"

"Because I can't."

"You can't?"

"No. I made a promise."

"A promise to who?"

"To her. To myself. To God. I swore that I'd stick with her, through sickness and in health, for better or for worse, 'til death do us part. That comes with the wedding."

"But nobody abides by that anymore!"

"So I've noticed. Nobody keeps their promises. Vows aren't honored unless they are on paper, and even then, they can be argued about in a courthouse. So what's the point? Well, the point is, it was a promise, Megan. My promise. Just because nobody else can keep one anymore is no reason for mine to be worthless too."

"But…but you're committing adultery with me." She hadn't wanted to say it, but she felt she couldn't not say it.

"I know," Nick said. "I haven't found a way to rationally justify it to myself yet."

"*Yet.*"

"Yeah, I know. But let's be realistic. That's exactly what I'm going to do. I can't divorce my wife, and I can't just cheat on her, so I'm stuck. The only thing for me to do is be a hypocrite and try to live with myself."

"So, what's going to happen with us?" she asked quietly.

He studied the patterns of sauce on his plate for a long moment, absently dragging the tines of his fork across them, scalloping them in places.

"Depends," he said.

"On what?"

"On whether a meteorite falls out of the sky and lands on my wife. Or she gets hit by a car."

There was a very uncomfortable silence, broken only by the tinking of other peoples' silverware and the low drone of their conversation.

Megan and Nick's eyes met, and held each other, and she wondered if this was going to turn into one of those soft-core porn movies they show late at night, where the two people having an affair hatch a plot to kill the spouse and inherit life insurance.

"So, what'd you do when you were younger?" she asked brightly, killing the uncomfortable mood. "You went to college?"

He chuckled. "Well, I tried that. Didn't work out. Went to Navy boot camp instead."

"You were in the *Navy*?"

"No, just the training. Shit, I'm going to have to confess a deep dark secret."

"Ooh, I like those."

"Really? Do you have any?"

"One."

"Tell me. You tell me yours, and then I'll tell you mine."

"Hmm, all right. I've slept with a married man."

"That's it?"

"What, it's not bad enough? That's a pretty bad one."

"Oh. Yeah, good point."

"So, what's yours?"

"Wait. What we're doing is the worst thing you've ever done?"

She thought a minute, considering it. "Yep. Yes, it is."

"Oh. Okay. Well, here goes then. I enlisted in the Navy under a false name."

"What, why?"

"Because I wanted the training."

"But…but can't you just—"

"Nope. If you sign up, you're in it for a minimum of six years. See, it takes one point five million dollars to train a recruit, so there's a commitment that comes with that."

"So you…God, you could get in trouble for that."

"And how. But I won't. They think the guy they trained was killed. Ancient history, and too long of a story. But I got one hell of an education, and after the fifty-two-hour graduation test— boy, that sucked, lemme tell you—I conveniently disappeared. Got killed, they think."

"Well, what can you do with all your training, if not—"

"I can do whatever I have to, if the need arises."

She realized she was sitting with someone very dangerous… she didn't want to think about it. The coldness of his tone when he said that…she decided to be intrigued by it, instead. She hadn't given herself enough time to form an opinion, so she just chose one and ran with it. It'd be better that way.

"So, you can sink a battleship?"

"Child's play. Hon, I could sink Molly Brown."

"You can kill a man in cold blood?"

"I don't know," he lied. "The opportunity hasn't come up."

"Tell me about boot camp. What was it like?"

"Oh, it was great. They beat the shit out of me!"

"Uhhh…and that was good?"

"Well, they didn't beat me up, not literally. I mean, they got me into shape really, really quickly. They fed us tons of really great food while working us out, so I got bigger in no time."

"You do have a great body."

"I know. I mean, thank you."

"That's my line."

"Was."

"You swine."

"Yeah, so, anyway, when we signed up, me and the other recruits, we were treated like kings. They really rolled out the red carpet for us, but once it was official, that's when all pretenses dropped and the fun began. The others were scared, but I don't know why. What'd they expect? To be pampered the whole time? I went in there knowing it'd be hell, and I took it all in stride, because that's what I'd signed up for in the first place. Some of those pussies started *crying*, though, for God's sake!"

"So, what did they do that was so horrendous?"

"Pshah! They started yelling at us. Ooooh, scary! This one sergeant screamed 'Don't call me sir,' and so everybody except me had to shout 'Yes sir!' I'm standing there rolling my eyes, and everyone else is panicking. 'I told you not to call me Sir! Now, do you understand me?' 'Yes, sir!' Idiots. So then, we have to take a piss test. I can't believe how stupid this was. It wasn't a test to see if we had any drugs in our urine, it was a test of *how we urinate!*"

"What?"

"Listen to this. They gave us a cup, and had us stand a few feet back from these urinals, behind a line on the floor, and told us to piss in the cups and then in the johns, without spilling a single drop."

"What in the—"

"Yeah, that's what I thought. So I watched the others, watched them all go half in the cup, and then spray all over the place trying to aim for the urinals. I looked at the sergeant, who was shaking his head, and I leaned forward. Caught the urinal with one hand, and just held myself there, still behind the line but with my manhood a lot closer. Did my business first in the cup, then in the john, while everyone else was still standing behind the line, missing, and feeling mighty stupid."

"My God. Common sense."

"You'd be surprised how common sense isn't."

"Boy, tell me about it."

"There was one of the guys, he was crying and trembling like he was having an epileptic damned fit, and spilled everything he was holding *in the cup*, all over the floor. Sarge started screaming at the dumb bastard, and it just got worse."

"That's pathetic."

"So then, we took a written test for the Nuclear Corps. The supervisor said it was two hours long, fifty questions. So I'm breezing along. It consisted of chemistry, physics, high level algebra, and geometry, which I've always been pretty good at. After an hour and a half, the supervisor sticks his head in the door, sees me sitting there, and asks if I'm done with all eighty questions. Eighty? He says 'Yeah, I told you eighty.' Of course he didn't, but who am I to argue? I turn over the last page which I'd thought was blank— stupid me not bothering to check—and sure enough, there are thirty more. By the way, these were all essay questions, not multiple choice or true/false."

"So how'd you do?"

"Eh," he said modestly. "I finished first and got the highest score. A sixty-three."

"Jeez. That's one point below failing."

"No, that's in high school. Sorry. I didn't get sixty-three *percent*, I got sixty-three correct answers out of the eighty questions."

"Oh."

"Yep. And that was the easy part. That was just the first day. More wine?"

"Yes, please."

They had dessert, tiramisu, and he told her about basic training. When they were finished, they went back into the bar to have even more wine and get to the good part.

"The graduation test. Good *God*, that was awful."

"Not just written, was it?"

"No, it was all physical. Fifty-two hours of battle."

"Fifty-two? That's…over two straight days. Did you do it in increments?" she asked, expecting the answer No.

"Megan, we went fifty-two hours straight with no sleep and no food. Just water."

"My God!"

"Well, what do you expect? This isn't a summer camp or a weekend retreat. This is supposed to make us capable of surviving worse conditions than that. We ran around in groups of five with M-16s that were like Laser Tag, but with simulated kick every time we fired. We were given shitty old-fashioned masks to wear and were then tear-gassed. Man, that burns. God. I do not recommend you ever get tear-gassed. We started off at the firing range, that was the only time we used live ammunition. We showed our progress with the M-16 and the .45, then went to blanks and Laser Tag, with live rounds whizzing over our heads. God, it was great.

"There was this one part, though, where we had to jump through a flaming hole, not like a circus animal. See, in Vietnam, on the USS Forestall, or is it the USS Forrestal? It's probably Forrestal. Can there be two? I doubt it. Anyway, an F-14 burned its way all the way through. Fighter planes are magnesium on the outside, and magnesium burns hotter than steel, and the fire cannot be extinguished until the plane is *dust*. They can't even be put out when they crash under water, because the fire draws oxygen straight out of the water itself. Well, when this plane was burning through the Forrestal, ten sailors managed to get out through the hole and escape. They were severely burned, but they survived. We are measured against them as the standard. We must be able to do what they did. So, we have to get through a burning hole that is four feet up off the ground, and three feet tall by two wide."

"Where is this? Annapolis?"

38

"No, Great Lakes, just north of Chicago."

"And you got all of that training without having to pay for it. You just split when it was over?"

"Sure did. Well, actually, some other guy did, and when it came time for him to put in six years running around the world in a submarine, beating off to his memories of getting laid at his last shore leave, he died in an accident."

"You faked your death?"

"It wasn't hard," he said modestly.

"How?"

"Oh, I forget. Maybe I'll tell you someday, if I remember."

"I see."

"So now you have the goods on me. I've confessed."

"Fear not, Sir Knight. Thy secret is safe with me."

"Cross your heart?"

"Hope to die."

"Good. Are you feeling a little tipsy?"

"I am. You?"

"A little." He was staring at her hungrily.

"And what do you propose we do about it?" she asked.

"Oh, a few options have sprung to mind."

"Before we go upstairs, can I ask you something?"

"We've been over this, Megan. Or do I have to kiss your ass again to make sure you're clear?"

"Oh, God, yes. You'll have to. I had no idea that would feel so good!"

"Me either," he lied. Very few women dislike it.

"And I was worried for a minute there, but yours didn't really taste like anything but skin."

"I get that a lot."

"What!"

"Kidding. Your toes tasted rather good."

"Oh *God*, that was wonderful, too!"

"Glad you think so, because I've had one eye on your pretty little feet all night, and I am just dying to suck on them right here."

"Are you serious?"

"Yeah, put one foot in my lap. It's dark enough in here."

"Doesn't matter, people will still see!"

"I'll cloud their minds so that they'll see nothing—a little trick I picked up in the Orient."

"Oh Jesus. At least let me take my shoe off."

The old man playing the piano glanced over every now and then, looking at the young woman's shapely leg under the table, her fingers clutching the arms of her chair, the man's head bent over her toes, and shook his head at the state of the world today.

"I still haven't asked my question," she managed.

"Mmm?" he said with her littlest toe in his mouth, his tongue circling around it.

"Your card said you had three days."

"Mm-hmm."

"Oh *God*, that feels so good."

He grinned and then started licking figure-eights around the second and third smallest.

"Oh *God!* It is impossible to hold a conversation like this. So…(ahem) will be you be staying here all three days?" She was trying to take deep, calm breaths. When he didn't answer, she continued. "Because I was thinking, it'd be better if you could come stay at my place."

He stopped, releasing her middle toe with a wet smack.

"Why's that?"

"Well, you wouldn't have to pay for this hotel. One. And two—I don't want to bring this up again if it bothers you, and if it does bother you, I'll never mention it again—but, let's say you and Mrs. Nick split up. You won't be rich anymore, and you'll need a place to stay. Just in case you and Mrs. Nick *do* break up, you can already have had all the practice of living with me that you'd need."

"Practice?"

"Well sure! Practice makes perfect."

"The money doesn't impress you?"

"Um, is it supposed to?"

"Does it?"

"Well it's nice, and this hotel's nice, and dressing up like this is nice, but it's not me. Remember what we were talking about earlier? About money just making you lazy?"

"I do. I rather enjoyed saying that."

"That's how I feel. I'd rather be snuggled up with you on the couch watching a movie…or snuggled up in *bed*, than being at fancy places with sommeliers and their goofy medallions around their necks."

"The money wouldn't be important? You're sure?"

"Of course not! Besides, you said it was your wife's money anyway. So, let her have it. Fuck it. I'd much rather have you, and I'll have you any way I can get you."

Nick broke into a grin of elation.

"I've been waiting to hear that all night," he said.

"You have?"

"Damn right, I have. And I am very, very relieved you finally said it."

"Well, what else am I going to say?" she asked. "You know I'm not one of those girls who have to have gobs and gobs of money to be happy. 'Oh, I'm so depressed, I haven't bought a pair of shoes in two whole days!' You know I'm not like that!"

"I only *hoped* that," he corrected. "I know it now."

"So what do you have to say about it?"

"Three simple words."

"…*Three?*"

"Yep."

"Not *those* three."

"Oh, no. Too early. I'll probably be saying *those* three, maybe, a week from now, if you keep up the way you've been."

"Get outta here!"

"No, I mean a different three. For tonight."

She raised her eyebrows expectantly, and she looked absolutely gorgeous doing so. Nick smiled.

"Let's. Go. Upstairs."

She grinned.

"About. Damned. *Time*."

"Glad you think so."

"C'mon, unhand my foot."

"Yeah, hurry, put your shoe back on."

"I *will* if you'll let me."

"I'm not stopping you. Shall we get more wine to take up with us?"

"Ooh, yes. Is there another toothbrush up there?"

"I'll ring the concierge and demand one."

"You do that. Ask him for some condoms too."

"Wait. How 'bout some champagne, instead?"

"Sure. And some Smucker's Strawberry for me to toss your salad with, while we're at it."

The pianist watched them leave, shaking his head.

Much, much later, with his cheek against her breast, he listened to the hiss of the champagne bubbles in the darkness, feeling her insides expand and contract as she sipped from her glass. Heard and felt her drain it, heard the click of it being set down empty on the nightstand beside her bed. Felt her hand, now free, rest upon his head, her fingers combing into his hair.

I'll fall in love with this man, she thought.

She felt, deep within her, that primal emotion taking root. It didn't scare her. It felt so right, and with a calm and rational mind she decided she *would* love this man, and do whatever she must to make him stay. It felt right. It felt perfectly natural. No other animal would accept this situation, a lesser female having claim to her mate. She would do what every rightful mate would do.

Stay with me and love me, she thought, caressing him. This was starting to look like a soft-core porn movie they show late at night.

She couldn't stop hearing the echo of his voice, as faint as a thread of wavering smoke, his sadness behind it. It felt so right. It felt perfectly natural.

There was only one way to keep this man. His words whispered in her ears, quieter than the sound of his breathing, but still there, unmistakable.

I swore that I'd stick with her.

For better or for worse.

'Til death do us part.

People say all the time that they'll fight for what they love, but somehow they rarely mean *literally*. I'll fight for him, Megan thought. And this isn't any soft-core porn movie. There are no convoluted plots to screw up and get busted. When they find Mrs. Nick, it won't look like an accident.

No interrupted burglary-whoops-homicide. No driving home late at night and accidentally going off a cliff. It could not be anything that the police could pick apart and find wasn't what it seemed, that it was really a disguised murder, a cover-up. And the only way to keep the police from finding out a murder was a murder, and not start looking for things like say, an unfaithful husband and his jealous lover, was not to disguise it at all.

The only way, she reasoned, is just plain kill her.

III

When she was sure he'd fallen asleep, she eased herself out of bed and tiptoed around the room, snooping. In the desk by the window, she found a few papers, antique stuff it looked like, a pad of hotel stationery with notes-to-self jotted down, some of which were endearing little questions about her—"What color roses? Screw it, get 'em all"—her name written over and over the way she thought only teenagers do.

Ah ha! A checkbook. A joint account at Wachovia, in the names of…she had to squint in the faint light from outside the window…Nicholas Coniglio and…you're kidding.

Gwynnevere Hutchinson?

She hadn't even taken his surname? Bitch.

Megan browsed through the responsibly-kept log of checks written, and found, well whaddaya know? Ol' Gwynnie takes art classes at the university here. That's a start.

She tore the second page carefully off of the pad, so she'd later be able to make a rubbing with a pencil and read all of the sweet things Nickie had written about here. Eased the desk drawer closed, silently, and went to his suit jacket—yet again draped over the back of a chair, and looked for his wallet. It was full of money and plastic, but she'd meant what she said earlier about money. She was digging business cards out of the middle pocket, trying to find a wallet-sized photograph. There *should* be one; everyone keeps those kinds of things… don't they?

Bingo! She tiptoed hurriedly to the window and leaned to see better. He wasn't in the picture. Just her. And you could tell just by this one shot what a narcissistic bitch Gwynnevere Hutchinson-Coniglio was. Blonde hair obviously slaved over. Waaay too much makeup.

Even though it was a candid shot, she was still displaying the body language of a model during a photo shoot. Beautiful woman, but sickeningly beautiful, the kind of woman that uses her face and tits to get her way. Not her ass, like a whore, but the hint and empty promise of it. Her face was intelligent, but not really intelligent so much as crafty and cunning. The kind of woman that Megan had always despised.

She put everything back the way she had found it, quietly folded up the sheet of hotel letter-headed paper and slipped it into the small purse she'd borrowed from Neve. Went into the bathroom and turned on the light. She looked at her reflection in the mirror, comparing herself to Mrs. Nick.

No, she wasn't as beautiful. Her hair was mostly straight, and down to her shoulders. Her breasts were not as large, but they were at least a handful, and perky. Her hips were narrow, her fanny a fanny or a bubble butt, not really an ass. Her legs were nice, her stomach flat, and her vulva a nice slit that looked like what you would slide a credit card through, instead of a Pussy or a Snatch.

She looked down at her feet that Nick seemed to love so much, wondering what the big deal was, and it occurred to her that a lot of people had second toes longer than the big one, or littlest ones that didn't even touch the ground or have toe-nails. Or they had bulging veins or were really long or really wide or had bunions, or—she had to chuckle—carbuncles.

She shut off the light and tiptoed back to the bed, easing her way back into her lover's arms. As if on cue, he muttered something in his sleep and moved, adjusting himself, put his cheek back on her breast and held her possessively, which she loved.

"*Te voy a comer*," he mumbled. She didn't know if it was sleep talk or another language. "Tu culo, tus nalgas, voy a comer, y tu chocha, y tus…"

She traced her fingers over his dark skin, lightly.

He sighed, a low rumble of deep satisfaction.

"Megan…" he said, and she smiled.

Despite Nick's urging, Megan could not just "call in sick." She apologized, and meant it, but she absolutely *had* to go to work and run her errands.

"Eh, that's okay, I guess," Nick said. "I've got a few things to do around town. Errands of my own."

"Careful," she said. "You're not supposed to *be* in town."

"Ha! Like you need to remind me. But I don't have to worry about Gwynn—that's my wife's name, Gwynn—I don't have to worry about running into her or her gaggle of friends because she's in class today until two, and the rest of them will all be buying shoes somewhere, or getting their nails done. I'll be discreet, though."

"We're seeing each other tonight," she said. It wasn't a question. He loved the way she said it.

"Oh, if we have to," he muttered, as if conceding.

"Knock it off. What time?"

"Come straight here from work, if you can. Don't get all dolled up. Just come as you are."

"But I want to be pretty!"

"Baby, you're irresistible as it is. I didn't have dreams about a chick in makeup and jewelry, and I didn't get thunder-struck in a records store by a Revlon ad." He took her in his arms and kissed her cheek, held her tightly. "I love your face as it is, *a cappella*."

She made that mewling noise that only girls make.

"I almost forgot," he said. "I got you something."

She looked at him in surprise as he went to his suitcase, dug around in it until he found a small jeweler's box, brought it to her.

"It's not much, but..." He gave her the box and watched her eyes as she opened it. The look on her face told him it was the best present she'd ever been given, and while that pleased him, it also made him sad, in a way. It was a necklace, a blue sapphire amulet set in silver, with diamonds, and a silver chain.

She threw her arms around him and started to cry.

"Hey! What's with the waterworks?"

She laughed while crying, said something unintelligible, and after a while he turned her around. Gathering up her hair, she let him put the amulet around her neck, fastening the clasp. She sighed.

"Now, get to work." He spanked her ass. "And hurry back. I am insatiable."

"Don't I know it."

"I'm already feeling the first pangs of Megan withdrawl."

She sighed again, "It's about damned time I heard someone say that."

They kissed, a loud smooch like husbands and wives do, and it felt so right. So natural. She left, feeling silly leaving in the morning, dressed as she was, and constantly touching the amulet, deciding not to let anyone see it yet. She drove home quickly, called Emmy to say she'd be just a few minutes late—"Good for you, hon, I'm glad to hear it"—and filled Neve in while she changed her clothes. She gave the Cliff's Notes version, omitting, of course, that she was going to find and murder Mr. Perfect's wife. Neve made her a cup of strong black coffee that Megan threw down in a hurry on her way out the door.

The exotic-looking young woman stood with the empty mug she'd been handed, smiling faintly at the closed door. She cast her eyes upward, not at the ceiling, but the sky beyond and the Heavens where she half believed God lived, and winked. Put the mug in the sink and went back to studying Fitzhugh's rebuttals to *Uncle Tom's Cabin,* the two books that said if cannibalistic Negroes hadn't ever been enslaved and brought to America, they'd never have become civilized and Christian.

So far, the basis for the essay she had to write on the subject was: what a shitty thing to say. She knew she'd have to put a little more thought into it. It's a dirty job, writing essays, but somebody's gotta do it.

What she couldn't wait for was to get it over with and move onto the horrible "War of the Worlds"–type mass panic of the 1970's when Johnny Carson made a joke about a sudden dirth of toilet paper, which all the idiots out in Whitey Audienceland took seriously and flooded the supermarkets to stock up in preparation for the Charmin Famine.

She'd just finished *Sociology for the South* and picked up *Cannibals All* when her kitchen timer went off, the alarm she'd set to warn her when it was time to go to her Bushido Japan class. She tidied up and grabbed her backpack, headed out.

In the stairwell, she passed a guy carrying boxes upstairs and did a double-take. She'd only caught a glimpse of him, but she was almost positive it was Megan's new boyfriend, out of uniform. She watched him from behind. Same height, same build, same cute ass…when he got to the landing and turned to go up the next flight he glanced down and met her eyes. Wobbled a little, and two of the smaller cardboard boxes perched atop the largest one slid off and fell. He overcorrected his balance and the rest of the smaller boxes fell off the other way, one bouncing down the steps toward her. The guy started cursing under his breath.

He had on the typical college-boy outfit, jeans and an ugly unbuttoned plaid shirt, untucked, with a white wife beater underneath, and a baseball cap on backwards. Neve, out of curiosity rather than helpfulness, retrieved the box that stopped rolling a few steps up from her, and carried it to him. He was still muttering irritably, bending down and holding the large box squeezed between his knees and his chest so he could use both hands to collect the other boxes. Coming up closer, Neve could see that the shirt wasn't plaid, but that Murano glass *millefiori* pattern. Different, but just as ugly. When he stood up, uncertainly balanced, she set the box she'd gotten on the top, and he turned to face her better.

"Thank you," he said, in a voice bit higher than Nick's. Up close, there was no way she could confuse him with the man she'd met two days before. The goatee and hair coming out from under the cap was black, and his face was pitted by horrible acne scars. Not just pockmarks, but *craters* in some places. On top of that, his eyes were brown and there was no tan line on his left ring finger. Puffy eyelids, too, from not enough sleep.

"Just moved in?" she asked.

"Yeah. Number 418. Wish we had an elevator."

"418? Hey, that's right above me."

"Really! Well, I don't make much noise," he said, and laughed a dorky laugh, as if something funny had crossed his mind.

Lord, what a dweeb, she thought.

"I'm Barry," he said. "What's your name?"

"Neve."

"Ooh that's an original name. Pretty, too."

"Uh, thanks. Well, see you 'round, Barry."

"Yeah, see ya! Hey, thanks a lot for helping!" Another dweeb laugh.

She hurried down the stairs, feeling a little creeped out by the way he looked at her. And to think she had confused him with that married guy! Her hunk radar must be getting rusty.

Barry listened to her footsteps die away, and smiled faintly, continued up the stairs. On the fourth floor, he found 418 and fished the key out of his pocket as easily as if the boxes he held were empty and glued together. He really had not wanted to drop the box, but it was the only way to get his neighbor to come up and talk to him.

He dropped the boxes off in the living room, which was sparsely furnished and barren-walled, went back down and got the rest of his things. Once the door was locked and the apartment secure, he went into the bathroom and stripped to the waist, tossing his clothes on the toilet lid. He chuckled dryly at his reflection, and began carefully picking at his hairline. Very gently, he gathered enough of a finger-hold to peel his skin away from his forehead. It started to tear over one of his eyebrows, so he had to do it more slowly. Frustratingly slowly.

Damn, I hate this part, he thought.

He peeled the pockmarked skin off one wide strip at a time, laying it out flat on the sides of the sink. Then he removed the cellophane-thin strips of plastic from his eyelids, what he used to make them look puffy.

His face always *had* to start itching in one place or another once the fake skin was on and he couldn't scratch. It came in handy, though, especially at times like just now. When he saw that Megan's roommate had recognized him, he had to think fast, get her to come up closer and get a good look at his disguise, hear him with Barry's voice and have her suspicions allayed.

Once the skin was off, the colored contacts came out and went in his little case full of disinfectant. He'd caught pink-eye way too many times to not take every precaution with his contact collection now. He'd leave his hair and goatee black for now. It would be a while before he had to be Nick again, and he still had to be Barry just to get out of the building.

He rinsed the residue of adhesive off of his face, then went into the living room to unpack and set up office. He'd padded all of his equipment carefully in the boxes, so none of it was damaged when he dropped it on the stairs, but he still regretted having to do that. Eavesdroppers and tiny surveillance cameras are not easy come by, and he couldn't just drop them off at some repair shop downtown.

Shit. He'd left the generator downstairs. Maybe he'd need Blue Tick to come and help him carry that thing up, because damn, it was heavy. Necessary, though. He couldn't have the apartment manager see the electric bill skyrocket when he had all the security cameras and monitors running, and get nosy, come around asking questions.

He stopped to have a cigarette, hating himself for starting back up again. He'd given up smoking for a whole two months, but one, there were so many opportunities to look cool and debonair that he was missing out on, and two, he'd grown antsy being this close to Gwynn, finally finding her after all this time. He couldn't *not* smoke.

He blew three smoke rings and watched them float lazily away, elongating and dissipating.

Everything was working out well. One tiny part was troublesome, though. He actually liked Bonnie, or Megan, whichever she'd rather be called. He hoped this wouldn't turn into one of those movies with a slogan like "He broke the only rule: never fall in love with your target" that seemed so popular nowadays. Stupidass movies. Like that was actually a rule somewhere in a handbook for hitmen or flimflammers or badguys in general. He started to laugh, shaking his head. How many movies had he seen that said that? Twelve? And how many others had a different Rule Number One?

Rule #1: Never trust a naked woman.

Rule #1: Never fall in love with your target.

Rule #1: Never put a car thief behind the wheel of the car you're going to blow him up in. Those had to be the worst lines Sean Connery and Ben Affleck ever said. The other one was from a movie poster, Rabbit thought. He decided he'd compile a list of Rule Number Ones that would fill an entire book, and publish it when this was all over.

Right, he said, stop thinking about stupid shit and worry about the task at hand. Megan. Yeah, he actually liked her, which could be a problem. He'd always felt that those inherently cool guys who got to go to bed with the really hot but shallow chicks, racking up tally after tally on their pussy scorecards, they were entitled to some renown as Players, but if he could win the *hearts* of those coquettish bitches—or better yet, the hearts of intelligent women such as Megan—that was worth so much more as an achievement. Chicks like Neve, while they may be gorgeous and have higher standards, are a dime a dozen.

Their looks aren't durable, and once they had faded, what good were they? They couldn't hold interesting conversations, didn't express any interest in productive hobbies, and couldn't appreciate the finer things in life (which, he adamantly believed, were *not* money, flashy clothes, and fancy cars.)

The problem with genuinely beautiful women like Megan was that he fell in love with them way too easily. And way too often. Just like now.

Despite all the lies he had to tell her, he could be himself with her. Well, not *himself* himself. But the false name and fictitious marital status aside, everything he had with her was genuine, once the seed had been planted to seduce her.

And she was a wild woman in bed. Good God daaaaaamn! She let him do everything he wanted to her, all the weird perversions he could not rationally justify, but was consumed with the need to act out, especially the toe sucking. And the habits he'd picked up in Morocco.

And on top of that, on top of her letting him commit all those depraved acts upon her person, she lived up to her promise of reciprocating. And top of *that*, she was the kind of girl that used the word "reciprocate!" That alone was worth his heart and his love!

Whoa. Stop thinking like that, Rabbit.

Evil thoughts, get out of my head.

He looked at his watch, saw it wasn't time for him to take his meds yet, but knew he could use them right now. Keep himself grounded, keep his thoughts from drifting away. Keep focused on the task at hand.

He went to the fridge, got out the half-gallon of Bacardi that he considered as essential to the mission as his Acho unidirectional microdish or his night vision goggles. Poured himself a shot in one of the big red Dixie cups he'd brought, reconsidered, and made it a triple. Got his daily dose of self-discipline/reality pills and downed them in one go from the cup, grimacing. Damn, he should've thought ahead and gotten some Coke to go with it. Dumbass, he thought. You can plan something as epically complex as this and you can't remember to buy *Coke?*

Putting the bottle in the freezer this time, he relit his cigarette and got to work.

IV

Megan couldn't believe the people she passed in the halls of the Arts Building. There was one rather attractive blonde girl in low-rider khakis, riding so low they revealed a good two inches of ass cleavage—no underwear—a spaghetti-strap baby shirt—no bra—a tattoo on the small of her back—of a *sunflower*, for Christ's sake—and of all footwear, flip-flops. Megan had always believed that flip-flops were appropriate footwear for the beach and the communal shower only. But here was some chippie trying to look sexy in her Britney/Christina/Whoever outfit and scuffing her feet as she walked in a trashy pair of flippity floppity flippity floppity fricking *flip-flops*.

"I'm going back to bed," the chippie said to the guys next to her. "I've got like, eleven hours of sleep in the last, like, two days, or whatever. And I'm like, y'know? Draggin' ass."

Draggin' ass? Oh, how articulate.

Megan made a mental note to tell Neve that if she ever used the phrase "draggin' ass" to contact the proper authorities and report her as possessed by an evil spirit. Either a priest, a root doctor, or a witch should be fetched with all speed.

There was also this chick (she could tell it was a female by the ways its jeans fit) who bumped into her without apology, whose arms were wreathed in bracelets from wrists to elbows, whose eyebrows were pierced with so many rings that at first she appeared to have glasses on, with a labret and two lip-rings as well.

I hate people, Megan thought. If Nick and I could be hermits in the Appalachians or the Catskills, I'd be happier than if it were a mansion in Beverly Hills. She wondered briefly if this made her a sociopath.

It was her lunch break, and if Gwynnie was in class until two, she'd have to be around here somewhere. Megan had to get a look at her. Once she knew what at least one of her classes was, she could come back and stalk her at another time. Find out where she went, what she did, and plan the best possible way to kill her.

It still did not disturb her that she wanted to do this. She wondered if it ever would.

Weaving through student traffic, she glanced through the square window set at eye-level in every classroom door. She passed bulletin-cluttered corkboards and rows of lockers that had been spray-painted with graffiti. Everywhere there was the musty smell of School, a stench that she thought she would never have to suffer again when she graduated. It was the stink not of learning and work and study, but of people. Lots of people clumped together in small rooms where they'd throw wads of paper and shoot spitballs. And call names.

Megan could've gotten a scholarship to any university she wanted, but couldn't bring herself to put up with so many people her age at one time, ever again.

Besides, what with bell curves, vanity universities with their fraudulent degrees, and student pride based on intercollegiate athletics, what was the point of enrolling when a better education could be found at the town library? If Bachelor's, Master's, and even Doctor's degrees were for sale (several in California, Florida, and Hawaii, India, fifty-six in Colombia—twenty-seven in Bogota alone) in exchange for a large enough cash payment known as an "honorarium" what good was any degree worth in the job market? Better to work in a record store than be a liar, a poseur, a fraud.

She came up short at the door to a professor's office on the art building's third floor. The woman from the photo in Nick's wallet was inside, on the other side of the glass panel that ran a foot and a half wide from the floor up the left side of the office door to the molding across the top, sitting on a desk and shamelessly flirting with a big man with a mustache and paint spatters on his shirt.

Megan's eyes bulged. There was no mistaking. That was Gwynn Hutchinson, Mrs. Nick and...

And she wasn't wearing a wedding ring.

Megan watched her toss her head and laugh at some joke that could not have been as funny as she made out, judging by her own exaggeration and the professor's uncertain posture and nervous smile. Gwynn playfully clapped one hand on his shoulder, then his cheek, and held it there.

Professor Edmund Braswell, the door's sign read.

Well well well.

What? A private tutoring session at your house, Professor? This evening? Why, thank you! It'll be an honor!

You would like me to pose for you, Mr. Braswell? You'd like to paint little ol' *me?* Why, certainly. In the nude? Oh, I'd love to!

My husband is at a long, boring convention for three days, Mr. Braswell. Or can I call you Edmund?

We've got the house all to ourselves, Eddie.

Megan left, furious. Sure, in the two-wrongs-make-a-right philosophy, this may have made their affair justifiable, but her outrage was at a "frigid" wife withholding sex from a wonderful wonderful man like Nickie, while paying off an "honorarium" behind his back. How could anyone forsake him, especially for some swine artist who was obviously so unsuccessful at his art that he had to make a living teaching it instead?

Quite rationally, in her own mind, she made a few changes to her plan.

"Sorry Vince," Rabbit said into his cell phone. "I don't really have much time to talk."

"Jesus, Nick, it's an emergency!" the art dealer shouted back. Vince was a little on the flamboyant side.

"Vince. Vincey. An emergency is a frayed elevator cable. It's a ruptured appendix. It's your true love tied up on the railroad tracks."

"It's *also* a major art collector stopping by right after we had a big sale and we have nothing really spec*tac*ular to show him! We had to lie and say we were fumigating the gallery and ask him to come back in two days! Then what are we going to do two days from now if you can't whip something up? Tell him we have radon?"

"Radon's passé," Rabbit corrected him. "Tell him asbestos. It's a retro thing. I see asbestos coming back in a really big way."

"*Oh!*"

"Calm yourself," Rabbit snapped, holding up and admiring the preliminary sketches for a nude portrait of Megan that he'd been working on from memory. The one he'd finally chosen was an erotic and provocative one of her touching herself. It would not be pornographic. It would be erotic and provocative. "It just so happens that I've come into five pieces. I can let you show this collector four of them."

"What are they?"

"Two of them are Cigouaves'. One is "Traiture" and the one you can't have is "Orgè D'Une." I like that one too much."

The reason the gallery couldn't have the second one was that Rabbit hadn't painted it yet. All he was looking at was a set of different poses so far. "There's also a Yingzhao, and two Derwatts. 'Man In Chair' and 'The Clock' have finally resurfaced. Been lost in France for decades."

"What are you talking about? Who's Derwatt?"

"Nevermind. So, you want the Yingzhao sculpture and the Cigoauves? The painting's of a juju woman."

"Sure, that'd be great. Your Cig-wahv stuff is getting real popular."

"Careful what you say, Vin. The walls have ears."

"Oh, knock it off, Nickie. It's not like this is cloak-and-dagger—"

"You're right, it's just fraud."

"You're just a big worry-wart, Nickie. That's what you are."

"Look who's talking. I got a fag calling me up screaming about an emergency like being short on supply is the Great Chicago Fire. I've got a big date tonight and I have—"

"Really? Who's the lucky lady?"

"None a yer business, Liberace. But if you'll let me, I'll get cracking on having these two pieces Fed-Exed so you can have them in time. Have some papers fixed up to say you got the sculpture from me through Immortelles."

"What's that?"

"It's a brokerage I want to establish."

"How do you spell that?"

"It's the funeral flower. Plural. Immortelles, LTD."

"Oh, how quaint. Selling dead people's stuff under that name. Get to Fed-Exing, you big freak. And enjoy your date."

"I will. And I will."

"Thank you, Nickie, you're a life saver."

"That's why I make the big bucks." He hung up, checked his watch. He had time, but he couldn't go wasting it. Yingzhao was a scam his father had started, Oriental sculpture and bas-relief in alabaster, jade, and cinnabar, all with a thin and angular signature carved into the undersides of their bases next to an imaginary symbol that was supposed to be mysterious and cryptic. Rabbit's little art projects were all based on studies of ancient works, then stained with this and that, or buried for a few weeks to imitate the patina of antiquity. Yingzhaos were then passed off as artifacts of unknown origin.

Jubal Cigouaves was Rabbit's *nom de guerre* in painting, and Vincent Kilgore's gallery dealt exclusively in the Haitian's—no, not Haitian, but Creole—portraits. White people seemed more ready to support a "diamond in the rough" these days than one of their own, and Rabbit was capitalizing on it.

He did not have time to be Jubal today, though. He had to be Barry to get out of the building and become Mr. Coniglio to get into the Heather-Leigh before Megan even had time to get off work. One might think it illogical to make so many complications just to settle an old score, but all this adventure was *so much fun*, and gave him spice and excitement to keep life thrilling instead of allowing it to go stale.

While the vendetta against Gwynn Hutchinson was his own egg on the face, the evil bitch who had evaded him so long finally turning up dead would mean probing, investigation, a list of anyone who might've had motive, and he really didn't need the police to show up asking questions.

No, seducing some needy, borderline sociopathic chick and dropping enough hints had seemed like an easy way to get the job done for him, and then she'd be caught and he'd disappear, having never really been here anyway—since the beef with Gwynn had begun way back when he was Jared Layton, a teenager in his parents' house, and that kid was "dead"—case closed.

Face wiped clean of egg by someone else's hand.

Problem with a plan like that, though, is that like, say, Communism and Democracy, and New Year's resolutions, or anything dependent upon Man being consistent, is that it only works on paper.

After last night, truly getting to know Megan as a person instead of as a tool he'd observed from afar and found satisfactory, he would dump the entire project, kill Gwynn himself, and date Megan openly if there was a chance it would work. Problem with *that* was, while he'd become expert at picking up chicks, seducing them, losing them one way or another for the sole purpose of winning them back, and losing them again, he had no clue whatsoever how to *keep* them. They don't bother to write those parts into the love stories, and Mom and Dad sure didn't provide an example while they were alive.

Whirlwind romances were, sadly, all he knew.

Looking at it that way, he finally thought he knew what Megan had said about practice making perfect. Too bad it wouldn't happen like that, at least not yet. Time enough after Gwynn was dead…and that asshole that he saw keying a stranger's car for no reason. Just because he thought it was funny. That piece of shit needed to be off the planet, just on general principle. And then there was that girl who was walking up to a restaurant with her boyfriend and jogged the last few steps to stand still at the door and wait for the poor sap to catch up and open it for her. Strawberry blonde bitch doing it just to subtly humiliate him, make sure that everyone who was watching, like Rabbit, knew who was wearing the pants. Rabbit couldn't believe his eyes. And she had done it with a big, shit-eating grin, splitting her face like a jack-o-lantern smile. What a shitty thing to do! She definitely needed to be put in her place. And then there was that other guy…

Whoa. Earth to Rabbit.

Evil thoughts, get out of my head.

He needed to get himself ready for tonight, then get Kilgore's shipment taken care of. He realized he'd picked up a pencil and had been writing Megan Delaune, Megan Coniglio, Megan Haggerty, Megan Lapine, Megan Danaher, Megan Layton, and even Megan Cigouaves while he was daydreaming.

Good God, he thought. Liberace's right. I *am* a freak.

V

"I was looking through a catalogue," she said. "And I was disgusted by the names of the colors the clothes were listed under."

She took a folded square of loose-leaf paper out of her breast pocket. Her shirt was white, button-down, with the cuffs rolled sloppily up and the collar out of whack, by design, with the amulet sparkling in the V. Her hair hung in a braid down the back, but she kept the same strands hanging in front of her face that Neve had arranged the night before.

"Care to see it?"

"Of course." They were in the Heather's bar again, this time in an out-of-the-way booth. No piano. "No, wait. To be honest, I'd rather you read it to me."

"In that case..." she unfolded it, took a sip of her wine, and began. Periodically, Rabbit made either snorts of disgust or low chuckles, while trying not to put a hand on the thigh beside him. (He knew he'd been a little too, um, exhibitive before and had reeled himself in a bit.)

"I started out just counting them, thinking it was about a dozen or so out of a hundred items, but when I hit twenty and had only gotten about a third of the way through it—"

"Read the damned thing."

"Watch it, buster!"

"Sorry, Tourettes."

She laughed, cleared her throat, and read.

"Coral. Seen it before, so it's not so bad. Cactus. Spearmint. Buff."

"*Buff?*"

"Yeah, Buff."

"What kind of a color is *that?*"

"It was somewhere between Ecru and Taupe."

"Was it now?"

"It was. Glacier. Didn't look like any glacier I've ever seen. Pond. Hibiscus."

"Wait. Hibiscus come in many different colors."

"Not on the planet this catalogue came from."

"Great sleepin' Jesus."

"Opal, but not Opal like an *actual* opal. Opal as in turquoise."

"You're kidding. *Turquoise* is turquoise."

"Preaching to the choir, Nicky. Okay, Flax. Flax isn't so bad. I can live with flax. Henna. Terra Cotta. Celadon. Cadet. Not cadet-blue, just Cadet. Ivory. Off-white. You see that shit? The Ivory was beige with little red flowers all over it, but they take an actually ivory-colored shirt, and name it Off-white. Their version of ivory was…yunno those elephants that come from, uh, France? Yeah, French elephants, as opposed to the African and Indian ones that have tusks made out of ivory that is the *color* of ivory? Not *those* elephants. The French ones with beige tusks that have little red flowers all over them. That's what this shirt is."

"Have you seen the elephants that come from Detroit? Up around there? I'd like some pants the color of *their* tusks."

"Ooh, yeah, that'd be nice. So, anyway, back to the atrocities. I'm not boring you, am I?"

"Of course not! Shame on you for asking such a stupid question."

"Just making sure. Okay, I got Ivory, Off-white, and—oh, you'll love this one. Worn Light."

"Worn Light? What the hell is that?"

"It looks like ivory."

Rabbit snorted a laugh.

"Oh, you ain't seen nothing yet," she said. "Oatmeal. Aubergine. Daffodil. Toast."

"*Toast?* You're shitting me."

"Would that I were. And it wasn't even brown. It was gray."

"Oh, for Christ's sake."

"Uh-huh. Wait'll you hear the rest of them."

"There's more?"

"I'm not even half-way through the list."

"But that's twenty already!"

"…You've been counting?"

"Huh?"

"You're right, that was number twenty. How'd you know that?"

"Well, I've always been good at that kind of thing."

"Wow, that's pretty cool. Can you count cards too, like Rain Man?"

"Yes, I can up to a point, but not as well as him. I'm working on it, though. Now, what's twenty-one?"

The truth was, he really wasn't interested in her list, and *was* getting bored with it, but he could see that she was enjoying this and didn't want to hurt her feelings. He had heard this was the kind of thing that people did in relationships, so he feigned interest.

"Okay, twenty-one, twenty-one…ah, Gunsmoke."

"But gunsmoke is so varied in color depending on the model of gun and time period. When some guns are fired, they give off a kind of anodized blue—"

"Um, are you trying to make sense of this?"

"Sorry."

"Ahem…next is Flag."

"Flag?"

"Yeah. There were four plaid shirts: Blue, Green, Amber, and then Flag. Flag was the red one. Why it couldn't just be Red is beyond me. Or better yet, why the ass that did the naming couldn't step up and have Blue and Green be something equally arbitrary like Fish and Traffic Light, y'know? Not be half-assed stupid, but gung-ho, full-throttle, all-the-way stupid."

"Pass the wine, please?"

"Why, soytenly. Okay, Artichoke…Seaweed. Iced Shrimp. Radish. Steel. Pebble. Mulberry. Dark Sage. Sagebrush. Big difference between Dark Sage and Sagebrush. Lake. Smoke. Harvest. Cayenne. Desert. And the last one, Light Pumice."

"Oh, hell yeah! I was just thinking the other day about how incomplete my life was that I don't have a Light Pumice suit. Thank God they finally got around to Light Pumice. By chance, do they have a Dill tie, or an ascot even, that I could wear with my Light Pumice suit, and be the talk of the town?"

"It's not available in a suit yet. I don't think they'll come out with that until after Labor Day. Right now all they have in Light Pumice is a windbreaker and a Greek fisherman's cap."

"Darn."

"Tell me about it. Oh, the humanity. By the way, what are the colors of your outfit?"

"The suit is Gunmetal, and the shirt is what used to be called Rust, but now is Antique. Wait, Antique is so five minutes ago. It's Vintage now. This is a Gunmetal and Vintage ensemble."

Megan was ever so pleased that he pronounced it on-somb instead of on-som-bull.

"It looks good on you," she said.

"Why, thank you. What's that you have on?"

"What, this old thing? My top is Mayonnaise and these pants are Charcoal. Wait'll you see my panties."

"What color are they?"

"Clear, but I call them Existential. You can argue whether they are real or imaginary, but the truth, if you want the truth—"

"I want the truth."

"I'm not wearing any."

"Prove it!"

"I will, later."

"More wine?"

"Yes, please. So, point of all this, I am toying with the idea of becoming a famous fashion designer."

"Toying, you say?"

"Yes, I haven't quite decided yet. See, I've made a list of the ten things I'd love to do with my life, and being a cashier in a records shop didn't make the cut. I started thinking about a grander scheme of things, and realized that cashiers don't have any paparazzi following them around twenty-four-seven. Their lives aren't monitored by gossip columnists and their relationships reported to every enquiring mind that wants to know."

He just blinked at her.

"I hate it when people do that."

"Do what?"

"Blink at me. Does anyone blink at the schmucks whose job it is to sit around and make up bullshit color names? Or do they give each other high-fives and get fat checks and medals pinned to their chests? Just like those bullshitters Andy Warhol and Basquiat and the rest of them, putting paint on canvas in the visual equivalent of gibberish, to get praised by ass-kissing sycophants with even less talent, but still eagerness to be part of a scene that claims to be culture. And people dare to call this art!"

He stared at her. In the silence that fell, under his steady gaze, she sheepishly huddled into her wine glass. He licked the tip of his index finger, touched it to the air in front of her and made a hissing noise.

"Sorry," she said. "Got a little carried away."

"Keep going. This is the good stuff."

"What?"

"Anybody can be charming and delightful for a couple of hours in the evening, but you don't get to know anyone, not really, until you find out what they hate. You've only been telling me what irks you, Megan. But there's some deep-seated hatred in there, bottled up inside that perfect little body, and I want a good whiff of it. You should've seen the look on your face just now. God, I'll bet you're capable of fury, real fuckin' *rage*, if you'd just let yourself go."

"Are you serious?"

"Are *you?*"

"What do you mean?"

"Do you really want things to change, or are you just a dreamer? Be honest with yourself. Are you going to take the steps to become one of your top-tens or just sit behind your cash register waiting for life to just drop into your lap?"

Her eyes flashed bright with anger.

"The way *you* just dropped into my lap? I—"

"Are you pissed off at me or yourself?"

"What the fu—"

"And if it's me, is it because I'm right or wrong?"

That shut her up. He kept on, smiling faintly.

"It seems like people these days are looking for a banner to fight under. Yelling that they're 'killing in the name of' and searching for something to fill in the blank. Well, Megan, I beg of you, don't be one of them."

"What the hell are you talking about?"

"Shit. I get ahead of myself sometimes. Just listen, bear with me. Invention is never born without necessity. And I mean real invention, not salad shooters and scrotal clamps. Real innovation must come out of bona fide need. Glory and triumph can never exist without adversity. Without hardship, sure, we continue to invent things, but at such a petty level. We branch out into the unimportant. With peace and safety and security comes only stagnation. Without the necessity of daily survival we have the time to become so bored that we need to stir up trouble and controversy over petty things. Am I making sense, at all?"

She stared at him a long moment, then nodded.

"Sort of."

"Good. So—"

"If what you're saying is, since we're not like animals, fighting every day just to be alive and have something to eat, having to constantly be on the alert because of threat of danger, because we can rest easy at night and not have to worry about anything really, not in comparison to any other animal on this planet, and because of that, because we have the extra time on our hands to be angry about whatever else there is, we pick stuff that really doesn't matter, then yes."

"Okay, good. Whew! I thought I'd lost you."

"You nearly did."

He paused, wondering if there was subtext there, and saw in her eyes that there was. Shit. He rallied himself and forged on bravely.

"Good, so, now, if you could change one thing about the world you live in, what would it be? Don't think about it too hard and say something you feel culturally obligated to say, like world peace or starving children in Africa, or something you really don't care about because it doesn't influence you in any way. Don't pick something—" He flipped through an invisible Rolodex until finding the invisible card he was looking for, plucked it out and held it up, pretending to read aloud.

"I wanna end world hunger and white slavery. Bullshit! What do *you* want to change, Megan?"

"…I want you to be single."

"Oh, come on! Is that the best you can do? You're bringing that about just by being here! Think bigger. Think on a *grand* scale. Put into perspective that nothing happens anywhere, ever, unless one person puts it into action. The world doesn't change because of committees sitting at Mahogany Row debating shit. They are accomplishing a grand total of zilch. The people who are actually getting things done are people like you and me.

"I'm not going to say ordinary people, because one, we are far from ordinary, and two, those sheep we classify as ordinary don't ever do shit except date, marry, spew out clones, and die. And the funny thing about it is that they all think they are anything but ordinary. They all think they are so unlike Ordinary People who have clear skin and straight white teeth, nuclear families and fresh-smelling laundry with no static cling, and their children play fair and chew with their mouths closed at dinnertime and then the grown-ups go off to have quiet sex in the missionary position and then fall asleep in each others' arms. But those people aren't ordinary at all. If they even do exist, they are complete freaks in this world. The everyday ordinary people are really people who think they are different, people who, like Steinbeck said, think they are just temporarily embarrassed millionaires, people with incredible talent and advantage that are going to be recognized for their imagined fabulosity one day, and in that way they're *all* the same…how do I always go off on these tangents? Where was I even going with this?"

"Um…something about people like you and me?"

"Ah, thank you. Honey, things happen in this world because people who are pissed off figure out a way to do something about it. They don't act out their anger by getting drunk and hitting the wife or shouting at the TV like 'ordinary people' do. And if you don't act to change what pisses you off, I mean actively, you waste your entire life. For God's sake, take advantage of everything life has given you."

"And what exactly," she asked patiently. "Has life given me?"

"Opposable thumbs."

"…what?"

"Think for a second. You're a human being, the only type of animal on this planet that's capable of changing its environment to suit its own preferences. Everything else has to adapt to any changes in its surroundings. We say fuck our surroundings. We make it adapt to us. Fuck that swamp that was Florida, we're going to drain it and sell Oceanfront. Fuck that desert that was Las Vegas, we'll irrigate it and put up monuments to gambling.

"And what's that? All our saying fuck it has taken its toll on the Earth? We've irrevocably damaged our surroundings and the clock is ticking down to our self-annihilation? Fuck it! We're gonna start terra-forming Mars! We'll move, no problem!"

Megan's eyes were fiercely bright, and her mind spinning. Rabbit could almost hear the cogs whirring inside her head, seeing the possibilities stretch out around her like reflections in opposing mirrors, just like he had one day years ago. At that moment he felt the way he imagined his mentor had felt when the preaching had taken root, when he had truly opened his eyes for the first time. Now he felt that almost paternal satisfaction of having created a truly self-aware human being.

He turned and caught the eye of one of the waiters who had been looking at him askance while he was talking. One of the pointless people who were pissed off at him for not making unexciting bullshit small talk in library volume.

The man hesitated a moment before coming over, for appearance's sake, making a point to show Rabbit he really didn't want to serve him, but *had* to. Rabbit made a mental note to kill him sometime.

"Yes sir?" the condescending waiter asked when he arrived. He looked strangely familiar.

"I'm going to need three chilled bottles of Veuve Cliquot Ponsardin sent up to my room, please. Make that five."

"Yes...*sir.*"

Did he just enunciate 'sir' as if he didn't mean it?

To be sarcastic?

Oh, I'ma have to do more than just kill this prick.

"Wait," Megan said to the doomed servant. He paused and assumed an air of longsuffering patience, a move that pretty much sealed his fate. "Settle an argument for us?"

He parted his lips and moved his jaw, taking the little knob of flesh on the inside of his cheek between his teeth, a habit Nick Coniglio made a note of and filed away.

"Who was Betsy Ross?" Megan asked.

The waiter thought for a moment.

"Sewed the first American flag?"

"The first United States of American flag," she corrected him. "We are not the only country in America. We've got North, Central, and South Americans who don't appreciate us calling ourselves 'Americans.' But that's not where I'm going with this. Who were the first cowboys?"

This he answered with more confidence.

"An outlaw gang in the old West."

"Where was the Gettysburg Address written?"

"On the back of an envelope," he said like a student reciting the most elementary of facts and stating it with the firmest conviction.

Megan slanted her eyes sideways at Rabbit.

"Do you consider yourself educated?" she asked. The waiter could barely conceal his outrage at such an insult, and he made a big production out of the effort he went to in concealing it.

"I'm working my way through *college* right now, so yes—"

"But Betsy Ross's contribution was a lot smaller than what you stated. She was just one of several flag makers in Philadelphia at that time, and really all she did was change the six-pointed stars to the easier-to-sew five-pointed star design. The story didn't appear until almost one hundred years later, and was told to promote her as a patriotic role model for young girls and a symbol of women's contributions to US history. If anything, her real contribution to US history was screwing Count Carl Emilius von Donop, a Hessian colonel on Christmas Eve and keeping him from going to help Rall fight the rebels at the Battle of Trenton the next day. But they don't teach that in history class.

"That cowboy garbage? You remember that from a Kurt Russell movie four years ago, and you foolishly assumed that the cowboy origin was factual because the narrator had a voice of knowledgeable authority. If that voice told you a fish was eligible for the Presidency, you'd believe it.

"Just like everybody who now thinks all Sicilians are part black because Dennis Hopper said so in one of Tarantino's first movies. Christopher Walken was torturing him because he knew Hopper was lying, and no one can lie to a Sicilian because they know all the pantomimes a liar will do to give himself away. So

Hopper said he'd read that the Moors, who are black, conquered Sicily and fucked all the women, changing the bloodline forever, and that's why Sicilians now have black hair and dark skin. Then he goes 'Am I lying?' So Christopher Walken shoots him.

"Then they put Morgan Freeman in a Robin Hood movie as a Moor from the Crusades and now it's an accepted fact. Trouble is, Moors *aren't* black. They are a mix of Arab and Berber. But nobody bothers to look that the fuck up. The only reason Dennis Hopper said all that shit was he knew it would piss Walken off so much that he'd stop torturing him and go ahead and kill him, but you accept it as gospel.

"And the Gettysburg Address was an old joke that idiots mistook as fact, just like Dan Quayle wanting to learn Latin so he could converse with Latin Americans. Where do you write addresses? On the backs of envelopes. Ha ha funny funny. And the dig about Quayle? It was a joke told by Claudine Schneider, the Congresswoman from Rhode Island, and she even admitted it was a joke. Didn't matter, though. You couldn't make the connection because you are so narrow-minded that you absorb every bit of bullshit that anyone says with a straight face."

"Now, you listen—"

"Cowboys," she continued, ignoring him. "Were an irregular body of guerilla soldiers, colonists, who, in late 1776, fought against Washington, on the side of the redcoats, between the Hudson Highlands and New York City in what was called Neutral Ground, No Man's Land. They were nicknamed the cowboys because that's how they ate, by stealing the cattle of local farmers. New Yorkers stealing cows. Next country boy with a hat who calls himself 'a real cowboy' is getting a fat lip.

"In fact, a lot of what I hear about the Revolution pisses me off because it was really nothing more than a bunch of discontented colonists taking advantage of a war in Europe to divide their masters' forces and relieve themselves of taxes. You could even go so far as to call them a bunch of lawless opportunists who couldn't handle a conventionally organized society, not even the one they managed to establish in the years following the Revolution, since the only reason it stayed together when the agricultural South said 'This is bullshit' was that the industrial

70

North outgunned them. Or am I wrong? If I am, O educated waiter who's working his way through college, waste no time in correcting me."

Rabbit stifled his laughter as the belittled man shifted his weight from one foot to the other and back again. Megan turned her attention fully to her lover, her body language dismissing the waiter, who still stood there, furious.

"*That's* what I'd like to do, Nick. I'd publicize the true stories and dispel the myths we were reared upon. All history has been fumigated in schools until it's nothing more than dates and names and ruins and multiple choice guesses, instead of real shit that happened to real people not that long ago.

"But I could never get anyone to listen to me without the empty validation of a college degree. If I had an honorarium, I could get myself a Doctor's and a couple of letters to put behind my name on a controversial book that people would take seriously."

"Good!" Rabbit applauded. "That's what I've been waiting to hear. Now, I suggest that this meeting adjourns to my room, this snooty do-boy fetches our bubbly, and we have ourselves a seventy-seven."

"What's a seventy-seven?"

"It's like a sixty-nine, only you get ate more."

She had to think about that one for a second, and while she did, Rabbit turned back to the waiter.

"Garçon, in case you've forgotten, that was five bottles of Veuve Cliquot Ponsardin I need sent to my room, posthaste. If you can hop to it and get them to the door before the lovely Megan and I arrive, there will be a crisp new dollar bill in it for you. So crisp, in fact, that it will slide right into the vending machine slot that you purchase your breakfast from without any hassle. Or the token machine in the video game arcade, if you decide to indulge yourself a little. You do only live once, yunno."

"I'm going to have to ask you to leave," the waiter finally choked out.

Rabbit stood up and looked into the young man's eyes, calmly, but only a few inches away.

"Now I know where I have seen you before," he said. "You're dating a strawberry blonde chick who makes you hold the door for her. Tell me how it is that you act like her little bitch but you dare try to be disrespectful to me? You have a cloak that you throw down before her every time she walks up to a mud puddle, but you hesitate when I call you? When I signal to you that I want something, you hop the fuck to it because you're a waiter and I'm a guest here. Do your job and kiss my ass all the way up to my room."

Megan stared at the two of them. This wasn't the kind of stupid male pissing contest where the air stank of testosterone. This was something scarily exhilarating. There was pure evil emanating from her boyfriend's pores that paralyzed the waiter, like a snake with a shivering chipmunk.

"Grow some balls, fuckboy," Rabbit said gently. "Stand up to that bitch and put her in her place. Now rehearse what you're going to say to her while you're getting my champagne, and don't ever act snooty at work again."

"Get out of my face," the waiter stammered.

Rabbit leaned forward and touched the tip of his nose to the tip of the waiter's.

"Honey," Megan said. "It's past our bedtime."

"Ah, right you are. Come along, darling, and you, garçon, do remember to send up our nightcap. While ruminating over our friendly discussion, I hope you'll see the light and change your major from whatever garbage it is to something that works at the development of the intellect rather than the memorization and repetition by rote of fabricated or essentially useless material. Good night."

Rabbit backed his nose away from the other man's and held out his hand for Megan, who took it and rose from her seat, and the waiter watched the two of them leave, not knowing what to think, but wanting a drink. He felt the eyes of everyone in the bar, his coworkers, the guests, and wished he were invisible.

VI

As much as he hated to think about it, Rabbit had gotten this idea from one of his victims, a Ukrainian prick named Velosh Bilowas. Well, it was a variation of the prick's idea.

He had tied Megan down on the bed, spread-eagled, and opened a Dobb kit, worn and old with a zipper that didn't close all the way. He duct-taped her mouth shut so he wouldn't have to hear her protests, and removed three devices from the kit, lubricating one of them with a tube of Sexx Grease.

Her eyes went even wider than they already were when he started gently easing the smallest of the three vibrators into a place she was, um, un*accustomed* to having a vibrator.

She was surprised that it slipped in so easily, and didn't hurt at all unless she clenched down on it. She looked up at him, somewhat fearfully as he took out the longer vibrator, began to toy with her a little, and slipped that in a more conventional place. The third device he strapped to her, positioning it right over her clitoris.

Then, gently, he peeled the tape off her mouth.

"Honey?" she asked. "What are you—"

She convulsed as he turned the smallest dildo onto the lowest setting. Gasped as he switched on the second one. Cried out as the first of many low-voltage jolts zinged into her from the third.

He kissed her briefly, and went over to the hotel room's desk, bringing back his sketch pad and a mechanical pencil. Pushing aside the phone and lamp on the nightstand, setting the pad down on his thigh, he started to draw her expressions.

Velosh Bilowas had gotten a system of pulleys together and a harness to hoist himself up off of the floor so he could hang suspended horizontally. He and his "team" finally agreed upon a height of two feet, because the girl who gave him a rim job could put a pillow under her head and not get a crick in her neck, and the two that went to work on his blowjob and hummer could easily keep their balance without bonking heads. The one that straddled his torso to lick his navel didn't get in the way of the two who were biting his nipples, and the one kissing him didn't interfere with the two on either side of his head, licking his ears. He had to settle for only four girls to handle his fingers and toes because there just wasn't enough room for each individual digit to be serviced.

He ended up with thirteen girls sucking on him at once instead of the thirty he'd dreamed up in a fit of stoned and drunken inspiration, which is just as well because the original plan would've cost a mint.

It was Heaven, or as close as he could get to it, for about fifteen seconds before Rabbit came into the room. The girls looked up in surprise, gasped, then froze as he pressed the index finger of his black gloved hand to where his pursed lips must've been under his black balaclava. They stared, terrified, at the silenced Heckler & Koch MP-10 in his other fist.

Bilowas started to shout, but quit when the machine gun's suppressed muzzle came within an inch of his face, and the prostitutes shrank fearfully away from it.

"Wszyscy weseli ludzie podniescie rece," Rabbit said in Polish, thinking it was Bosnian for "Get into the truck outside. My men will escort you." He would find out later that the man who coached him with useful phrases had a sense of humor. The girls blinked for a moment and shrugged, deciding for themselves what he meant, and obeyed.

They had all been lured out of small towns in the Ukraine and Moldavia, like many others, by promises of employment, and were worth up to four thousand dollars American. Most were shipped to Israel, Germany, the US, Japan and Switzerland. There, they would have to "work off the debt" and earn back the amount paid for them before they could be set free, but the way the books were kept, the debt wasn't even close to paid off until the girls stopped pulling clients.

These girls in Bosnia, though, were supposed to be luckier. In Prijedor, Milorad Milakovic's Sherwood Castle, the debt was a mere fifteen hundred American dollars, but the price of each "gig" was the equivalent of only a few packs of cigarettes.

It could have been a lot worse, of course. They could've gotten stuck at Artemdia, a club in Banja Luka, that catered entirely to cops, and cops, it is sad but true, can be the cruelest and most sadistic of all.

A few years from now, in 2000, these two outfits would be busted but Milakovic would still be free and able to operate, and he would even try to sue for compensation, to get back all the money he had lost when his slaves were set free.

That same year, Josip Loncaric, former cabdriver from Zagreb in Croatia, turned slavery warlord with even his own airlines in Albania and Macedonia, would also be brought down. His Chinese wife and business partner was his link to the Triads, and was adding her own people to his stock. They smuggled Kurds, Iraqis, Iranians, Indians, and Asians to work eighteen hours a day in restaurants or the sweatshops of famous Italian leather companies.

There would be an estimated twenty-seven million slaves in the world at the turn of the century, between fifteen and twenty million of them in Pakistan, India, Bangladesh, and Nepal, generations of families all passing on debts to their children and their children's children because of exorbitant interest and crooked accounting on loans taken out generations before.

These thirteen girls would not be much of a dent in the problem, Rabbit knew, but it was a start.

The girls hurried from the room, from one slavery to what they expected was another. Rabbit stayed, wanting to do this slowly, maybe with a nutcracker, crushing this piece of shit's knuckles one by one, and followed by his testicles, but he just didn't have the time.

Instead, he blew Bilowas' crotch into a ghastly ruin with a short squeeze of the trigger. The slaver shrieked. Another short burst of muffled fire pulped his kneecaps.

The thrashing body hung half on the floor, and collapsed fully when both arms were blown off.

Rabbit cut a notch in his belt. That's one down.

Sadly, the manic crusade he'd embarked upon did not last much longer. The thirteen slave women he brought to Navarre and housed until they could support themselves, putting them to work in one of his little projects, the conditions of which beat the shit out of a sweatshop any day. After that, though, the third attempt to free a decent amount of women at one time became a bloodbath.

Most of the bodyguards of a certain ambassador were killed, but enough were left alive after all but one of Rabbit's fell, and several of the women were seriously wounded—enough to make them useless as prostitutes.

With only one mercenary left standing beside him, Rabbit realized the futility of the whole venture, and retreated. He'd managed to get one or two, and the occasional three, away from their miserable lives, but that just wasn't enough for the risk involved and the money spent.

The first time had been just outside of Antigua Guatemala, at a place called El Zodiaco. He figured it was called that because you'd get crabs or something, or there were scorpions under the mattresses. Whatever the reason, there weren't too many virgins, and he gave up trying to make jokes as soon as he walked into that horrible place.

There was red foil on the walls, incense burning, and smoked mirrors. Wobbly tables and vinyl booths sticky with old sweat. A dirty tiled floor, high heels clicking and shitty music coming out of an old radio.

A heavy-set woman led a skinny, grinning white teenager upstairs while his friends giggled at a table below, elbowing each other in the ribs.

What was funny—not Ha-ha funny, but odd—was that the women all looked miserable and out of shape, while the boys dressed up as women were really into it, strutting around and having a great time, wishing they really were women, and looking smoking hot. Even though their penises were pulled back with string and taped between their buttocks, aside from that of course, damn, they looked good. For whores.

They were the ones who did sit-ups and squats and jumping jacks to keep their figure. They were the ones with the affected daintiness and the feather boas, who'd chat the clients up at the bar, touching their knee for emphasis, fingertips lingering. The women were just used-up and vacant, at least as Rabbit saw.

There was a huge owl that he had thought a statue until it spread its wings and flew across the room, startling the teenagers on their little South-of-the-Border summer adventure. These were just kids in maybe their freshman year of college. They didn't know any better. Like him when he was their age. They didn't deserve to die for being there, so he and his men left and came back a little later.

In total, twenty-four women made it to the free world, and seven of them went right back into prostitution immediately.

Figures.

Megan lay helpless, trembling on the bed for a long time after Rabbit had turned the vibrators and shocker off, removed them, and untied her. She had no idea how many times she had come. She lay still, tingling, as unable to move as if her bones had liquefied and drained out of her pores. She felt herself rolled over as he got into bed, felt his arms go around her and hold her tightly, and dimly felt his breath in her hair. Before too long, she was fast asleep in his embrace.

It had been a few years since Rabbit had last seen Anabela's ghost in his dreams, and though his love for her had eventually faded, as had the memory of at exactly what angle her lips curved and what shade of brown her eyes had been, his soul-consuming hatred of Gwynn Hutchinson had not dimmed a single watt.

He glimpsed her face out of the corner of his eye, vanishing into a crowd or behind a corner, taunting him for the split second it was there, at least once every day of his life.

Gwynn, who he'd thought a friend, was a lying bitch whose con game made him a laughing stock, whose accomplices had killed Anabela Quiñonez in their attempt to get at him. All of the accomplices were now dead, and they'd died badly, but Gwynn kept escaping him.

The thing about Gwynn, no matter how obvious her bullshit was in hindsight, men fell for it willingly, and life had a way of making things fall into place around her pathological lying, making whatever story she'd concocted seem plausible.

Somehow, she always managed to keep her head above water, just barely, until she met Jared Layton, a young rich kid as naïve as they came. He had thrown a house party in a foolish bid to earn new friends, and that party had lasted two weeks because nobody left.

Daddy was one of those liquidators who sell rich people's assets for them when they find themselves in a bind and need cash for whatever reason, and he kept a decent percentage. Of course, Daddy was a crook, so of course, Daddy was rich. Well, actually, Daddy was dead, and so was Mommy. Which meant that Jared was rich.

Jared hadn't gotten very far as Jared Layton, but as Mike Lapine, Will Danaher, Warren Haggerty, Nick Coniglio, and Chris Hammond, he had accomplished much.

As Rabbit, though, he was nuttier'n a fruitcake.

The biggest problem he'd found with assuming new identities was resisting names like Oliver Clozoff, Phil McRacken, and Mike Oxmall. The second biggest problem was that his attention to detail was so committed that every identity had to be so markedly different that they seemed like different people instead of just one guy with different names. They each had different habits and catchphrases that made them unique, and he was constantly improving them by noticing traits other people had and finding ways to work them into his own characteristics. The trouble was keeping them all in order and not getting them mixed up. A tremendous amount of trouble for something his one surviving mercenary found not only unnecessary, but a real pain in the ass.

Meds helped, but Rabbit didn't always take them. Whenever he stopped, he tended to get erratic and a bit misguided, and came up with hare-brained plots and schemes like, well, the one he was in the middle of now, trying to kill Gwynn without getting his hands dirty. His plots had ranged from dropping a safe onto her from atop a tall building, installing a fake mounted moose head in her apartment that poison gas would shoot out of when she walked by it, and any number of Rube Goldberg-style chain reaction contraptions that would blow her up, make her fall through a cunningly disguised trapdoor into a shark tank, or shoot a harpoon into the bull's-eye he'd painted onto her forehead while she was asleep.

Now, it was debatable who was crazier, Rabbit or Gwynn. She would masturbate in front of a mirror, for example. She had good reason to, sure, but still.

Now that she had a decent bankroll and was finally sober, she could successfully ape the dress, style, and mannerisms of Hollywood starlets to the point that she even kissed like them. Her meticulously cared-for dyed blonde hair had the same sensually tangled look as an A-lister who'd just been slept with on-screen.

The extent of her lying prowess? She was taking three classes at the University of Tampa, and she wasn't even enrolled.

The first day of each class, she just showed up. When the professors told her she wasn't on the roster, she feigned confusion, listened to their advice to ask down at the Bursar's office, and came back confidently the next day. Still no.

"What?!" And she pretended to furiously run back and forth between them trying to sort this out, badgering the professors with her plight until they were finally convinced—"Oh, they're deliberately messing with me, I don't know why, maybe because they're overweight and they have a chip on their shoulder..."

And when Fall Quarter was over, she barged into the President's office and demanded the problem didn't happen again, because she'd be damned if she missed the first few essential days of class again, and she'd be *damned* if she let anyone call her a liar. And like that, problem solved.

Hey, with all the scholarships and grants available those days, even a fricking *werewolf* is entitled to a higher education. By using a little initiative, she'd managed to get what she felt she was *owed*. She deserved a medal. At least, that's how she saw it.

Her job, until she could make the connections and become a lobbyist and then a political fixer/white-washer, was public relations for the school, taking calls from disgruntled students and the parents of students, then talking them in circles until they were convinced they were either in the wrong, or that something would be done to appease them, but it would take a while, what with all the red tape.

From there she would finagle her way into other classrooms, and she made sure to take the kinds of classes that would sharpen her already Machiavellian people skills, not the useless crap that served only in the amassing of credits.

Jared Layton was a distant memory that washed ashore in her mind only rarely, but when it did, it brought a smile. Her luck had been great since she pulled that little stunt. Quite a few times, trouble had found her and people around her died, but she always managed to escape. It must've just been the state of the world today, that death was always lurking just around the corner.

Not once did she make a connection.

She was being careful this time around, though. She'd be in no danger here. She'd be ready if trouble came, but it wouldn't come. Things were going too well for there to be any hiccups.

She ruminated over this while scrubbing her face in the shower with her face cloth, and then her nape with her neck cloth, in her shower stall with no door and poorly-aligned ugly tiles. She lived in a one bedroom efficiency apartment just off campus, but there were certain amenities that made up for it. The waist-high railing set into the wall for handicapable people was perfect for her to drape all the rest of her rags and keep them neatly organized. She used her crotch rag next, and then her back exfoliator, and then two loofahs—one long, one short —and a pumice stone.

Of course, her face cloth needed a facial scrub of crushed apricots and vitamin E, while the others were all working up a splendid lather with ginger nut and jaffa cake body wash. The shampoo that was honored enough to be used on her hair was a concoction of cucumber and coconut oil, and the conditioner was nothing short of an avocado-mint-grapefruit blend, fortified with over sixty multiprovitamins, whatever the hell they were.

When she was finally convinced she was clean, she threw on a black and crimson silk brocade robe with a mandarin collar, tab buttons, and side vents up to the waist. Changed her mind when she saw her reflection and knew that was a look for lounging around the place, not doing important things like her nails. She switched to her sheer silk shawl with the red velvet burnout pattern and the knotted fringe.

She checked herself from all angles, decided to leave one breast exposed, and went into her kitchenette/living room where three outfits were laid out on a chinoiserie table, under a Bagues chandelier, with all the corresponding nail polishes and eyeliners, mascaras, blushes, and lipsticks.

The vinyl-tiled floor had bubbled and cracked in places, and was marred here and there with cigarette burns, but she'd covered the blemishes up with Aubusson carpets and nineteenth-century Persian rugs.

The efficiency had been sparsely furnished, but she'd moved the garbage it had come with into a storage unit with a bright orange roll-down door, cramming it in with the rest of her stuff, and replaced it with divans, armoires, chiffoniers, Lumiere buffets, Louis Quinze fauteuils, and a French Provincial four-poster canopy.

The walls were pockmarked with poorly-spackled holes from the last tenant's misses at his dartboard, and fist dents from the one before that, but she'd distracted her eyes from them by hanging sconces, a gilt-worked futtock plate with mahogany deadeyes, an antique samisen, and an exposed gears pendulum clock. From the traverse rod over the sliding glass balcony door—if the railed ledge outside could be called that—she'd hung raspberry and cream French silk draperies.

She turned on a three thousand dollar stereo, playing White Zombie's "Devil Music Volume I," poured a glass of cheap whiskey from an elegant crystal decanter, and stood before the table, debating the three outfits.

She had two and a half hours, just enough time to get ready for her date with Professor Brascombe, or whatever his name was, and one night to seduce him without actually sleeping with him and get him addicted to crack, or she'd have to actually reach into her own pocket to come up with this month's rent.

And she'd be damned if she spent another dime on this shithole.

Christ, she thought, I need a vacation.

It had been a Yingzhao she'd managed to pawn at Vincent Kilgore's art gallery—Kilgore n' Friends—that had given her away. (Rabbit had put an APB out on any and all Yingzhaos under the pretense of building a private collection.) Kilgore's partner had shaken his clean-shaven and shiny purple head, putting some disappointment into his poker face.

"Ooh, no, honey. One look at that's all it takes."

"What do you mean?"

"You think that's antique? Before something can be antique it's first got to be old." This is what's known to the masters of the ancient art of haggling as 'Jewing down.' Gwynn was a journeyman, herself, but most of her mind-bending powers were useless against this man because he was queer as a football bat, and therefore immune.

Lavon Gilbert (and that was pronounced Gil-*bair*) was flaming gay, with all of the grossly exaggerated effeminacy that in no way resembles femininity. Lavon—or as he preferred to be called, "Peaches"—didn't just swish a little when he walked. Every step he took was chiropractically suicidal. His gesturing, which he probably assumed helped him to get his points across during conversation, was as boldly (and unnecessarily) dramatic as that of a street mime. A queer street mime.

His shiny, shaven skull tapered toward the rear, making the back of his head grotesquely concave, and, all political correctness aside, there was just no other way to say it. The man had a snout. His maxilla and mandible both jutted forward, his lips always hung open naturally, and he had small teeth and long tracts of mottled gums that made for a strange smile.

Yet, somehow, he was very, very popular.

He was thin, impeccably dressed with the exception of garish jewelry, and his skin had the purplish sheen that suggested the reason he had been featured on the cover of Poz magazine more than once.

Therefore, he covered all the bases and ranked highly in the most fashionable subspecies of American mankind: a gay black man living on borrowed time, and the only thing that kept him from blowing apart in a strong wind like a doll made of ash was the Cocktail he took daily—AZT, Norvair, Viricept, 3TC, Retonivir, et cetera. He wasn't dying of AIDS, he was "Poz," and he wasn't "sexually active, spreading disease to others and effectively committing murder," he was a "gift-giver."

According to a sickening trend in the "gay community," life was so terrible when faced with the fear of catching HIV that one was better off just going ahead and *trying* to catch it. The lie was that by bringing it upon yourself, you automatically stepped up another rung on the evolutionary ladder, forcing your body to adapt and survive. A Poz who'd pass on this opportunity to a Neg "bug chaser" was a good Samaritan, somehow.

Vince carried on as if he simply a*dor*ed Peaches, but even he secretly thought this "gift-giving" was a sinister glorification of "Tag, you're it!"

The whole time Gwynn was negotiating the sale of a forged antique, she had in the back of her mind "Peaches? Fucker doesn't look like any peach *I* ever seen. Eggplant, maybe, but no fuckin' peach."

"Well, look here," Peaches said eventually, after much haggling. "As an antique, it is forty-weight, pure-D bullshit. As art, though, I'd say it might bring in a couple hunnerd—"

"A couple *hundred?*"

"Whoa there, Miz Thang. I'm tryin' ta work wicha here. Straight up, I say you tryin' me coming in here wittis fake-ass—"

Gwynn hissed and raised a hand, palm out, the international sign for Shut the fuck up. "As you say in the vernacular, save me the rap." She'd just learned the word "vernacular" two days ago and couldn't stop using it, the way she had to check the time every five minutes whenever she got a new watch.

Peaches folded his arms across his bird-like chest and tapped the bejeweled fingers of one hand against the elbow it held. Assumed a belittling I'll-hear-you-out expression.

"The only reason I'm selling my dead grandmother's art is to make this month's rent. Rent's seven hundred and fifty. You know it's worth more'n that, but I'm tired of arguing, so look, gimme a break and help me at least keep my apartment—"

A straight man would've bought that. A wise straight man would've known it was bullshit and *still* bought it. As previously stated, Peaches was gay, though, and therefore immune.

"Girl, the only way you're gonna get seven an' a half for that there is coming up with a better story than that rent crap. Tell me you blew your allowance in Vegas or Atlanick City an' Daddy's gonna skin your ass. Something. Anything. Try again."

She stared at him hard for a moment, then pretended to give up. Closed her eyes, grimaced, and wrung her hands.

"I got ripped off."

"Ripped offa what?"

"...A thousand tabs of ecstasy."

Peaches winced. "Ooh no, girl, you didn't!"

She nodded, playing Gullible Li'l White Girl like nobody else could, and Lavon Gilbert fell for it hook, line, and sinker. He sympathized, gave her a long girl-to-girl lecture on how to spot a con game, and paid eight hundred dollars for the Yingzhao, which they both knew was worth thousands and they both knew she'd never get more'n a couple hunnerd for.

As soon as she was gone, Peaches told Vincey and the two of them rejoiced, then notified the private collector who'd advertized his interest. Rabbit flew into town to see if the piece was one his Dad had sold off or one that had been taken in the burglary. In the interrogation that followed, the truth came out about Yingzhao, and shortly thereafter, Jubal Cigouaves was born.

Knowing that Nick Coniglio might be too easily recognizable to Gwynn, he snooped around town for her as Chris Hammond, a good-looking artist type with tattoos and goatee and longish black hair, often seen chain-smoking and drinking strong coffee from tiny cups at an outdoor café just off campus, brooding. Something about brooding, with your John Lennon sunglasses on, it's a lot more convincing than pretending to read a newspaper and you can watch people for an hour without them ever noticing. Woe be us all when the cops figure that out.

It was very convenient that Gwynn turned out to be an art student, because Chris fit right in while shadowing her through the art building. His jeans were torn at the knees, his leather jacket and combat boots scuffed and worn, and his Che Guevara t-shirt obviously slept in. He could sit cross-legged on the green outside with his sketch pad open across his knees, drawing under a shade tree, and watch her from afar without raising any suspicion. No one would ever bet against him if he said she couldn't spot him. The only way she'd even look his way was if he was wearing a mirror.

In the meantime, Rabbit sold other Yingzhaos through the gallery, along with several paintings he had done before but re-signed as Cigouaves, mostly paintings based on National Geographic photographs he'd cut up and mixed-n-matched until he had scenes of Ethiopian women and Zulu men, whoever, doing whatever. Women with their used-up banana breasts and their necks thirteen inches long, supported by gold rings, lip-plates clacking together as they talked. Masai warriors in their brilliant red that made almost Tuscan color schemes with the mustard yellow of the plains and the dark green of the occasional tree.

The paintings had all been adapted enough to be passed off as something poignant and, regardless of the depicted people's true origins, Haitian. Most of them had subtle references to poli-tics underneath the façade of religion, like the large wooden phallus in "Agove Minoire" being not only limp but vermiculat-ed, and the female *loa* it represented slumped against it in defeat. "Maît Carrefour" and "Grand Bois d'Ilet" were both sunrise scenes with the figures turning away from the light, only in the former, a single child was looking at the sun with hope and wonder. "Baron Samedi" was the only one of twelve that he had never sold. Maybe it was too subtle.

Rabbit wanted to try branching out into other cultures and keep the work under the name Cigouaves, but he knew the idiots who were buying his paintings would probably balk at a Haitian doing the Irish "Morrigu" or the Turkish "Rose and Butterfly" fable, so he had to resist the urge to improve. Oh well.

Even if it did catch on, Rabbit would need something else to pursue, because once he had attained something he'd worked toward, anything, it became worthless. The chase and the fight were all that mattered, because the hunger remained after his triumph.

He often got depressed when thinking about it, wondering where he was going and what he'd accomplish, and that invaria-bly led to thoughts of death and how no matter what he did in life he'd end up the same way, win or lose. So, he drank. In the

magical feelings of inflated self-importance that came from alco-
holism, he found irresponsible adventures and things to fight
for. Like the hearts of women.

Every long, drawn-out courtship and conquest was a purpose for him keep living, and living well, instead of just exist-
ing, and every victory brought him redemption. At least for a
little while, anyway. Then he'd become stagnant. If there was no
opposition for him to defy, he'd get to thinking about life again,
and then he'd feel the emptiness and futility once again, for
which there was but one cure. The girl next door. And the girl
next door's sister.

And all of these girls, ignorant of the futility of their short
meaningless lives, dwelt in their own private worlds with drama
and soap-opera complication and problems for him to solve and
feel useful. These poor, sad little puppets and their so-called in-
trigues, there for his fleeting entertainment.

He even tried the reassurance of religion once, the placebo
for hope, but his depression surmounted even that.

"But Father, what about *after* Judgment Day?"

"Well, we will have one thousand years of peace on Earth.
We, the faithful, will be left after all of the sinners and nonbe-
lievers are roasting in the lake of fire, and the world will be ours
to enjoy."

"For a thousand years?"

"Yes, my son."

"Okay, I'm willing to buy that. What about after?"

"Er, what do you mean?"

"What happens on New Year's Day, January first, year one
thousand and one?"

"Ummm…"

"Does it all start over? Good, evil, both of them, wars, famine, and God sees if we can do it right the second time around?
Or actually, third time around, considering this is our second
attempt following the Flood, and we're not doing so well this
time either?"

"I don't follow."

"Christ."

"Don't take the Lord's name in vain."

"Sorry Father. Okay, what about Heaven?"

"What *about* Heaven?"

"What happens there? What will we do?"

"We'll sing and pray and praise God."

"What, that's it?"

"What else is there?"

"That's what I'm asking you."

"I'm still not following you."

"Well, if that's what Heaven is, why don't we just do that now? That can't be all there is to it, or we would be happy to just drop everything and do that. But instead, we do other things to be happy. At least the Muslims have a Paradise that sounds like it would be fun."

"Blasphemer! I rebuke you, Satan!"

"Christ."

"Don't take the Lord's name in—"

"Shut the fuck up, Father."

And that was the end of that. This "hope," this *faith* seemed like nothing more than an anesthetic self-deception, and Rabbit gave up. Chose instead to distract himself with self-inflicted burdens the way others wore weights on their feet while jogging, or corsets under their clothing, burdens self-imposed for no other reason than the pleasure of them being removed. He picked fights just to have an enemy and a threat to overcome—usually someone deserving of his wrath anyway, not some innocent on the street.

This adventure promised him everything he needed, though. The more time he spent with Megan, the brighter the future looked, and the warmth of pride filled him as he watched her through slitted eyes, like just last night, tiptoeing around the hotel suite and finding the clues he had left her. Like the phony checkbook. The hotel stationery. The photograph. The...uh-oh, she'd found the sketchpad.

He watched her leaf through it at random, leaning against the window in the moonlight, seeing her own face contorted in ecstasy, stifling a gasp. He knew he should groan and roll over or something. Do *some*thing so she'd panic and put the pad down, hurry over and get back into bed with him, but he couldn't. He was frozen and paralyzed, as if in a nightmare, unable to do more than watch.

Megan turned the pages toward the front of the pad, looking at the earlier ones. Her body. Sketches for "Orgè D'Une." More sketches. And this was what he'd been afraid of. But he couldn't move, knowing that if he did, he'd be obviously awake and she would know that he'd been watching. Then she'd ask what these sketches were all about, and he'd have to tell her. No, he told himself, better she think he was asleep and see what he'd been stupidly careless about leaving in the open. At least she couldn't question him about it in the morning without giving herself away. But if he didn't stop her now, she'd see…

Aaaaaand she saw it.

Gwynn.

But not Gwynn like a husband would draw her.

Gwynn with her head bent back so far that her neck-bones splintered through the skin of her throat, his fist in her hair.

Gwynn with her mouth gaping wide, his knife buried to the hilt in her heart.

Gwynn impaled on a large wooden stake, a six-inch diameter fence post bulging through the skin of her belly and coming out from between her probably-fake breasts.

Megan stared, her eyes wide with shock.

Rabbit wilted, wanting to shut his eyes tight, but unable to. Wishing so badly that he could erase those images from her mind. Keep those dark parts of him a secret. And then he saw Megan grinning.

She could only take the first blank page after the last one he had sketched upon, but she wanted badly to take the whole thing as a souvenir and hide it away for no one to see but her. She settled on the one page, though, tearing it out slowly and gently and rolling it up tightly to keep it from creasing. It had the indentations of three faces, all of them impressively accurate.

Before she replaced the pad she looked again at all the pictures of Mrs. Nick, savoring them.

The last thing she did before she crawled back into bed was steal Rabbit's undershirt from the tangle of clothes on the floor and shove it, wadded up, into her bag. Something of him to smell when he wasn't around.

He stirred as she came to him, rolled over with his eyes lazily half-open, arms spread to welcome her.

She started to tell some lie about why she was awake and had only barely gotten her mouth open when he pulled her to him and kissed her fiercely. She purred as their tongues writhed together, feeling him grow instantly hard against her belly, and she reached down to take hold of him. His hardness jumped in her hand, insatiable, and she felt a desire for something all of a sudden that she'd thought disgusting until now.

She moved until she was on her knees, straddling him, holding him by the shaft and wetting the swollen tip between her legs. Reached a fumbling hand out in the dark and found the tube of glop he'd lubed the vibrator up with earlier. Biting the cap, she twisted the mashed tube until it was open and spat the cap into the shadows.

Hesitating only an instant, wondering Do I really want to do this? And then saying Fuck it, she reached around and worked the mouth of the tube inside her bottom, squeezing. Better to just say Fuck it, go ahead and do it instead of having time to reconsider and chicken out. The glop was a quick-relieving anesthetic, and the pain of having the tube's threaded plastic mouth inside her had dissolved within moments. She pulled it out and tossed it away, rose up on her knees to bring the dome of his cock underneath her, tease herself with it, and then slowly inch it inside of her.

Slowly, millimeter by torturous millimeter, she sat down farther, easing him deeper inside.

Rabbit tensed and strained, having never in his life felt anything tighter envelope his surgically-enlarged penis, not knowing whether to be mystified or repulsed by how... *different* it felt.

God, I feel dirty, Megan thought.

What a dirty, filthy little whore.

And it was beautiful.

VII

Across town, Gwynnevere Hutchinson was sitting on the lap of one Professor Edmund Braswell in his den, holding an altered cigarette lighter with a five inch flame to the end of a crack stem and telling him to keep on sucking until she said When.

A disappointingly short time later, the baggy of crack was all gone, and she was lying to him, saying "No, sorry, I don't have any more. But I know where we can get some."

"This late?" Professor Edmund Braswell—call me Eddie—asked hopefully. He found himself repeatedly swallowing air, knowing it would give him gas later, but unable to stop.

"He won't be too happy to get a call this late, but if he's awake...well, he definitely won't give us a break. Most likely charge us an extra fifty or something, if I know him like I think I do. He's an asshole, thinks he's God's gift."

"Well, he is if he has more of this stuff. Wow, this is some wicked shit. I haven't even done coke since I was..." he caught himself before he said 'your age' and sounded old to her. He was only thirty-eight, but girls in their early twenties tended to drop the "only."

"I can get some," she said, scooting off of his lap and pretending to accidentally put her hand down on his crotch to steady herself. "Whoops! Sorry!"

"Umnh...that's okay," he managed.

"But the thing is, I don't have that much cash on me. I guess if we can get another eight-ball for three, three-fifty, that oughta last all night."

"Three *hundred* and fifty?"

"Yeah, what'd you think it was gonna be?"

"Eightballs were only two hundred—"

"Well, yeah, back in the day," she told him, her body language saying *D'uh!* but her tone conciliatory. "But inflation's a mother. Besides, you're thinking of coke. This is crack. And what's more, this is the *bomb* as far as crack goes."

"Honey, whatever it is, I'm in love."

91

He was already grinding his teeth, and his expectations for the night had changed entirely. While he'd been fairly convinced this gorgeous, exquisite creature would put out for him—was hoping against hope that she would—all he wanted now was to smoke more crack with her. He even doubted he could get it up right now if she started dancing around the house bare-ass naked, but that didn't mean he was unhappy.

He darted his eyes around the floor, stood up and started lifting couch cushions.

"We may have dropped some," he said. "Look around and see if you can find any."

"Edmund. Eddie. You know we didn't drop any. This is what people always do when they're done smoking crack. They get up and look for more."

Braswell held up an ancient petrified crumb of a potato chip, ruffled, with ridges.

"This looks like it could be—"

"It isn't."

"We could try it."

Gwynn knew he'd be finding crack between his teeth when he flossed. Mission accomplished.

"Best I can do, Eddie, I can score half an ounce for six-fifty, seven hundred."

In reality, five hundred would do it. She'd cooked it all herself, and the lineage of the coke she'd made it from (her term, lineage, meaning coke bought from the money made by selling other coke) traced back to pounds she'd convinced Jared Layton to buy for her.

You don't get rich by paying your own rent. You don't get ahead by being honest.

"No bulk rate?" Eddie asked. "Price doesn't go down the more you buy?"

"Sweetie, this is the consumer lever. This is retail. Maybe I could talk him into a little leniency *tomorrow*, during the *day*, but right now…"

He bit. "So when the bank's open tomorrow morning at eight o'clock sharp we could get an ounce for one grand? To keep here? You come over and smoke some with me whenever you want?"

Eddie was a sly fox, he was. He knew how to keep this chick coming back at night to see him. He'd have her eating out of his hand, he would. Might even get her addicted! Oooooh! Then she'd be his, all his!

Gwynn smiled wryly. "If only. More like eleven, twelve hundred at best. And that's if I can work some kind of magic on him, but to be honest, I've never really been good at stuff like that…That's why I like you, Eddie, I can be myself with you, not have to put on that stupid act I see other girlies doing."

Ed wasn't even paying attention to that. He was doing math in his head. Finally, he spoke up.

"I've got three hundred and, I think, seventeen dollars in the house. You think we could get by with that? For now, I mean, until the bank opens."

Gwynn smiled wider. "We might. You want me to call him up and see?"

The morning of Nick Coniglio's final day at the Austin convention, Megan called in sick.

"That's great, honey," Phil said into the phone. "If it's some kind of horrible illness that keeps you bed-ridden for a few days, don't worry. We'll manage to get along without you somehow or other."

"Paid leave," Emmy said, calling from the second-hand turntable she was repairing.

"Emmy says she'll dock your pay."

"I did not!"

"Yeah, I know. Slave driver," he muttered, shaking his head. "Uh-huh…Uh-huh. Okay, hurry up and get well. Bye."

When he hung up the phone and came out of the office's open doorway, Emmy giggled in her Beavis and Butthead voice.

"You said bed-ridden, huh-huhuhuhuhuh!"

"Ridden. H-huhuh! In a bed. Huh-huhuhuhuh!"

They kept on at this until they were interrupted by the front door's jingle bells. They looked up to see a beautiful girl come in bawling her eyes out.

"What the...?" Phil muttered.

The girl's voice hitched like a badly scratched CD. "Is Me—is Me—is Me—is Megan—"

Phil and Emmy looked at each other. The girl was dark-skinned and lovely, or at least had been before the dam burst and her face flamed scarlet under gushing tears and mucus.

It was a contest of wills between the husband and wife, whose duty it was to hold the poor dear and comfort her, and get her grief and snot all over them. Arguments in facial expressions and telepathy were batted about in the air between them, their eyes alternately squinting and bulging in rebuttal.

Finally, Emmy made the universally recognizable face of I'll-reward-you-with-some-of-*this*-later-on, which he answered with an expression that is for no one else but a husband and wife, so the meaning must remain unknown, lest it fall into the wrong hands. Suffice to say, Phil had called Emily's bluff, and she had conceded.

She went to the poor distraught young woman and tried to take her in her arms, but was resisted, so she grappled with her.

"Is Me—is Me—M-M-M—" the girl blubbered.

"Megan!" Emmy snapped. "Say it!"

Phil rolled his eyes. His wife was never any good at this kind of thing.

"M-m-m-m-Me—"

"Is Megan here? No, she isn't! And we don't know where she is, and even if we did, she's busy!"

"Emmy," Phil said.

"Shush!" she hissed at him over her shoulder.

"I n-n-n-need to ta-ta—"

"Quiet you!"

The young woman tried to break away, but Emmy braced herself and swung sideways from the hips, one way and then the other.

"Megan!"

"Get a hold of yourself!" Emmy shouted, gave one more sharp wrench to the left and the two of them went down, knocking over a particleboard CD tower and scattering jewel cases all over the floor.

They wrestled for a moment before the girl's head cleared enough to remember a few good holds she'd picked up from reluctantly watching WWF with ex-boyfriends. Phil hung back respectfully, wondering if that was a figure-four leglock the crazy chick had gotten his wife into, until Emmy screamed like her leg was getting dislocated. He started forward, but the dark-skinned girl took the advantage she'd gained from her submission hold and let go, rolling to safety, bolting to her feet, and scrambling out the door.

Emmy looked up as Phil got to her, gasping for breath and grinning madly. He shook his head at her.

"Bet she won't try that again!" she choked.

"Chrissakes, honey."

"What?" she asked.

Neve crashed through her apartment door into the hallway, hair flying as she looked around frantically for anything, any kind of clue. She remembered the card Megan had gotten when she spotted the roses in the living room and ran into the bedroom to find it. The card was on the mirror, held there by a corner, wedged underneath the frame. She'd known it would be there, or someplace like it, where Megan could look at it every day.

Thank God for the ever-predictable Megan.

She snatched the card and hurried out to the living room while reading it.

Heather's. Okay. Nick Coniglio.

She pushed over a stack of magazines and stuff piled in a corner to get at the phone books on the bottom. Hillsborough, no, that's *here*. Pinellas County, that's the one. Across the bridge in St. Pete. She tore through the pages, overshooting the Hs and overcorrecting when she backtracked, accidentally tearing a page and thinking, Just watch it be the page I'm looking for. Watch the tear be right through the number of the place. But it wasn't, thank God.

She found the number for the Heather-Leigh and repeated the number aloud, over and over while she went to the portable phone. Her hand was shaking so terribly while she punched in the number that she had to start over twice.

Finally, "Heather-Leigh Hotel, front desk."

"Nick Coniglio's room please," Neve blurted.

"Just a moment."

Rabbit was kneeling on the floor in front of the bed, Megan's trembling legs draped over his shoulders with her thighs clamped to the sides of his head when the phone rang.

"Please," Neve whispered.

Rabbit couldn't hear anything but his own pulse inside his head, and the roar of Megan's through her flesh mashed against his ears. Megan heard the ringing distantly, as if it came across vast gulfs of time and space.

"Please," Neve whispered urgently.

Megan's eyes cracked open, her breath hitching in her throat, and bit her bottom lip. Maybe it was some kind of telepathy, or maybe it was the vibration of philotic particles between two familiar beings on an astral plane, or maybe she just wanted to be talking on the phone to somebody while she was being eaten out to see if she could carry it off without giving herself away. Whatever it was, Megan decided she had to answer that phone.

She reached out her arm and she stretched and stretched until her fingertips just barely grazed the plastic cradle and pushed it away. It rang louder then, somehow more insistent. While she definitely did not want to stop Rabbit so she could inch further up the bed, a weird feeling crept into her stomach and she knew something was very wrong.

"Please!" Neve shouted, her voice quavering.

Megan scooted her ass up farther on the bed and Rabbit followed, like an animal eating up a trail of food toward a hidden snare.

Her fumbling hand knocked the handset off the cradle and it bungee-jumped over the edge of the night stand, the cord stretching taut and elastically snapping back up, the receiver clattering against the cabinet doors. Baring her teeth in irritation, she butt-walked sideways, bobbing Rabbit's head, but still, he hung on. Reaching over the side of the bed and groping, Megan heard a tiny voice scream her name.

Bolting upright in alarm, she wrenched her lover's head and tumbled him over the side as she twisted.

"Jesus fuck!" he shouted as he hit the floor.

"Ooh, sorry, baby." She leaned over the side and caught up the phone, combing her fingers through her hair as she answered it. "Umnh, hello?"

"Megan!"

She winced and held the phone away from her ear.

"Megan! I need you!"

"What the hell for?"

Rabbit's head came up halfway behind the edge of the bed, his eyes glaring, one hand massaging the back of his neck. Megan couldn't reach him with her hand so she stuck out her foot and caressed his hair with its underside. He spun and caught it like a dog, his fangs clamping into her heel.

"Ow! Jesus!"

"Megan! Come home, please! I've got a big, big problem!"

"*You've* got a problem? I was just getting eaten out righteously and now I'm getting rabies!"

"What?"

"None of your business. Now, what's going on?"

"I can't say over the phone."

"Then it's nothing I want a part of," she lied. She'd help Never no matter what it was, but at least she tried to bluff a little. Neve knew she could count on her, though, if she pressed. Megan was such a selfless person that she'd actually stop the love of her life from giving her oral to throw on her clothes and go help a friend.

"Please, Megan! I wouldn't be calling if I didn't need your help! There's no one else I can trust with this!"

"What about your boyfriend? What about Serge?"

"Sage."

"Whatever. Him."

"Meg..." Neve was giving her a look, a wide-eyed scowl and a sideways tilting of her head. Even though she couldn't see it, Megan somehow knew from Neve's tone what look she was getting.

"Ohhh..." She stared absently at Rabbit, who was shaking his head, terrier-like, with her foot still between his teeth, a low guttural growl deep in the back of his throat.

"So, can you come? Please?"

"Shit."

"Oh, thank you, Meg! I knew I could count on you! I knew I could depend on you to be there for me! Thank you so much!"

"Yeah," Megan muttered. "Don't mention it."

Neve heard the click and a dial tone, sagged with relief. Looked up at the ceiling, through it at where God lived, and gave him a tight-lipped smile.

After all the apologies and pleas for forgiveness and understanding, Rabbit watched her vanish, hastily dressed, shutting the door behind her. He was still holding his neck, massaging it. He bit the little knob on the inside of his cheek and chewed meditatively for a moment. Also practiced something else he'd seen someone do: crack his knuckles using only the thumb of that hand. Made it easier to twirl a pencil or a cigarette or whatever between his fingers the way he'd seen Val Kilmer do in the movies.

He decided it was Chris Hammond who chewed as a habit and Barry Dimick who nervously cracked, making an effort to remember it while he opened up the suitcase he dragged from atop the wardrobe and took out everything he needed to be Dimick, Gonzalez, and Batman.

The door swung open, flooding the small room with light, the sudden displacement of air swaying the squares of white that hung in rows from clotheslines. Neve led Megan into the darkroom, shut the door and flipped the switch that bathed the room in nightmarish red light. Megan recoiled in horror when she saw what she thought she'd been prepared for.

They were slumped in one of the many empty tubs along the end of the far wall, arranged almost like a parody of Michelangelo's Pietá, one sprawled face up across the other's lap, unnervingly still. The one who was in the Madonna position was a scrawny Hispanic that Megan had seen once or twice and likened to a scarecrow eloped from a pumpkin patch. The other, the one lying sprawled in the Jesus pose, was Sage Gurrier—*Saizh Gooryay*, to hear him say it—his face frozen in a ghastly rictus.

The both of them were naked in the tub.

Megan approached slowly, her hands pressed to her mouth, her eyes wide. Neve said nothing as her friend crossed the darkroom, peered with revulsion and yet fascination at the wound above Sage's left eye. Gunpowder smudged around the edges of the star-shaped hole, and the arms of the star showed where gases had lifted the mulatto's skin away from his forehead. Contact wound, the forensics team would call it.

"*You* did this?" Megan asked, not turning around.

Neve nodded dumbly, knowing her roommate couldn't see her, nodding more to herself.

The other corpse's wound was under his left armpit. Unbidden, the scene played itself out in Megan's mind. Neve coming in for a tryst with her boyfriend, thinking the note she had found was meant for her. Hearing the sounds and flicking on the sanguine light.

"Where did you get a *gun?*"

"I had it. I been carrying it for years. It works a lot better than pepper spray."

Megan nodded.

Shit, now what?

"I just *lost* it, Meg."

"Apparently."

"What're we gonna do? We gotta get 'em outta here somehow."

"This makes me an accessory."

"Meg!" Neve hissed. "It makes you a friend!"

"The police kind of frown on friends like that."

"Meg!"

Bonnie Ophelia Delaune turned and stared at her roommate, then her eyes wandered around the darkroom as she thought. This part of the Arts Building, the photography wing, wasn't soundproofed, but at this hour, bright and early in the morning, only the night owls with special privileges from the staff would have been around to hear the shooting. Plus, it wasn't a big gun at all, just a little travel-sized semi-automatic, the kind for women and small children.

Neve said that she wasn't sure how long ago it had been; the images were kind of disconnected in her mind. It had been dark out, still. She'd run from the scene, fleeing down the corridors and out into the night, hiding in one niche for a moment and then dashing off to lay in the dirt behind a hedge somewhere else. Hiding from whom, she wasn't sure. Probably God.

Running and finding places to hide on campus, then panicking and running off to find better ones, scrambling desperately just to get away. Jumping at every shadow. Feeling the terror and paranoia that accompanies everyone's first murder, and regarding every scurrying ant in the grass with a deep sadness. The quiver of every leaf in the night breeze was the sound of some imaginary witness in pursuit, and the twittering of birds serenading from power lines made her feel as lonely as only a fugitive can feel.

Snapping out of it eventually, though, she realized that if she didn't do something about those bodies in the darkroom, and *soon*, this feeling she had gotten just a taste of would be very real.

The sun was starting to come up. Since it was late October, it wouldn't be too long before businesses opened, and there was only one person in the world she knew she could trust enough to ask such a favor of. Megan was always at work. She never missed a single day. She would be at Big Beat already, sitting outside and chain-smoking, waiting for whoever to come and open the door.

It wasn't too far away from where Neve was hiding. She'd get there in no time if she hurried. Already out of breath, Neve got up and started to run.

"I'll help," Megan said. "On one condition."

That startled her roommate. Meg was usually a pushover. She'd never be expected to put up an argument...unless it was all that dick she'd been getting made her start to develop a backbone.

"What is it?" Neve asked.

"You help me with something else later on."

"Oh Christ, of course I will! Anything, you know that! But we have to move!"

"Cross your heart."

"Jesus! We don't have time—"

"Do it." Her voice was unexpectedly firm.

"Jesus. Cross my heart, scout's honor."

"Okay...we'll need...hell, I don't know, a bag or..." She was scanning the darkroom, and coming up with nothing. Neve sighed helplessly.

"They're gonna be heavy, aren't they?" she asked.

Megan nodded, absently fingering the amulet beneath her shirt. Then, Neve's face brightened.

"That cart! There's a janitor's cart I see every now and then with a big ol' thick yellow bag in it. It's got to be either parked somewhere in a corner or—"

"Let's go."

They hurried out of the darkroom, through the rooms of the photography department and out into the hallway. Heavy silence hung down both directions. The stairs were only a short distance to the right, switchbacks leading down to the third floor and up to the third and fourth. They ran to them and went up, neither of them remembering seeing the cart anywhere downstairs, so not bothering to check there. Megan thought that, with her luck, the damned thing would be locked up in a closet somewhere.

Pausing at the third floor to glance around the corner, seeing nothing, they kept on up to the fourth. With quailing stomachs, they raced down the hall looking through the small windows in the classroom doors, hoping it might be on the other side of one of them. By the time they got to the far end, the fear was setting in again.

They took the steps downstairs five at a time, didn't bother stopping for a closer inspection of the third floor, and when they rounded the corner on the second floor they almost tripped over—of all things—a good-sized dolly that neither one of them remembered seeing earlier. They glanced at each other, thinking the same thing, and seized the metal arch above the handles, turned and dragged it behind them as they ran back to Photography.

Even more surprising, they came across a couple of bungee cords, lying like snakes in the middle of the floor. The girls' eyes were wide with appreciation of these gifts from Fate. Neve snatched them up thinking no one could be this lucky.

Oh, thank you, God!

On top of it all, a ream of heavy duty garbage bags just happened to be leaning against the wall next to the darkroom door by the trash can when they returned. Conveniently large garbage bags.

The plan did not need to be discussed between them, as they both had made it up independently on the spot. Shaking the bags loose from each other, they both hastily went in and dragged the bodies out of the tub and stuffed them headfirst into a bag that—God be praised—was almost as long as they were tall. It took them a minute to get them laid out straight inside, tight against each other, and they both found that more repulsive than the fact that they were handling two dead bodies.

Once the bag was stretched all the way to the feet, Neve and Megan struggled to right them. Neve didn't remember what the stiffening of dead bodies was called—either rigor or livor mortis—or which of them set in first, but they were definitely getting stiff.

She avoided even looking to see if the other rumor was true, that if a man died with a hard-on it remained erect. The very thought of two stiff dicks made her shudder.

They wrestled their burden upright and dragged it against the concave spine of the dolly, and Neve, the stronger one, held it there while Megan hooked the bungee cords and stretched them around and around until they were taut, hooking the other ends and securing the bodies about the knees and midriffs.

Before casting off, they glanced back at the tub. In the red light the blood looked just as conspicuous as it would in the sunshine. Neve looked around the darkroom again, at all the jugs of different chemicals used to develop photographs and fuck with them artistically. Think think think. Shit. If they stuck around to clean up before wheeling the bodies away, they'd surely be caught. If they took care of the bodies first, someone would come in and see the blood before they got back.

She snatched up a bottle of hypo-whatever-it-was-called, developing fluid, some stuff Sage had told her could be used in place of P2P—phenyl-2-propanone—to make crystal meth, because she noticed a warning symbol on the side that said it was flammable.

Highly flammable. She twisted off the cap and sloshed the stuff on the wall and over the tub, dousing every splatter of blood.

She'd read about something the police had now, luminol, this stuff you spray that'll light up a spot where blood had been washed away, even if it had been long ago. There was nothing you could use to conceal spilt blood anymore.

"What is that stuff?" Megan asked.

"Never mind. Start pushing them outta here, I'll be with you in just a minute." She was digging a cigarette out of her soft pack.

"We don't have time—"

"I'll explain later! Start moving!"

Megan scowled, teeth bared, but turned and leaned the dolly back on its wheels, grunting at the weight. Put her shoulder into it and pushed. The dolly wobbled, and in a flash she realized what Neve was doing and had an idea.

"Wait! Before you do that! Use one of my cigarettes instead!"

Neve looked at her blankly.

"You smoke the same cigarettes as Nick, and his go out if you don't keep puffing on them. Mine will burn all the way to the filter. Use mine!"

Neve nodded, somewhat surprised, and reached out to dig Megan's pack out of the pocket she swiveled her hip to indicate. It wasn't coming out easily, and Megan was straining to hold up the dolly, but she didn't say anything, knowing that whatever she did say would slow Neve down more.

Finally, with most of the cigarettes mashed inside the pack, they came free and Megan shoved the dolly again. It wobbled just like before, panicking her, and she tripped while overcorrecting its yaw. She managed to catch herself, but the dolly shot out ahead of her and she scrambled to keep up with it, almost dropping the handles. As soon as she was stable with the weight a bright flash and hiss of flames made her jump with fright and drop the truck altogether.

"What the fuck!"

Neve turned from the fire she'd started, the bottle of hypo-something in one hand, dripping.

"Ohhhh shit," she said, and then a bolt of rippling flame caught the thin stream of dribbling fluid and raced up it into the bottle, setting it ablaze in her hand. She yelped and flung it away, regretting it an instant later. "Oh shit."

"Why the hell'd you do that?" Megan shouted.

"I thought it was gonna blow up!"

Neither of them moved, both thinking the bottle still might —as soon as they reached for it, *bam!*—so they stood wringing their hands like two children who'd played with matches and didn't know what to do about the forest fire they'd started. Not much had spilled out onto the floor, but the bottle's mouth was still belching little yellow tongues, the puddle glowing with ripples like waves surging across a tiny sea.

"Ohhhh fuck."

"Scuze me."

They jumped, shrieking, tripping over themselves and hitting the floor as they tried to turn and see who'd spoken. A woman chuckled at their fright and pushed past them with a fire extinguisher, proceeded to fill the room with white smoke.

"You two might wanna get somewhere," she said.

They scrambled to their feet and hurried to right the dolly, getting in each other's way like a pair of bungling Keystone Kops. The fog was billowing about them like a smoke screen and they took advantage of it, rushing the bodies out of the darkroom and crashing into everything along the way.

As they collided with furniture and equipment in the next rooms of the Photography Department, Megan risked a glance backwards, seeing no one.

They turned around and started pulling the dolly behind them instead of pushing, and found the going much easier. Making it to the hallway, they looked in both directions before yanking the dolly hard into the doorjamb, splintering the molding. They cursed and tried again. This time they glanced it off the other jamb and spilled out onto the checkered vinyl floor.

Cursing louder, and then shushing each other, they rolled to their feet and tugged the dolly up and after them toward the stairway, running full tilt. As they made the turn at the corner, the wheels slid and the base of the dolly fishtailed. They let it keep going, not knowing how to take a dolly down stairs, having never had to do it before.

The wheels bounced off the aluminum checker-plated concrete steps, the weight gaining speed, and the handles of the dolly just slipped out of the girls' hands. They watched in horror as it jounced down the stairs, the metal truck clanging again and again and again, the bodies under the tearing plastic jumping like chicks trying to bash their way out of eggshells.

At the landing, instead of stopping, the dolly rose upright, fell forward to crash against the wall, and ricocheted. Falling backwards against the railing's corner, it turned, tipped, and clattered to the concrete landing. Bounced a little, slid, and seesawed at the edge of the top step on the last flight down.

The deafening noise echoed through the halls, and through it came a sprinkling of distant "What the fuck was that?"s.

Panic again cut through their paralyzing fear, and they rushed down the stairs to put the bodies back on straight, shake out another black bag to slide over them and the dolly's backing, covering all the holes and exposed flesh.

"Need a hand?" a voice asked, the same as before.

Neve and Megan gasped, looking up at the top of the stairs. A woman stood there, the one who'd come into the darkroom. She looked Hispanic, with long curly black hair that cascaded over her shoulders and looked greasy, in baggy work pants and men's work boots, with a rumpled blue Belmont-striped white button-down shirt tied beneath her breasts.

She looked messy the way an actress or a model would be made to look, with a black smear across half of her forehead and a dark smudge on one cheek where she'd absently wiped sweat from her face with the back of a sooty hand, or scratched an itch, or whatever. It looked the way chicks are made to look for photos of girls who pull their own weight. Megan wasn't sure why she was thinking that.

Maybe because she was a handsome woman with obvious strength who was showing up like Deus Ex Machina.

"Eyes are stinging from all that smoke," she said, coming down the stairs. "I can barely see. But it's not bad enough I can't help you carry whatever it is you've got there." Her accent sounded Cuban, heavily, but nice.

"Uh, we…" Neve looked at Megan. "We've got it all right. Thanks, though."

"Oh you do, huh? Is that why it looks like a tornado hit back there? Shit, I need some Visine. You got any?" She came down the steps toward them.

"No, sorry," Megan said, rallying herself. "But yeah, we'd love a hand with this thing, at least to the first floor."

Neve shot her an alarmed look, but Megan made faces back that read She can't see us distinctly, so we'll be okay, and *really*, you wanna carry that thing?

The Hispanic woman bent down when she reached them and gathered up the dolly. One wheel was hanging at a wobbling angle, and it would be a problem dragging it down after her, so she heaved the entire load up and laid it across one shoulder instead. The girls stared.

"Heavy," she grunted, but it sounded like she only meant it for their benefit. She wasn't struggling to hold the weight of two dead men. At all.

Students had appeared at the base of the stairs, drawn by the noise, but stepped aside when the woman came down with the other two following. They turned the corner when they got to the floor, and went to the glass doors of the Arts Building's entrance.

"Mind getting that for me?" she asked.

Megan felt awfully stupid at having to be asked, and went to hold one of the doors with her head down and followed the woman and her roommate outside. Setting her burden down, Señorita turned to them and smiled a crooked half-smile.

"You should be able to get it from here."

She sauntered back inside.

Neve and Megan stared at each other for a long time, not knowing what to say, until more students came drifting to class and the girls remembered their fear. They nervously started pushing the dolly along the paved walkway that led toward the edge of campus closest to their apartment, both of them jumping twice at the bangs of newspaper boxes' metal doors slamming shut.

Megan almost lost it again when a girl came walking past them from behind, glancing their way, and it was Mrs. Nick herself. Megan restrained herself, though, barely, and Gwynn Hutchinson marched on with three stolen bottles of hypo-something in her backpack, wiping the pink and irritated corners of her eyes, still smelling fire extinguisher fog.

The door of 318 swung open, the girls staggering through, and as soon as it was shut, they both sagged against it, sighing deeply.

"Thank you, Meg."

"Yeah. Don't mention it."

They dragged themselves down the hall into the living room, collapsed into their rattan chairs and Neve dug out cigarettes, handing Megan hers. In black and white, Rabbit watched them fish their lighters out of tight jeans pockets, heard from the speakers the rasp of the grindwheels against the flints as if he was next to them.

He lit a cigarette and twirled it between his fingers like Val Kilmer, practicing, blew smoke rings at the monitor, and waited, absently stroking the lines around his mouth where his goatee used to be, like an amputee fingering his stump.

Neve got up after a few minutes to get a couple of longnecks out of the fridge, brought them back and handed one to Megan. Her roommate wasn't fond of beer—would sneer and say that it tasted like piss that somebody farted in—but she sure appreciated it now. Drank half of it in one go, and visibly relaxed.

"We might have to move them," she said eventually. Neve nodded slowly.

"Been thinkin' that, too."

"When the busboys go to throw the trash out..."

"Yeah. They might see them in there."

"I know, but what do we do? Dismantle them with chainsaws?"

They fell silent again.

The Dumpsters behind Allegra's, Rabbit was thinking. He'd seen them stopping there on the GPS tracker, their little green blip courtesy of the sapphire amulet around Megan's neck, pausing a moment and then moving much faster through the alley towards home as if they were no longer encumbered by the weight of the dolly.

That must be it. Walking distance from campus, a secluded area, close to home. Convenient.

"I'm sorry," Neve said.

Megan didn't answer.

"Why did this have to happen?"

Rabbit smiled.

VIII

With the developing fluid, Gwynn had almost everything she needed. Distilled drinking water; no suds, no scent ammonia; lithium strips out of size D Coppertops; muriatic acid; red phosphorus from a certain brand of drain cleaner; ether from a certain brand of starter fluid; iodine crystals; ephedrine pills; and a few other ingredients, things she didn't have to reach too far to obtain, and she could be back in the meth business. Meth beat the shit out of having to sell crack on 22nd Street or Nebraska Avenue. Not even Tamarind back in West Palm was as bad as parts of Tampa. Plus, college kids aren't as big on crack as they are on crank, since crack didn't help much for cram sessions, and getting more than one professor hooked on butterscotch cubes would be an unlikely accomplishment.

Plus, Guavaween was coming up. There was a high demand right there, what she was needin' was supply.

Best get cracking.

On top of that, the forty-five days were almost up for the acid to be ready. Either tomorrow or the next day, she wasn't sure. Dozens of mason jars hidden away, rye grass seed moldy and rotting in darkness, fifteen pounds worth of the one of the most horrible poisons known to man. Well, provided she'd done it right. If she did it right, all that work would yield her a whole gallon of LSD.

One whole *gallon*. One tiny drop was worth five dollars, and how the hell many droplets were in a gallon? She could've sworn it was on a measurement chart in the dictionary, but she couldn't find the damned thing in the cluttered pigsty she called a bedroom. Efficiency, my ass, she thought. More like a hole in the wall, she could've told them, the people who came up with the term Efficiency, but nobody asked her.

She racked her brains. Gallon, quart, pint, cup, gill...ounce ...drop? Droplet? What came in between?

Ahh, fuck it. She'd have to do math anyway.

Last night had been the first time in a long while that she'd smoked the crack she made. Had to hand it to herself, that was some pretty good shit. She was still tweaking off it. Hadn't gotten a wink since leaving Braswell's house.

She had to laugh. He couldn't even get it up after he'd smoked it all. Didn't even seem to *want* to get it up. When she bade him farewell, he was down on his hands and knees, studying the floor like a goddamn bird hunting for worms. Coming up with pebbles that had been shaken loose from the treads in his shoe soles, bits of God-knows-what that had accumulated since the last time he'd vacuumed, even toenail clippings. Packing them into the stem she'd given him as a present.

Well, that's not entirely true. She hadn't given him the pipe. She'd pretended to forget about it sitting on the end table and he snagged it, thinking that he'd pulled a fast one on her and gotten away with it, just like she had wanted him to.

Now, as her eyeballs jiggled and her heart started to flutter, she felt the high waning. Good, now I can get some damned sleep before I go to work. She checked her watch. Shit! She was supposed to be in answering phones in less than twenty minutes!

My, how time does fly.

She glanced at the cabinet in her kitchenette where the batch of crack was. Tried to look away, but her eyes kept sliding back to it. There was another pipe in her bedroom, the glass one she smoked weed with.

No!

Don't even think about it!

But I'll be a zombie at work. How am I supposed to talk on the phone and represent the university if I can't…well, maybe…No! Resist! Be strong!

Wait. Who'm I kidding? I can resist this shit, it's nothing. I did it before. I'll only smoke this one little bit to get me through the day. That's all. A little dab'll do ya. Now, where's my lighter?

Megan called the Heather's, putting the room number as an extension, and the phone just rang and rang. She hung up, redialing without the extra numbers, and a moment later the front desk picked up.

"I'm sorry," the man's voice said. "Mr. Coniglio has checked out."

Megan's eyes burned as she hung up the phone, tears gathering that she tried to blink away.

Shit. He's gone. The last day, and he's gone.

God damn you, Neve.

Seeing the two phone books on the floor out of the corner of her eye, she went over and started flipping through them. Pinellas County...aaand no. Hillsborough...shit. Unlisted there, too. After a moment, she thought of looking under H for Hutchinson, and Christ, there were a lot of Hutchinsons in the both of them. Absolutely none named Gwynnevere, or even with the initial G.

Shit.

She was at his mercy. She had to wait for him to call or show up. And what if he didn't? She pushed the thought into a dark closet and shut it in there. Lit another cigarette, and after the second drag, went to the fridge and got another beer, took it into her bedroom. There, she took out all of the pages she'd taken from Nickie's hotel room and consolidated them, unfolding the new ones from her pocket and laying them on her bed next to the ones with the shiny dark gray of graphite already revealing their messages.

She got the pencil and her chessboard, took them to the bed and sat down cross-legged on it. Laid one piece of paper on the chessboard for a solid backing, and started rubbing. The indented images of her own face appeared in white against the gray, and she smiled, stared at them for a long time when she was done. The next one was hotel stationery. When she'd finished darkening it, she leaned back to lie against her pillows, falling into them, and started reading. Some of the things he'd written about her she had to read two or three times, slowly following every loop and jag of his handwriting with her eyes. Imagining his hand pressing a very lucky pen against the piece of paper that had lain on top of this one. That same hand that held her, caressed her. The hand that...

She let go of the paper with one hand, rested it on the buckle of her belt, fingers starting to knead on it absently. Stopped abruptly, sitting up and grabbing another sheet of stationery again. Rubbed the edge of the pencil lead to bring out the words and doodles, then pushed the chessboard aside, loosened her belt and freed the button of her jeans. Lay down on her stomach with her feet up in the air behind her. Set the page before her on the bedspread and snaked her hand into her jeans.

Neve had gone back into the alley nearby to give the bodies in the Dumpster another look. Paranoid, thinking that maybe the garbage bags covering them wasn't enough. Maybe the dolly being in there would arouse suspicion. She knew it would if she found it in *her* Dumpster.

They'd just heaved the thing up over the rim and dropped it in there, took off running, glad to be rid of the bodies and not reconsidering until later.

After such a terrifying morning, Megan wanted nothing but to lie in Nick's arms, feel his massive...

What the f...?

She frowned, leaned closer to the paper, squinting.

Squinting at the word "darkroom."

Very shallow indentations from a much-earlier page on the pad, barely legible.

In the darkroom...at (obviously numbers, a time) bring... My Dear, meet me...darkroom...My Dearest.

Written over and over and over. In someone else's handwriting. She stared at the words for a long time, drawing a complete blank, her mind processing nothing. Just reading and rereading, feeling a mounting fear. Who could've written on that pad other than Nick? Who would've? It wasn't him, though. She knew it wasn't his handwri—wait a minute.

Echoes of conversations came back to her, and the short hairs prickled on the back of her neck. Nick's voice, saying "I can copy a sculpture, a lamp, a portrait, or a signature."

Megan stared at the incoherent jumble of words.

This was practice.

Oh. My. God.

Neve's voice. "I found the note, it said 'My Love,' had Sage's name at the bottom, who the fuck else could it be for? Well, now I know. His *boyfriend*."

But where did you find it, Neve?

Sage just left a note lying around for you to find?

Then his fag lover couldn't have found it, could he? If you found it, then obviously, the other guy didn't. And if he didn't, then how'd he know to meet Sage in the darkroom? Unless...

And why was there a dolly right by the stairs?

And why were there bungee cords? Really, why?

And big, big garbage bags, bigger than the trash can? Why were all these things just conveniently there for us to find?

Oh. My. God.

No, that's ridiculous. Get a grip on yourselfthere'sjustgotta beareasonable explanationforallthisyou'rejustbeingparanoid—

The front door flew open and slammed shut, startling the shit out of Megan. She yanked her hand out of her pants just in time for Neve to come flying into the room, eyes wild.

"Meg!" she choked.

"What? Christ, what is it?"

"Goddamn bodies are gone!" Neve hissed.

"*What?*"

"The dolly's in there, and the bungee cords, all the garbage, but—"

"But no bodies?"

"They're *gone!*"

Blue Tick watched the young man die, cold and expressionless, got up and went to the pedestal in the middle of the room. He hated having to do this part. It was funny the first time, but now it was just stupid.

He grabbed the handle that dangled from the end of a miniature confetti cannon, picked up the three New Year's Eve party horns in his other hand and stuck them between his lips.

He was a giant of a man, six and a half feet tall, almost three hundred pounds of swollen muscle and pitiless cruelty. His shaven skull gleamed with sweat in the dim light, and his eyes were small and cold, almost like those of a fish, his lantern jaw stubbly, a shadow of a beard threatening to overthrow his pencil thin mustache and soul patch.

The other captives stared with bulging horrified eyes as Tick yanked on the string and fired the cannon, at the same time blowing hard. There was a deep *blum!* and shrill *pwaherrrrrrrr*s as the long paper tubes unfurled and lanced out like frogs' tongues. A burst of black confetti belched from the mouth of the cannon and fell in a glittering shower over the fresh corpse strapped to its dentist's chair.

Blue Tick could shrug and say the Devil made him do some things, but Rabbit was the one who made him do this.

Every. Damn. Time.

Christ.

Rabbit was a cool little dude, sure, but sometimes, man, he was madder'n a March hare.

The kid who'd just died was one of five teenagers Rabbit had caught in the middle of the night dropping cinderblocks off of an overpass. He had read in the Tribune a few weeks before that a man had lost his fiancée when one such block crashed through his windshield. The woman he was going to marry and at least make a stab at spending the rest of his life with, gone in one instant of meaningless evil.

There was a chance that these kids weren't the same ones who did it that time, but did it really matter? They were guilty and needed to die horribly.

Rabbit and Tick had been out that night in an SUV they had stolen from whoever had stolen it first, and were driving around, looking for victims to practice on. That is what they called it. Practice.

Torture wasn't something people just knew, see. There were books on the subject, the kind of instruction manuals bound in human leather and written in blood, yadda yadda yadda, that weren't available in the local library. They had scruples, though. Their victims would have to be caught in the act of doing something bad. It would've lacked merit otherwise.

It was, indeed, an art. Rabbit was so into it as an art form that he had gotten himself what Blue Tick referred to as the Smithsonian Institute Collector's Edition Torture Kit, an impressive array of instruments with beautifully-stained mahogany handles, contained in a rather nice briefcase with every tool set in a sunken niche matching its shape. Blue felt and everything. It was nice.

The kid who had just died was the third to go. The second went in a merciful way; ventricular fibrillation they call it, when the heart fails and there is a massive release of epinephrine, usually caused by great fear.

In layman's terms, the little wimp got literally scared to death. It happens. Wet his pants, too. This happened when he watched his first buddy give up the ghost, get confetti showered upon him, and his executioners turned their attention to him. The first instrument hadn't even touched him, yet.

"Tough guy," Rabbit had said to the others. "Big men who kill people you don't even know, but you wet yourselves before I even touch you."

Now there were only two left. Blue Tick had been called on his cell phone before he finished with the last one, interrupted while prying off toenails to come into town and remove two corpses from a Dumpster.

"The girls did it, or you?"

"They did. Not very well, but they did it. If I hadn't been there to help, they'd be sitting in a cell right now."

"The GPS working?"

"And how. I got her movements to within a few feet. More than worth the money."

Rabbit wasn't acting himself, Tick noticed. Seemed erratic, like he hadn't been taking his meds again, or took too many of them. Something.

"You gonna be by later?"

"With bells on."

"Good. See you then."

Tick decided he'd dispatch the last two quickly when he got back and bury the bodies outside the tiny house they'd gotten out in the middle of nowhere, emptying a certain phosphate fertilizer over them before shoveling in the dirt. The graves had been dug in advance, deep pits covered over with screens and disguised much like deadfalls. Handy prefab graves in the woods outside Tampa along I-75 for quick and easy corpse disposal.

There were many.

The only concern he had was the bum that had been camped out in that alley, wrapped up in a blanket. They noticed him, but Rabbit just winked, raised a finger to his lips and said Shhh.

"Shush bout what?" the vagrant asked. "Dumpsta-divin' ain't no crime. I git dat calzone, dat fechinee alfredo, goddamn meatballs every day. Ain't nare cop come an' shake me down fo' it."

"You smoke cigarettes, Mandingo?"

"When I can, dog."

Rabbit—well, technically, Barry—dug his pack of Reds out of his pocket and tossed them to the bum.

"Well, I just quit, so here you go."

"Thanks, bwana. You know, you all right."

"Yeah, I get that a lot. I can't give you my lighter, though. I'll need it later today when I start back up again."

The black guy laughed—not a crackhead's cackle, like Rabbit and Tick half-expected, but a deep, healthy, bull-chested laugh. He sounded like maybe he hadn't been homeless long. They couldn't tell though, because of the way the blanket was tented around him, but suddenly he didn't look so downtrodden. He might even be as big as Blue Tick, if the breadth of those shoulders meant anything.

The bum grinned straight white teeth at them.

"You two go on, enjoy yo' spicy meat-a-ball!" he said, gesturing with a tilt of his head at the large package that Tick held, which was now leaking purge fluid, and a bit of blood.

It was that flip *So, what?* attitude that'd gotten Rabbit through everything since Tick had first started running with him. Where anyone else would be on the defensive and making witnesses suspicious, Rabbit just cracked jokes, putting everyone at ease. While there was something wrong about that bum, their spidey-sense didn't tell them he was a cop, so they took their dead bodies and left him in peace.

Now, Tick went to the huge industrial fridge and got himself a Bud, sat down on one of the cheap-ass plastic chairs the room was furnished with. He looked at the two captives, deciding whether he was going to shoot them both and get blood all over the place, or stab them and get blood all over the place, or just strangle them or bonk them over the head with some blunt object.

Funny thing about language, he thought. If you want to describe a really violent death in a cutesy way, you can. Takes the edge off the horror of what you're talking about. It's not so bad if you say you're going to take a blunt object, bonk someone over the head with it, and smoosh their skull. Put their little tootsies in a vise and squish them all up.

He gestured with the bottle, offering it to the last two kids with a pumping of his eyebrows, then grinning as he withdrew it and saying "Psyche!"

Thinking as he took his first draught, Christ Almighty, that sick kid is rubbing off on me.

That's two down, Rabbit thought, changing his clothes. His phone rang.

It was Vince, and Rabbit had to think for a minute to remember who he was supposed to be with that crowd. Oh yeah, I'm Nick for them. He absently decided that he ought to make up some kind of chart so he didn't get confused.

"Nickie!"

"Hello, Vince."

"'Traiture' is fabulous! The collector loves it!"

"And the Yingzhao?"

"He thinks it's cool, but he doesn't understand it."

"It's the Pleiades, tell him. Titled 'Aharaigichi.'"

"Gesundheit."

"Never mind. So he's going to buy?"

"Yeah, we're haggling. He's trying to Jew me down to twenty-eight thou."

"Oh, what a tragedy."

"Well, it has to be more than that, I mean, how am I supposed to get broken off a decent chunk at a measly fifteen percent? I mean, come on."

Rabbit really wasn't in the mood to listen to this guy's drama, but it really was the only way to keep up relations with Lavon Gilbert, his lead to the "gift-givers." It was, in a convoluted way, how he'd stumbled upon Megan.

117

Now, time out a minute.

A local Poz named Manny Cordoba had been boning a bisexual mulatto, "helping him" to catch the Hiv, as Rabbit was fond of calling it. Said mulatto was also continuing to sleep with an unsuspecting girlie, and said girlie was the roommate of a cute but repressed brainiac with tons of potential.

To arrange events that would not only eliminate two degenerates, and by the hand of someone they'd sinned against, would not only be a fun little project, it would also be hitting two birds with one stone. It would help two modern girls grow the way modern human beings certainly needed to, and prepare them for being pawns in another fun project.

Killing Gwynn for him.

It was complicated, and that was the point. Occam's Razor: the simplest answer is often the most likely. So what detective would really believe in something as ridiculous as the truth? Besides, Megan had to experience, rather than hear voiced in abstract ideas, that Law and Order were horseshit. That her mind was held in a vise of institutional thinking that kept her from making distinctions between arbitrary matters of opinion and actual laws. Laws being, say, gravity. Thermodynamics. Physics, et cetera. And matters of opinion, dependant entirely upon a viewer's vantage point, like, say, beauty, holiness, faith, and courage. And murder.

Time in.

"Um, Nick?"

"I'm sorry, what?"

"Jeez Louise! Are you paying attention to me?"

"No, not really."

"Well, I never!"

As it usually did when Rabbit neglected his meds, his attitude did a sharp about-face. The fact that he was on the phone with a mincing cocksucker made his face suddenly burn, stinging bile rising up to sour the back of his throat.

Lips writhing back to bare his fangs, he turned and hurled his phone against the wall, shattering it into a hundred thousand slivers of plastic. The red haze that clouded his eyes dissolved and he realized he was grinding his teeth again.

"Hel*lo!* Earth to Nickie!"

"Yeah, copy that. Roger. Go ahead."

"You still there?"

"Uh-huh. Sorry about that, Vincey. Got a lot on my mind right now."

With the cell phone held between his cheek and shoulder. Rabbit opened his freezer and got out the Bacardi bottle, thinking for a second that he really had destroyed the phone. Thinking a couple of drinks from now he'd have enough self-control to not want to throw anything, much less do it. He got out a Dixie and poured himself a tall, steadying, redeeming drink.

Thinking, God, I hate myself like this.

Opening the fridge after dropping some ice cubes in and thinking Fuck! I still haven't bought any Coke!

"By the way," Kilgore was saying. "We drew up some papers saying we got that Yingzhao from Immortelles, Ltd, as per your wishes."

"Good. I'm going to send you a lot more, soon. Various antiques. I just have to go pick them up."

At Gwynn's apartment, as soon as.

"Great. Hey, when can I have a look at that other Cigouaves you mentioned?"

"Orgè D'Une?"

"Yeah, it just sounds so tasty."

"I'll let you know."

"Please do it soon. This buyer won't be around forever."

"Oh, the humanity." Click.

Staring into his drink, Rabbit had a brilliant idea.

Checking the monitors, assuring himself that the apartment beneath him was empty, then seeing the girls down the street on the GPS tracker's screen as a green blip, he slipped out of 418 and ran down the stairs. The doors in this place here remarkably easy to unlock, especially considering the wide array of tools he had to work with. He was inside 318 in less than a minute.

Hurrying into the kitchen, he peeked into the fridge and scanned the shelves. Bin-fucking-*go!* Coca-Cola Classic, two liter bottle, more than half-full. He confiscated it, scribbled a note to Megan on the Post-It pad next to the phone, reconsidered and crumbled it up. Stuffing it into his pocket, he headed for the door. In the hallway, he stopped.

Making a yes-no tilting of his head, debating the wisdom of staying a moment longer, he decided it was worth it. He went into the bathroom and switched the toilet paper roll, so that the end piece was in front instead of behind. For some reason, he just couldn't stand it when it was the other way, even in someone else's house. How girls could live with it the other way made no sense to him. Girls and gay guys, it seemed.

Then, swallowing hard, he turned and went into Megan's room. Standing inside the doorway, he breathed deeply, smelling her. He closed his eyes, savoring it, and when he opened them, he noticed the rubbings that lay on her bed. He smiled, proud of her, and went to inspect them.

It took a moment of looking at the pages through her eyes to see what she'd seen, the stupid careless mistake he'd made. She could not possibly have missed it, clever girl that she was. The only thing he could do was take the page and have her wonder if she'd imagined the whole thing, a product of a very long night and a very stressful morning.

Now hurrying out of the apartment, wadding the page up and shoving it deep into his pocket, he fumbled while relocking the door, and couldn't get back to his own lair quickly enough, thinking they'd come around the corner any second and catch him.

The whole time he stood in his kitchen, waiting for the hissing foam to fizzle away after topping off his drink, he cursed himself. Careless, stupid, over-confident dumbass! What the hell was the point of planning ahead like a paranoid nutcase for every possible contingency just to let go and slip up like *that*? The chances Megan could have let a clue like that get past her were slim to none, obviously, because he never would have chosen her in the first place if he thought she wasn't a borderline genius.

Now he was debating whether he should just dump the whole damned thing and kill Gwynn in a mock-burglary or an assault-whoops-homicide. Sure, they were messy, but not as messy as a stupid plan like this.

Good God, what was I thinking?

IX

"You've got to be kidding me," Professor Monga said. Lloyd D. Monga was a little man with a high forehead and a milkstain mustache, who stared at Braswell from behind half-moon glasses at his desk.

"Nope, nope, lovely. Everything about her." Edmund Braswell seemed to have forgotten how to blink.

"Have you gotten any sleep since you met her? Because you really don't look like it."

"Been up all night. And after she comes by to see me later, I'll probably be up for the next two weeks!"

"Smoking crack."

Braswell winced. "That sounds so...so...the way you say it ...when you say it like that. You know what I mean?"

"No."

"Trashy. It sounds kind of trashy when you call it 'smoking crack.' It wasn't like that at all."

"You're out of your fucking mind, Ed."

"Look, if you *tried* it just once, you'd see what I mean."

"No."

"Listen to you with your closed mind. C'mon, have I ever steered you wrong?"

"Yes."

"Oh, lord, do you have to keep bringing that up?"

There had been a brief business venture between the two of them and Ed's brother-in-lay, Murray, for which Lloyd had been convinced to put up most of the capital. It was a furniture store, named Sofa King, and because he was the larger contributor, he was the one who got to pose for the ad wearing a crown and one of those red velvet capes with ermine and what looked like vanilla bean specks in it.

The problem with this was the same curse that had followed him from the maternity ward all through his life, right up to the very minute of this conversation. His name, surname first, comma, followed by his given name. All his life, from Day One.

Monga, Lloyd.

It never got funny, *ever*. But that didn't mean people stopped laughing. The stigma followed him to every listing in the phone book, every billboard, every bus stop bench, and the last straw was when it was brazenly scratched into the glass at the front of the store, under the name Sofa King: "We Taw Did."

"I didn't bring it up, Ed. You did."

"That's it, blame me."

"Ed, listen to yourself. You're trying to get me on *crack*, of all things."

"What I'm trying to do is open you up to a new and wonderful thing."

"Just like when you took me to that gay bar."

"Hey, you've got to admit it eventually. You are as bisexual as the day is long."

"I am not bisexual. I am asexual. I haven't been with a woman because they don't like me, not because I secretly want to suck men's dicks."

"It's obvious, Lloyd. You must be hurting inside."

"Yes, I'm hurting!" he shouted. "I'm hurting because I'm lonely! But I'm not like you, Ed! I don't need love so badly that I'll do what you do! I'm not like you, so for God's sake, leave me alone!"

"Jesus, just listen to that anger. Anger at the shame and fear you have to live with—"

"No, Ed! I'm not that way!"

"—because of the feelings you repress—"

"How many times I have to tell you?"

"—and conceal even from yourself—"

"Do you memorize this crap from fag brochures?"

"—lifelong psychological battles—"

"I have students to worry about, Ed. Ed? I have papers to grade. I have a lesson to prepare."

"—must be tearing you apart, man."

"You know you haven't blinked once since you came in here? Not once."

"Fine, fine, you want to go on living your sad—"

"Get out, Ed! Getoutgetoutgetoutgetout!"

"If you change your mind about coming to this party…" Professor Edmund Braswell said, moving toward the door.

"Never!"

"Suit yourself."

The door opened, swung shut, and Monga was alone once again.

"He'll come around," Braswell muttered outside.

Lloyd started nervously sorting through papers, not sure what he was looking for, then sighed and dropped them all on his heavily-doodled desk blotter. He picked up his phone, called his home and checked the answering machine. No messages.

Same as yesterday, same as the day before.

Same as tomorrow.

Reaching down to tug open the bottom drawer of his desk, he brought out his Humphrey Bogart black fedora, set it on his balding pate at a jaunty angle, and took a stogie out of his cigar box. Stuck it in the corner of his mouth and chewed on it meditatively. He did not smoke.

Dammit, he thought. I'm going to call Ed back in here, aren't I? God damn it.

"Ed!" he shouted.

Braswell opened the door and swung in with it, his eyebrows arched, trying to hide a smile.

"You were standing right outside?" Lloyd asked.

"No."

Pause…

"Nice hat."

"Thanks."

"You need me for something?"

Lloyd sighed deeply, took his cigar out and looked at it for a moment.

"Yeah," he mumbled. "Tell me about this girl again."

Time out. Flashback to a month or so ago.

Lips turning black from too much wine, Rabbit stared from his balcony at the spot where the legendary Roland held an entire Saracen army at bay, all by his lonesome, single-handedly killing one hundred thousand and change and not calling for help until it was too late to save himself. Details vary.

What every storyteller could agree on, though, was that this indeed was the spot. The great hero fell right over there, after blowing three blasts from his great horn Oliphant to warn the rest of the French of the ambush—the third peal was so loud that birds fell dead from the sky—and then dropped his magic sword Durendal and collapsed onto the heap of dead he'd piled high in the mountain pass.

Right over there.

That's the spot, yessiree.

Okay, historians were now saying that it wasn't the Moors who'd tried to trap Charlemagne's army in the mountains, AD 778, but Christians. Basques, in particular, avenging their burned city Pamplona.

Tom*ay*to, tom*ah*to. The important thing is that this is where it happened, Roncesvalles, this pass here through the Pyrenees on the Spanish side of Navarre, heading back into France. Don't leave without visiting the gift shop.

Tourism is what the other side of the pass, Basse-Navarre with its frivolous villages like St-Jean-Pied-de-Port, thrive upon. The restaurateurs, hoteliers, hiking excursion planners, and castle curators all live for the blessed tourist. Yet while the wines on the Spanish side are rich and magnificent, Rabbit noticed, the ones from the French side are expensive crap, and while Pamplona does wineskins like Murano does glass, all the "traditional" souvenirs in Basse-Navarre are made in China.

This side, though, called Navarra, is cheaper and generous, and Roncesvalles offers itself not to tourists, but pilgrims, a great many of whom came now more than ever before to see the monastery they had there and be healed. Chants came hauntingly from that monastery both day and night and lulled Rabbit to sleep if he drank too much.

This province, now shared by France and Spain, was once a kingdom nestled between them—and was called, by one of its last kings, a flea between two monkeys—was now home to seventeen former sex slaves that now spent work hours assembling false antiques. They put together armillary spheres and Caird astrolabes, wooden arabesque-framed mirrors, and Bagues chandeliers. They had just clocked out.

The other seven freed women who had abandoned liberty and returned to prostitution had either hiked across the Pyrenees into Basse-Navarre and fucked their way to Paris and Le Wherever, or migrated south, deeper into Spain and out of Basque country.

Either the lifestyle had become so engrained that they knew how to do nothing else, or they had been whores by nature from the very beginning.

Whichever was the case, to hell with them.

He had felt like Moses must have when the Jews started bitching, the day those seven women walked out on him, but he tried to understand. Admittedly, it had been a tumultuous few weeks—what with all the chases, escapes, the heroism, infamy, the works—and maybe they felt that being whores offered more stability.

The monks' chanting soothed Rabbit as he drank wine from Estella out of a pretentious souvenir wineskin from Pamplona. It had been left sitting in the sun for a day to soften the seams, then filled with wine to absorb the goatiness flavor and then be poured out. He loved that 'goatiness' was a word there.

Rabbit disliked it and felt stupid having it, preferring his hip flask for the conveyance of emergency booze, but he was laying low for a while, and so he needed to blend in as much as possible. Blending in meant looking like an American tourist, and that meant buying a wineskin and carrying it around with him because Hemingway did that, and "Papa" was just as big there as he was in the Florida Keys.

He put the down the wineskin and his copy of the *Codex Calixtinus*, the world's first (known, anyway) travel guide book, written for pilgrims hiking the Pyrenees. It told where the potable and the non-potable water was, mapped out all the mountain passes, warned of false pilgrims and told how to avoid them, and so on—a fascinating read, truly—he put it down and picked up that day's International Herald Tribune to see if he'd made the news.

Ahhhh. Interpol looking into connections between a string of whorehouse raids, shootings, kidnappi—

Hold the phone.

Kidnapping?

Who's been kidnapping sex slaves? Not *me!* Must be somebody else. Gotta be a coincidence, all of these seemingly-related whorehouse raids, shootings, and removal of women, and whoever these *other* guys were, *they* had to be the ones doing the abducting.

I, however, am the one doing the rescuing.

Kidnapping. Sheesh.

The notion of an anonymous press release flitted briefly across his mind, a formal correction for posterity's sake, but he dismissed it. Though angry, he still took the time to carefully fold the paper back up along the same creases it had come with, grabbed his wineskin and went back inside. Kidnapping. Fuck.

The girls had disappeared off to wherever newly emancipated sex slaves go to unwind after work.

Rabbit checked his reflection in one of the arabesque mirrors leaning against one wall, their frames drying, and winced at the color of his lips, went into the bathroom to brush his mouth. Then, minty-fresh, he locked the place up and went forth into the street to look for the girlies.

He found Mischka and Gretchen in a quiet bar, both chain-smoking at a wobbly table for four. He went through the polite formality of asking if he could join them, as if they were in a position to say No.

I have a question," he said in German. They both gave him their undivided attention.

Gretchen was a redhead, a notch or two above plain-looking, small-breasted but well-assed, with the kind of face a man would find enchanting after only one drink.

Mischka, however, was not. She had a mannish quality, not ugly so much, but rather blunt, if that can be a description. Yet for some reason, men looked at her and damn if they didn't want to screw her. When men saw one of their friends dating an ugly woman, and asked what the hell he was thinking, and he could not explain what had attracted him to her in the first place, it was because she had whatever this woman had. Whatever it was, Mischka had it.

"Do you feel kidnapped?" Rabbit asked.

They blinked at him, then looked at each other.

"What I mean is, do you feel just like you did before I came and got you? Am I just another master to you, like the men that bought you? Be honest."

They both looked back and forth from him to each other, trying to second-guess him and wanting to say whatever it was he wanted to hear. Finally, Gretchen answered in a halting Deutsche, knowing only a bare minimum of it.

"You don't make us, er, go to bed with you."

Gee, he thought, no shit. But that doesn't tell me very much. It isn't easy to gauge inflections and hidden meanings when the speaker speaks only a little of the same language.

"Go on," he prompted.

"Um, we don't know where we are go."

"What, you mean after this? You go wherever you want. The world is your oyster."

Gretchen hesitated, so Mischka jumped in for her.

"We good. Me?" she added, touching his arm from across the table for emphasis, her fingertips lingering. "Very good. Happy. Came for job, got caught, now look for job more. Have kind of job now," she said with a yes-no tilting of her head, then touched his arm again. "Thank you."

"And you?" he asked Gretchen.

She glanced at Mischka again, to get up the nerve.

"You want, me happy work for you."

"What do you mean?"

"I do good, keep you satisfy, whenever you want."

"Are you kidding? I just got you out of that life!"

"Okay, okay," she assured him. "I don't mind."

Rabbit threw up his hands, got up and stormed out of the bar, muttering under his breath. Gretchen looked at Mischka, and Mischka shrugged.

At that moment, while checking out Parisienne girls along the Rue des Moulins, three men vacationing from Eastern Europe stopped and stared at two prostitutes. Sensing their gaze, the women looked over and froze. Two of the men, the Bosnian brothers Viktor and Anton Brasi, grinned, but the third's face turned to stone. He was with his own brother when these two whores were chosen out of a lineup to be an ear-licker and a nipple-biter only a few weeks ago.

His name was Vladimir Bilowas, and he was a gangly, shaven-headed man with gin blossoms erupting at the end of his sharp nose and putting some color in his otherwise pale face. His cobalt eyes narrowed and he pushed his way between his friends, advancing on the women and pulling his tazer.

"I give up," Rabbit told Tick in his muscle-bound henchman's room. "These broads aren't going to change. They're just like those dolphins that got freed back in the Eighties, you remember? Swam out into the ocean and frolicked for a while, then came on back when they got hungry. These women were a lost cause before I started."

"I ain't gonna say I told you so, but I did."

"Go to hell."

"Can't blame you, though, after the Kinonas girl."

"Quiñonez. And thank you very much for bringing up that painful memory. Why not gouge out my eye and skull-fuck me while you're at it, you insensitive shithead?"

The nipple-biter flew headlong into the lamp, phone, and clock on the hotel room desk, scattering them and plowing face-first into the wall. Without even time to groan, she was yanked up and backward, her hair coming out in clumps from Bilowas' fists. A knee came up and slammed into her gut, doubling her over, and she vomited all over the room's periwinkle blue carpeting.

"So, what then?" Tick asked.

"If they want to keep on like this, let 'em. Pack up everything and let's go somewhere else."

The ear-licker's arm was bent back behind her, her elbow inching slowly toward her spine. Tears glistened on her swollen face, running blood and mascara together on her cheeks.

"Where you wanna go this time? Beirut?"

"Nah, nowhere special. Back to Florida for a while, I guess. Check the messages, see what's been going on."

"When do you want to tell the girls?"

"Mischka already knows," Rabbit said, jerking a thumb over his shoulder. "She's behind that door, eavesdropping."

They both heard the creak of floorboards in the hallway, somebody hurrying quietly away, but not quietly enough.

"How do you *do* that?" Tick asked, impressed.

"A little trick I picked up in the Orient."

"Huh. So, what you think? Maybe we oughta go tonight, then?"

Anton Brasi let go of the ear-licker's elbow and she collapsed into Viktor's arms, crying out. He grabbed a handful of black hair and hoisted her up by it. Looking deep into her swollen eyes, he whispered something, kissed the tip of her nose, and let her fall.

"Now," Bilowas said, panting heavily, his pointy nose and shaven skull making him look like a buzzard. "I ask you, one more time."

"Yeah," Rabbit muttered. "This town's too dull anyway."

Okay, time in.

"Cracka," Blue Tick was saying to himself in a Cuban voice. "Las nigh, cracka, I see choo geev a choo peanuh bottah to tha beeg negro. But tonigh, cracka, tonigh choo geev choo peanuh bottah to *me*. I like tha peanuh bottah too."

The two remaining hostages looked at each other with wide-eyed frowns, thinking What the fuck is this nutbag doing now? Talking to himself while he's conjuring shit up in the shack with his toolbox.

"No, no, please, Sancho!" Tick chirped in a high pleading voice, then putting on an angry, brutish face that the hostages guessed would be tha beeg negro, but was interrupted by his cell phone ringing. He dropped his tools and stretched across the bubbled linoleum to reach the tiny phone, so ridiculously tiny when he held it in his giant, meaty hand against his enormous round head.

Beep!

"Shit Plop n' Doodle Burgers! Would you like to try one of our award-winning Deluxe Shit Plop n' Doodle Burger Combos today?"

"Abandon ship, Tick."

"Say again, Red Leader, say again."

"Abandon ship. Abort. I've decided to just go ahead and do it. Scratch the stupid plan, it's not going to work, so it's going down the old-fashioned way."

"Um, are you sure that's a good idea? Are you in a responsible frame of mind right now?"

"You're goddamn right. I wasn't when I came up with this hare-brained scheme. I was on my stupid meds, which I stopped taking the other day."

"You *have* been acting kinda funny, lately."

"That's them wearing off."

"Don't they take longer than a couple days to—"

"Dude, the facts are irrelevant. I'm heading over to the efficiency right now, and I'll call you in a few hours once the hen squats. Go ahead and send those kids on to the next life."

Rabbit hung up. Staring now at his half-filled glass, absently wondering if it was half-empty, he felt himself flip-flop. Although silence reigned throughout the apartment, his ears rang maddeningly, and his head buzzed like a scrambled channel, his eyes registering static.

He stood in the kitchen, feeling the linoleum floor waver beneath his feet, and for balance he reached for the glass instead of the counter it rested upon.

Just as his fingers touched the glass and smeared rivulets of condensation, an ice cube cracked with a noise as definite as that of a driven nail, solidifying his determination, and he poured the rest of his drink down the drain. And good riddance, too, he thought.

While he might be the life of the party the more he drank, while he knew he got braver, smarter, funnier, more charming, and better-looking the deeper his drinks came and the faster they were emptied, he also knew he was impetuous, reckless, and ultimately, stupider. Every day may have been magical, full of adventure and self-importance and superstitiously misplaced significance, almost completely withdrawn from reality, and certainly not of the mindset necessary for choreographing successful murders.

He looked around the apartment for something he could transfer his addiction to, something else he could take up to excess so he wouldn't miss drinking quite so much. He had cigarettes stashed somewhere...no, shit, he gave them to that bum in the alley. Chewing gum? Did he have any? No, just breath mints. Shit, he had to find *something* or he'd be left with nothing but his teeth to grind.

He grabbed the pen that had been sitting on the counter next to the phone book, on top of the sheet of paper where he'd copied down all of the numbers for pizza delivery and Chinese takeout. Now the pen's official function was the Thing That I Twirl Around My Fingers Like Val Kilmer Does. He had one up on ol' Val, though. Not only could he do it *really* fast, it was one of those click pens that he could thumb the button on, unsheathing the nib, without breaking stride. If he got restless and wanted a drink or a cigarette while practicing, he could distract himself by trying to manage two clicks, and then he could try to break that record. And look like a goddamn lunatic if he did it in public.

Another goofy-ass thing he'd do was eat spaghetti, twirling it and eating with his left hand, his non-dominant hand, while playing Tetris on his cell phone with the other. He could do it without getting any sauce on his shirt, and win the game, but he ended up with indigestion from eating without chewing.

Going in the bedroom, he opened his suitcase full of weapons, the few necessities he'd brought into town with him, and chose the even-fewer necessities he'd take with him now. Lessee, Mauser SP66 three-round sniper rifle...no. Good old-fashioned Mark II fragmentation grenades? No. James Bond style Walther PPK with obligatory silencer? Yesyesyesyesyes.

Two Asp extendable batons with Velcro strap-on forearm sheathes? Ohh yes. Throwing knives? Ye—nahh, that's probably overkill. They were fun, though, and as much as he'd wanted to, he had never gotten to kill anyone with them yet.

He got changed into his Maria Conchita Juanita Garcia Gonzalez outfit, knowing that, as a Hispanic chick, he'd attract less attention while breaking into Gwynn's efficiency. It was illogical, sure, but for some reason, anybody that might see him would be less suspicious of a woman picking a lock than they would seeing Barry or Chris doing it.

He shaved again, just to be on the safe side. He wouldn't want to be waiting so long on a stakeout that he started to show stubble. He then applied some concealer and a little shading to change the shape of his cheeks, accented his lips a little, and put on a bra with falsies that he could hide stuff in.

He really wanted a foam pregnant-lady belly, like that shoplifter in that Jane's Addiction video, so he could carry all kinds of weapons around in secret, plus a change of clothes in case he needed one, but he just couldn't find one. Maybe there would be a way to find one on the internet in a few years, once it got off the ground and people started using it for more than just chat rooms.

A pair of jeans one size too small showed off his good rear-end and strong legs without him having to tuck his artificially-huge manhood wherever the drag-queens put theirs. His bulge wouldn't be that obvious down one leg, as long as he didn't get down-wind of a woman with perfume on.

He chuckled at the thought, then realized how bad off he'd be if that did happen, a vision of being out in the open popping into his head. Broad daylight, dressed up like a chick with his surgically-enlarged wang standing out almost halfway to his knee.

Everybody pointing. Oh yeah, way to blend in.

He swapped them for a baggier pair of jeans. Grabbed one of his ugly buttondowns out of the closet and did it up half-way, sloppily tucked it in, and rolled the sleeves up to his elbows. Pulled the tight picoted skullcap over his hair to contain it, and then fastened his wig to it.

The asps he stuck in his bra, underneath the falsies where the underwires would hold them in place. The pistol he stuck in his bookbag, along with his lock-picking set, bottle of chloroform, and a rag. After a moment of reflection, he also got one of his two stun guns out of his suitcase, just in case.

Ready now, he locked the apartment and went down the hall to the stairwell, remembering to put a little swerve in his bop and trying not to feel like a fag while doing it.

As he hopped lightly down the steps, taking them three at a time, he heard low voices coming from below. For a moment, he felt a fear that his disguise would not hold up, but when he had rounded the switchback at the third floor landing he saw two young men who suddenly stopped talking and looked away from each other, doing the whole we're-not-suspicious routine. *Whew!* Rabbit relaxed, remembering that in this world almost everybody seemed to be hiding something, and most did not have the time to scrutinize him. He bopped down toward them, and they stepped aside to let him pass.

Bopping the rest of the way to the ground floor and swerving out the door with a confident swing in his hips, he stepped aside for Neve and Megan as they almost crashed into him. They did a double-take, and he winked. Flashing them a toothy grin, and walked on.

They stared after him, Megan wondering if she should catch up with Señorita and thank her for helping them earlier that morning, and Neve frowning at the shirt Maria Conchita Juanita Garcia Gonzalez was wearing. Without a doubt the ugliest shirt she'd seen since...

Yesterday.

The ugly guy who'd moved into the apartment right above them, who was that height, that build, same cute ass...hmmm. Must be his sister. Looking so alike, wearing that same hideous millefiori shirt, just without the disgusting pockmarks that Whats-hisname, Barry, had all over his face.

She mentioned it on the way up the stairs, and Megan tried to give a shit, but couldn't. Then they got safely into their home and tried to have a Coke while talking about the word "darkroom" on the stationery rubbing, but—?

Rabbit felt like he was in some kind of time warp when he walked into Gwynn Hutchinson's secret lair. He hadn't seen all these things in years, but they had been a part of his home and so he knew them as one knows his long-lost mother when he spots her across the counter in a small town diner. What song was that from? Didn't matter. He was too busy staring in wonder at the chinoiserie table under the Bagues chandelier that had been in the dining room outside the kitchen door, and the Aubusson carpet and the nineteenth-century Persian rug, and the divans, and the armoires, and the chiffoniers, Lumiere buffets, Louis Quinze fauteuils, breakfronts, high-boys, and grandfather clocks all crammed in without hardly any floor space between them.

God, those raspberry and cream French draperies that used to be in the den were now hanging from a *traverse rod,* for God's sake. That gilded futtock plate and the antique samisen had been on the walls of the library, and that Benares vina in the corner, and that exposed-gears pendulum clock. That ornately-carved hourglass, that Goethe barometer, that Galileo thermometer. That Caird astrolabe. That armillary sphere.

That cunt.

This was his home, boxed up in a tiny room. They weren't material possessions, they were his *stuff.*

He picked his way through the maze of what had once been his and ransacked whatever hadn't. The cupboards in the kitchen, the fridge, the drawers. In the bedroom he found his parents' bed. His bed. The aircraft carrier. It was unmade and still looked good. Black and gold Greek keys for a border, leopard print on one side of the duvet with a striated red on the other, the linens made of cotton in Germany but somehow managing to look like silk. Trying not to look at it, he tore through her laundry, and her bureaus and credenzas that used to be in *his* bedroom.

Finally, after finding nothing he hadn't expected, he settled down on her bed and smelled her scent, took out his asps and his gun and got comfortable, waiting for her to come home. He waited.

And waited.

X

Gwynn squatted inside a storage unit with a bright orange roll-down door, fussing over the contraption she'd put together in the light of a battery-operated lamp sitting on a dresser. She'd run six feet of quarter inch plastic tubing from a hole she'd drilled in a PVC dome cap through an ice-filled Styrofoam cooler set on a ratty sofa underneath a blacklight, and into a two gallon bucket on the floor.

The dome cap had an elbow sticking out of it to accept the tube, and she had just set it onto the mouth of a mason jar, and put the jar into a saucepan full of boiling water. She switched off the lamp, plunging the storage unit into eerie purple light.

Now, the steam rising up out of the jar was being forced through the tube to the Styrofoam cooler, condensing the steam into liquid. That liquid was now passing under the blacklight, where it glowed a bright green, showing it was potent. If it had been a pale yellow, like last time, it would've meant another month and a half down the drain. Out of the tube's end, the liquid, indistinguishable from water, trickled slowly into the bucket.

Yay! A fortune!

This would take a while, though. She had forty-four other jars to go through, and when she was done, she had to responsibly dispose of all the jars because they were highly poisonous, and just touching the sludge inside them could leave a person insane and hallucinating for the rest of her life.

So, of course, these jars were destined for the grass along the side of the highway, where she could just chuck them out the window of her VW Beetle as she drove back into town.

She wanted to smear that gook all over the door handles and combination locks in the Art Building, as revenge for getting fired from her job that morning, but then a shitload of people would be tripping for free, and she couldn't have that. The last thing she'd be was some kind of charitable institution.

But she just had to get back at that school for firing her just because she talked a little fast to callers on the phone that day and cussed them out a little and made up a bunch of such obvious bullshit that tuition-paying parents would never believe unless *they* were tripping. Hey, so she'd been up all night smoking crack and doing bumps of cocaine right there at her desk, so of course she got a little excitable on the phone, I mean *d'uh!* Hel*lo!* She didn't get all judgmental when her coworkers drank too much cough syrup during flu season, now did she?

"May cause drowsiness," she muttered. "Christ."

She'd show them, though.

Guavaween was—what?—next weekend? Yeah, the Saturday before Halloween. She'd make enough money to not need this stupid school job. Then she could—whoa, Gwynnie. Don't count your chickens. Isn't that how you got here in the first place, lugging a ton of furniture around with you everywhere you went? Unable to just skip town like the old days because of all this, for lack of a better word...*baggage?*

Shit, stop talking to yourself, Gwynn.

Rabbit lay on the bed in the darkness, twirling his pen in his left hand, clicking the button, twirling it around another circuit and clicking it again.

Good God, stakeouts are so fucking boring.

Anton Brasi had Gretchen on all fours, her face pressed down into the floor, bare ass up in the air and bruised with his handprints.

Mischka was up against the wall with her pants down around her ankles, Viktor taking her savagely from behind, and she was trying her damnedest not to sound like she didn't love it.

There was another man in the room along with Vladimir, sitting on a cot with a sketch pad, making adjustments to his portrait whenever Saaja spoke. Saaja was Finnish, blonde and fair-skinned, and she was somehow even paler as she sat on Vladimir's lap and described Nick Coniglio. Vladimir lightly stroked her skin with his fingertips and occasionally brushed his lips gently against her. The whole while she sat rigid, trembling, cooperating fully and wondering if she was going to die anyway.

This was back in early September. The next day the slave traffickers were huddled over an atlas, scanning multicolored Europe and wondering where the hell Florida was.

"Fuck, this is boring," Gwynn mumbled, sweating, stepping outside for a cigarette. Forgetting that there was a sun hanging low in the sky on the other side of the orange door, she was momentarily blinded when she raised it.

"Dammit!" She let it slam back down so she could pull her five-hundred-dollar sunglasses out from where she'd hung them in her skin-tight Gargamel baby tee. Once they were on, she lifted the door again and slipped under it, letting it fall behind her.

She lit a Gauloise, an imported French cigarette, and let it hang out of the corner of her mouth.

"What, you live in there?" a voice asked. She spun around, startled, and faced a man and a woman. They were dressed like some kind of Goth, but not the usual black-wearing vampire wannabe types.

The man had long brown hair, elbow-length and rather poorly cared-for, and wore what looked like a red doublet. He was skinny, but would probably use the word "gaunt" to describe himself, the same way it wasn't getting close to evening, it was "nigh unto the gloaming."

The woman wasn't so much chubby as "zaftig," not so much sickly pale to the point of bluish as she was "cyanotic." Her hair was a snow-white Chelsea cut, her fingernails long and painted hot pink until the quick ended and white the rest of the way. Her eyes were bright blue, her lips blood red. She wore a gray sundress with a chatelaine girding her waist, with something silver dangling from it, some talisman.

Gwynn smiled.

"Well, actually, yeah, I do live here."

Rabbit daydreamed about unscrewing the bulb from the bedroom ceiling light, gently worrying a hole through the delicate glass with a needle, and submerging it in gasoline until it stopped bubbling. Screwing it back in, and leaving.

But when Gwynn came back home and flicked on the light switch, and the white-hot filament ignited the fuel inside the bulb, the explosion would destroy a lot of these antiques along with her, not to mention burn down the entire building and kill or at least render homeless a bunch of innocent people.

So, that's a no go.

He thought about powdered aluminum, red phosphorus, gunpowder, and a little rewiring, and her hairdryer. But no. That would make too loud of a boom, and the neighbors would call the police, and he would still be without all his furniture because he couldn't come pick it up.

He thought about poisoning whatever it was in his Mom's crystal decanter, but he didn't happen to have any poison on him, so that was out, too.

He thought of all the ways that he could kill her without his presence actually required, because he was sick and tired of sitting around waiting for her to get back from wherever the hell she was, and he'd read all of her stupid magazines with their relationship advice columns, their misleading ads, and blowjob tips cover to cover and back to back and Jesus fucking Christ, what was taking that bitch so long?

He checked his watch. It was getting on evening already! If she'd just come the fuck home he could pop her twice in the fucking head with the PPK making no more noise than a little *ping!* and he could stick her in the bathtub so her fluids could drain instead of soaking through the floor and dripping on the nose of the guy who lived downstairs.

Then he could come back tomorrow with a big ol' U-Haul truck and carry his stuff out with Blue Tick. And *then* he could have a legitimate business selling antiques instead of forgery, gun-running, and piracy.

But no.

Goldilocks wasn't coming the fuck home.

He shifted a little on the bed and was suddenly fast asleep.

"Yeah, I had a place to stay and a car and all that," Gwynn said. "But my boyfriend, you see, I thought he was cheating on me and I confronted him about it, and we got in this big, big fight and he threw me out. So I packed up all my stuff and put it in here until I get a place to stay and I went out looking but would you believe it? I went into this one place and when I came out, my car was towed!"

"Oh," the two Goths said, wondering what they'd gotten themselves into.

"Well, all of my money was in the car and I don't know who towed it, or to where, and I had some change left and I called the towing people to see if they took my car, but they all said No. So now I'm living in here while taking the bus up to Dale Mabry where I can pay the monthly rent for this unit by dancing in this seedy place called the Fleshpot and I hate it, yunno what I mean? It's just so degrading, but, like, what *else* am I gonna do, yunno?"

Mistress Charlotte and Lord Dave looked at each other, both feeling not so much charitable as spellbound, the two of them having a strong affinity for hot chicks in distress.

And this poor urchin was very, very hot.

"Um, do you think," said Dave. "That if no one seems to have your car, then maybe it wasn't towed?"

"What? It had to be towed. I mean, it *had* to be. Because one minute it was there outside and the next it wasn't."

"What he means is," Charlotte chirped at her. "Someone probably stole it."

Gasp. "*Stole?*"

By the time the mason jar's added water boiled out of the sludge, and it was time for a new jar to be put on, Gwynn had gotten a place to stay with them and their entourage of unemployed mooching friends.

Of course, actually staying with them would be horrid, but the opportunities there were boundless.

She excused herself and slipped under the orange door again, after only lifting it a few feet off the ground so they couldn't see inside. She carefully ladled out some of the liquid acid in the bucket and funneled it into an empty Pepsi bottle, making sure to get not even a drop of it on her skin.

When the bottle was full, she grabbed a duffel bag full of plastic vials, some empty, that the acid would go into, some full of crystal meth, and some of crack. She zipped it up, changed the mason jars so at least one would be steamed while she was gone, turned off the blacklight, and went to the door, placing a drinking glass against the metal and putting her ear to it.

Mistress Charlotte and Lord Dave turned out to be a couple with a swinging relationship (with whatever weirdos would go to bed with them) but neither one wanted the other to know the designs they had on poor little Gwynn, so they were carrying on a rather convoluted discussion about how they ought to do something to help and taking forever to get to the point because neither of them wanted to be the one to come right out and say "Maybe if we play our cards right, we can fuck her." All that she managed to pick up through the glass in the moment she listened.

She went out the way she'd come in, interrupting them, trying not to laugh at their We-weren't-just-talking-about-trying-to-fuck-you faces.

"Had to grab a few things," she said sweetly, turned, and locked up the storage unit.

"Well, you know, the reason we're here in the first place," said Dave. "There's this really great party at this club we go to on Seventh in Ybor, called Baroque. Us and a bunch of our friends are going. We came down here 'cause we don't have enough room in our house to store all our party stuff, so we stick it here. If you want to come with, you can pick out something for yourself to wear."

"Really? Wow, that'd be swell! Now, hey, is that Baroque as in 'irregularly shaped' or as in 'pertaining to the styles of Europe after the Renaissance and characterized by exuberant decoration?'"

The Goths stared at her a moment, then beamed.

"Uh, the second one," Charlotte said.

"Oh cool."

She followed them to their unit, watched them go through the trunks full of costumes that were wedged among big gibbet-like structures for sadomasochism. There was even a pillory and a cangue. Gwynn had learned about these things from the huge framed history lesson pictures on Rabbit's bedroom walls when she was in his house. Big documentary-type things with footnotes, about the American Revolution and the Serenissima and Columbus and all kinds of stuff.

While Dave got out what he was going to wear, Charlotte held up various things for Gwynn to choose from. They ended up agreeing on a black and burgundy cotton Prom corset with matching hoop skirt and a paisley shawl with tassels.

"Ooh!" exclaimed Charlotte. "And the finishing touch! You can't be without one of these!"

She held up a papier mâche Venetian Carnivale mask, with stiff jester's cap whatchamacallits curling down from the top of it. Little jingle bells dangled from their ends, ringing.

"You're right," said Gwynn. "I can't."

Their house was an ugly bungalow, turquoise and pink, with a wraparound porch and jalousie door and louvered shutters. It would've been ghastly anywhere except Florida, as would the plastic pink flamingoes that stood guard on one leg in the front lawn.

It was very hard to believe Goths would live here, instead of in some haunted rundown mansion with a dead tree out front. The squatters, sure, maybe. When she mentioned this, they informed her they weren't Goths at all, dear God no, ha ha, but steampunks.

"Steampunks?" she asked, trying not to include "What the fuck are" in her question.

"We're really into science fiction and alternative history and horror," Lord Dave said.

"Retrofuturism from a Victorian era standpoint," Mistress Charlotte corrected. Ahhh.

Inside, more pastels, and instead of anything made of actual wood, everything was either T-one-eleven or woodgrain contact paper on particleboard. It was the Floridian version of the American Dream: if you paint a turd turquoise and pink it is somehow no longer a piece of shit. It reminded her of oranges, the worst in the batch dyed bright orange so they at least looked good.

Half a dozen affectedly morbid wastrels sat inside, drinking wine, chain-smoking, and arguing over their paperwork and trading cards in a fantasy role-playing game. They didn't look up as their hosts came in.

"Guys! Hey, everybody!" Dave called.

"You're fulla shit! That's six hunnerd life points, *easy!*" one of them said.

"But don't forget the wounds you sustained—"

"I'm a fourth level yeoman cleric! That got automatically healed."

"The fuck it did."

"Oh, I am *so* gonna get you back—"

"Can't do a thing with 'em," Dave said to Gwynn, trying to be offhand, but ashamed at being ignored and having no backbone to do anything about it.

"Hey, mind if I take a shower?" she asked.

"Yeah, yeah, knock yourself out. Last door on the right, towels under the sink."

Once she'd locked the bathroom door behind her, she quickly browsed through the medicine cabinet, looking for Percosets, Demerol, Xanax, anything. She came up with Ritalin and Sinequan, that's all, but it was better than nothing, so into the duffel bag it went. Then she tallied the available cleansing agents and came up with a grand total of two. Some unimpressive soap, and a Shampoo-Conditioner-Two-In-One.

Oh good God.

Fuckin' Philistines, we got here.

Gritting her teeth, she peeled her sweat-soaked clothing off and didn't bother adoring herself in the mirror. Got into the shower and washed the soap off under the hot water for a bit before letting it touch her bronze skin.

When she came out wearing her tight cotton briefs that looked like hot pants and a Gasparilla t-shirt that she'd had in a side compartment of the duffel bag, she walked in on eight people, naked, in a circle holding hands.

"Oh, just in time!" Charlotte called. "Hurry up, you can join us!"

Oh really, can I?

"Our religion," Dave said. "We have to give thanks and offer a sacrifice to the Goddess before we go out tonight."

"Sacrifice? Where? You got a goat in the microwave?"

"Ha-ha, no. Wine! We poured a glass for her." He jerked his chin toward the table that Card Game Of Doom had been played upon. A glass of red sat alone among the papers.

"You go on ahead," Gwynn said, walking to the table, dropping the duffel bag.

Charlotte tried the guilt maneuver. "But we do this all the time, and everyone who lives here does it. If you're going to be staying with us, you can't insult our religion—"

"I'm Muslim. I'm not allowed to show my body."

"But you said you're a stripper, didn't you?"

Rolling her eyes, Gwynn grabbed the tail of her t-shirt and lifted it up, flashing her boobs at the eight steampunks only for an instant, then dropped it and reached for the glass. Before any of them could shake off their star-struck surprise, Gwynn had drained the wine and smacked her lips, considering the aftertaste.

"Mmm. January…maybe even November of last year. November wasn't a very good month. Okay!" she added, addressing the coven. "When's this little shindig start?"

They looked at each other, glanced down at each other's nakedness and broke the circle, realizing their ruse wasn't going anywhere and started putting their clothes back on, muttering about getting gypped.

"This Baroque place you mentioned. They got drugs there?"

Dave was sitting down, legs up in the air, tugging his pants on. "I wish. There's a couple people in there, selling this or that, but mostly it's BYO."

"Not anymore," Gwynn said.

They all looked at her blankly. "Wha—?"

XI

There is an old saying that Gwynn Hutchinson had heard once but paid no attention to: you can shear a sheep many times, but you can only skin him once. She continued to pay no attention to it at the Baroque Club later that night.

Bizarre figures moved jerkily in the strobe light to British voices chanting behind pounding beats and strange, ethereal music. There were both women and cross-dressers in corsets, from underbusts and Amazons and bodices to full-body affairs that almost completely restricted movement, and all manner of gowns and costumes. Some men wore bondage gear, some in only a few pieces and some in full regalia.

Some wore damask waistcoats and ramillies—the powdered white wigs with curl-rollers on the sides and the pigtails with the little bows—and stockings and buckled shoes, and they bowed to each other with flourishes and kissed one another's rings.

At regular intervals, there were ancient torture devices such as the wheel, the rack, and the gibbet, where a victim's pants were pulled down and either their asses were spanked or their genitals whipped with a silken cat-o-nine-tails.

On the side opposite the door, across the dance floor (where nobody really danced, *per se*) were more modern toys for mild electrocution, clamping, and so on. There were giant canopy beds with black velvet drapes along one wall, on which strobe-lit shapes grappled with each other. Restaurant-style booths lined another wall with their own black drapes for discretion or seclusion.

Nosferatu, Type-O Negative, and Marilyn Manson were all heard in the length of time it took Gwynn to be doing steady business from the moment she walked through the door. Aside from the drugs themselves, she also sold crack stems and tufts of pre-shredded Brillo pads for the curious and the unprepared, those who'd only expected to drink or snort a bump of coke off of each other's car keys or fingernails.

Before too long, the crowd was lit more by the sustained flames of cigarette lighters than by the sweeping shafts of party lights in the rafters.

Face concealed beneath the Carnivale mask, she had a hell of a time trying to smoke a Gauloise in one of the booths, so she finally took the damned thing off and threw it onto the table. The two guys across from her in Victorian and bondage couture who were negotiating the purchase of two hundred-dollar vials of acid stared at her startling beauty.

Barely managing to pull themselves together, they wrapped up their little transaction and rejoined their friends, describing her to them in wonder. One of them, a young woman barely legal, that everyone had nicknamed Dorothy, looked curiously at the half-drawn drapes enveloping the booth they'd just left.

Charlotte, her middle only fifteen inches around inside her red leather corset, clomped from the bar in her red platform heels over to the booth, a carafe of wine in one hand and two glasses in the other.

"Busy?" she chirped, sticking her head in with a smile. "I brought you a drink."

She held up the carafe, and Gwynn snatched it.

"Aw, you shouldn't have."

Charlotte watched with unbelieving eyes as the carafe was drained, gulp, gulp, gulp in one long go, leaving only the lees in a thin trail of color, and then that was gone too.

"That's a little more like it," Gwynn managed, handing the empty carafe back to Charlotte, who took it and stared at the two empty glasses in her other hand, hovering less than two feet from Gwynn, still halfway through the motion of sitting down beside her. "Mm, that really hit the spot, thanks."

Trying to salvage something, perhaps her dignity, Charlotte cleared her throat and asked if she could get a little somethin-somethin out of that bag for herself, whatever was handy. Gwynn gave her a look.

"Now, honey, really. You know what a fix I'm in. I'm trying to scrape together a little something of my own so I can get back on my feet, and that's just not going to happen if I give it all away for free, now is it? I tell you what, maybe I'll let you get something out of the next batch, how's that sound?"

Charlotte mumbled something and backed out of the booth, set the glasses and carafe down on the coping of the short wall bordering the dance floor, not seeing the beautiful young woman everyone was calling Dorothy stride past her toward the booth.

"Ya don't get rich by paying for drinks," Gwynn was muttering, putting another Gauloise in the corner of her mouth. She lit it with an ornate Zippo she'd stolen from one of the squatters back at the house. "You don't get ahead by waiting your turn." She sucked on her teeth with a loud smack, and turned to look as someone else came through the curtain.

She caught her breath.

The girl was tall, but young, still just eighteen and amazingly gorgeous. Her long black hair was in a French braid with a red bow tied at the end, near the small of her back, and her ample breasts stood out more with her abdomen constricted beneath them. If Gwynn had known anything about corsets, she could describe this one as an Edwardian blue gingham cotton underbust, breasts covered in the same frilly white lace that comprised the very short skirt. Her strong legs were spider-webbed in white fishnet stockings, and on her feet were red patent leather stripper stacks.

The both of them stared at each other for a long moment, each admiring the beauty of the other without trying to show it.

"Shop's closed," the girl said finally. "Come buy me a drink." And she was gone.

Gwynn blinked at the gently swaying fringe of the velvet curtain that marked the girl's passing.

What in the—?

She blinked some more, wondering if it had really happened. Then, either affronted pride or curiosity made her zip up the duffel bag and hang it over one shoulder, draping her paisley shawl with the tassels over it as a formality, a perfunctory attempt to conceal it just to satisfy the security in the place.

Slid out of the booth and stepped into the play of the lights, the hoop under her skirt ballooning back into shape. Remembering her mask, she reached back in to get it and strapped it to her head underneath her hair. Turned around to look for this impetuous girl and put her in her place.

There she was. By the bar.

Now, Gwynn was not gay. Sure, she'd messed around with another girl back in reform school, but who didn't? That didn't make you gay. Sure, she thought about that girl every now and then, but she chased those evil thoughts out of her head and resisted that voice, that traitor that said Yeah, you liked it, you little dyke. She wasn't gay. At all.

But there was the girl, Dorothy, with her legs that went all the way up, that perfect ass just barely covered by the ruffles and picots of the skirt. She stared at that exquisite profile, torn between the urge to publicly belittle that proud girl and the longing to *be* her.

The girl looked her way. Smiled faintly.

And Gwynn went to her.

"Dorothy?" she asked. "Is that you?"

The girl looked at Gwynn's eyes behind the mask and said nothing. For the first time in her life, Gwynn felt inept.

"Take that off," the girl said.

Gwynn hesitated, about to tell her that she took orders from *no one*, but for some reason found herself obeying. She lifted the Venetian mask carefully up off of her face, letting her hair cascade down as the head strap came away. They looked at each other again, appraising, and finally the girl said "My name is Enolah."

"I'm Gwynn."

"I don't like this crap wine everyone's drinking, Gwynn. This moricaud. I like Narcisse. Why don't you get us a bottle, and we'll go off and talk."

Gwynn looked at Enolah's blood red lips, at her flawless white skin. She smelled her perfume through the haze of smoke and sweat, a faint thread of white oleander and something else.

She wanted to say something clever and cutting, but when her breath passed through her throat and her mouth moved she heard herself saying "You have a bottle of Narcisse back there you're not doing anything with?" Then noticed with embarrassment that she hadn't spoken loud enough, turned to lean across the bar and shouted for one of the bartenders.

A skinny kid dressed in a tabard nodded in her direction as he fixed a rum runner, handed it over, got paid for it, and then came with his eyebrows raised and his mouth open to Gwynn, putting two fingers behind his ear and bending it toward her.

She repeated herself and he nodded, going to the wine rack. Conscious of Enolah watching, Gwynn swung the duffel bag forward under her arm to get at one of the zippered ends where the money was.

"I been meaning to get a new handbag, but, uh—" Gwynn started to say, trying to be funny, but her attempt fizzled out and she went quiet. The flap came unzipped and the wads of cash started to fall out, but she managed to catch them before they embarrassed her further.

She had close to three grand already, because once the word got out that there were hundred-dollar vials for sale, a line had formed at the ATM outside, and those going into the courtyard out back to smoke crack or into the bathroom to snort meth always came back before too long.

By the time she had gotten eight twenties out of the bag, the bartender was back with a bottle and a corkscrew saying "A hunnerd forty-seven."

They both watched the little silver man that was the corkscrew raise his arms until he was waist-deep in the bottle's cork, arms up in rapture and exultation, and then the arms were forced back down and he said *Pop!* Gwynn wondered if she was the only one who thought shit like this, and paid for the bottle.

Enolah carried the bottle and two glasses, leading Gwynn across the middle of the dance floor. Girls in skirts like the one Gwynn had on would see Enolah coming and step out of her way, curtseying low, and she nodded her head to each of them.

They got to the black canopy beds on the other side, and Enolah flicked a hand dismissively at the group of Goths sitting on the middle one. For a moment, they just looked at her, then they looked at each other, slumped a little and climbed off the bed. A few of the more androgynous ones smirked derisively at Gwynn for no good reason at all, as if she were the one being kicked off the bed. Her lip curled at them in disgust, then she noticed people drifting toward the booth she had occupied, like cartoon people pulled along by a visible, snakelike thread of fragrance, only to find the booth empty and walk away, disappointed. She saw how much money she was losing, remembered how much she had spent on wine for some *teenager* who —she turned back to Enolah, saw her white form shimmering in the lights, leaning back on the black pillows ten feet away.

Swinging the duffel bag onto the bed, she lifted her skirt and clambered on after it, feeling less ladylike that she would have wished. She had nothing on underneath, having taken off the briefs so she could have them halfway clean to wear home tomorrow. Maybe her nudity was in shadow, but the hoop under her skirt that held its shape made her look ridiculous, and she gritted her teeth at the idea of mooning the entire club.

Enolah grinned. "Is this the face that launched a thousand ships?" She had to shout to be heard.

"That's not funny!" Gwynn snapped. "Goddammit this is embarrassing and you got me into it!"

"You'll get over it. C'mon, you don't have much farther to go."

"I could be back there making money, but—"

"That sound you just heard? That was my heart breaking."

Gwynn stopped to glare at her, gnashing her teeth, and Enolah put on a solemn face and played an imaginary violin. Nothing enraged Gwynn more than her pride being wounded, but the girl dispelled it with a come-hither crook of her finger. Gwynn rose up on her knees and folded her arms. She was still trying to reconcile herself with whatever-this-was or whatever-this-might-turn-into with another girl, in a public place, no less. It may be the Nineteen Nineties, and world was changing, but it hadn't changed *that* much yet.

The carafe she had drained so quickly might've affected her judgment, she was thinking.

Enolah put on a face that made Gwynn think of a beautiful witch casting a spell on her, and she tried to be cocky and dismissive, but knew it was working.

"Oh, catch me, quick, before I swoon."

"You're too far away. How can you fall into my arms from way over there?" She raised the two empty glasses that formed a cross in one hand. "Thirsty?"

Gwynn haughtily lifted her chin and walked on her knees to the beautiful witch's side, and flopped down dramatically next to her. Enolah laughed.

"My hands were full. I wasn't ready. Comfy?"

"No. I want this damned net thing off."

"Hang on, hold these." Enolah handed her the bottle and glasses and scooted down. Uh-oh, Gwynn thought. What do I do, tell her No? Tell her Wait, I'm not wearing any panties, don't go in there? Maybe she won't see anything. It's very dark in here. She was suddenly tingling all over, just like years ago, when she thought Omigod, it's really going to happen! Omigod, it's going to happen!

She frowned, and dropped one of the glasses to pour wine in the other while Enolah ducked out of sight behind the skirt. The glass was half-full when she felt the girl's soft warm hands touch her skin, felt her hot breath. Then she cried out, spasming and spilling most of the wine on her bosom.

"Hold still!" Enolah called, then tickled her again. The rest of the wine sloshed over Gwynn's throat and breastbone as she thrashed about, giggling.

"Hold still, I said!"

Back arching, she shrieked with laughter and fell back, shuddering, then went suddenly rigid.

"Oh," she said curiously. "Hmmm." And then she hummed quietly to herself while the springy hoop was unfastened and then tugged off. She pushed her hands against the mattress and lifted her bottom so the hoop could be slip out from underneath her, and Enolah reappeared after a moment, holding up what looked almost like a birdcage.

"Looks like this might've been what caused all the trouble," she reported, and swung it over her shoulder. It bounced off of the duffel bag and disappeared over the edge of the bed.

"Um, could you bring that with you when you come back?" Gwynn asked. Enolah put a finger on the bag, raising her eyebrows, and Gwynn nodded.

The beautiful witch grabbed it by the strap and dragged it as if it weighed a ton, and when she'd crawled far enough, she collapsed like Gwynn had.

More wine was poured, and what had spilled on Gwynn's bosom was getting sticky. She hoped it would get licked off of her before too long.

"Talk to me," Enolah said. "Fascinate me. And pour me some of that wine. Did you know that we, as a people, don't drink nearly enough?" She sat up and leaned against the pillows, holding the other glass.

"You jest."

"Wine, I mean. We rank thirty-fourth in the world, in *per capita* wine consumption, in between Slovakia and Latvia."

"It's 'cause I go for the hard stuff. I tip the scale."

"But the problem is, out of all the hundred fifty eight countries in the UN, we rank an appalling *forty-ninth* in literacy. I say there's a connection."

"Okay, so—here you go—" Gwynn said as she interrupted herself to hand Enolah her filled wine glass. "If we drink this, we'll be able to read better?"

"*Merci.* No, but we'll be more inclined to try."

"*Salute.*"

"*Prosit.*"

"*Skoal.*"

"*Slainte.*"

"*L'Chaim.*"

"You did not just say that."

"I was joking.

"Are you Jewish?"

"Hell no!"

"Better not be, because I'm the spokesmodel for Einsatzgrup Tampa."

"You can't be. I thought I was."

"There can be only one."

"We'll duke it out later. Your place, 'cause mine's a mess."

"Maybe," Enolah said. She started absently moving with the music. I'm losing her, Gwynn thought.

"Going back to that wine-literacy gibberish…"

"Yes?"

"I want to test it out on you."

"*On* me?"

"Um-hmmm, only I read Braille."

"Ooh, what a smoothie. You make that one up all by your lonesome?"

"Sure did. They don't call me Super Charming Vixen Gwynn for nothing."

"You're a dork."

"*What?*"

"I can't believe I let you talk to me."

"I am *not* a *dork*."

"Are too."

"Am not! I'm not the one who opened the courtship with almanac statistics on fucking *wine*."

"Courtship? Is that what you call this?"

"Not anymore!"

They drank in silence, Enolah thoroughly enjoying the tension. After a moment, Gwynn just had to mutter "Dork."

"Turn on some of that charm you mentioned, Super Charming Vixen."

"You should be so lucky."

"You remind me of my roommate."

"You have a roommate?"

"Of *course*. You think I'll stoop to cleaning and paying rent?"

"I know what you mean."

"Shit, I'll foster a child and get *him* to clean before I do it. Ha! I can see myself now, with a handkerchief tied around my head, on my knees scrubbing the floor."

"So, what about your roommate?"

"He's a hypochondriac. A malingerer, even. Always whining for attention and—"

"I don't whine!"

"His medicine cabinet is a damn treasure chest."

That shut Gwynn up for a minute.

"Besides that, he's got heating pads, ice packs, braces, crutches, trusses, an *eye patch*, for Christ's sake. And every week he's sick with something new. Neurosis of the liver, typhoid fever, trick knee, bad back, once he even had malaria. He gives all my friends 'remembrances' when they come over, like souvenirs for the last time they see him. Little trinkets or knick-knacks to remember him by. It's pathetic."

"And I remind you of this guy, huh?"

"Oh, just in the face. He's really, really cute."

"Awww. S'about time you said something nice."

"I won't be making a habit of it."

"You're a real bitch, yunno that?"

"Look, if I wanted your opinion I'd be in the bathroom reading a wall." She drank, looking at Gwynn over the rim of her glass and winking.

"Ooh, you make that up all by your lonesome?"

A cigarette appeared in Enolah's hand, seemingly out of thin air, and she proffered it to Gwynn, draining her glass.

"Thanks, but I have my own."

"Not like this, you don't," she said, smacking her lips and holding out the empty glass for a refill.

"Oh really? What is it?"

"A dipper."

"*Sherm?*"

Looking maligned, Enolah put the hand with the cigarette to her breast. "You wound me."

"What is it, then?"

"A dipper. Stick the tip of it in liquid PCP and suck hard on the filter to saturate the tobacco. I've been saving this in the freezer until tonight."

Gwynn took it gingerly, examining it, and when Enolah gestured with her glass, she filled it back up for her. She took out her stolen Zippo, but Enolah stopped her.

"You can't light it with an open flame, you'll kill us all. Gotta use the end of another cigarette."

"I knew that. Here, hold these." She handed her the bottle, finished her own glass, and dropped it on the pillow between them, reached for the duffel bag and hauled it up to her. Unzipping several compartments looking for the pack of Gauloise, she exposed an impressive bit of contraband, pretending to do it carelessly, but really doing it to show up the beautiful witch. Ooh, you have a dipper? Wow. But look at what *I've* got.

"Coke?" Enolah asked, pointing at the meth vials.

Gwynn shook her head. "Glass. Take one."

"Don't mind if I do." She plucked one out of the pocket and sat up, popped the top off and tilted it to pour a bump onto the tip of her long red pinkie fingernail, daintily lifted it under one nostril and sniffed.

Gwynn wasn't sure why, but she found it very sexy to watch. Rummaging around in the bag, she finally found the cigarettes, took one out and lit it.

"Damn," Enolah said after hitting the other nostril. "This is some good stuff."

"Thank you. Made it myself."

"Ya don't say." She prudently put the cap back on.

Gwynn put the dipper in the corner of her mouth, touched it to the end of the Gauloise and puffed it to life. The first hit made her start to cough, but she didn't dare lose her composure again. Wasn't happening. No sir. She held it the best she could, her lungs quaking against her ribs where they were squashed in by the corset.

She handed it to Enolah, who hit it like it was nothing, it seemed. Handed it back, casual as can be. Ashamed of how easily the girl handled it while she struggled, Gwynn steeled herself and tried again.

Sounds whooped and echoed inside her head, the music suddenly sounding very different, and she felt herself pulled out of her body and snapped elastically back in. She held the dipper out to Enolah again, who was pouring herself another glass and made her wait. Her extended arm swayed a bit, the hand shaking. Gwynn fought to control it. It seemed to take eons for Enolah to fill her glass and set the bottle against the pillow, finally turn and take the dipper.

Again, when the glowing orange cherry brightened, the girl's expression didn't even change. She smoked it like she was toking an extra long drag off of a cigarette. When she finished and offered it back, her chest gave a perfunctory little spasm, like it was doing it only to make Gwynn feel better. Enolah reached over and took the Gauloise out of Gwynn's hand, brought it to her sensual blood-red lips, and while Gwynn hit the dipper again, it occurred to her that she'd never once seen the girl exhale smoke.

Wow, she thought. Mushta held it so long her lungs assorbed it. Asssorbed. Hee hee! Isn't that funny? Even my thoughts are slurring.

She took another long hit, watching beautiful wisps of lazy white smoke curl out of those beautiful red lips. The lights were sparkling in the girl's eyes, the strobe making her flawless white skin shimmer.

Gwynn felt herself falling hopelessly in love. She watched the girl leaning back against those pillows, propped up on one elbow like a Roman goddess, lifting her glass and drinking in profile. Gwynn could not stop staring, openly adoring her.

Enolah noticed and smiled faintly, reached over and took the dipper between her ring and pinkie fingers because the other two were holding the Gauloise. Flicking the ash off into the sheets, she turned her hand to put the glowing end in her mouth and Gwynn thought *Hee-hee!* She's so fuckered up she's gonna smoke the wrong end!

But when Enolah looked at her and beckoned, she realized Oh, stupid me, we're gonna do a shotgun. D'uhh! Ooh, I'd love to accidentally brush my lips against hers in a perfectly innocent shotgun and have it be that magical moment when I look into her eyes for a moment, then throw the dipper away and we lose ourselves in each other.

She leaned in, her lips parted, letting the filter slip into her mouth, and she kept going because she wasn't going to miss an opportunity to kiss this goddess, or at least touch her lips with her own, if only for a nanosecond. Before she could even brush against those blood-red lips, though, her mouth and throat and lungs suddenly burned as she filled up with smoke, and fell slowly backward, feeling water-logged and heavy, feeling like she was drowning. The pupils of her eyes shrunk to pixels, and she saw explosions of color like she'd see when she rubbed her eyes too long, when she couldn't sleep and was bored and rubbed her eyes to look at all the pretty explosions and keep rubbing until she got to that checkerboard pattern and—hey.

Where'd Enolah go?

When she was able to, Gwynn rose unsteadily and crawled to the foot of the bed, reached and held onto the black velvet hangings to steady herself, absently realizing they weren't really velvet. She inched forward a little and fell off of the edge that she'd forgotten about, landed in a heap on the floor next to her hoop. Like an embarrassed cat, she bolted to her feet and looked in every direction, hoping no one had seen her, and fell again as the momentum carried her backwards.

Struggling to right herself, grabbing a hold of the drapes again, she looked back at where she'd been and saw only her glass lying there.

She stumbled toward the dance floor, her equilibrium yawing on its axis, and she realized she couldn't walk there without everybody seeing her. Instead, she hung a right and made her way toward the modern torture exhibit, the entire time listing to the port side.

It felt to her like the world was a windshield that she was pressed up against, and she the wiper that rubbed back and forth across it.

"Hey, there she is!" somebody called. The words came to her across an enormous distance, and she thought because of the darkness and shafts of light that speared past her all around, and the winking strobe lights, that she was in outer space, moving at warp speed. And these were all planets. And I'm a star. No, hee-hee! A heavenly body.

Then she collided with a table and knocked a bunch of glasses onto the floor. They shattered in slow motion, scattering a million droplets of alcohol and a hundred thousand shards of glass that glittered in the lights like a galaxy, all moving so slowly she could have counted them if she'd wanted.

Many shapes came toward her, strange beings that seemed hostile, and they made noises for a while until she found herself stumbling along with a few of them. A pretty blue light appeared and was brushed against her arm. It tingled. She held out her other arm and the pretty electricity thingy started at her fingertips and tingled its way up her arm to her shoulder, across her throat and down her first arm.

A goblin-looking girl with pimples leaned in and kissed her. She didn't mind that the girl was ugly. She also didn't mind all the guys that kissed her and passed her around. She felt awfully popular.

She was moving again, stumbling along with other people helping her. Where were they going? She didn't care.

After traveling light-years along the bar side of the dance floor, being led through crowds of inconsiderate people who didn't move out of the way quickly enough, she found herself on the side where she'd been dealing. The side with all the booths instead of tables. She closed her eyes for a moment, felt herself being lifted and pulled and pushed and when she opened her eyes weakly, she was shackled up to the gibbet that she'd seen people get spanked on.

She was facing the wall and a strange-looking girl with stark white eyes staring out of a painted-on raccoon mask, green lipstick and a short mohawk was peering at her and saying No, she's too fucked up. Better take her down.

And for some reason, pride maybe, Gwynn forced her eyes open wide and leaned toward the freak.

"I'm okay," she hissed.

"Uh-huh, sure you are."

"I'm fine!"

"It's your funeral, then."

"Kiss me."

"What?"

"Are you deaf?"

"What did you say?"

"I said kiss me. Now."

"Yeah, you're pretty out of it." The freak disappeared. Gwynn craned her neck to look over her shoulder, but the view was blocked by all the curls in her tousled hair. She felt something brush her hair on the other side and she turned to look, her face colliding with someone else's.

"You've been a naughty little girl, haven't you?"

"You dunno the haff of it."

The ugly man that was leaning over her shoulder sighed heavily, and his breath was sickly sweet.

"You spilled all our drinks back there."

"My bad."

"Apologies won't fix anything. We're thirsty."

"Oh, kiss my ass."

"Hmmm. With pleasure."

The face withdrew, and over the music she heard a burst of derisive laughter, felt her skirt gathered up and lifted, and she felt a draft on her legs.

Then her ass.

She felt cold lips pressed against one cheek, and remembered suddenly that she'd taken off her underwear so she'd have something to wear under her jeans on the way home tomorrow. She had them in her duffel bag with—

The duffel bag!

Smack!

She felt the sting of a cupped hand on her ass.

Smack!

Her eyes filled up with tears and she bit her lip.

Behind her, the man wound up and put his weight behind it this time, and the pain jarred her, buckling her knees, and she sagged. Hanging from the manacles that secured her to the gibbet, she felt the edges biting into her wrists, but couldn't stand to take the weight off of them. Another vicious slap rocked her and she cried out, again, and again, and again.

The face reappeared over her shoulder, the Breath returning. "Enjoying it, toots?"

She felt his hand, hot and red, rest on one of the hot and red cheeks of her ass. Another hand, wet and clammy from holding a drink, rested on her other cheek. It was soothing and repulsive at the same time.

"Look at Miss High an' Mighty, now."

The hands tightened, fingers digging in, pulled her cheeks apart, spread her wide open, and she never felt so naked in all her life.

"Well well well, whatta we have here?" the Breath came in staccato gusts of silent laughter, sounding to her like Muttley from the cartoons. She tried to think about that instead, about Dastardly and Muttley in their Flying Machines, think about anything at all to take her mind away from wherever she was. You'd think I would be numb to all this, she thought. You'd think so, but no. Quite the opposite, in fact. Hyper-sensitive would be the word.

"Yunno you need to get yourself a new ass," the Breath said. "This one's got a hole in it."

"Hey, what're you doing?" another voice shouted. A knight in shining armor, come to save her. Come to rescue the maiden fair.

Gwynn felt her ass unhanded and her skirt drop to cover her again. The man behind her was gone and she felt a rush of air coming in to fill the space he'd filled. Someone stepped in front of her, eyes full of concern. Lord Dave.

"You okay, Gwynn?"

"Yeah," she mumbled. "I jus' wanna lie dowwwn a minute, have a drink."

"Okay sweetie, I gotcha. Everything'll be fine. I gotcha."

She felt the manacles open while he supported her around the waist with one arm. She sagged and someone else had to come and help her stand.

"I gotcha, I gotcha. We gonna walk now, okay?"

He put one of her arms around his shoulders and someone else took the other. Then she was moving again, her weight entirely on…or were these the same people as before? The ones that were spanking her? She didn't know why she thought that, but she just couldn't tell.

People were pointing at her. And laughing.

She closed her eyes for just a second, and a second later felt herself being lifted and pushed and pulled, and when she opened them she was on the same bed as before. There was something she was supposed to remember, but goddammit, her ass hurt and she was stoned like she'd never been stoned before.

She must have grimaced in pain because she heard people saying Oh, her ass, yeah, her ass, we'd better flip her over, and many hands lifted her and she was turned over like a rotisserie chicken, and laid back down with her face in a wet spot that smelled like spilt Narcisse.

The Good Samaritans lifted her skirt, telling her It's okay, it's okay, we're doctors. And there was a draft on her ass again.

"Oh boy," somebody said.

"Yeah, they got her good."

"Third degree burns, extensive damage beyond even the subcutaneous tissue. You all thinkin' what I'm thinkin'?

"Yeah, dude. We'll have to operate."

"Okay, people. We need this to be a team effort."

"No fair," Gwynn heard Charlotte say. "Since I don't have a dick, I never get to rape *any*one."

She felt her legs being pulled apart, remembered what someone told her once a long time ago, Just go with it and it won't hurt so much, and once it's over it'll just be a memory.

Something heavy lay across her and pushed her harder into the bed, her face harder into the spot that smelled, and now tasted, like spilt Narcisse. Once again, there was a face leaning over her shoulder, breathing heavily into her hair, and it was the Breath again. Whispering sweet nothings into her ear with Lord Dave's voice.

She didn't count how many had her.

She didn't bother.

XII

Rabbit woke up in the dead of night, his stomach growling and his body twitching in minor delirium tremens. He checked his watch, grateful that he was the Hispanic chick because she wore a Timex with a glow-in-the-dark feature, rather than Nick, whose six-thousand-dollar "chronograph" was about as useful as tits on a boar.

The green light that flashed on said it was three-seventeen in the AM. And this dumb bitch didn't keep squat in the fridge. He'd found leftover pizza surrounded by bottles of booze and girlie-drink mixers. And in the cupboards, granola. Yay.

He put the wig back on and straightened himself up, got all his stuff together, and left the efficiency, locking the door behind him.

Outside, the air was cool and palm fronds clattered together in a pleasant breeze. He decided to walk back to his apartment rather than try to flag down a cab, and went down the concrete stairs to the parking lot. While he did love walking at night, and always did it when he couldn't sleep, he really would have rather to be dressed as a man this time.

Swinging his bag over his shoulder, he crossed the parking lot, stepped over the short hedge along the sidewalk, and cut across the street, hoping there'd be a place to grab a quick bite to eat along the way. He called Blue Tick to tell him Never mind.

Half an hour later, Gwynn Hutchinson passed in a taxi, staring blankly at her place out of a backseat window and wishing she didn't have to go all the way back to the storage lot to pick up her Bug, and wishing even more that she didn't have to drive it back.

"Whutchoo talkin' abow, bwah? Puss'ass shit!"

Rabbit couldn't stand people talking that way, but he always heard it in this country, somewhere, and he heard it now as he came upon an intersection. It was like fingernails on a chalkboard, these voices of the ignorant and vulgar, who had a catachresis for just about every damn word in the English language—like "stipulate" as in: "Lemme stipalate whut Ah'm sayin'

163

so's you can be sheperdized"—and then they'd grossly mispro-
nounce the words they actually *did* know the meanings of, like
"ejamacate."

"I'm jes *sayin'* doh! Da devil ain't workin' no damn spookism,
feel me? Mah ontee tell me out da Bible dat da devil be gittin'
unda you wit some secret-ass shit!"

"Mah nigga, save da rap. Doanchoo be comin' at us wit dat
Kairos. Save dat shit fo Sunday!"

They were talking about *church?* Seriously? Even though Rabbit had long since become a heretic and a blasphemer, he still
hated nothing more than a hypocrite, and tasted bile when he
saw a gold cross on a gold chain around the neck of a gangster
or a whore.

Rabbit got to the corner and saw them out of the corner of
his eye, heading right his way. He glanced in their direction just
to see if there were cars coming, and did a sharp double-take.

There were four of them, and judging from their attire, they
were either going to or coming from a basketball game. Their
shorts were down their legs halfway to their knees, showing their
boxers. Their gold-capped teeth caught the orangish glow of the
streetlights and glittered just as brightly as the cubic zirconia in
their barbaric ornaments.

And all four of them were white.

"Wooo-wee! Check out da ho!"

"Hey boo! Whutchoo doin' out here dis late?"

"Makin' summa dat green? Summa dat cheese?"

"Lemme git summa dat! Hey boo! Git ova heah witchoo bad
self!"

They were now cakewalking their way toward him now, each
of them with their own outlandish strut.

Rabbit started across the street and jumped back at a shrill
horn as a car came blasting by from the other direction. The four
wiggers' taunts redoubled, some gibberish about da ho gittin' run
tha fuck ovah.

Rabbit swallowed hard, feeling his face burn scarlet, and he
knew he couldn't say anything. His voice would betray him because he couldn't fake a woman's voice with his own crimping in

anger. They'd know he was a man and there'd be no way to explain.

He looked both ways, waited a moment, and just as the wiggers got close enough, he bolted across the street, making the cars that were coming have to slow down. There was no way they could follow him yet without making the cars slam on their brakes, and even then, they might still get hit.

Sprinting down the crosswalk, he was bathed for a moment in light, and every step made him more furious that they'd put him in this position. He could hear them calling after him, and he wanted so badly to pull out the PPK and let them have it.

He didn't stop running, knowing that if they caught up with him they'd tease him and fuck around and somehow they would find out he was a man and jump him instantly. He could take them, of course. He would be outnumbered only a paltry four to one.

He was proficient in *jeet kun do* and ninjitsu, and even if he wasn't, he had two batons to *ken po* their stupid asses with, a stun gun to drop them to the ground and make them piss all over themselves, and a gun to blow their brains out.

All of which he'd happily do if…if only…

Fuck it, why not?

He slowed halfway down the next block and turned. They were coming. There'd be a few witnesses, people driving by on their late-night errands, and anybody looking out their window to see what had woken them, but all that would mean was the end of this disguise.

Campus was spitting distance away, and students were coming to and from cram sessions at the library, or keg parties, and he'd give them something juicy to talk about.

He dropped the backpack and pulled out the two asps. They came running, fading in and out of orange light as they passed the lampposts, their shadows shrinking from long to short behind them, then long in front, and back again.

"Hey, you 'fraidycat ho! Whutchoo runnin from?"

And just as they reached him, tugging their shorts back up to keep from tripping themselves, he sprang.

165

Two feet of steel snicked out of the black handles and he swung in midair. One's forehead split above the browline, and the one beside him took his on the cheekbone. Landing among them, the asps struck shins and elbows and broke one collarbone in the time it took one bystander's dropped cigarette to hit the sidewalk.

Striking a double blow both forehand and back, he staved in one's ribs and shattered his breastbone.

Pivoted on his heel and jabbed a knee with the knob-like tip just inside the patella, dislocating it.

He staggered as the second wigger with the fractured cheek-bone kicked him in the back, but turned quickly and parried a thrown punch, batting the fist aside and crunching two of the knuckles.

Another punch came from the other fist, but he ducked and sidestepped, backhanding him across the side of the head, and then smashing him across it with all his might. The wigger stumbled, then swayed on his feet.

In the light of the lamppost, Rabbit saw that his hair was cut in a fade, mostly bald on the sides of his head. He wore a visor, backwards and turned upside-down so the bill jutted diagonally up from behind. Under the line of that visor, on the nearly bald side of his head, a dull gash slowly filled with a dark line of blood. It didn't come gushing out. A few drops fell, bright red in the light, freckling the white of his jersey, spreading wider as they soaked into the fabric.

For a moment, he was the last wigger standing, the others groaning on the pavement, but he was already dead.

Rabbit turned and started walking fast, sheathing the asps with a ringing *snick*, and snatched up the straps of his backpack. Kept walking.

A gigantic black man, dressed as a bum, watched from the roof of a nearby building. He grinned widely, and his white teeth gleamed in the darkness as he turned and ran, leaping from one rooftop to another, following silently along as the Warrior Woman cut across lots and through alleys, disappearing from the scene. He lost track of Rabbit once, but caught the sound of a Dumpster's lid dropping behind the coffee shop Bodega, and when he made it to the spot he had heard it from, he spotted a young man vaulting over a chain link fence.

A young man dressed just like the young woman. With a bookbag just like hers. Hmmm.

Curiouser and curiouser.

The giant black dropped down into the alley and ran to the Dumpster. Lifting the lid, he pulled a small Mag-light out of his back pocket and shown it on the garbage. Amid Styrofoam cups and stale pastry, orange peels, apple cores, and coffee grounds, he saw a curly black wig and a large bra with foam-domes.

"Tsk tsk tsk!" He reached in and pushed the evidence down further into the garbage, spread some banana peels and other crap around on top of it to conceal it better, and dropped the lid down gently again. Hauled himself on top of it, reached up for the eave of Bodega's roof, and vanished into the night.

Inside 418, Rabbit stripped off his blood-spattered clothes and dropped them in a garbage bag, sprayed some bleach all over them to scramble the DNA they carried, so, if it was found, it could not be linked to the wiggers, tied it off and dropped it on his way into the bathroom.

He was still starving, but he'd have to go out again and get something to eat. He was not about to burglarize one of his neighbors, sneak in while they slept and quietly make a sandwich, though he had done it before and it was actually quite fun.

He took a hot shower, then a freezing cold one, and when he came out with a towel around his waist he checked on the monitors in his living room to look in on the girls. Both were asleep, though not too deeply. Neve was murmuring anxiously and Megan could not keep still. His eyes lingered on her sadly, sorry he'd brought this on her. He reached out and touched her face on the screen.

Rewinding the tapes that had been made with the eavesdroppers, he listened to the lamentations of a first-time murderess, the consoling by an accomplice, the fear and confusion that had followed his burglary, and eventually, the conversation about him.

It's a funny thing about people, when someone starts to lose her mind a little, she'll think that she's seeing everything clearly for the first time. And when someone else really does begin to see everything in her life clearly and know that something is horribly wrong, like knowing in her heart that at least three people who recently entered her life are one and the same, and they are plotting some bizarre scheme in which she is coerced into killing people for them, and they are watching her at every moment in her own home, she'll think she's going crazy.

Neve said she really didn't believe the dream story that Mr. Perfect had seduced her roommate with, said it was just too hokey. Megan smiled apologetically and did her best to argue that no matter how skeptical she was at first, she had and still wanted to believe, maybe because she'd always half-believed and half-hoped that telepathy and precognition and even pre-sentimental dreams were real, and had always wanted to meet ghosts and aliens and everything else since she was a little girl, but never had, and it took some of the fun and mystery out of life.

And, she admitted, she had been waiting a long damned time for the miracle to happen.

Well, here it was, the miracle, and while she still may harbor a germ of doubt, she had him and would do anything she had to to keep him.

And that's where Neve came in.

"But you want me to help *murder* this woman?"

"You murdered two people today, didn't you?"

"But—but that wasn't murder. That was a—"

"A *what?* A crime of passion? It sure wasn't self-defense. It certainly wasn't an accident. Talk about the pot and the fucking kettle."

"But you're talking about *planning* something!"

"You're goddamned right I am. Think about it, Neve. If you had planned what you did this morning, we wouldn't have had all the trouble of covering it up. You wouldn't have had to involve me and make me an accessory to murder. And this bitch has to die. She's a cheating cunt who doesn't deserve what she's got and I do, and I'm going to take him from her. And if we do it right, we'll get away with it."

"Over some guy? Over some dick you got—"

"He is *not* some *guy*. He is the man of my dreams and I've never seen anyone like him, and I'm not about to let him go. I'm not about to go back to my lonely miserable life. Not so that whore can have him and not appreciate him."

"But why not get a divorce? It's so much—"

"He's Catholic, Neve."

"So what? Catholics get divorced."

"Try telling him that."

"But he's committing adultery! Isn't that a sin?"

"Yeah, it is, and don't you dare remind him of that because then guilt'll set in and I'll lose him forever."

"Megan, I understand how happy you are, but you gotta accept that he's married and you can't have him. You just can't. Unless he gets divorced, which you say he won't, he's someone else's. She got him first, for better or for worse, so he's stuck with her."

"*No.* We didn't climb to the top of the food chain by giving up. I found him, and now I have to keep him. I have got to *make him mine*. His whore wife is fucking around on him and I'm going to catch her on her way back from someone else's bed, and I'm going to *kill* her."

Rabbit listened to Neve staring at her friend. He could actually hear her eyes widening. Then he heard Megan lean forward, her eyes gray and cold.

"And you're going to help me do it."

XIII

The next morning, Phil and Emmy greeted Megan with a strange look that made her wary.

"Uh, hey guys."

They made tight-lipped smiles and nodded.

Surprising them, she looked them square in the eye and said "Out with it."

Phil sputtered. "Well, ahhh, just wonder—how is, um, how are things going?"

"Fine."

"What he means is," Emmy tried. "We, er, have, well, it's like this, yassee—"

"Oh, gotcha."

"What?"

"You want me to go get you guys take-out, right?"

Phil and Emmy looked at each other.

"Wha—"

"Huh?"

"Take-out?"

"You're stoned again, right?" Megan asked. "Got the munchies and need victuals."

"Humph, no. We—"

"Of course not!"

"Then what is it? Spit it out."

"You, ahh, had a friend," Emmy said. "Um, come looking for you. Here. Yesterday. Very upset."

"Very," Phil said.

"And, well, things didn't work out all too good." Emmy looked uncertainly at Phil, then started boldly. "I wasn't really tip-top on my people skills."

"You were stoned."

"Er, okay, yes. Yes, I was. And totally unprepared for this very distraught young lady who came in crying her little eyes out and screaming for you, and I tried to subdue her, and—"

"*Subdue?*"

"Well, yes, you see, I told you I wasn't tip-top—"

171

"On your people skills, gotcha. Was she dark? Dark skin, dark hair, really pretty? Wearing, say, really tight blue jeans and a red gingham haltertop that looked kinda like a big handkercheif? Denim jacket?"

"Uh, yes. Yes, she was."

"Yesterday morning?"

"Yes. Early."

"Okay. There's no problem, is there?"

"What? Oh, no, not on our end. Why, have you heard something?"

"Yeah, somebody slipped something in her drink the night before at a party and she was disoriented a bit, that's all. She's fine now."

"Oh. Oh, dear. Is she, though? Fine, I mean."

"Absolutely. Needed somebody to talk her down, that's all. Has no recollection of you guys, and if she did, she'd think it was a false memory or something."

Emmy and Phil both sighed with relief.

"Oh, well, that's good."

"Yes, yes," mumbled Phil. "Glad she's fine. Just, you know, concerned. Well, good. Good! Okay, well, let's get on with the day, then."

Emmy looked at him for a second and some more spousal telepathy passed between them. Megan had a good time watching the facial discourse, trying to hide her amusement. Phil turned to her once again.

"We did miss breakfast, ahhh, feeling a little—"

"Peckish," Emmy put in.

"Peckish, yes. That take-out you mentioned? That doesn't sound like a bad idea. You hungry, Meg?"

"I could eat."

"Well, why don't you go pick us up something? Here's a few bucks." He pulled his wallet out of his back pocket and handed her a ten and a twenty.

"Anything in particular?"

"No, no. Whatever. Surprise us. Just no pizza, no Allegra's, we've had that stuff *ad nauseum*."

"Chinese?" she suggested.

"Whatever, whatever."

"Surprise us," Emmy said.

"Oh! Before I forget," Phil laughed. "How're you feeling? Still sick? Or did you get over it?"

Megan smiled. "Oh, I'm a little sore, but other than that, I think I'll live."

"That's good, that's good. Really happy for you."

"Very," Emmy added.

"You just let us know ahead of time, take off—"

"Are you getting sick again anytime soon?"

"How're the flowers holding up? You know you should put sugar in the water—"

"Ice."

"Or aspirin, that works too."

"Was he a gentleman?"

"He damn well better've been, or I'll—"

"Now dear—"

"Well, he better."

"Chinese it is, then," Megan interrupted. She went to her stool behind the till, got her bag, and the bells on the door jingled as she left. Phil and Emmy looked at each other again, surprised, thinking Damn! Is this the same Megan?

"Wow," said Phil.

Emmy nodded. "That boy must have some real—"

"Watch it."

"What? I was only—"

"Don't be getting any ideas."

Emmy made a wide-eyed mocking gasp, spread the fingers of one hand wide and placed the tips of them on her chest. "Well, I never."

Neve heard all about the horrible murder later that day—or at least, she thought she did. All she could make out from the gossip she overheard was that it wasn't far from school, late at night, and it was done by a girl with long dark curly hair. She assumed the details that didn't match up with her killing Sage and Manny were due to the inability of people to repeat a story accurately. See: the game Telephone.

Murders last night, murders the night before; two bodies, four bodies; tom*ay*to, tom*ah*to. They were all talking about her, and she knew it. Long, dark, curly hair. But there were plenty of girls like that around here. What about Señorita Whatever? She even lived in the same building! Right *above* her! It could have been anyone, anyone at all!

But they were talking about her.

She couldn't concentrate in class, and the discussion about the "Freeport Heresy" of 1858 and the Panic of '57 somehow jumped all the way to cakewalks and comb tests of the Post Civil War Era.

"Miss Jackson," the professor said, startling her. "You seem very attentive today. Maybe you can tell the class was a 'comb test' was."

He had on that smug expression that she loathed.

People were staring at her, and that threw her off.

"Um, in the South...it was—"

"You did seem to be zoning out a little there, Miss Jackson. I'll—"

"It was discrimination among free blacks, some picking on others because they didn't have as much white blood in them and they looked too much like monkeys."

The professor's eyebrows jumped. So did a lot of the students'. Well shit, Neve thought, you want me to sugar-coat it? That's the way they'd said it then.

"If you could pull a comb through your hair without it snagging in your kinky, nasty wool, you got to go to the good church, and if you didn't have that good hair, you went to the shitty church. You want to talk about Redbones and High-Yellahs?"

"Please try to tone down that language, Miss Jackson. And since you brought it up, the Redbones, or Zebras, the contemporary names for people that are half-black, half-white, have another name. Can anyone tell me what it is?"

A few hands went up, but Neve just said aloud, "Mulattos are half-white, half-black. Quadroons are a quarter black, three quarters white. The High-Yellahs are Octoroons because they're only one-eighth black. But what do you call someone that's half-black, half-Vietnamese? A nook? A gigger? You dunno? Well, I dunno either, but you better not trust him to do your laundry." Pause. She pretended to tap on an invisible microphone. "Tough crowd. Hey, this thing on?"

The rest of the room stared at the bitterness in her voice; the prof worried some kind of racial argument was about to start in his classroom that he'd somehow get blamed for, and all you had to do in Florida was have your name in the same sentence as "racist" and your career was over.

"And since you brought it up," Neve continued. "A cake-walk was a Southern black contest where the boogie with the stupidest, weirdest walk won a cake. They thought they were being fancy, just like when they make up those stupidass names for their kids."

A collective gasp, and more than a few giggles.

"Miss Jackson!"

"Naviance," she said quietly. "My dumbass name is Naviance Anquamette Moné Jamario Jackson. That's the kind of name boogs think is fancy."

"Jesus! I think I'm going to have to ask you—"

"I was just leaving." She stood up, holding her unzipped backpack open under the edge of her desk and sweeping her text book, notepad, and folder into it with her other hand. She felt everyone staring harder, but what'd she expect? She'd acted badly and had no one to blame but herself, and she knew it.

Her hands were trembling, her knees knocking together, but she shouldered her bag and made her way up the row of desks to the door.

"With the vulgarities aside," the professor said, trying to re-capture his students' attention. "Yes, she's right. Interestingly enough, the cakewalk is where we got both tap-dancing and the phrase 'take the cake.'"

She let the door swing slowly shut beside her as she sagged against the wall, taking a deep breath, and wondered why in the hell she'd done that.

"Get a fuckin grip, Neve," she whispered. "You're not going to act like this during Jap History, too, are you?" She suddenly became aware of the guy watching her and spun in his direction. He sat against the wall by the water fountain, a book bag next to him, with a sketch pad open across his knees. She turned and hurried off the other way, down the hall.

Rabbit brushed his long Chris Hammond hair back behind his ears and rose, closing his art book and stuffing it into the bag. Nodding to himself, thinking Neve wasn't going to be very stable at all.

A young woman in a lavender hotel uniform with gold braid picked up a ringing phone, saying "Heather-Leigh Hotel, front desk."

She heard an ethnic—not foreign, but ethnic—type of voice speaking, and she smiled brightly as if the caller could see her. A little trick they taught her at phone-answering school. "One moment."

Consulting her computer, she clacked a few keys, pursed her lips, hummed, clacked a few more, and smiled brightly for her caller again.

"I'm sorry, Mr. Coniglio has checked out."

On the other end of the line, Vladimir Bilowas hung up the phone and looked up at the eight other men standing in his motel room, scowling.

"Om zorry," he said, imitating the girl. "Meezder Koneeglio hass jegged out."

A package arrived at Tampa General Hospital, addressed to "The 3 Wiggers Still Alive." It was heavy, and it made a sloshing sound when moved. Suspicious, the head nurse opened it, frowning at an aluminum jug full of turpentine. A note was enclosed, written in a girlish scrawl with circles dotting the I's.

"Dear Gangsta Wannabes, this little gift is to help when all the brass in your mouths turns each other's dicks green. Hasta luego! Z."

Gwynn passed the night at the storage unit, squatting in the eerie purple light, her eyes glowing yellow and staring emptily at the bright green juice trickling along the tubing. She smoked a Gauloise watching the sun come up, carried everything to her

Bug, and drove home, watching her speed, staying carefully inside the lines.

At her apartment, she undid the knots of her corset, absently realizing that she had been in it all night long, with her ribs squeezed in against her lungs, felt the relief of them expanding again. Let the skirt fall to the floor and kicked it away.

Walked like a zombie into her shower stall. She cut herself a few times while shaving her legs, but didn't seem to notice. Didn't mind when she stained her towel with blood.

She anointed her body with lotion, smeared cream on her face and wiped it back off with tissues, put on astringent with balls of cotton and fumbled with her curlers until she dropped one and started to cry.

The tears stung and twisted her face, sobs rising up out of deep inside her and racking her body until she was gnashing her teeth and slapping herself hard across the face, again, and again, and again. The sobs died away, except for a few half-hearted aftershocks.

She dried her eyes and finished with the curlers. Yawning and stretching and yawning again, she started for the bedroom before she remembered to brush her teeth. She scrubbed so hard with her brush that her gums bled. Scrubbed her tongue, over and over, and the insides of her cheeks. Spat into the sink and pretended it was clear, like nothing had happened.

Staggering finally into the bedroom, she fluffed up her pillows and pulled down her bedspread, starting to climb in.

And stopped.

She sniffed.

Scowling, she hurried back to the light switch and flipped the ceiling lamp on, padded back to her bed and climbed onto it on all fours, sniffing it all over like an animal. She found them, on or around her pillows. Long, greasy, curly black hairs. And her bedspread smelled like a man.

She sucked her teeth with a low smack, sat up.

"Somebody's been sleeping in *my* bed," she muttered quietly.

*   *   *

177

Naviance Anquamette Moné Jamario Jackson did not make it to her Bushido Japan class. Locking herself in the apartment, she drank. A lot.

Starting with just a beer, she ran the gamut all the way to her adoptive father's bottle of corn-squeezins that he'd given her as a joke on her twenty-first birthday. Since the beers just made her go to the bathroom over and over, she switched to low priced and lower quality fortified wine, and quoted Thurber's wine lover, raising her first glass of it to an invisible audience and describing it as "a naïve little domestic, but I'm sure you'll be amused by its presumption."

Less than ten feet above her, Rabbit laughed and raised his own glass in acknowledgement, took a draught and set it back down next to his easel, where he resumed painting.

Neve's bottle lasted less than ten minutes. She followed it with shots of Goldschlager, absently wondering as she always did if she should be straining the stuff through her colander and saving up all the gold flakes, then shrugging, convincing herself that it was probably pyrite anyway.

Then she got whimsical, deciding to conjure up some blender drinks.

Her adopted mother, Mrs. Ramsey, used to make the world's best Bloody Mary, which Neve improvised with a pre-fab mixer by Major Peter, a forkful of horseradish, a dill pickle spear, a celery stalk, and a handful of sweet onions and pepperoni slices.

The blender drowned out whoever that was on MTV6, the last bastion of music videos, but she half-knew the song and kept singing along anyway. When that was gone, she made daiquiris with the broccoli in the drawer of the fridge that she and Megan had bought God-knows-when in a short-lived effort to "eat healthy." She poured the whole batch down the sink after the first sip.

Started drinking Bacardi straight out of the bottle, instead, and by the time Megan got home from work, she had polished off the squeezins and was shouting gibberish at her.

"Been watchin' the news!" Neve declared. "Was hopin' ta see sompin' 'bout what we did. 'Scuze me, but I'm slurrin'm' speech a li'l. Well, can't help but notice the 'news,'"—here she made little quotation marks in the air—"don't tell you shit 'cept what they need to keep you in suspense so you don't switch channels before they show the next commercials!"

Megan went to one of the rattan wicker chairs and sat down, not saying a word, thinking it best to ride out whatever tirade Neve wanted to go through instead of trying to calm her down—something she'd learned from three or four abusive relationships with other drunk assholes.

"And don get me started on everthin' *else* on TV!"

Too late, Megan wanted to say.

"My late *boyfren*," Neve spat the word. "Him an' all the rest of the swine I dated, could recite all this superficial bullshit about the sports teams from their hometown, but not a damn thing about its history, or any important stuff like where its water supply was, or the power sources, or any planned construsssion.

"But his favorite football and basketball team, pro and college, man, he had that rootless loyalty to them and talked about how We was goan to da playoff, We was doin' this, We was doin' that! It was *We* were changin' our colors to yellow and purple in deference to come coach who died in fuckin' Nebraska or some shit. Acted like his manhood was in question if he can't tell you every fact an' stat on every player. *No*, mothafucka! Your manhood is in question 'cause you suck dick!"

Neve's quivering lips were flecked with foam, and her eyes blazed with such rage that Megan had to force herself not to look away, force herself to meet Neve's gaze evenly. Like a dog, even an angry one, Neve looked away first. Started moving around the living room while she continued her rant.

"And art! Faggot's takin' art classes an' he doan know shit about it! All he know about art an' music an' theatre is the personal lives of all the actors and actresses divorcing each other and what hotels got trashed by what band that can't play any song longer than three minutes with more'n three chords!

"Then we got people like *you*," she said, turning again to Megan, who braced herself. "Sure, I ain't no virgin," Neve said. "I've had sex. But I never gone to bed with no married man! I don't give a shit if he ain't happy with his wife, I ain't about to be no homewrecka! You got me thinkin' about murder today, how

179

it's just a matter of opinion. You look at it one way, it's murder, you look at it another, it's self-defense or it's revenge or a duel or a fittest-survive-type-of-thing. Kinda like Rashomon. But doing it to get rid of thy neighbor's wife, that's just plain *wrong* no matter which way you slice it."

Megan's eyes were gray, and hard. She thought about how she hadn't heard from the love of her life, not since she ran out on him, how she had no link to him at all, how alone she felt and needed his arms around her, especially now. She felt all of her newfound happiness evaporating, and steeled herself.

She reached over the arm of her chair to pick up her bag off the floor, and took out Neve's travel-sized semi-automatic.

Neve stared, wondering how the hell Megan could have gotten it.

In a voice as cold as her eyes, Megan spoke, holding the weapon casually in her lap. "No matter how you slice it, you did it, and I helped you, so you're going to help me. You want to call it murder, go ahead, call it murder. I don't give a shit. At Nuremburg, they called it taking orders. Since I'm the one with the gun now, maybe that's what you can call it."

Neve stared at the gun and at those cold gray eyes.

Megan smiled. "You smell what I'm cookin'?"

Neve swallowed, and swallowed again.

Thinking *Who are you?* You're not my roommate.

Who *are* you?

"Stick your finger down your throat," Megan said. "Puke up everything you've drunk, then drink water until you're choking on it. Then, I dunno, do jumping jacks or something, but you'd better be sober before the sun goes down because we're killing our neighbor's wife tonight. Don't forget that you promised to help me do what I needed in return for being your accessory. I quote: cross my heart, Scout's honor."

Neve was weighing her chances of getting the gun back. Taking inventory of her abilities, what parts of her body she still had enough control over.

"I know where the bodies are," Megan lied, surprising Neve, who was so transparently paranoid that Megan knew she'd fall for it. "I told Nickie about it yesterday, while you were in the shower. I told him, and he went to get the bodies out of the Dumpster and move them to a better place."

Above them, Rabbit chewed the knob inside his cheek, shaking his head and stifling a laugh.

Close, he thought, but no seegahhh.

"I played like I didn't know when you came back from checking on them. Didn't want you to know and freak out even worse. So don't think you can take this gun away from me, this *murder weapon* of yours, because while Nickie will do anything to help his lover, his future wife as soon as his present one is dead, I really don't think he'll help *you* if we end up falling out. I really don't think those bodies'll stay hidden if you decide not to be my friend anymore.

"The bullets that are sitting in those bodies match the ones in this gun, *your* gun, and you got motive like it's going outta style. Let's see, what else? Oh!" She slapped her forehead as if she coulda had a V8. "The eyewitness! Poor little roommate you forced to help you move the bodies from the murder scene, where there was a mysterious fire, and I can think of two people who'd back me up that you were acting mighty suspicious yesterday morning while you were looking for me. So, even though I'm the one holding onto this gun, I really don't need it. Not to get you to keep your promise. And you don't have to call it murder," she added.

"Calling it 'taking orders' didn't help them much at Nuremberg," Neve said quietly.

"That was a trial," Megan reminded her. "If we do it right, if you do everything I tell you, there won't be a trial. Now, get to swallowing that finger, Naviance."

Rabbit laughed.

"How..." Neve stammered, wavering. "How you know where she'll be? Nick's wife, I mean?"

Megan snorted. "Where you think I been all day?"

XIV

Gwynn finally awoke after a day of nightmares, and the ghosts of them still flitted about in the edges of her vision. She felt a hundred thousand parasites wriggling inside her womb, each trying to pierce an egg, felt a million different diseases all fighting each other as they swam through her veins. Felt like no matter which one of them won, she was fucked.

And as she plotted her vengeance against everyone under the roof of the pink and turquoise clapboard bungalow, she couldn't stop thinking about a girl ten years younger than her getting away with... with...and *blowing* on the dipper instead of sucking on it! So obvious now that she thought about it!

Making the orange cherry light up at the end of it because she blew when it was in her mouth, and she didn't have to take any of that smoke into her lungs.

Tricking her with something so simple, then shotgunning her that monster hit that floored her, the whole time toying with her like she was some mere mortal.

Some...some *kid* getting away with...and her being stupid enough to fall for it, too! Her! Genius of bullshit! Improvisational mastermind!

How she'd ever find that bitch again, she couldn't even begin to guess. That minx would never be foolish enough to go back to Baroque anytime soon. And of course, neither would Gwynn. It was all up to chance. Mistress Charlotte and Lord Dave, on the other hand, were as good as dead. Ditto for whoever was in the room with them when she struck.

Rabbit wasn't the only one in the world who knew about light bulbs filled with gasoline.

Or better yet, she'd take an entire mason jar and open it over the water supply entering Baroque next Saturday night. Everyone who drank from a glass that had been washed in that water, everyone who washed their hands in the bathroom, everyone who took part in her torture or let it happen and everyone else for good measure would spend the rest of their lives in... wow, she couldn't even imagine what it could be like, how they'd suffer.

Sure, other people down that water line would trip for the rest of their lives, too, and end up in a mental hospital (if they were lucky) and the workers at the water treatment plant would no doubt get the worst of it, but hey. She didn't know any of them, and she'd be long gone by then anyway.

Her beeper went off, somewhere beneath her pile of dirty laundry, and she realized before she even found it who it must be. Professor Edmund *Call-Me-Eddie* Brascomb, Braswell, Brassnuts, whatever his name was, wondering what happened to all the crack. She found the beeper, checked the green display, and grinned at all the 911s after Eddie's home number.

"Right again, Dragon Lady!"

She started looking for the handset to her phone.

Lloyd Monga paced back and forth, chewing on the cigar and tonguing it from one side of his mouth to the other. He'd left the Humphrey Bogart black fedora at the office, and was wearing the Indiana Jones brown one with the brim pulled low over his eyes. He stopped pacing for a moment by the end table in his den, staring at the retro rotary dial phone.

"Ring," he muttered.

Professor Edmund Braswell sat in his own living room, having beeped the lovely Gwynn for the umpteenth time, staring at the novelty phone with the clear shell and all the lights that would come on when it rang, and said Fuck over and over and over until it sounded like a chicken clucking.

Thinking Did she try to call when I was beeping her, and she got a busy signal? Did it piss her off, and now she won't call me at all? Or could something've happened to her? Oh shit! Did she get arrested? Are they leaning on her now to give up a bigger fish? She wouldn't give them *my* name, would she? *Would* she?

"Ring!" he shouted at the phone.

Neve was getting nothing but false starts in the bathroom, her throat having gotten used to that finger after all the times she'd unswallowed lunch to keep her nice figure.

Hearing this, Megan poured her roommate's glass out in the sink and filled it with two parts milk, one part mustard, and stirred as she carried it into the bathroom. Neve was making coughing noises over the toilet instead of heaves. She looked up when Megan came in and held out the glass.

"Drink this, fast as you can."

Neve took the glass, looking at it skeptically.

"Chug it down. Trust me, it'll sober you up."

"Milk?"

"Do it."

"What's this other stuff?"

"Trust me, Neve. Drink it. Drink it down in one."

Neve gingerly brought it to her lips, smelled it.

"Drink it!" Megan snapped, her face twisted with rage. Neve's eyes went wide and she gulped half of it down before her eyes went somehow even wider, and she turned her head and doubled over, her face in the toilet. Megan caught the glass, not letting any of the potion spill onto the floor, and set it down on the lid of the toilet tank while Neve convulsed.

"Shhhh," Megan said gently, gathering up her friend's hair to keep it out of the way. "Shhh. Attagirl. You'll be okay."

"Oh God," Neve croaked between heaves.

The spinning had begun.

"You're going to go out and commit murder like *that?*" Rabbit asked the painting before him, listening to the commotion coming out of the speakers and the floor. "I don't recom*mend* it."

He chewed the knob in his cheek and regarded the folds in the sheets he had painted. They were off-white (not ivory) and badly tangled, as if she hadn't kept very still while lying in them. He was sure he'd captured the raw intensity in her flushed and sweating face, but this technicality of sheet folds and the shadows between them was starting to piss him off.

One second, the deep trenches between those folds needed more cobalt blue in the gray to give depth, and the next, it was so dark that the whole crooked line distracted the eye from the subject, Megan.

The only other thing he wasn't a hundred percent confident on was the arrangement of tiny birthmarks on her body. He knew they formed little constellations here and there where they peppered her skin like freckles, but he wanted them to be exact.

Everything else was exact, down to the number of creases in her parted lips, so there was no way he could be off even one degree on this. They don't call it perfectionism for nothing.

He grinned, a thought occurring to him.

He had to somehow stop Megan from trying to kill Gwynn with her wasted accomplice in tow, because that was just plain foolish, and he wanted her to not go ahead with the plan anyway because every moment that went by made him regret involving the both of them in this. This was a man's work, nothing for girls to dirty their manicured hands with.

Besides, any accomplice, more so a drunk one, ended up being a codefendant. Too many cooks spoil the broth, they say. He had to stop them from going out, had to get another good look at those birthmarks, and had to make love to that baby girl one more time. It wasn't just that she was incredible in bed, when he was with her he felt drunk with love.

So, the most logical solution to all three problems was to just knock on her door and take it from there. Tell her Honey, I've missed you so much, and the Missus went out for a few hours somewhere, probably to sell crack to an art professor, and we've got some time to kill.

Hold me.

Or better yet, Honey, I left my wife.

Hold me.

If he'd known that Megan was lying, had no intention of going out that night, had been at work all day, and only said all that to get Neve to start sobering up and pull herself together...yeah, he'd still be going down there. No doubt about it. This voyeurism with the monitors really wasn't his cuppa tea, anyway.

He took off the dark blue thread one more time and stepped back, looking at his painting as a whole. He considered it for long moments from different ways; through the eyes with which he imagined the anonymous buyer would view it; through the eyes of Kilgore, the dealer; through the eyes of his darling Megan. Through the eyes of his father. With or without a millimeter-wide shadow with a hint of blue in it, he saw that it was good.

And a moment later, he saw that it was good with or without the extra birthmarks. In fact, they might be a distraction, so to hell with it, no birthmarks. And then he realized with more than a little surprise that he was done. 'Orgè D'Une' was finished.

He'd been niggling over all of these nitpicky little details so much that he'd not bothered to step back and see that he was already done, and stop messing with it before he ruined it.

He chuckled, face flushing with the joy of having finished another painting, being satisfied. He cleaned his detail brush and dipped it in the same fuchsia he'd used to color the gums around Megan's bared teeth.

Down between the shadows of a fold in the lower left-hand corner, Rabbit signed "Jubal Cigouaves" in scriptina and started cleaning all of the brushes while Neve's misery came up through the floor.

XV

The phone finally rang.

Braswell snatched it up off the cradle, the pretty lights going out, and he shouted "Hello!" perhaps a little too eagerly. A split second later, and "Gwynn! About time you called!"

The phone finally rang.

Monga started to snatch it off the cradle, but caught himself, forced himself to wait until the third ring. He tongued the cigar over to the other side of his mouth, pulled the brim of his fedora down lower, and answered.

"Talk to me. Ah, Eddie, how are ya?"

He listened for a minute, his eyes going wider and wider, and he started looking around the den, making sure his house was suitable for company. *His* house? A small party *here?* With a real-live hot chick in his own home? Mother of God! Christ on a stick!

"W-why yes! Sure, not a problem! What?"

He frowned. Sure, it had sounded good, what he could've sworn he'd just heard Braswell say, but you never know with a guy like him. The implications.

"You think we can what? A threesome? Gosh. You think we can? I don't know, Ed."

Thinking I'd love to get laid, sure, but…

Thinking you never know with a guy like Ed.

"So, when you gonna be here? Okay. She knows I live right close to campus, doesn't she? Good. Well, hey, should we have dinner first? I can walk on over to Allegra's from here and get take-out, have it waiting, you know, on plates. For when you get here. No? Okay, then. Right…right…I'll see you then."

He hung up the phone, spun about and rose up on tiptoes, bending his legs a little and doing an attempt at moonwalking, grinning like a madman. Trying a pirouette, he took off his hat and flung it in the general direction of his hat rack. Took a few steps and hurdled the back of his sofa to land seated in the middle, and put his crossed feet up on the coffee table, his hands behind his head.

After showering and getting dressed in a Nick Coniglio outfit—gunmetal double-breasted suit with verdigris French cuff shirt, no cufflinks to slow down his undressing, and the wedding ring—he grabbed a briefcase out of the bedroom and put a few accessories inside: the tube of anesthetic lubricant in case she wanted to try that one thing again (*wow*, he couldn't stop thinking about it), the silken cords he'd tied her up with the other night, a pair of handcuffs, and the smaller of the two vibrators to prime her with.

These were along with the basic toys he never left home without, because one just never knew when the need for them might arise—like nightvision goggles, stun guns, and lockpick set. Better to have them and not need them...

Checking the monitors, he saw that Neve was in her bed and Megan was smoking a cigarette in the kitchen, waiting for her coffee to perk. Rabbit knew that since he had stopped smoking recently, Megan would taste to him like an ashtray when he kissed her, so he popped a breath mint into his mouth that he could pass into hers when they kissed. Locked the place up and went downstairs.

Taking a moment to get into character, he took a deep breath and knocked on the door, smiling as he listened to Megan's approaching footsteps. Saw her shadow darken the floor underneath the door crack, and the tiny pinpoint of light in the peephole blotted out. Heard her gasp.

The four locks clicked hurriedly and the door flew open, Megan springing out into the corridor to throw her arms around him, to mash her lips against his. They stumbled backwards and thumped into the door across the hall, laughing in mid-kiss.

"You shaved," she murmured, and rubbed her lips and cheek and throat against his smooth chin.

"I managed to get away for a few hours. We—"

"Shut up and get inside."

She dragged him into the apartment, slammed and locked the door. Pulling his face down and kissing him savagely, she pushed his jacket off his shoulders to fall to the floor, started unbuttoning his shirt.

He walked with her down the length of the hall, not so much kissing as making out, not so much caressing as groping and petting and pawing. He pulled her shirt up out of her jeans, fumbled at her leather belt and button fly and finally got them open, shoved her jeans and panties unceremoniously down over the swell of her ass and left them bunched there over her knees. Kneaded her, hard.

Neve peeked dizzily out her door, saw Megan's snow-white bubble butt and ducked back in.

Rabbit's shirt was only half-unbuttoned, but Megan had lost her patience in it while her other hand squeezed the front of his slacks. She started tugging on his belt and trying to pull his zipper down at the same time, and with a sudden wrench the zipper came down too far, losing the copper teeth of one flap and popping the button off.

"Oh God, I'm sorry!"

"I don't care."

"But your wife'll see!"

He didn't have time for a lie. "I don't care!"

She fished her hand into his pants and seized him, yanking him free. He grunted, slid his hands up her back under her shirt, under her bra, and around under her armpits to mash her breasts and twist her nipples.

She stood on the heel of one shoe with the toes of the other and pushed, rising up on the toes of that shoe to step out of it. Did the same with the other and then stepped on the legs of her jeans like climbing a ladder, pushing the denim to the floor. Stepping out of it, kicking it out of the way, pulling him with her against one wall of the corridor, she locked her arms around his neck and gave a little hop, wrapping her legs around his waist.

He held her under her upper thighs, steadied her back against the wall. Reached with his fingers to guide himself into her, and she released his lips with a smack, panting.

"God, yes. Do it. Neve's in her room, but—"

"I know," he said without thinking, and rammed himself hard into her. She gasped, her tailbone slamming into the drywall, her eyes scrunched shut, her mouth open, short grunts escaping her every time he slammed her into the wall as plaster dust came sprinkling down from the crown molding above them—until she cried out, tightening around him and shivering, and when she finally went limp in his arms he carried her down the rest of the hall to her bedroom, kicking the door shut behind him.

He dropped her onto the bed and climbed on with her, the two of them taking off the rest of each others' clothes. It wasn't until he was only in his socks that Rabbit remembered his briefcase in the hallway.

"Time out," he muttered, jumping off the bed and going to the door. Throwing it open, he startled Neve, who was in the living room going through Megan's bag. She gave a little yelp when she saw him, dropping the bag and covering her face with her hands, then peeking between her fingers at him.

He gave her a little wave.

"Say, you haven't seen my clothes anywhere, have you?" he asked. She was staring at his, um, manhood. He just smiled and shrugged. "I'd lose my damn head if it wasn't screwed on tight."

He slid across the floor on his socks and grabbed the briefcase and his jacket, came back and walked right up to Neve, intimidating manhood and all, who backed up two steps and was flat against the wall.

"You won't find your gun in Megan's bag," he said quietly. "So stop looking there. Why don't you take a few aspirin and have yourself a little nap?" He winked and started to walk back to the bedroom when he remembered something and came back. "Another thing. The police are looking for an *Hispanic* chick with long curly dark hair. Tampa General got something from her today, a taunt in Spanglish, and that's what everybody was talking about. Not you. So chill out and get some sleep. You look a bit peekid, Neve."

He smiled at her, a crooked half-smile.

And suddenly, she knew.

He walked back into the bedroom and slipped in, shutting the door behind him, Neve watching his ass the whole way. Cute ass. Crooked half-smile.

Strong chin, now that the goatee was gone.

Just like that Hispanic chick who now lived in this building all of a sudden, wearing the same ugly-ass shirt as the guy who'd just moved in, the one with the same build, the same goatee. The one she hadn't seen since the girl showed up, and Nick Coniglio by sheer coincidence decided to shave…and that guy with the sketch pad, always sitting around drawing something somewhere, always just around. All this weird shit happening in just the past few days when out of the blue, Mr. Wonderful showed up.

Neve looked upwards, not at the sky beyond, and the Heavens, but at the ceiling. The floor of the guy who'd moved in right above her. She leaned against the wall, feeling the floor swaying beneath her.

This was stupid.

She was drunk, and she'd gotten drunk because she was paranoid. This was all paranoia. There was no way on Earth this could be real.

The headboard of Megan's bed started banging against the wall, and Neve came back to reality, or as close to it as she could. Hell! Why not go up there? Knock on the door! And if her dorky new neighbor—what was his name? Barry?—if Barry answered the door, then she was wrong. No, wait, it could be a family, two brothers and a sister.

No, that's just as stupid. If Barry was up there, she was just drunk enough to come on to a guy like that, use her feminine wiles to get in and have a look-see.

And what if she was right?

She dismissed the idea. She wasn't right. She was being paranoid, and she was doing this to prove to herself that she was wrong.

Stumbling across the living room and down the hall, she unlocked the door. Megan was starting to holler again. Christ! But then, seeing that monster she was getting boned with, Neve could understand.

She slipped out into the corridor and went to the stairwell. She had to hold onto the railing to steady herself going up those stairs, and it was slow-going, but she made it. In the hall on the fourth floor, she walked leaning for support against one wall to

418, making these little hops with her shoulder whenever she had to straighten up to pass a door, then falling back to lean again. It was weird, how she made her way down the hall, door by door, thinking she was getting somewhere but it seeming like she always had the same amount of doors between her and the one she wanted.

Pushing off with her shoulder, hop…land, slide. Next door, hop…land and slide to keep herself upright. Each time thinking she hadn't pushed off hard enough and was going to fall short, crash right into the doorknob. Scared, thinking then that whoever lived there would answer the door and see her moving like a zombie, maybe freak out and call the cops.

But she made it. Came falling back on her shoulder against the wall just in the nick of time on the other side of the door.

And all of a sudden, she was at 418.

Deep breath. Steady hand against the molding around the door. Fingers comb hair out of face.

Knock-knock.

She waited an eternity, then, knock-knock-knock.

Another eon passed.

Knock-knock-knock-knock-knock-knock-knock.

She put her ear to the door, hoping she would hear something, and she did. Hey! That's why Barry's not answering! He's getting laid! Well good for you Ba—

Waitaminute.

It may not have been that loud, but she could hear that it sounded a lot like Megan had started to sound when she had left. And what were the odds? What were the odds of two people, two girls in two apartments one on top of the other getting laid at the same time and making identical noises?

Then Neve looked at all the other doors along the hall and thought about all the rooms on all the floors and decided that the odds were pretty good, since screwing was really not all that uncommon. It is, after all, what everything on the planet was supposed to do, and everybody was doing everything they could to make it happen. And that is the kind of thing that happens in apartments, on the weekends especially.

But then again, Neve thought, what are the odds of Megan specifically getting screwed in two different places at the same time? Because that was Megan's voice, without a doubt, saying Jesus, Nick.

Please don't stop, Nickie.

Not Barry. Not saying Oh, oh, oh *Barry*. Omigod, Jesus, fuck me, Barry! Oh God, Barry, don't stop.

She was saying Nick. Nickie.

And it was her voice, no doubt.

Neve tried the doorknob, but of course, it was locked. She made her way back down the hall as quickly as she could, sliding along the wall and pushing off with her shoulder, but this time not gauging distances or force of push and falling back into jutting hinges and moldings, or ricocheting off, stumbling and weaving, catching her hip on doorknobs and staggering, hearing doors open behind her and not giving a shit anymore because she was on a mission.

In the stairwell, she tripped over her own feet and fell, hitting the concrete steps and aluminum checker-plating, not tumbling down, luckily, thank God, but sliding, and that still hurt like a mother.

She vomited again when she fell sprawled on the landing, but didn't stop moving. Grabbed the railing at the switchback and hauled herself up, held onto it tightly and made her way down, still heaving, her head reeling, but she kept moving.

Hit the third floor, collapsing on her knees, but kept on moving. She crawled on all fours to 318 and managed to get inside.

She lay on the floor of the hall for a long time, waiting for the ride to stop, waiting for the planet's centrifugal force to stop trying her hurl her off into space, and she listened to Megan getting pounded to smithereens in her bedroom.

Finally, when she could stand again, Neve staggered to the apartment's utility closet where the bare necessities of tools were kept in a cobwebbed toolbox on the floor, and gift to Megan from her Dad when he'd hoped she'd someday learn how to use them. She always figured that meant he'd wanted a boy.

They'd never been touched, were pristine inside the toolbox, and she selected what she thought she'd need: a foot-long black pry-bar, a flat-head screwdriver, and a small saw with a pointy, tapering blade for those hard-to-reach places.

Taking them to her room, she climbed up on top of her dresser and, pushing with one hand against the ceiling for balance, started stabbing the screwdriver up through the popcorn ceiling, raining dust down into her eyes. It stung, but she was drunk enough to disregard the pain. She just shut her eyes tight and kept stabbing, perforating the sheetrock.

When he thought she'd done it enough, she shook her head and swatted her hair to get the dust and crumbs out, blinked until her eyes were clear again, and stuck the screwdriver through her belt as if she were sheathing a dagger. Now, she sawed. Now, she pried. Slabs came off in her hands, exposing joists and drywall screws. She kept pulling bits away and dropping them onto the floor, trying not to make too much noise, until she finally thought to turn on her stereo.

In Megan's room, Rabbit lay quivering on the bed, and they only faintly noticed that some hip-hop band had come on suddenly, way too loud, with the bass turned way up. No surprise there, they both thought. Neve had to be sick of hearing them and wanted to drown out their noise.

Oops, sorry Neve. Didn't think you were conscious.

Neve had pried the seam of a sheet of plywood up off of the upper side of one joist, rupturing the lousy quality floorboards above her, and followed that seam as far as she could go without losing her balance.

Surely, if someone was indeed up there, having sex, they would've noticed this. The thumping of bass in her room could never have drowned out the grinding and squeals up uprooted wood. She got down and moved her dresser to get farther along the seam, and carefully went back to her task, heedless of the mess she was making, striped orange in the sunset light from the venetian blinds.

Rabbit had Megan's wrists handcuffed behind her back, tied her ankles to the legs of the bed with the cords, her legs securely opened wide. She lay face down, the lubricated vibrator gently easing in and out, preparing her for something much larger.

In one of the two spartanly-furnished bedrooms of apartment 418, with splintered floorboards popping up even farther, an area of the floor opened up like a crocodile's mouth, nails jutting down along the lip, and Naviance Jackson squeezed herself slowly up out of it, a feat unlikely in (probably) every state except Florida, home of the paper walls and cardboard roofs that somehow managed to pass inspection.

Megan cried out, Rabbit easing himself slowly into her, in black and white, and her mouth gaped in a silent black and white gasp that Neve remembered making once or twice with Sage, only never saw, and never dreamed of seeing in black and white on a small TV screen in a stranger's apartment.

Never dreamed of seeing her roommate...

She looked in horror around the living room, her body trembling uncontrollably, and then she heard it. A whisper, as clear as a word spoken right beside her, a sweet nothing whispered into an ear an entire floor beneath her.

"I love you, Megan."

And if that could be heard...Neve's mind reeled and she stumbled backwards as if struck. Her vision blurred as stinging tears clouded her eyes. The world closed in around her, buffeting her with police sirens and the ringing clank of jail cell doors slamming shut, the rap of a judge's gavel, gunshots in the darkroom.

She stifled a wail and fled, down the hall to the door, fumbled with the locks, desperate. Finally managed to get the door unlocked and flung it open, fled out into the corridor. Fled down the stairs, slipping and falling and catching herself, then slipping again. Down flight after flight of stairs, dizzier and dizzier from spiraling until she fell out of the building and onto the sidewalk, into the orange light of the setting sun, into the surprised looks of people passing by on their way to Wherever.

Got to her feet, sobbing, and fled. But to where? There was nowhere to go.

Fled past the front lawn and closed curtains in the windows of Lloyd Monga's house, where he had company.

XVI

"Here, guys! I've got chips! And salsa!"

Lloyd came into the den with two large bowls, one full of Tostitos Mild and the other piled high with tortilla chips. Ed rolled his eyes, and Gwynn tried not to, wondering Is that a smoking jacket?

It was a smoking jacket. A cheap knock-off of the one Hugh Hefner wore. Ed thought Hey, it wasn't as bad as that damned hat. At least he wasn't wearing the frickin' hat. Chips and salsa. Christ!

Lloyd put the two bowls down on the coffee table and started rubbing his hands together and grinning.

Gwynn smiled at him from the couch, next to Ed Braswell, who looked embarrassed.

Gwynn could smile at anyone.

"So, Lloyd, that's your name, right? Lloyd?"

"Yes! Yesyesyesyesyes. Lloyd. That's me."

"Have a seat, Lloyd."

Lloyd plopped down on the other couch, the one across from his two guests. Gwynn turned her smile up another few hundred watts and patted the couch cushion beside her, inviting him to come sit next to *her*, and Lloyd flustered.

Spineless, ingratiatingly, he apologized and told them how stupid he was a dozen times as he came around the glass coffee table, kneeling one knee on the couch so he could face her. He flustered some more, backing up because he thought he'd sat too close to her, then came back because he'd scooted too far away, apologizing, apologizing, sorry.

"Lloyd!" Braswell snapped.

"Hmmm?"

"Sit still."

"Oh! Ha-ha, yes, sorry, sorry, yes…So—"

"Wanna smoke some, Lloyd?" Gwynn asked.

"What? Oh! Crack. Yes. I'd love to, thanks."

Vladimir Bilowas, Anton, and Viktor smiled at the waitress as she set their plates down in front of them. The restaurant had come highly recommended by the concierge at the Hilton, where the three of them were bivouacked. The six other gun-toting henchmen that Bilowas had stationed at a motel were out scouring the countryside for anyone even faintly resembling this Coniglio guy. According to them, every young guy around campus resembled him more than faintly, what with the goatee and the moviestar hair.

"Cotoletta di tacchino," the waitress said as she served Anton. "Very good choice. Careful, hot plate."

Anton nodded, putting his finger on the dish's rim.

"And for you," she said, moving to his brother.

Vladimir had not been able to stop staring at the girls he saw around town, and now he was unable to stop thinking about some of them. They looked like, a lot of them—granted, some were freaks—but a lot of them looked like Barbie dolls. And not just in the hair and the faces and the small breasts and the narrow waists and tiny feet, but, well, even their skin, they looked almost, *plastic*. They really did look like dolls.

Especially Deanna here, the waitress. Strawberry blonde and, while pretty, looked wholly artificial. Her teeth were way too white, her skin so made-up it looked nonporous, the smile frozen on as if she'd made a face and it stuck that way.

Bilowas saw how fake that smile was and knew Deanna could hold it there through anything.

*Any*thing? He smiled at the thought.

These girls, he'd seen them touring Europe on vacation, but never seen them up close. To him, they always seemed to have thought that the world was the way they were told it was by the Barbie people. Ken always took the copilot seat in the pink biplane. Ken always rode shotgun in the pink Corvette. Barbie was the one in charge of everything, and he always had a little smile when he thought about those dolls being designed by men, and girls growing up with eating disorders so they could fit those men's fantasies. Oh, yeah, Barbie's in charge, all right.

Bilowas knew it was that sense of entitlement that made it harder to lure American girls into his world, much harder than to lure an impoverished girl from an isolated little village somewhere, but it was a lot easier to force them into it. It only took one beating to break a girl who'd never been spanked as a child. A real woman was a lot more trouble.

Viktor was reading his mind from across the table, and he smiled, nodding in agreement. Yeah, Deanna here was definitely coming with them, and they'd enjoy the hell out of breaking her in.

"Okay, enjoy your meal! I'll be around if you need anything!" The waitress smiled even more brightly, which must've put her in serious danger of spraining something, and they smiled back, watching her perky little ass as she walked away. Their eyes met when she was gone, and they spoke casually in Polish, the language they had in common, as they ate.

"She'll do."

"And she'll come quietly after she understands."

"I get that impression. And they are a dime a dozen here, it looks like. Something good'll definitely come out of this trip."

"Maybe we could get some with a phony foreign-exchange student program. They seem awfully naïve, especially for a lot of superior-acting bitches."

The lights suddenly went out with a resounding *boom!* like a cannon had been touched off, the restaurant plunged into blackness, unsteadily illuminated only by the small candles flickering in the center of each table. There were cries of alarm from all except Bilowas and the Brasis, who whipped instinctively out of their seats to crouch with their backs to the hanging tablecloth, pistols drawn from the concealed holsters under their jackets.

There was momentary panic with attempts to quell it vainly made by know-it-all men offering their opinions about fuses, but more observant fear-mongers pointed out that even the lamp-posts outside Allegra's front bay window were out. Even the streetlights, and even the businesses across the street. A transformer, then, all of the self-appointed damage-controllers suggested. The disaster did not really strike until those patrons that were truly afraid of the dark announced that they were going outside, and the restaurant staff said Hey, not without paying for your meal, you're not, and we need light to do that, so sit the fuck back down and enjoy your dinner, folks.

Things went downhill from there.

XVII

"Jesus, what was *that?*" Gwynn screamed, bolting to her feet, and was a second later tackled from both sides. She and her two would-be suitors all lost their balance and fell, crashing through the coffee table, which exploded into a million shards of glass and a hundred thousand tortilla chips. Sandwiched between them, she was sheltered from much of the glass, taking gashes only on her elbow and flank. The other two, however, got cut all to hell.

Where the crack stem and batch of butter cubes landed, Gwynn didn't give a shit. The second after they fell through the round plate of glass and landed in the collapsed base of the table, the two professors let go of her, screaming, and she scrambled up from between them. Without even bothering to feel about on the couch for her handbag, she tripped and stumbled and crashed her way through the darkness, trying to find the front door.

The blaring noise from Neve's radio cut off, along with the lights coming through Megan's window and under her bedroom door. Rabbit assumed that a cute little brown squirrel had blown a transformer off of a pole somewhere nearby, thinking Noble sacrifice, you brave li'l guy! That hip-hop shit had gotten old quick!

Megan, however, stopped him. Listening.

She sat up, his face still in her lap, and looked at the stars glimmering outside her window, the anemic pink haze over the horizon. She had never seen the stars through that window. Ever. Always, they'd been outshined by the city lights, and now they twinkled like the stars over the Gulf on a clear night.

"Transformer," Rabbit said, eager to get back to it.

"No...look."

Before he could, the noise of the frightened neighbors had spooked Megan. She swung her leg over Rabbit's head and scooted off the bed, feeling in the dark for her bathrobe.

"Honey, what—"

"Neve!" she cried.

"She's asleep, baby. Passed out."

"How do you know?" She found her robe and was pulling it on when she suddenly remembered him saying *I know* in the hallway, and she stopped, turning to him in the dark. "How *did* you know?"

Rabbit heard the faint hint of suspicion in her tone, under-coating her wonder. He thought fast.

"I'm psychic."

Pause.

Fuck, he thought. They can't all be gems.

"No," she started to say. "How did you—"

"Holy Christ!" he shouted, hoping to derail her train of thought as he looked over his shoulder out the window. "That's a lot more than a transformer blown! What in the—"

"You're changing the subject."

"Look, I saw her when I went to get the toys in the hall. She was headed to her bedroom and she said—"

"She saw you *naked?*"

"Yeah, and she didn't throw herself at me, so I figured she was pretty much out of it. I mean, what other possible explana-tion could there be?"

"Good point. And she said...?"

"She said she was about to pass out. There."

"Okay, but then later, she turned on the stereo so loud that if she was actually conscious in there..."

"What?" He couldn't see the look on her face, but could tell what it was by her tone. It was Uh-oh.

"What?" he repeated.

"I'll be right back." She stood, pulling the robe on the rest of the way and tying the sash while doing the Stingray Shuffle, moving toward the door and sliding one probing foot along the floor and then catching up with it with the rest of her body.

When her hands were free, she reached out to feel for the door jamb and groped her way out of the bedroom. As soon as she was gone, her footsteps moving cautiously away, Rabbit felt about on the floor for his briefcase. Finding it, pulling it to him, he got the night-vision goggles out of their disguise—some extraneous parts that made them look to the casual eye like a fancy camera—and slipped them on.

Seeing the room clearly, albeit green, he went to the window and looked out, feeling ever so pleased with himself that he could do so. Outside, he saw people milling around in confusion, and checking every telephone pole he could see through the glass and the screen, crappy range of vision though it may be, he couldn't see any downed wires or blown transformers anywhere nearby.

"Oh shit. *Nickie!*"

Megan's scream brought him around sharply, and in a flash he crossed the room and saw her backing out of Neve's doorway. She didn't look afraid, well, not of physical harm, so he stayed put, not wanting to rush to her where she might feel his goggles by grabbing and hugging him or something.

"What is it?"

"We gotta find Neve, honey. Quick."

"You sure she's not in there?" He started forward.

"Oh God. Yeah, hon. I'm positive. She's gone."

Her words were loaded with meaning she thought only she could understand, but Rabbit paled. He set his jaw and nodded in the dark.

"I'll go get her," he said.

Megan blinked in surprise at the direction she'd heard his voice from, at the quiet assurance her man had spoken with, and it filled her with pride on a deep, animal level. That pride was quickly supplanted by a confounded amazement as she listened to him move quickly about in her bedroom without any bumps of his knee or stubs of his toes, just the ruffling of his clothes as he found them and picked them up off the floor, the muffled squeaks of bedsprings as he sat down and hurriedly got dressed. No cursing when he put his feet through the wrong trouser legs or buttoned his shirt sloppily. She heard him not even bother with the zipper of his slacks, just his belt, as if he remembered perfectly and it was no big deal. She heard the snap of his briefcase latching.

Shod footsteps, as dauntless as a mountain goat's, came out of the bedroom and toward her, quickly. She heard something else right before he reached her, but didn't have time to wonder what it was because his warm lips were suddenly on hers, maybe a centimeter off at the most. A quick kiss, and his footsteps were hurriedly receding, him calling over his shoulder.

"I'll be back with her as soon as I can, and I'll find out the story with the lights. I love you."

The door opened, and a second later was shut. She stared into the darkness, her mind a riot, a dozen fears and wonders colliding and ricocheting inside her head, and one joy outshining them all—"I love you!"

Rabbit effortlessly weaved between the crowds in the corridor and the stairwell without breaking stride, feeling like the kid in the fantasy books with the Cloak of Invisibility.

"Scuze me, scuze me, pardon me, gang way. Hey, take your half out of the middle, why dontcha?"

More than a little irritable, thinking What the hell is that drunkass bitch up to now?

Up ahead, he saw some guy goose a woman on the ass, then grope her breast as she turned around to yell at him. He managed to back out of her arm's reach just in time to not get swatted, the both of them on the landing in between the first and second floors. The guy was laughing at her, and she was shouting bloody murder at him.

Rabbit smiled, and pushed his way through a few people, setting his briefcase down when he got to the landing. With a sharp blow of his palm to the temple, he stunned the guy and staggered him back a step, almost knocking him over the last flight of stairs. He grabbed the guy's belt, yanking him back, then pulled his pants down to his knees and shoved him into the flailing arms of the angry woman.

Happier now, he snatched up his briefcase and hurried down the last flight to the ground floor, through the confusion of bodies, and out the door.

Megan found the flashlight in the utility closet, turning it on to see the toolbox open in the yellow light. Hurriedly, she made her way to Neve's room, dreading what she'd find she had stepped on when she first entered, and was dumbstruck when she saw what her roommate had done. Shining the light up at the ceiling, she gasped.

People were outside with candles and flashlights, suddenly becoming neighborly with people they'd lived next to for years, and never seen, speculating about what could have caused the blackout and then recounting anecdotes. Some even went so far as to quote parts from the Bible that dealt with the End Times, which were "obviously close upon us."

Rabbit rolled his eyes. That's what they said in the Seventies, and during Vietnam, and during World War Twice, and during the Dustbowl, and during the Depression, and during the Great War, and he knew that they'd been saying it every year leading up to that.

He expected people to start bringing out drinks any minute now. It always annoyed him how people would congregate like this, coming out of their homes to finally meet their neighbors for the first time, then retreat once again into self-imposed captivity and never keep their promises to drop by and see each other once in a while—in fact, not even make eye contact when they passed each other in the days to come. He'd been in many a tornado or sinkhole party or been trapped in the rain with a bunch of people under a building's eave enough times to know and be disgusted by the way they all come out of their shells only to dart back in again as soon as the rain lets up.

He patrolled the streets, wondering how the hell he was going to find that dumb girl, when a thought snagged him. What was it shehad said while ranting? Superficial info, water supply, power sources, history, blah blah blah. *Power sources.* Yelling about how guys didn't know about them as if she did and everybody should, and suddenly, Ooh look!

Coincidence! The power's out! Ehhh, probably nothing, but worth a shot, so off Rabbit went toward the area he remembered the map saying housed the closest substation. If memory served him correctly, it shouldn't be too far away, over the back of that one building in the alley where he and Megan had taken their first walk. Where she and Neve hid the bodies.

Circumventing the buildings that would block his view of the substation, he guessed a few times and correctly found himself at a fenced-in, graveled weird Thunderdome-looking place with a bunch of creepy tall monster shapes squatting in the green darkness. Each one had a four-foot-tall plinth for a base, then a huge coil he couldn't see very well, topped off by what looked like a steel plate. Above that, maybe nine feet up, was a large metal ring, and cables rose from it connecting to some scary-looking shit that radiated more cables to the other big electricity squatting monster things.

Helixes of barbed wire ran along the top of the chain-link fence, but he could see where it had been pulled out of shape where it met the wall of the building that housed the generator. Pulled out of shape as if someone had snagged it while climbing over, and their weight had left it drooping.

Rabbit nodded. Barbed wire was not there to keep people out, but to slow them down. And if their mind was made up about getting in, it wouldn't slow them down by much.

"Neve!" he called, and a moment later felt stupid.

She wasn't there. She'd run off somewhere, but not here. And whoever shorted out the Thunderdome was long gone. But he called out again anyway.

"Neve!"

There was no answer but a soughing breeze, the faint sounds of distant traffic. He opened his mouth to call again when he suddenly heard it, a long crunch of gravel, something sliding slowly, and he spotted the shape in the green lenses of his goggles. His nape hairs prickled, his fingers squeezing the links of the fence as he leaned closer and strained his eyes.

It wasn't her. It couldn't have been. It wasn't even a woman. It was propped against the powerhouse wall and was sliding down slowly, feet digging one sloppy trench through the gravel. It spoke.

A hoarse stage whisper, terrifying.

"Killlllll meeeeee."

Rabbit ran.

The circle of yellow light waivered on the painting, the flashlight held vise-like in Megan's trembling hand. She stared at her own face on the canvas with three expressions on a three-headed naked body.

One biting her lower lip, one with eyes scrunched tight and teeth bared, and one with mouth agape in ecstasy. Hands together concealing her vulva, arms squashing her breasts together as her body trembled.

Her eyes cut to the signature in the folds of the sheets and widened even more.

XVIII

Rabbit came up short, panting heavily, not knowing what to do. The first instinct was to run and get help—did Timmy get electrocuted, Lassie, did he, girl?—but the wraith's chilling words finally registered in his head and he realized that he wouldn't want to be rescued and kept alive if they swapped places. He played the sight back in his mind, trying to see it clearly, from a distance, and he was startled to realize that the guy was naked. Guy, girl, he wasn't sure which. He didn't see a hoohoodilly, but then again, he didn't really see breasts, either. He saw an ass, and stared at it in his mind's eye for a moment.

It could have been either. Man or woman.

But naked? In a substation?

Whoever it was had tried to commit suicide, he was certain, because for some reason, people like to knock themselves off in the buff. He knew, because he'd found himself naked and still alive before, hung over out in the woods and crusty with dried blood. This was after Anabela had been killed.

Strange days.

He remembered it being an act of defiance, somehow, exposing himself outdoors, exposing the small penis he'd always been ashamed of, and not some kind of sexual thing. He just couldn't explain it. But he knew that sometimes people killed themselves naked, and whoever that poor soul back there was, they were naked, so he or she must have tried to die back there and it didn't work, and now whoever it was, was desperate because now it was too late, but not too late enough, because they weren't dead and it was far too late to change their mind.

Like the guy who jumps off the roof and only breaks his back, then has to live thirty more years in a wheelchair that he can only move by blowing through a tube. Like the guy who tries to blow his brains out but misses, putting the gun to his temple instead of over his ear or in his mouth, and only blinds himself.

Rabbit swallowed hard.

The Good Samaritan isn't the guy who calls an ambulance and saves John Q. Suicide's life. He's the guy who puts him out of his misery.

He turned back around and started running.

Gwynn moved from one knot of people to another, listening to them talk, piecing together what may or may not have happened. They would all find out over the next several days that it had been a person, their identity withheld, committing suicide at the substation nearby, who had misdirected massive amounts of electricity—one point twenty-one gigawatts, or something like that—and caused the city-wide blackout.

Pictures of the steel plate would be shown in the newspapers with two footprints burned into it, and also of the ring suspended above it with eight black fingerprints where the person had grabbed a hold and completed the circuit.

Reporters assured the public that death had been instantaneous, and many grumbled that they wished it hadn't. They wished upon her all of the pain in the world for the inconvenience she had caused.

Far as Rabbit knew, death should've been instantaneous. There was absolutely *no* reason that this leathery-skinned thing he looked down upon should still be alive, but alive it was, and whimpering.

It had definitely been a woman, and he could recognize her somewhat in the green of his goggles.

He sat down and slipped off the detachable heel of one of his shoes, taking out his broken-down syringe and snapping the pieces together. From the heel of the other shoe, he took one of the four small vials he had hidden there. Each one was there in preparation for a different contingency, should some plan of his ever go wrong. The one he selected was full of heroin in liquid form, for him to shoot himself up with if ever he was mortally wounded and preferred to overdose and check out more comfortably.

It would be easier to break this poor thing's neck, he knew, but he would rather she end her life feeling immense bliss instead of horrible pain, and the high she would experience would be as close to Heaven as he could get her.

He hurriedly prepped the needle, slipped it gently into her arm and pushed the plunger. A few seconds later, she tensed as the rapture came over her, and the wretched sight of her blurred as his eyes teared up. A short moment passed, and her breathing slowed, and her heart stopped.

"I'm sorry, Neve," he said. "God, I'm so sorry."

Megan stood outside in the street with her flashlight and hundreds of other people with their flashlights. She shined hers in the faces of people approaching, momentarily blinding them and making them curse her. Her body trembled as if stricken with an ague, and she kept her jaw clamped shut with fear that if she relaxed it for just an instant, she'd start screaming like a nutcase. Her fear was not unfounded, because a sob welled up inside of her that she had to keep swallowing.

Black shapes kept pushing passed her, bumping her backwards and forwards without either concern or apology, and terrifying her, giving her the unshakable feeling that she'd be knocked down and trampled to death by an uncaring crowd that wouldn't even know until daylight what they had done.

A rapid succession of shoulders battering her head almost knocked her glasses off, and made her lose her balance, and then it started.

"Nickie!" she screamed. "Nick Coniglio! *Nick!*"

Startled people came and tried to console her, but she recoiled from them and screamed louder, more desperately. Disaster voyeurs, the sick types of people who gather at crime scenes and the sites of horrible accidents, started to gravitate toward her, some only passively hoping to see blood, but all actively interested in the pain and misfortune of others. Gwynn went like many did, like cartoon people lured by a visible snakelike thread of fragrance, pulled along blindly.

The three sex traffickers came at a run, not knowing what to think, and not believing their luck.

They all crowded around the frightened little girl, watching her have her nervous breakdown. Several of them had trained their camcorders on her, hoping there was enough candle-power from the flashlights to get a good video, and the tiny red lights that meant Recording hovered in the dark around her like the laser scopes of sniper rifles.

"Nick Coniglio!"

"*Jesus*, honey! What is it?" someone called, and people turned to see the slim dark shape came pushing its way through the crowd, occasionally mildly tazing people who didn't move quickly enough.

Flashlight beams found their way to him, shining in his eyes and blinding him to make him grimace and curse, and when he beat his way to her side the lights played on both of their faces.

"What happened? You okay? What is it?"

"Nickie! What—Nick, what are you—"

"Christ, honey, let's get inside." He turned and snapped on the crowd that pressed him and his lover. "What is the matter with you fucking people? Get your goddamn lights out of our eyes!"

Megan's frantic pawing at him made her hard to hold onto, and he had to hug her tightly to him with one arm while swinging his briefcase with the other arm to clear the way. She suddenly went still, though, looking straight into Gwynn Hutchinson's face, all yellow and bright in the wash of the lights.

"Nick Coniglio," Megan said again, just to see.

"Honey, stop saying my name!" Rabbit snapped.

Gwynn's eyes didn't show a flicker of recognition, not even of mild curiosity. The boy she'd known as Jared Layton looked entirely different as a grown man, and with what may have been blood matting her blonde hair down, she didn't look enough like the vixen he'd been hunting to catch his eye, especially considering what they'd just gone through and what they had on their minds.

Not at all like a husband and wife, Megan thought, and she was suddenly very calm. While she didn't know what in the blue fuck was going on, she did know what she was going to do about it. She cooperated from then on, no longer struggling, and went along with him as if he were a bell ram.

They fought their way to the apartment building, oblivious of the three human traffickers following close behind.

318 was dimly lit by the soft glow of candles, their small tongues of flame flickering nervously in some unfelt draft. They entered silently, Megan leading Rabbit by the hand. They shut the door on the Darkness Party behind them but didn't bother to lock it.

Megan led her lover back to the bedroom, let go of his hand, and stepped away from him, taking the briefcase.

"Get naked," she ordered. He couldn't help but smile, relieved that she had forgotten, at least for a moment, about Neve. He obeyed, enjoying the way she shone her flashlight on his hands and illuminated his progress. When he stood before her, trying to make out her face behind the glare of the light, she gestured with it toward the bed.

"Cuff yourself like you'd cuffed me. Face down."

He arched an eyebrow at her.

"*Do it.*"

Whoa.

He raised his hands, placating, humoring her, climbed onto the bed and found the cuffs in the circle of yellow light. Feeling a trifle stupid, but also a bit exhilarated to surrender control to someone else that he trusted, he locked a bracelet around one wrist, fed the chain through the bars of the headboard, then snapped the cold metal around his other wrist.

Megan found the silken cords her feet had been tied with at the two corners of the frame, still fastened at the other ends. She grabbed one and seized a hold of his closer ankle, yanking it to her.

"Spread 'em!"

He laughed, and cooperated. She bound him securely, both legs, then climbed onto the bed and lay over him as he had lain on her, only fully clothed.

Whispered in his ear.

His smile froze.

Anton Brasi was the closest to the bedroom door when the voice startled him. He understood very little English, and even if he were fluent, Rabbit's esoteric Scooby Doo reference would be lost on him.

215

"I'da gotten away with it too, if it wasn't for you meddling kids!"

Rabbit trying to be funny, cut the tension of the moment, but Megan didn't laugh. She said nothing, and the three killers in the hallway stood frozen.

Megan got off of her lover, off of the bed. He craned his neck to look over his shoulder, tried to see her out of the corner of his eye, the flashlight dancing over him and the walls and the floor as she looked for something. He strained his ears trying to make out what it was she finally found.

Her breathing was harsh, shallow hisses between clenched teeth, ominous, raising goosebumps on his skin and making even the men outside keep still.

Then she climbed back onto the bed, lay across him again with her chin on his shoulder, her hands fumbling with something and brushing across his back. She whispered again into his ear, her voice sibilant and terrifying, and tinged with madness.

He opened his mouth to protest, calm and soothe her, to explain, but the lies caught in his throat.

And then he felt it.

Her hand, fingers slippery, groping at the crease of his rear end and fumbling toward his anus.

"Oh God, no."

"What? You can dish it out, but you can't take it?"

Fear swallowed him, and he found his voice.

The men outside's mouths dropped open, startled by the horror and panic in their enemy's voice, this man they'd heard so much about. His begging, in a language they understood little of, but in a tone they knew all too well.

Then, Megan coldly reassuring him. "Now, don't you worry. Liking this won't mean you're gay."

Then, the screaming.

Bilowas grinned, stood up straighter, and sensing him relax, the others relaxed also. They made their way into the living room, their footsteps masked by Rabbit crying out, and plopped down on the rattan chairs and the small couch to wait their turn.

"Hey, it's not so bad, is it?" Megan asked, taunting as she plunged the dildo in again. "I liked it, and I don't even have a prostate, so you oughta be *loving* this. Yunno, it wouldn't hurt so much if you'd relax."

Rabbit sank his teeth into one of the pillows to stifle his sobs, and only a whimpering escaped.

"Don't clench up so much," she told him. "Relax, Nickie, or whatever your fucking name is. Ooh!"

She'd reached underneath his belly to grab a hold of him, and taunted him even more when she found him hard. He couldn't help it. Prostate stimulation is not a strictly homosexual pleasure, it's working the male G-spot, but in his ignorance Rabbit felt shame and humiliation and terror that maybe he *liked* it, and Megan fed those thoughts with relish.

The pushing from behind forced his hardness into the soft resistance of the mattress, and Nature took its course in under a minute. From somewhere deep inside of him, the most wonderful feeling swelled and radiated along every nerve until he tingled all over with ecstasy, and though he felt he might explode with rapturous joy, he hated himself for it.

He tried to hold it back, but that only magnified the intensity. When he came, his scream made Megan grin wickedly and the whoremongers blanch in disgust, looking at each other thinking *Christ!* Did he actually *enjoy* that? So, he was a faggot, then.

Their new contempt for him made them look forward to killing him even more, and to making him suffer before he died.

In the bedroom, he convulsed, groaning in a sad mixture of pleasure and self-loathing. Megan sat up and eased herself off of the bed. She'd taken Neve's gun outside with her when she went to look for him, and set it on the nightstand within reach when she began his punishment. Now she retrieved it, wedged it into the waistband of her jeans, enjoying the feel of it there and the power it represented.

"I'm going to go have a closer look at all your toys upstairs, Nickie dear. I won't be long. Don't go anywhere."

She blew him a loud kiss, picked up the flashlight where it had rolled off of the bed onto the floor, and left the room.

Vladimir, Anton, and Viktor watched her nimbus of light recede down the hallway, heard the door open and close, and they smiled at each other in the dark.

XIXX

Rabbit wept. His face buried into the sheets, his teeth grinding as he gnawed on folds of sweat- and tear-drenched bed linen, he spasmed and wrestled with the unholy thoughts that screamed in his head. The views of others that he'd taken on as his own—though he would denounce such a thing and deny he'd ever done it or ever would—shrieked inside of him on one side, screaming Faggotfaggotfaggot while the other, quite calmly, imitating the voice of Reason, said Free yourself from your self-deception. Give up the futile torturing of your poor soul, put away the false shame you think you feel and accept the fact that you liked that. There's nothing wrong with it.

Accept that it felt good, because it did, and you do feel great, and even though you got to feel it from the hand of a woman, which is perfectly natural, you might as well go the whole way and have a guy do it.

Might as well. Faggot.

And between the two, his tortured brain huddled, desperately trying to shut out both voices.

Thinking *Evil thoughts, get out of my head!*

And suddenly he froze, the tingling inside of his belly turning to ice, because that wasn't Megan who had come into the room with candles, chuckling.

She heard the voices coming through the speakers when she entered 418, first thinking What kind of batteries are these things running on? And then That isn't English and it sure as shit ain't Spanish. Who the fuck is *that?* Is there a TV on somewhere? And then Holy shit, there's somebody in my apartment!

She ran to the monitors, saw the three men standing next to her bed, looking down on Nick spread-eagled and helpless. Saw what must've been pistols in their fists. Saw one of them leaning forward over him, his voice turning cruel, and just as they had not understood what she'd been saying, but known exactly what she meant by it, she knew what he said.

"Oh yeah?" she heard Nick say in English. "Well, get in line, motherfucker."

The shape bending over him wound back and cracked him in the side of the head with the butt of his pistol, making a sickening *thwack!* and her lover cried out. For a fleeting instant, she thought Why should I care? But it's a funny thing about people, you have great sex with them and it doesn't really matter how they betray you.

Megan bared her fangs and looked desperately around for something, anything, caught sight of the uprooted flooring in the dim glow from the monitors and had an idea. Ran into the room that was right above hers. It was dark, but she quickly visualized her own furniture in this room, where it was placed, and figured where the three men were standing.

Lifted her shirt and pulled out Neve's travel-sized semi-automatic, pointing it at the floor and squeezing.

The trigger didn't budge. Dammit, the safety!

The men underneath her were loud now, their voices coming up through the floor beneath her as she dropped the flashlight and fumbled for the button, found it, turned the gun on. Then, quickly checking the monitor in the other room again just to be sure, she aimed once more at the floor, breathing a silent prayer, and fired.

The men in 318 all jumped at the sudden bang right above them, looked up at the ceiling. Not a mark on it; the bullet had lodged in a floor joist. Another shot, and this time crumbs of plaster spat down, making them flinch. With a gasp of relief, Rabbit realized immediately what must be happening, and he almost laughed, but shouted instead.

"They're sixteen inches apart, Megan!"

"What?" came a voice from above, surprising the sex traffickers.

Rabbit shouted again over his shoulder.

"You're hitting the gridwork that holds the floor together! The joists! But they're sixteen inches apart, so just aim a few inches to the side of your last shot!"

Pause.

Bam! The shower of splinters and plaster came raining down on Viktor and Anton as the hot wind of a bullet blasted between them. The three men scrambled, the two Bosnians rushing out of the room and Bilowas diving over the bed onto the floor.

Megan jumped as higher caliber bullets punched through the floor in the living room, and she squinted through the doorway at the monitors, trying to see where everyone was.

Uh-oh.

She jumped out of the way just as a volley from the living room came up diagonally through the bedroom floor, hit the floor rolling just as splinters and dust spat from where she'd landed, and she rolled right into the open suitcase containing Rabbit's "bare necessities". Another two shots punched up through the floor above Bilowas, and another volley from the Brasi brothers. Struggling to get back up, Megan saw the broken-down Mauser sniper rifle, and the knives, and grenades, and thought Holy Christ.

Bigger guns; lots more oomph than this little pea shooter. But what the hell is going on?

The whine of a ricocheting bullet, and the rushing of hot air a few feet past her; splinters flew spinning from the window sill and landed in her hair.

Choking down panic in a snarl of rage, she seized the James Bond silenced Walther PPK from the suitcase, checked the safety, finding it on, and thumbed the button, hoping that was all she'd have to do, and rolled to her feet.

Imagining where her bed would be, she decided the best place to be if she were the other guy would be crouched under her writing desk, so she squeezed off three more shots in its general direction, making no more noise firing the gun than the crunches of the bullets tearing through the floor, then ran across the room to the open doorway firing diagonally like the men in her living room had.

In 318, the Brasis dove out of the way again, giving Megan enough time to reach the monitors and see who was where. Deciding quickly, she darted back to the bedroom and fired at where she'd seen Bilowas creeping, hunched over. A muffled cry came up through the floor and out of the speakers, followed by Nick's voice calling up.

"Ha! You winged that cocksucker! Whoops, oh shit! Shoot him again!"

She squeezed off another shot next to the last one.

"Two feet to the right! No, left! I meant left! No, never mind! He just ran out of the room!"

A couple more shots punched splinters up through the living room floor, but squinting at the monitors again, Megan could see the three figures tripping over themselves and shit on the floor, dragging each other to the hallway and the front door.

She ran to 418's hallway and fired at the floor, the kick of the gun bringing it up so the next three successive shots pockmarked the floorboards in a straight line up the middle, and out of the corner of her eye, she saw one black and white figure fling his arms out and fall into the jamb of the kitchen's archway. Glancing at the monitor, she saw the two others loyally reach for him, but she fired again and her victim's shadow parabolaed backwards.

The other two gave up and bolted for the front door again, and the next three times she pulled the trigger she heard only hollow clicks.

"Honey, get down here!" Nick's voice shouted. She started to run for the door but caught herself, turned around and ran toward the room over hers, stopping to pick up her flashlight along the way. In the bedroom, she dropped to her knees over a bullet hole and put her lips to it.

"I'm out of bullets!"

"I've got a suitcase up there with—"

"Okay, which ones are the bullets that fit this gun? The James Bond-looking one?"

"Just bring the whole suitcase!"

"It won't—hold on!"

She shone the light on the arsenal where it was spilled on the floor, got up and ran to it. She wasn't about to go out into the hall where her neighbors might be, and where the two others badguys might definitely be, and the suitcase wasn't about to fit through the new trapdoor that Neve had made, but she'd seen a bookbag that might help.

Tearing through the suitcase, she found two empty clips and a dozen boxes of ammunition, several of them different. Taking them all into the living room, her arms awkwardly full of too many items, she went to the bookbag and dropped everything.

Picking up the bag by its straps, unzipping and upending it, she spilled its contents onto the floor next to what she hurriedly started shoving in to replace them.

A minute later, Rabbit heard a squealing, creaking, a grunting, then a resounding crash through the wall in Neve's room.

"Owwwww! Fuckin' shitbitch!"

Rabbit's eyebrows jumped so sharply they almost came off of his forehead. What the hell—?

A moment passed, then the ruckus continued as Megan struggled to her feet, stumbled out of Neve's room. Her apartment was a mess and many of the candles had fallen to the floor, but this wasn't the movies, where even so little as a dropped cigarette would ignite extra-flammable draperies and Megan would have to hurriedly unshackle her lover as the place became a holocaust around her. She was picturing this as she rushed into her bedroom, thankful that no flaming rafters were threatening to give way right above her, thinking that that much excitement in this weird adventure would be pushing it.

"Who were those guys?" she asked as she frantically searched for the handcuff key on the floor.

"I don't know yet," Rabbit said.

"You don't know? People are trying to kill you and you don't know who they are?"

"Hey, they could be anybody. It's a big world out there," he muttered, shaking his head.

"Oh, Christ! How many enemies do you have?"

"Baby, my ass hurts, my head hurts, I'm really not feeling up to doing higher mathematics right now."

"Oh, Jesus."

"You find that key, yet?"

"I'm looking! I'm looking!"

There was a brief silence while she continued searching, and then something occurred to him.

"Meg, the case is right by you. The briefcase."

She looked, and nodded.

"Open it up and get out the metal box, my lock-picking set, and hand it to me."

"You have a lock-picking set?"

"And how. Could you get it for me, please, before all the bad guys come back?"

She unlatched the briefcase, quickly rummaging through it until she found what looked like an oversized cigarette case. "This it?" she asked, holding it up and shining her flashlight on it. A sobbing cry from the hall startled them both.

"Yeah, yeah, that's it. Give it here and go see who that was. We don't have a lot of time."

Megan reached over and dropped the case in between his cuffed hands, leaned toward the doorway and shined the flashlight down the hall. Carefully, she could make out the guy she'd clipped twice lying half out of the kitchen, looking like he'd just come to and couldn't get up.

She propped the flashlight on her nightstand so it illuminated Nick's hands and the case he fumbled with, then took the case from him and opened it.

"Which one?" she asked, looking at all the picks lined up.

"Uh, tilt it a little bit more…third from the left."

"Here." She plucked out the slender needle and put it between his thumb and forefinger. "I'll be right back," she said.

She got Neve's little gun back out of the backpack and went out into the dim light of the hallway. As she came closer to the gasping man it was unnerving to realize, belatedly, that she had shot another human being, a person, and just not a blur on a surveillance monitor, a phantom on the other side of a floor like he'd been only minutes before.

It made her flesh crawl, but in a strangely exciting way. As she came to stand over him, and his eyes found hers in the gloom, she felt as if she stood at the very edge of a cliff, looking down. Felt that strange combination of fear and vertigo and the manic urge to fling herself out into empty space, like she always felt when standing in a high place.

"Please," Viktor said quietly, his strong accent making the word sound like "bliss," but she knew what he meant. She felt the world around her reeling in chaos and tried not to reel with it. "Please," he choked.

This is it, she thought. Back up or dive off.

Point of no return.

She saw the fingers of one hand curled against his hip, glistening crimson in the dim light from the kitchen's flickering candles, his other hand clamped to his shattered collarbone.

Good or Evil.

Mercy or Death.

Weakness or Will.

Back up, or dive off.

"You done haff to," Viktor gasped, his eyes wide with pain and fear, his head shaking weakly from side to side. Fuck what Jesus would do, Megan thought. What would *this guy* do, if we swapped places? He would rape me, first. He'd torture me.

She swallowed, her throat dry, and felt the tiny gun heavy in her hand, and growing heavier.

"Please."

She raised the pistol and shot him.

Rabbit snapped upright, startled, with the handcuffs swinging from one wrist where he stood in his pile of clothes. He allowed her a moment, letting her first murder sink in, and pulled his pants the rest of the way up. It wasn't easy. He could barely stand. But there wasn't any time for pain just yet.

When he hurried out of the bedroom with his briefcase and the backpack, she was still standing at the end of the hall, looking at the shape that slumped over into the kitchen. Spellbound. It was not the time to come staggering up behind her. He called softly from the darkness instead.

"Honey? Megan?"

"I'm okay," she said, not looking away. "Ears are ringing still, but..." She stared at the smear that had until recently been a man's brain in childlike wonder. "I killed somebody," she whispered.

"If we don't move now, we'll have to kill a lot more people, and every one of them ups our chances of getting killed too, or worse, incarcerated. So we have to move right now, okay? You understand?"

She nodded.

"Will you help me walk, Meg? We'll iron all this other stuff between us out once we get where we're going, but first we have to get there, okay? Truce?"

"Uhhh...sure."

XX

Emily Coleman was a child again, curled fetally and staring up at her mother, who was swathed in cerements that bulged at the seams, her eyes clouded over like a dead cat's. Things were moving underneath the fabric, rising and receding, but she could not make them out. There was an eerie whispering that came and went, sounding sometimes like breath on her cheek, and sometimes distant and faint like flies buzzing in the crawlspace under the floor where the body is hidden. Sometimes the voice was desperate, imploring, and sometimes hopeless like the ghost of someone long dead who'd sinned and repented but had no absolution.

Emily shivered and sobbed, unable to look away from her Mommy and her bulging seams that stretched and stretched until they finally burst, and she was showered with maggots and scorpions and scarabs, pulp and chunks and wisps of putrid, leprous flesh. Somebody screamed, and suddenly the scene was blown away like smoke by a strong wind, leaving behind a view through the peephole of her front door, the wide-angle lens view that distorted the two shadowy figures ringing her silent doorbell.

The image shook as the taller of the two pounded on the door, looking back over their shoulders at Death coming for them.

The pounding became louder and more insistent, then— "Christ!" Phil grumbled beside her, throwing off the sheet that covered them and shaking the bed as he struggled to get up— and suddenly she was awake, blinking in the darkness, wondering why the familiar comforting lights weren't on around the room; the red stick figure digits of the alarm clock on the night stand, the little plug-in lightbulb that fit into the socket across the room, the television muted with silent people doing whatever they were doing until the timer went out on the sleep feature.

The only light at all was the flashing red dot in the jewel case of Pink Floyd's *Pulse* CD.

Bangbangbangbangbangbang.

Phil stumbled and cursed in the blackness, wondering aloud why he couldn't see anything, wondering why whoever the hell it was banging on the door in the middle of the goddamn night wasn't ringing the goddamn doorbell.

With that, Emmy came fully awake, alarmed with the sudden realization that whatever it was had to be very, very bad. She jumped up out of bed and fell over something.

"What was that?" her husband snapped.

"Me," she groaned. "Owwww, that hurt."

"Honey, the lights aren't coming on."

Phil was doing the click-click, click-click of testing the light switches, flicking them over and over.

Bangbangbangbangbangbang.

"Hold on!" he shouted.

Then there was the sudden rasping of a window sliding up and, even though neither of them could see anything, both of them were now staring wide-eyed at where they knew the window to be, at something that could hear them watching in the darkness.

And spoke.

"It's okay, don't panic."

And of course, panic seized them, their throats crimping in cold terror.

"That's Megan at the door," the voice said. "We're not here to rob you or anything, Mr. Coleman, so you can put the gun down."

Phil went even stiffer, the pistol he held becoming very heavy in his right hand, wondering How the hell did he know I *had* one?

"Stay calm. I promise we won't hurt you."

Bangbangbangbangbangbang.

"Put the gun down, Mr. Coleman. It's all right."

Phil didn't move. His eyes were wide with fear.

"Shit. Have it your way."

Something stung horribly and Phil lost all control of his body. The pistol he held slipped from his nerveless fingers as all of his bones became water, and he dropped like a ragdoll onto the carpeted floor.

Emily stared into the blackness, paralyzed, as she had been in her dream, listening to the noise of someone pulling himself up and through the window and sliding into her bedroom, and with horrifying surety making his way around the furniture that even she had stumbled over, walking to where she'd heard her husband fall and pick the gun up off the floor. Walk without hesitation out of the room, down the hall, and into the living room where the front door was, eerily at home in complete darkness.

Bangbangbangba—

The clicks of the door unlocking and the swish of it brushing the carpet when it opened, muted conversation in hurried tones, and the soft clunk of the door being closed.

A car could be heard screeching round the corner nearby and coming up the street. Its headlights cast a yellow glow through the bay window at the front of the house, and Emmy could see two figures at the end of the hall, getting brighter as the light grew, their shadows stretching out long behind them into the kitchen. The light hurt their eyes, the man raising a visor from of his face, and with another screech the car halted, half-spinning in the Colemans' front yard, bathing the living room in yellow light.

The man shoved the girl behind him, stepping toward the bay window, and then explosions shattered the quiet. Splinters and shards of glass burst into view as the two figures dove onto the floor, and plaster dust spat out of the suddenly pock-marked walls.

Emily shrank back, cowering against her dresser and covering her face with both hands. The deafening chatter of gun-fire made her ears ring, and she started rocking back and forth, voice keening.

In the kitchen, the row of cookbooks turned and jumped next to the stove, a glass jar full of uncooked spaghetti exploded, and from the faucet burst twin geysers of tap water, their spray arching into the living room. Wooden chairs bucked and splintered into view, then danced back out.

She heard another commotion in the room with her, the two people hurrying through, crashing into things and cursing. They were right on top of her now and she pulled herself in like a turtle, trying not to be noticed. Someone outside was running toward the window the intruder had opened—two someones. The man in her bedroom scrambled to the window and fired three loud flat bangs out of it.

"Oh Christ, Oh Christ, Oh Christ," she heard Megan's voice whispering above her, and in her mind's eye she could picture the girl wringing her hands.

The front door crashed open and the house got deathly quiet. An instant later, the car's headlights, illuminating the devastated living room and kitchen, went out.

Stealthy footsteps could faintly be heard, fanning out into the living room. Breaths held, Rabbit started helping Megan ease herself up and through the window. As the footsteps quickened, Emmy heard her Employee of the Month whisper "How'd they *find* us?"

In the passenger seat of Vlad Bilowas' rental car, a typewriter-sized GPS tracker pulsed faintly with one small pixel of green light, and next to it, a map of the Greater Tampa area was crumbled in a massive confusion.

When Vladimir and Anton burst into apartment 418, finding no one to shoot at, they stared in wonder at all that they *did* find, and while Anton stared at the monitors, seeing the rooms he was just in through different eyes and wondering if his brother was still alive, Bilowas called to him.

"I've seen one of these in a magazine!" he said, pointing at the GPS tracker.

It was a gift from God.

Now Vlad, Anton, Sergei, Constantin, and Laszlo picked their way in the darkness through the wreckage, while Wladzu, Yuri, and Mikhail ran around the sides of the house to cover the backyard.

Constantin was in the mouth of the hallway leading to the bedroom, with Laszlo close behind, when a fist-sized object clocked him in the cheekbone under his right eye, staggering him. Rebounding upward, the grenade—called a flash-bang, since that's all they really do—hit with the ceiling and went off. With a terrifying *boom!* the living room lit up with a flare as bright as ten thousand suns, blinding Laszlo as the grenade came down in front of him.

With their heads turned, Bilowas, Anton, and Sergei were all luckier, only stunned for a few moments, their eyes scrunched shut in pain.

Only Constantin could see, through squinted eyes with the explosion behind him, Rabbit striding forth with his pistol raised, a pair of ridiculously expensive designer sunglasses on.

Rabbit fired twice, blowing Constantin's brain out the back of his head. As the Ukrainian fell, Rabbit had a clear shot of Laszlo, clutching his singed eyes and screaming. A third shot plowed through the Balkan's bared front teeth, his upper palate and throat, and spattered the connection of his spinal cord to his cerebellum on the shirt of Sergei, the tall Muscovite behind him.

As the light faded, Rabbit saw the machine gun—*machine gun?*—in Bilowas' hands swing in his direction, and his eyes went wide behind the shades. He had just enough time before the first shot to squeeze his own trigger once more…and nothing happened. The pistol was jammed.

Serves you right, faggot, he thought.

Not even five seconds had passed since he threw the flash-bang. Megan was only halfway out the bedroom window, scared of falling and hurting her head. Constantin's body had only an instant earlier hit the carpeted floor. Laszlo was still in midair. The gun bucked in Bilowas' fist, spitting fire, and splinters of wood and plaster exploded from the wall beside the hallway's entrance.

Rabbit leaped backwards, hitting the floor and heaving his legs up and over his head, rolling clown-style back onto his feet in the bedroom door as bullets chewed through the walls and into the corridor. He managed to sidestep the volley that blasted past him in a hot wind, jumped up onto the bed and, giving a little hop for momentum, dove at the window Megan had just squirmed through.

She was standing on the path of mossy stepping stones that led to the patio in the back and the kidney-shaped swimming pool, staring wide-eyed down the barrels of two upraised Kalashnikov AK-47s at the two men who held them. Eight seconds had passed since the flash-bang.

One second and two-thirds since Yuri and Wladzu had risen from behind the air conditioning box they'd cowered in the lee of when Rabbit fired out of the window. Megan had only gotten as far as "Oh, fu—"

Sergei joined in, firing down the hall at the bedroom, and Emily Coleman pitched up and backward over the dresser and against the wall.

Rounds punched through the wall on either side of her, careened off course through the studs and faux brickwork out the other side and between the gunmen and their prey just as Rabbit came hurtling through the window, shattering glass and wooden sashes, and crash-tackling Megan out of the way.

With a yelp, she flew into the tall hedge that bordered the Coleman's property, the small branches of the leafy wall stabbing into her, breaking off in her hair and shirt as she fell through, into the tangle of larger branches.

Rabbit landed half on the mossy stepping stones, scraping gashes on his forehead and the palms of both hands, and half in the muck between the aluminum rain gutter's terminus and the leaky spigot jutting out from the house; that muck where the ground was always wet on the side of every house.

Both Wladzu and Yuri started firing blindly, their shots wild because the clouds of grit and dust spitting out of the faux bricks had stung their eyes.

And Rabbit, knocked half-senseless, stared at the small beetle twitching on its back not an inch from his nose. Legs frantically grabbing at the air, dying because it could not right itself. Next to it, ants were excavating the thorax of a dead bee. And beyond that, whole civilizations of mold and fungus thrived on the stones. A whimsical, quiet little voice in his head whispered How different the world looks when you might be a faggot.

Shut up, he thought. Jesus, shut up.

Mikhail shouted from the backyard patio to Stop firing, and after the clips had finally emptied, they did. For a quick instant of breathing space, Mikhail hesitated, then risked a look around the corner of the house. Yuri and Wladzu were coughing and blinking hard in the darkness, wiping their eyes. He could barely make them out.

"Don't fire! It's me!" he called, watching the dim white squares of stone beneath him as he ran to join his fellows. At that moment, Megan was sprinting up the front lawn of Mr. and Mrs. Kemp's house, having high-stepped the lower branches inside the hedge to get over them and onto the stronger main ones, and from there fighting her way to the other side.

At the road, she edged along the hedge's front side to peer around the corner, her heart throbbing in her throat, choking her. The men who had just fired were in shadow. She couldn't see whether they'd be facing her way or not. She bit her lip and decided to risk it. Made a mad dash across to the Colemans' driveway and ducked behind her car.

"Oh God, what happened? Jesus, what did I do?" she whispered, near-hysterical.

More shouts in some foreign language stung her out of hiding, and she crept to the driver's door of her little Toyota. She quietly prized the handle up and pulled the door open, lunging inside to jab the button down that turned on the interior lights, cursing when she was just a split second too late.

Miraculously, none of the gunmen saw the flash, so after a moment of holding her breath she slid inside and carefully extended one leg to press the toe of her shoe to the button as her finger moved aside. With that covered, she eased herself into the driver's seat, pulled her door in close to her and sat there, motionless, too scared to make the noise of starting the car.

"What was I thinking?" she whispered. "What the hell was I *thinking?* What have I done?"

The enormity of how much her life had changed in the past week alone suffocated her, making her sobs shallow and painful. The realizations that she'd tried to ignore stabbed into her chest and throat. She had been seduced. Lied to. Used and spied upon. She'd lost her comfortable and stable monotony, her...

Waitaminute.

Writing epitaph poems and making suicide pacts with her teddy bear, masturbating herself to sleep every night. *That's* what she'd lost.

She'd been seduced. She'd been lied to.

Okay, where was the problem with that? She'd gotten laid.

She'd been spied upon. Because someone wanted to see her and hear her at all times. Sick as that may be, it beats her being invisible!

She'd killed someone.

…Uhhh…

She'd shot someone in cold blood.

…Um…

She was a murderess.

Her concerns were suddenly blown away, like thistle-down, because three figures came out of the Colemans' front door, barely visible, one limping. She shrank down behind the steering wheel, trembling, knowing that they couldn't see her door was slightly ajar but still praying that they wouldn't.

Praying that her shuddering leg wouldn't shudder so much that her toe came away from the button it pressed. Those three men each had one hand against the front wall of the house, and their forms were dimly silhouetted against the faux brick façade, then the garage door right in front of her, then the faux bricks again, and a moment later they were swallowed up in the shadow between the hedge and the house. She let her breath out, not even knowing she'd held it.

The backpack full of weapons was still sitting on the floor of the car, in front of the passenger seat.

"Is that him?" Bilowas asked, shifting his weight to favor his wounded leg.

"Can't tell," Yuri said. "It's dark."

"Well, no shit, it's dark."

"Whoever it is, he's full of holes," Wladzu said proudly. "We both emptied into him."

"Now, why the hell would you do that? What did I tell you about wasting bullets? Do you know what those things cost? You shoot somebody once or twice, okay, maybe he'll live, but any more'n five is gravy."

"We could still shoot him again anyway," Anton spat, kicking the body hard.

"This is just one dead body," Bilowas reminded him. Maybe it's the guy who killed my brother, maybe it's the bitch who killed *your* brother. Either way, one of us is still unavenged. If this is the guy, then where is the girl?"

Anton started to speak when he was cut off by a blood-curdling scream from inside the house. They recoiled, startled. On the other side of the shattered window, Phil Coleman, having shaken off the dregs of his tazer-induced coma, knelt on the floor in the darkness with his wife's bullet-riddled body in his arms, the unmistakable smell of a lover's skin stained with the stench of blood.

Just that instant, Megan started her car and shut the door. The noise was not drowned out, but it went unnoticed. Shifting into reverse, she sliced backwards in a tight arc that almost backed her into the badguys' rental car, slammed on the brakes and cut long furrows into the lawn.

Then, with one hand poised over the headlights' switch, she shifted into drive and stomped on the gas, the car sliding from side to side on the grass before finding purchase. When the tires bit, the small car surged forward and almost crashed into the hedge, but she cut the wheel sharply and hit the headlights, bathing the narrow alley toward the backyard in yellow light and startling the shit out of the six already unnerved gunmen. The front bumper came less than two feet from the legs of the closest men before it was jolted to a halt by the air conditioning box, which came half-uprooted with a hard *bang!*

The impact made her car shut off, which cost her a few seconds, but instead of losing them now she skipped ahead to the shooting, rising up half-out of the window with the pistol and firing wildly at the shapes as they ran. They were floating blobs of purple light staining her dazzled eyes, but she did manage to clip Yuri in the elbow as he ran, and caught Sergei right in the seat of the pants, pitching him headlong into Bilowas. The both of them went down.

The breech of her pistol locked open, and Megan cursed, throwing it back inside and calling to Rabbit, who, with his eyes scrunched shut against the glare of the lights, was smacking his lips and crunching granules of dirt between his teeth, trying to spit them out. He really didn't feel like getting up, yet.

A shot from the backyard crazed the windshield into a spider web, blasting through the car to shatter the rear window. With a yelp, Megan ducked back in and spent those precious seconds restarting her car. Another, braver shot exploded the left headlight and lodged in the battery behind it.

Miraculously, the car roared back to life and she whipped back out of the alley, this time missing the rental car by a coat of paint. Dirt and sod flying as she made her three-point-turn to get onto the road, she cursed herself for not thinking to disable the other car in time. She didn't bother to try now.

Inside the rental, the tiny green pixel moved in a small arc, then away in a straight line down the street as Bilowas and his henchmen ran past Rabbit's prone form into the front yard.

He swallowed hard, reached out a finger for the capsized beetle to grab a hold of, and turned his hand palm-up to the sky.

In the darkness, its carapace opened for its delicate wings, thin and graceful and grossly incongruous to its bulk. He blew on it, urging it away, and watched it fly into the shadows, then sagged onto the stones, groaning.

The man inside still screamed, and Rabbit listened quietly for a long time.

XXI

"Fuck. Fuck. Fuck. Fuck. Fuck," Megan was chanting, like a mantra, as she turned back onto the main road back toward her apartment, not knowing where else to go.

Who *were* those guys?

What the hell did they have against Nick that they'd chase him down all over creation and—

How'd they find us at Phil and Emmy's house?

Her mantra had accelerated to a fast and steady rhythmic fuckfuckfuckfuckfuck, but switched now to an alternating Poor Emmy/Poor Phil, occasionally punctuated by her palm hitting the steering wheel.

Abruptly, she went silent, staring at the road outside of her spiderwebbed windshield. Ahead of her, driving at murderous speed not to escape but to *enter* the university district, the traffic was not looking too pleasant. It occurred to her that there might be looting, rioting, people taking advantage of the darkness and confusion. It wasn't safe. Shit, *nowhere* was safe.

She felt like she did in the recurring nightmare she used to have as a girl, like she'd fled some implacable enemy until there was nowhere left to run, and she was all but cornered. All the world was against her and now there was nothing left to do but turn at bay and sell her life for as high as she could.

She wondered briefly if that nightmare had been a premonition of this moment. Briefly, because she saw in her rear-view mirror that one of those fast-moving cars was coming up behind her. She moved a little closer to the curb and slowed down, giving whatever maniac was in there room to pass. The approaching headlights slowed, also. She watched those lights in her rearview, the lights blinding where her back window used to be, then in her side mirror, then turned in her seat to look over her shoulder. Sat up a little to lean out of the window, then realized a little too late.

The car slowed even more, drawing up not alongside her, but nosing toward her, and before she could pull her head back in the strange car rammed its front right side into her front left, the impact jarring her up and backward, sending her sprawling onto the floorboard of the passenger seat.

Her Toyota was pinned to the curb. Stuck wedged in between the passenger seat, the console, and the dash, with the backpack of goodies jabbing into one shoulder blade, her legs frantically grabbing at the air.

Then came a volley of bullets shattering the windows and punching through the car's body, raining pebbles of green-tinted safety glass and shards of metal and plastic onto her. Wisps of foam and batting jumped out of the driver's seat and floated down.

She just barely managed to pull her knees in tightly to her chest before her legs would have been cut to ribbons, but it was unconscious; her body was going fetal as the terrifying thunder of gunfire deafened her, the wind of the rounds whizzing above her head giving her no air to scream with.

In an instant of daring, she risked reaching a hand up to tug on the door handle and the door swung open—to grind against the curb less than one foot away, giving her no exit and turning on the interior lights to give them a clear view of her.

Desperately, she snaked a hand underneath the passenger seat to grasp the lever that rolled the seat forward and backwards, but not familiar with the car's layout from this angle, she misjudged and was steadily tugging on a part of the seat itself.

The firing stopped. The only sounds inside the Toyota were the panting of Megan's breath and her frantic tugging. From outside in the darkness came the clicks of car doors opening and softly chunking closed. She gave up pulling on what she thought was the seat lever and squirmed in the small cramped space, desperately working a hand underneath her into the backpack.

She had just gotten her fingertip on something cold and hard when she sensed them just outside, six shadows standing on the grass beyond the curb and looking down on her, blotting out the stars. Heard them muttering amongst themselves.

Then suddenly the passenger door scraped loudly across the curb and dug a wide trench into the grass and the dirt, and Megan lifted her head to look at the pants and shoes of the men who would kill her.

She felt an urge to swallow, that for some reason, she fought hard to resist.

"Stiff upper lip, kiddo," she heard her father say.

"Don't ever let them see you cry," Mom added.

She rolled her eyes to look up at the indiscernible faces above her, seeing only an arm extending into the circle of light, with a fist at the end of it and a gun in that fist, aimed at her eye, inches away.

What would Dennis Hopper do? she thought.

Mind racing, she kept digging her hand into the backpack, hoping to pull the pin off of a grenade that would blow them all to smithereens instead of just her. Thinking if it happened, they'd all laugh about this later in Valhalla and drink a toast to her bravery.

Stall them stall them stall them stall them—

On a whim, a split second before he pulled the trigger, she pursed her lips and made a loud smack, blowing a kiss up at whoever it was.

A moment of silence, of uncertainty.

A low murmuring of surprised laughter and disbelief, and the man with the gun growled something, stooping, and grabbed a hold of Megan's dyed-black hair with his free hand. She yelped as he began to pull her up by that fistful of hair, struggling to turn over and push herself up on her own so it wouldn't hurt as much. She kicked hard to get her legs underneath her, feeling some of her strands coming out by the roots and her eyes blurring.

Then her hand came out of the backpack, knuckles white, clutching a small object in her dainty fingers.

As the Bosnian lifted her, still growling guttural gibberish, she came to eye level with the man's belt buckle just as she got her feet planted firmly beneath her. Her teeth bared in a snarl of fury, eyes blazing slate grey, she pulled the pin from the flash-bang and seized his belt, yanking the waist of his pants from his belly and stuffing the grenade inside, stood up to glare into his eyes with the tip of her nose mashed against his.

She saw Anton Brasi's light brown eyes go wide before she shoved him backwards, hard, pushing off with her feet and falling with him.

Vlad Bilowas, leaning heavily on the shoulder of his henchman Wladzu, didn't see what happened. To him and the others it just looked like another futile last-ditch effort anyone worth their salt would make. They all stepped back to give Anton room to tussle, still enclosing the two of them in a semicircle. Just watching, but still at the ready.

But when they hit the grass, Anton and the girl didn't tussle. The mad, desperate clawing was not at each other. Anton let go of his Kalashnikov and was trying to get her up off of him. She was trying to get the gun and scramble away, when suddenly she just gave up on the gun and pushed against him, all of this taking maybe two seconds, tops.

Anton got one hand into his pants and toward his crotch just as she launched herself up and backwards into the car to sprawl across the two front seats when *bam!* His lap exploded in blinding light, his scream drowned out by the deafening roar.

Cars screeched and sideswiped each other, their drivers startled by the blast, and the gunmen staggered back, dazzled, and didn't see Megan wriggle out of the shattered driver's window with the backpack slung over one shoulder, roll off the hood of the rental car and run like fuck down the road.

Part of the mob outside of Allegra's had long since shattered the front windows of the jewelry store two doors down, ransacked the place, and bloodied each other over the spoils. After that had been exhausted, latecomers broke into Big Beat, carrying off guitars and CDs held in pouches made of their shirts held out in front of them. Now it was the furniture store's turn—people finally getting the chance at that daybed or loveseat they'd had their eye on, and not about to waste it.

Megan ran past them, having seen the damage but not caring yet. She'd gotten a stitch in her side, just below her appendix, two blocks back, and her feet were blistering inside her shoes.

She couldn't care about that yet, either.

240

Pushing through the bystanders waiting for the store's glass to fall, she slipped into the alley and held out a hand like she'd seen the bad guys do, feeling the wall as she ran the way a cat might with its whiskers.

Emerging in the space behind Allegra's where the Dumpster was, where she'd hidden two dead bodies the day before, she almost ran headlong into the bum that lived back there. That bum—standing with a flashlight in one hand, and a cell phone like Nick had in the other...? Did everyone have one of these new phones except her?

He towered over her. She came up to where his navel must be. He stepped aside in no hurry and she wheezed Excuse me, running by. He stood watching her go, trying to remember if that was the same girl he'd seen before, but the phone rang like he'd expected it to, and he dismissed the girl from his mind. Pressed a button and put the phone to his ear.

"Why aren't you here yet?" he asked.

XXII

Gwynn was already making her way toward the black Jeep Wrangler to ask for a lift when its interior lights came on, the driver trying to see street names on a map. In the backseat was another young man like him, muscular, and not quite punk, not quite Goth, but somewhere in between.

The Jeep was bare-bones, no top, not even doors on it, and that's how she happened to get a good clear look through the crowd of people and see who was riding Shotgun.

Whatshername.

Enolah.

Hair braided in that long queue, breasts not as pronounced as when she'd worn that corset, but still a good size, face with no makeup and still as creamy white as alabaster. She was wearing a tight black t-shirt with a white symbol standing out in stark relief between her breasts.

Her lips pursed to receive a cigarette, the glowing orange tip flaring for an instant, and then the interior light went out and the orange pinprick was all that was left of her.

Gwynn gnashed her teeth and pushed and shoved her way through the handful of aimlessly milling imbeciles still blocking her from leaping at the Jeep, seizing Enolah by her braid and yanking her out onto the pavement.

The vehicle's horn blared, startling all the human cattle that had drifted in front of it. Bathed in the headlights, some of the slowpokes stopped and stood defiantly, shouting obscenities, then scattered as the Jeep roared, lurching forward.

Gwynn lost her chance, but the Jeep couldn't just haul ass down the road because with all the other cattle either milling about or hurrying past, bent on dark errands, it was nothing but short bursts of progress.

Start, stop. Start, stop.

Running, she caught up with them when they'd stop just to be left behind, cursing, only to see them stop again a tantalizingly short distance away. Thus, they gradually made their way up toward the corner, across from which the edge of campus lay.

Finally, they were brought to a complete stop by the mob that congested the entire intersection, and were surprised to see people going in twos and threes with sofas held between them. Sofas, some daybeds, armoires, vanities, a few moving along singly with lamps and things like that. None of them cared about right-of-way.

"Shhhhhit," the driver, a skinhead named Duane, muttered. The other one in the back, Stan, with the longish brown hair, dug a cell phone out of his pocket and hit a speed-dial number. He was just opening his mouth to speak when Gwynn came flying past, and out of nowhere, Enolah swung out of her seat, hanging from the roll bar, aiming a kick that didn't get to land. Her leg was not even halfway extended because moves like this only work in the movies, and the two of them collided, both falling bodily to the blacktop.

"The hell—?" Stan choked, rising out of his seat with the cell phone to his head. Peering overboard, he saw them both making stunned attempts at getting back up, Enolah with skinned elbows and Gwynn with spinning head. Duane put the Jeep in park and, standing, vaulted over the roll bar to land at Enolah's side.

The teenager's exquisite lips were curled tightly against her bared teeth, the pale blue of her eyes isled in livid white.

Gwynn snarled, gathering her legs beneath her, then gaped as Enolah did in lightning-quick real-time what she'd only ever seen in kung fu movie slow motion. Rocking on her back, her legs kicking up into the air, Enolah reached backwards over her shoulders to push off the asphalt and her entire body whiplashed in midair. She landed in a crouch, her body cocked, and in a blur of blinding speed she busted Gwynn's lip with a quick two-piece, stepped in with a haymaker and knocked her out cold, spilling her back onto the street.

"Who is she?" Duane asked, stepping forward to prod the blonde's head with the toe of his boot.

"Dunno," Enolah said. "But I kept looking in the mirror and there she was, lit up red by the brake lights and running up on us." Enolah inspected her knuckles and then rubbed her bottom. "I can feel my ass tuning black and blue right now. Stan, gimme something or I won't be able to sit down."

Stan was still frowning, mouth open with the phone to his head. Duane was frisking the unconscious girl saying over his shoulder "If it hurts, you'll just have to wear it. Can't be slowed down."

"Keep that stoic crap for yourself, Duaniac."

"She's got a wad of money stashed in her bra," he said, ignoring her. "Big enough to choke a horse."

"But no ID?"

"Not yet."

"The fuck you looking at?" Enolah snapped at the bystanders. One of them shone the beam of his flashlight on Gwynn's face, the rivulets of blood that snaked down from her slack mouth.

"Holy—"

"That's the chick from—"

"The plot thickens," Enolah said, grinning.

Megan burst in through her apartment door, not wondering why or even bothering to notice that all of the candles were burning again. Not still, but again. They had all been prudently snuffed out before she and Nickie had left, her supporting him on her shoulder until he could overcome his "sea legs."

What brought her screeching to a halt was the empty space in the hallway kitchen. There was nobody slumped there on the floor, back propped up by the jamb. There was nobody lying there any whicha way at all. *He'd gotten up*, she thought.

He's in here, somewhere, hiding.

With a bullet hole in his face?

No, wait. He was dead.

Not unconscious. Dead.

What's that smell?

There were still blood splatters on the floor and wall, but no dead body, and that dizzying smell, she realized, was bleach.

"Where is he?" a deep and terrifying voice asked, and she jumped half out of her skin, her eyes finding the huge shape that stepped into the hallway. She shrank back toward the door, half-open behind her, eyes bulging, with her heart in her crimping throat trying to work its way out of her open mouth.

"You're Megan, right?" the monster asked. "So where is *he?*"

"W-w-who?" she stammered.

"Christ, listen to you, playing all innocent. Who do you think? Rabbit! Nick! Where's Nick?"

Her hand was reaching into the backpack.

"Honey, he's not upstairs, he's not with you, and he's not answering his phone, so where is he?"

"He's…h-h-h-he…"

"Jesus. Breathe into a bag or something."

He started moving toward her and she dropped the backpack, her fist coming out of it with one of the empty pistols.

"Stay there!"

He stopped, his hands coming up slowly to chest height. "Whoa, Nelly. Calm down, now."

"I'm calm," she said. "I'm mellow fricking yellow. But who the hell are you?"

"I'm Rabbit's partner. They call me Blue Tick."

"*Blue Tick?* What kind of a…oh, like a blue tick hound, or something?"

"Yeah, because I ain't nothin' but a hound dawg. Long story, and it can wait for another time."

"And you ain't never caught a rabbit?"

"That's just a coincidence, his name being Rabbit. Nothing to do with the song."

"Well, great. Fascinating, really. Why don't you tell me what's going on?"

"I got a better idea. Why don't you tell *me* what's going on, since what I know can wait, while what you know explains bullet holes all over the place and dead guys in your apartment."

"Where is he, anyway?" she asked, indicating the spot on the floor with a jerk of her chin.

"I bundled him up and threw him out the window. We gotta go down and collect him before we leave."

"We?"

"Yeah, *we*, sport. Or do you want the police investigating all of the apartments that have windows in a vertical line up from the corpse they find? We can put this wreck and the one upstairs back together later, when we got some free time. All it takes is a little bit of elbow grease. But I watched one of the tapes upstairs, I saw some of what happened. I know that you know something, but I don't know how much. What I do know is that you left with my little buddy and you'd better tell me where he is now, and stop pointing that fucking gun at me."

"Um…it's empty anyway."

"I don't give a god *damn*. You don't point guns at people, loaded or unloaded. You know what they say down at the gun club. Safe shooting is no accident."

"Okay," she said, lowering her arm. "There are more guns upstairs. We need to get them."

"I already did. They're in the truck. Wait a minute, what do *you* need with more guns?"

"I've been shooting at people tonight."

"No shit." He sounded amused, now.

"Yeah, and I'm out of bullets in all of the guns I know how to work. These guys, no matter where I run to, they always keep showing up."

"These guys?" All business, again.

"Those guys you saw on the little TVs upstairs."

"But who are they? This guy I found here, I've never seen him before."

"I dunno, and Nickie said he didn't know either."

"Shit, we keep getting sidetracked. Where *is* he?"

Megan paused. In the dim light from the candles behind him, he couldn't read the expression on her face. Couldn't tell what she was feeling, if anything.

"I think he's dead," she murmured.

"*What?*"

"They were going to shoot me," she said quietly, as if speaking only to herself. Going over it, finally having a chance to play it back in her head and see it all. "But he came flying out of the window just in time and pushed me out of the way. I couldn't see because I was in the hedge, but they just kept shooting and shooting. When I finally got to the car and tried to run them over, he just lay there. He wouldn't get up. So…so I took off."

"What the hell are you talking about?"

"He got shot saving my life."

Tick nodded bitterly, with a mixture of annoyance and admiration.

"Yeah, he *would* do something like that. Dumbass. Come on, you take me to where this happened, and keep talking."

The five of them stood over Anton Brasi, who lay rocking to and fro, his screams now dwindled to keening mews. They stared down at him, silent, trying to see past the purple blotches that stained their vision, the slowly fading afterimages of the flash.

Only Bilowas really knew him. The other four were only hired thugs, but they were still stricken by watching him suffer. Bilowas, though, standing with one hand on his bald head, was watching his friend die. The second of two brothers he grew up with.

Thinking nothing but Oh, God.

OhGodOhGodOhGodOhGod.

What'd I do? Oh, God, I got my friends killed.

Over avenging my brother, who I guess I never really liked that much anyway. Oh God, now what?

Do I put him out of his misery?

Do I take him to a hospital where the police can get him and lock him up forever?

Oh God, I'm sorry, Anton.

Oh God, I'm sorry, Viktor.

It was Sergei who finally broke the silence. He'd been looking from the crying man to the blood and gore on his clothes that had until recently been part of his buddy Laszlo, who always knew the funniest joke for whatever moment, and had it ready. He looked back and forth while he held his left buttock and the wadded-up shirt he stuffed in his pants to staunch the flow of blood. There were two wounds there, one entry, one exit, where the bullet had glanced off his pelvis. It hurt like a bitch, but he'd live, and he might even dance again.

He was lucky. And he knew it.

"It's been fun," he said.

"What?" Wladzu asked.

"It's been fun, but here I call it quits. *Spaciba* and *dasvidaniya*."

"What the fuck do you mean?"

"I mean, I'm not cut out for this shit. Apparently, *we* are not cut out for it. Sure, we can stand around in a club and intimidate bitches and beat up drunks who get out of line, but how many men died tonight?"

"Coward!"

"Fuck you. Laszlo's dead. Viktor Brasi, and now his brother, look at him. Constantin, dead. And me, I could either be a cripple or a eunuch right now. Fuck you. I know when it's time to quit."

"You gutless—"

"You *brain*less! A woman did this to Anton! And didn't you say a woman took out Viktor and got you in the leg?" This last was directed at Bilowas, who finally looked up.

He opened his mouth to speak, and shut it. From Anton the keening broke into staccato sobs and then a high-pitched wail. Bilowas' face cracked and twisted in misery. He pointed his Kalashnikov at his friend and squeezed the trigger, letting off a quick burst that shattered Anton's skull, splattering blood and brain and splinters of bone with clods of dirt and grass all over them. Silence fell at last.

In surprise, the others stared at his face, at the two runnels of tears curving down his face and glistening in the Toyota's light. He took a deep breath before speaking. "If you're coming, get in the car. If you're not, get outta of my sight." He stooped and picked up the dead man's AK.

Sergei watched the four of them walk round the small Toyota, what was left of it, and climb back into the rental car. Vladimir cranked it up, and they took a moment to consult the GPS and the map, and drove away, Sergei watching them all make a point not to look at him.

When they'd merged with the traffic up ahead, Sergei looked around him at the houses, at the windows he knew people were trying to watch him through. He sighed, started limping in the direction the car had gone, hoping he might meet someone who spoke Russian.

The press of "humanity" was too thick for the Jeep to progress any further, so they gave up and the three of them decided to abandon ship and carry Gwynn limply between them, shouting "Emergency! Coming through! One casualty! Anyone know CPR?" through the crowd and into the alley. There wasn't quite enough room now, so Stan motioned for them to lay her down.

"I've always wanted to do this," he said, stooping to gather a fistful of her hair, and began to drag her by it through the narrow darkness.

"Freak," Enolah muttered.

"Hey, this is a perfectly natural male exhibition. Freud said something about it."

"I said something about it, too. You're a freak."

"Exhibition of dominance."

"Are you going to rape her when you get her back to your cave, Thongor the Mighty?"

"Naw, I'm gonna eat her."

"You would."

"I'ma eat her wit' relish."

He dragged her the rest of the way in silence, the only sound the rasp of her clothing on the concrete. When they emerged behind the buildings, the giant frowned down at them.

"The hell is this?"

"It's our hostage," Stan told him proudly.

"Your...hostage."

"It's a long story."

The giant stared at him for a moment, then shook his head. "Kids."

"Okay, so what now?" Duane asked.

"Shit, with this fiasco we've got now—" he turned sharply at a sudden noise, and the two black shapes coming from the other way dropped their burden and shrank against the alley walls, hands pulling out what had to be guns. The suddenness of it made the giant and his three accomplices also leap aside, silenced pistols coming out, Enolah aiming from behind the Dumpster nearest her, and none of them hearing the rapid but stealthy footsteps coming up behind them until three more gunmen burst from the mouth of the alley. With curses of surprise, and confused haste to reposition themselves, there followed an uneasy silence in the dark.

Enolah had scrambled up on top of the Dumpster now, and everyone was covering each other, breaths held. The black giant grinned.

"I can't *believe* this happens as often as it does."

Duane called "We got no beef with anyone here!"

"We don't either!" Blue Tick said.

Silence again.

None of the three newer guys spoke.

"Everybody be cool!" Stan shouted. The giant rolled his eyes. The magic words to make everyone even *more* tense, and Stan has to say them.

Megan and Blue Tick just aimed at anyone up ahead of them, neither knowing nor caring who was who. Stan was backed into a corner, his gun sights moving from one to another of the three silent ones, aiming at them all in a circuit. Enolah was jittery, her pistol in both hands held out stiff-armed and jerking from one target to another and back. Duane and the giant were back to back and keeping one target each: Duane—Bilowas, and the giant—Megan.

Just then, Gwynn Hutchinson started to stir.

"Uh-oh," Duane said quietly.

One hand came up to cup an aching head, fingers burying themselves in her tousled hair. She groaned, then sat up suddenly and cried out. "Jesus fuck!"

Deafening gunfire and staccato bursts of light split the enclosure, shots clipping the concrete and spitting gravel and dust. The din lasted not even a second, and a second later all that was left in the cloud of choking dust and gunsmoke was the echo of ricochets ringing in the dark, and it was over.

Rewind.

The giant stumbled forward when Duane's body jerked and danced against his back. Tick dropped sideways, pulling Megan down with him and yanking Viktor's corpse up as a barrier—and not a moment too soon, because two of the bullets that came whining past thunked wetly into it. Stan put four rounds into Mikhail, pitching him against the side of the Dumpster before Yuri cut him down and was in turn shot dead by Enolah. As the bodies of his comrades fell from beside him, Bilowas turned and

251

bolted back into the alley, where another sudden blast and flash of light blew him back out and off his feet.

And dead silence. Gwynn was hugging her knees, trembling, and Enolah's breath whistled as she took deep, rapid draughts of air between pursed lips. Even the noise of the mob in the streets had stilled, a thousand eyes turned toward Allegra's.

On the ground behind Viktor's earthly remains, Megan and Blue Tick slanted their eyes at each other.

"Who farted?" Tick whispered. "Was that you?"

Megan frowned and blinked. "What?"

"Smells like something died."

"*What?*"

"Listen to you, trying to sound all innocent again."

"I…I didn't…*fart?* I didn't!"

"Well, I sure didn't."

"Well, I didn't either!"

"You trying to say you don't smell that?"

For a second, her trembling subsided, and she took a tentative whiff. Grimaced.

"Could be gas leaving the new bullet holes," she said, glancing at Brasi's corpse.

"Oh, sure, blame the dead guy."

"What?"

"Okay!" he shouted. "We're going to run along now! Real peaceful-like, so nobody has to shoot us."

Enolah was still staring at Yuri's dead body lying half-out of the alley, at the blood bubbling darkly out of his chest and throat. The giant lay still, playing possum under Duane's body, listening intently.

XXIII

I'm a faggot.

Rabbit limped across somebody's front yard, chewing on the knob inside his cheek and listening to the voices argue inside his head, all of them so familiar by now he couldn't tell which one of them was his own. Shrinks call those voices our inner troupe of actors that we call upon to play their appropriate parts according to the audience of the moment. The mutiny of that inner troupe is what they call schizophrenia.

Up until now, that troupe was busy, and now that he finally had time alone, time to think and torture himself, the important things like getting hunted and shot at by strangers, and the innocent bystanders that get killed or worse—find themselves suddenly alone—all that was abruptly on the back burner. He kicked a pink plastic lawn flamingo and winced.

I'm a faggot, he thought.

No, no, I'm not! Prostate stimulation is a—

Yeah, go on lying to yourself, dicksucker.

Hey, anal pleasure's a far cry from sucking on—

The hell it is. In for a penny, in for a pound.

Admit it, you liked it.

Well, yeah, but that's perfectly normal!

Uh-huh, yeah, you tell yourself how normal it is while a hot slippery dick is slamming itself to the hilt in your booty. Sure, it's normal enough. How many queers are there these days? Enough to welcome you anywhere you go. They can't all be wrong, now, can they? Wouldn't it feel good to finally admit it? That you're bisexual? You wouldn't have to put on that macho act anymore, overcompensating, always overdoing it and making it so painfully obvious to everyone else. You could finally let your guard down.

Stop messing around with all the girls and be truly happy with just one guy...

Snuggle up to Blue Tick, that big teddy bear...

Jesus! Shut the fuck up!

Evil thoughts, get out of my head! Get out!

Faggot.

Shut up!

That's why you suck on toes. Like ten little dicks.

Shutupshutupshutupshutup!

"Okay!" he shrieked at the star-spattered sky. Legs braced wide, arms outflung, he glared up at the heavens. "Okay! I'm a faggot! I'm a goddamned faggot! Megan fucked me with a dildo and I liked it, so if that makes me queer, *so fucking be it!*"

Trembling, he felt an enormous, intangible weight lifted off of him, just like the first time whispering his confession through the worn grating in a dark booth and hearing the priest absolve him. The guilt and shame exploding joyfully up and out of him just like it did back then, back when there was truly something of Catholicism in his heart; when you got past all the rituals with the monstrance and the wafers and the smoking censers swung by kids in scarlet and lace, there was really something to it. Personal salvation.

The voices were blown away from inside of his head, like smoke by a strong wind, like thistle-down, and he was finally *free*. He listened to the wind and the night-birds and the distant chaos, staring up at the vault of the sky, staring at infinity, and realized it didn't matter one iota whether he was a fag or not, not in the grand scheme of things. It wouldn't ever make any kind of difference at all, in anything.

Then the front door of the house opened, and the man who owned the lawn where he was standing came out with a flashlight, standing on his shadowy front porch.

"Me too!" he cried. "Yunno what? I am too!"

Rabbit stared at him, watching him jump down the three short steps from the porch and come toward him with his arms outstretched, shouting "Come inside with me, my brother!"

Rabbit snapped "Get the fuck away from me," and went on limping across the yard, feeling an even greater relief that he wasn't really a fag after all.

Whatever the black giant and his three accomplices had been up to before the blackout had interrupted them hinged upon a nine-volt battery, an alarm clock, a blasting cap, and four kilos of

Composition 4 plastic explosive. While the plan that went along with that bomb was out of commission, the bomb itself wasn't.

Enolah's eyes darted from Yuri's sprawled dead body to the mouth of the alley, trying to use ESP or X-ray vision she didn't have to pierce the concrete and see the hidden gunman who lurked beyond it.

Gwynn Hutchinson looked out from behind her knees into the darkness that was cut only partially by the giant's dropped flashlight. Blue Tick and Megan both peered over their barrier, straining their eyes, and then it happened.

Somewhere on a side street near the alley, very close, a monstrous thunderclap shattered the night, and a hurricane of flames was belched up into the black sky. The shock wave, an invisible brick wall passing through people on the street like light through glass, picked them up and hurled them along, dashing them to jelly against buildings even hundreds of feet away, and one of them flew like chaff on the wind out of the alley.

Megan and Tick had half-risen, shielding their eyes from the flare, and in that moment the giant saw them clearly. In an instant as bright as broad daylight, he recognized the mammoth henchman of the little guy he'd been following and the girl who had hidden the dead bodies the two men had carried off.

Then the unseen gunman hit the ground in front of him and slid on his rear for a space before flipping over and rolling. Then both Megan and Tick were blinking hard and staring incredulously at Vladimir Bilowas and Gwynn Hutchinson, both lying sprawled on their backs, and then the black man, and wondering what in the blue fuck had just happened.

It took a while to get everything sorted out, and it would be as tedious in the retelling as it was in occurring. There was confusion and much argument as to which unconscious person belonged to whom, and then there were the introductions, at which time it was revealed that the black giant was in fact an Australian Aborigine, not a negro, and a man of parts, not a bum. He called himself Jim Crowe, and Megan laughed, appreciating his pseudonym, and Crowe appreciated that she appreciated it, since no one else had ever seemed to catch the joke.

Removing themselves and the two unconscious prisoners to a safer place away from the fire and the rubble and death, they spoke at length and revealed as much as they were willing to reveal about themselves, until Blue Tick indicated Bilowas, prostrate on the ground, and announced that he'd give a bajillion dollars to know who the fuck *he* was, and they all whirled, startled, at the owner of a voice coming from the shadows, saying "I vill tell you who he iz."

And they stared as Sergei the Muscovite limped into view.

Shortly thereafter, all of them were crammed into and hanging out of the black Jeep, which, as Jeeps do, held up rather well under the circumstances. Shortly after *that*, they saw Rabbit limping in their headlights all covered in dirt and blood and blades of grass, and when they pulled up alongside him in the road, he blinked at them all until Tick said "It's a long story."

Rabbit and Blue Tick drove Gwynn and Vlad Bilowas to the house out in the woods, where they could be stored until it was decided what could be done with them. The simplest answer was to put two bullets in each of their heads and plant them, since that always ensures they don't escape and come back to hunt their captors down one by one, like in the movies. Killing people isn't that simple, though. In the heat of the moment, sure, but in cold blood, unless you're a real prick, just shooting someone isn't easy, long-overdue vengeance or not.

Megan went with Jim Crowe and Enolah to drop their new friend Sergei off at the hospital, and then the three of them that were left went to a motel outside of town, where there was still electricity. The two girls bunked together, since Megan really shouldn't be left alone, and ought to lay low for a while, considering the state of her apartment, and the two of them had a lot to talk about.

Since Crowe and his one surviving accomplice both had cell phones just like Rabbit and Blue Tick—the four of them agreed that they were handy devices and were certain everybody would have one in the next few years—they exchanged numbers and met up the next day.

"No, don't kill him," Crowe said the next day.

"Why the hell not?" Rabbit asked.

"Because he's involved in white slavery."

"That's exactly why I *will* kill him."

"No, I want to show you something first."

"What?"

"You'll see. We have to wait until tonight."

"Why? What's happening tonight?"

"We're going to a party."

Blue Tick called some people he had worked with for a few years who were now stationed, at least for the foreseeable future, in Coquina, on Florida's other coast. In peacetime, they dabbled in carpentry and renovations, and could be counted on to pop on by and replace a destroyed ceiling and patch up bullet holes in an apartment. They tended to charge more for labor than the average carpenters and detail workers because of their discretion, since their primary occupation involved the putting of bullet holes in walls in the first place. And other things.

In addition to paying for materials and labor, Rabbit had a fruit basket sent to their boss. It seemed like the thing to do. Then he poured himself a stiff drink and made a few more calls.

Before going to the party, Crowe gave Rabbit a pill he called Granosal, something that would help him distance himself from what he saw in order to handle seeing it better.

"Cum grano salis," as he put it.

Megan stuck around and believed them when they said Neve was probably laying low for a few days, just like her, that she'd probably come around.

As soon as the pill took effect, Rabbit found himself, while not high in any normal sense of the word, not quite caring so much. Megan wished Crowe could have spared one for her.

While she was with them, lying low, she didn't say a word to Rabbit, and avoided making eye contact with him.

He didn't push it. He just had another drink.

Blue Tick was doing voices again, talking to himself, this time quoting a Jamaican he'd once heard in the county jail, while cleaning his guns.

"It was up on dee roof, me an' meh *paht*-nah, we was smokin dat pheema-bobbit-all like it was crack, mahn." He'd noticed Jamaicans never say "mon" like white people do when they try to do the accent. They always say "mahn."

"Then Lucien, he get da waaa-el look in 'is eye, an' get to 'is feet an' he run, fast as lightnin' and take a flyin' leap offa da roof to splatta like kay-chup all ovah da street."

"What's that from?" Megan asked.

"Hmmm?" he asked with eyebrows raised.

"What you're saying. It's from a movie?"

"Oh. Nah, somebody said it once and I thought it was funny. It's a habit I got from Rabbit—Nick, you know him as Nick, that's right—he always does it and it sort of grew on me."

"Is his name not Nick?"

"His name's Rabbit. Why, I dunno. I call him Bad Habit Rabbit after this public service skit on TV back home that they used to have. Stupidass skit about this fucked-up druggee rabbit that goes on a picnic with the Eat-well Kids and they get him to clean himself up a little. Man, it was dumb."

"And he's that rabbit?"

"When he doesn't take his meds, yeah, kinda."

"What meds?"

"Ehhh, stuff to keep him on Earth, yunno? I don't really want to talk about him. That's a conversation you should be having with him."

"I really don't want to talk to him."

"Yeah, I figured. Sucks, though. He really liked you. In his way, he liked you a lot."

"What's the story with him? Honestly. What the hell was he doing upstairs from me, spying on me and painting weird pictures and going through this whole bizarre act pretending to be married to someone who doesn't even know him?"

Tick made an exasperated face and heaved a sigh.

"No idea," he lied. "When he's not on his meds and he starts drinking, he does some strange shit. Fruttier'n a nootcake, that's him. Yunno, we went on a tour of whore-houses all over the place so he could free women forced into sex slavery. Just got back from doing it all around Europe. *Dangerous?* My God! We're the only two who made it back alive out of fourteen guys. But that's what he does. He picks a crusade and goes off to fight it. I can't complain, he pays well and I get to travel."

She nodded, not knowing why.

"He's got this screwball view of life," Tick went on, trying to smooth things over without appearing to. "He read somewheres that everybody dies three times; the first, when you physically die; the second, when they dispose of your body; and the third death's when somebody says your name for the last time. That kind of messed him up, why, I can't imagine. Because, who cares, right? You're dead. But it really affected him and he's doing all these things to make sure he prolongs the time between the three.

"Since nothing we do really matters, not when you come right down to it, that after we die, we're just a memory, and then that fades away into nothing, it doesn't matter what we do at all. Like we really can't accomplish anything that will last, there's only the here and now. And so he's made it his job to improve the here and now for people. *Some* people. Like rescuing those girls who just wanted to improve their lives by going to Europe or the States and got roped in. He punished the guys who took those girls' lives away from them, and then he did the best he could to make their lives better, maybe through some kind of selfishness in wanting to be remembered, but who cares what the reason is? He did a good thing.

"I've seen him give a Coke to a homeless kid on a hot day, and I've watched him kill a guy for pissing all over the seat of a public toilet. How do I tell you 'the story with him'? Honestly? He's just Rabbit."

He seemed to realize something, and put down his gun for a moment, looking straight at her.

"Yunno that cowboy movie that came out a couple years ago? With Kurt Russell and Val Kilmer?"

She blinked in surprise, nodded.

"Well, they talked about one of the bad guys as having a great big hole in the middle of him that he can't never fill, and he's trying to get revenge for being born. I think that's him. Nothing he does will ever be enough to make him happy. He needs to always be fighting for something. And when he wins, then he has to go fight for something else. I got the feeling you had put an end to all that, though. He was talking about quitting, just throwing in the towel and settling down with you." Not entirely true, but so what? What harm could it do for her to hear that? "Like how he was going to improve your life by making you into more than a clerk in a used-CD shop."

"What? How?"

"I dunno. I was only listening with half an ear. Something about an honorarium, whatever that is."

She didn't say anything for a long time.

XXIV

On a pedestal, trussed up like a turkey with a red rubber ball gag strapped into his mouth, a young boy sat shivering even though the air was hot around him. His name was Timothy Lee Hahn, and his picture had been on milk cartons all over Connecticut for more than a year, and mailed in bulk to every house in the continental US for six months. He was just fourteen.

Most runaways up and down the Eastern seaboard who flee "abusive parents" "intolerant" of their "sexual orientation," who come to South Florida seeking acceptance by the "gay community" are eventually found in the canals that separate coastal cities from the inland swamps. Usually it's when a drunk driver crashes his car into a canal that the police bring in the heavy equipment to haul it back out and dredge the canal while they're at it. That's when they often find the remains of youngsters who had disappeared.

Some of them are never found, like Timothy.

Timmy was naked except for the straps that bound him and the tubes draining blood out of his femoral arteries, feeding the taps mounted in front of him.

A tall, thin man pulling one of those taps filled a champagne flute with Hahn's "naïve domestic." If he had wanted a "vintage foreign" there was a twenty-something on a similar pedestal not too far away.

"Getting a little chilly up there, arncha?" the man laughed, raising the glass in toast with his pinkie finger extended. "*Arncha?* Bottoms up!" and drank, staining his upper lip crimson.

"Influence," one bizarre, androgynous figure said to another, approaching with two empty glasses. The both of them appeared to be nude except for Krishna-like headdresses fronted by a single splaying peacock feather. Strings had been tied around the domes of their penises to pull them backwards, underneath and tucked between their buttocks, taped there. This was concealed by tight latex undergarments of a color and texture that blended into their painted skin.

The one who had spoken was solid gold from head to toe, except for the blue, green, black and yellow of the peacock feather and his own jet-black eyes. The other was a creamy white, from which two bright blue eyes sparkled. The both were unnaturally thin.

"Hey girl," the golden one said to the man at the taps. "Be a dear and fill these up for us?"

"My pleasure."

Timmy Hahn watched in horror as more of his blood was drained. He grew dizzier, and colder.

"Influence," the white one prompted.

"Yes! Thank you. Influence. You see, to a corrupt man, there is no greater pleasure than the corruption of others. You'll see it everywhere. Some halfway worldly person trying to be the mentor of an innocent, getting him to do something so trivial as smoke his first cigarette, and when he chokes, the truer victory, the far more significant accomplishment of then convincing him to smoke the second, and the third. Getting someone to—ahh, thank you sweetie," he, or rather it, said to the man at the taps.

The two epicenes graciously accepted the glasses and turned to go, and the tap runner watched their buttocks as they strolled away.

"Mm," Gold said, savoring his first sip. Ivory tried not to grimace at his. Went on listening attentively.

"Getting somebody to not only agree with your views, but renounce their own thoughts and echo yours instead—" and here he elbowed Ivory in the ribs—"Like you no doubt did long ago, because continuing the cycle of corruption is to justify your having been corrupted in the first place. Ooh, look! There's Peaches and Vincey! Let's go say hello."

Lavon "Peaches" Gilbert and Vince Kilgore were mingling with others resembling Gold and Ivory, they themselves clothed far more extravagantly. Peaches' gaunt form was draped in a long saffron robe of embroidered sendal with a yellow cowl, and gold thread tassels swung from the hem of his wide sleeves and trailed behind him on the floor.

Kilgore out-dressed him, in a gown of dove-grey linen with a gauze hood, pearl stomacher, and pink-slashed sleeves. From his enameled collar of white and damask roses hung a long chain of pear-shaped pearls—a chain by which he allowed Peaches to lead him around whilst drinking from their crystal goblets, wine "as dark as the bruises of love."

Taking a sip and nodding at something he was being told, Peaches licked his fat purple lips with a mottled gray tongue. He could barely hear what was being said over the music, but he'd long ago become a master at pretending to listen, which annoyed Kilgore no end. His eyes drifted away a moment, then drifted back, and did a sharp double-take.

"Vincey!" he exclaimed, cutting off the epicene who was speaking, stabbing a bony finger at a newly-arrived group of people in street clothes, obviously newbies. Kilgore followed his gaze.

"What?"

"Vincey, who dat is?"

"Well, as I live and breathe, that's Nick Coniglio! *Here*, of all places!"

"Naw, who dat *wit* em? See tha girl?"

They all looked, even the gold and white epicenes who had just arrived. They saw Rabbit, they couldn't help but see him, and Jim Crowe and Enolah, Crowe in a fuchsia zoot suit with an ostrich plume in his hat and Enolah in her Dorothy outfit again, and the petite girl with the glimmering black hair. All but Kilgore and Peaches were watching the men, or Enolah, wondering if she was a man. Hoping she was.

"You see her! You *see* her! It's her!"

"I'll be damned," Kilgore said. "It's her."

"Who?" asked the golden epicene who had been interrupted, but the art dealers hurried away without answering, swooping like vultures down upon the wide-eyed girl.

"Bogeys at three o' clock," Crowe said, warning Rabbit, and turned to greet them with a false but convincing smile. Rabbit saw, and repressed a shudder. The art dealers met them with vigorous hugs and kissy-kissies in the air, but they really only had eyes for Megan. The formalities of greeting the guests they already knew were finished with a perfunctory swiftness, and now they peered down at the startled girl, grinning in a way that alarmed and frightened her.

Their appreciation went unexplained for a moment too long, and Megan found her voice.

"Um...yes?"

"It's you!"

She looked away, feeling the weight of their gaze like a dog would. Kilgore turned to Rabbit, clapping him on the shoulders.

"I can't believe it! *You!* Here! Of all the people who'd come to the Royal Nonesuch, I never ever *ever* thought I'd see *you!* And you brought the model herself! Since getting the new Cigouaves today, we've just been staring at it for hours! It's...it's just breathtaking! And here she is!" He turned back to Megan and knelt before her, seizing her hand to hold it between both of his. "Milady, you are, without a doubt, the sexiest woman I've ever seen. *We!* That *we* have ever seen! To have seen you in that pose, dear God! But you seem so shy now, so innocent, like a delicate porcelain doll. The juxtaposition, one so shy in such a pose—oh! Magnificent!"

Now all in that little group, and the group that the art dealers had just left, and several bystanders stared at Megan Delaune in baffled curiosity. Enolah especially, frowned in skepticism.

"So, you liked it, then?" Rabbit asked in feigned modesty, relishing the moment.

"Liked it? I adore it! We've even brought it here to display tonight with some others! You'll see. And we even found just the frame for it. It's *smashing!* Egg-and-dart turning into keel molding in an antique bronze finish. Come and see!"

He rose and pulled Megan after him, hurrying through the throngs of bizarrely-costumed partiers. The others followed, curious, Rabbit keeping his poker face but beaming inside underneath it.

Pushing through exotic and fetishistic drunks, dancers, and schmoozers, breathing in smoke and a myriad different perfumes, they finally came to a wall whereon hung seven works of art. Or rather, seven paintings, for six of them were each quintessential of different major art movements inflicted upon the art world throughout that century. Inflicted by mountebanks making a pretense of being artists and abetted by charlatans making a pretense of being art critics, all playing at a charade claiming that paint splashed on canvases with no regard for color or form signified some kind of elusive talent.

Dada was represented, as were DeStijl, Cubism, Abstract, Fauvism, and Pop. Had those six been alone on the wall, art-fags would have been arguing the relative merits of each, trying to one-up each other in their praise of the Emperor's New Clothes.

If it hadn't been for the seventh painting.

Every nouveau Beau Brummell and art-fag that stood viewing the display was gathered before "Orgè D'Une" by Jubal Cigouaves, the Haitian Sensation. Openly astounded. And it was before them all that Vincent Kilgore opened the velvet rope and pulled Megan, situating her beneath it for all to gawk at.

From where she stood, Enolah couldn't hear all of the praise that Kilgore was heaping upon her and the portrait, but she had a clear enough view to note the likeness, and see this timid little girl in the same light the artist had. She watched poor Megan's face flame scarlet, and smiled, then pulled at her lower lip for a while, deep in thought.

Crowe was watching Rabbit watch Megan and the people, and he saw how pleased the little man was. The Aborigine tapped him on the shoulder, gestured for him to follow with a tilt of his head. Rabbit went, his pleasure vanishing.

As they fought their way to wherever Crowe was leading them, Rabbit noticed many people he'd seen around Florida, either in the newspapers at society functions or on the street or at parties he'd attended. People he never would have thought might be a part of this ghastly scene. People he never would have guessed. Yet here they were, cavorting in debauchery with each other, drinking blood, torturing people on gibbets and wheels, fuck-suck-and-cornholing each other in plain view of God and everybody under the party lights.

"You're the artist, aren't you?" Crowe asked.

Rabbit started to protest, but the man waved a dismissive hand. "You've got your hand in a bunch of different things. I'm impressed, really. And I think I'd like to impress you back."

They stopped an epicene who was carrying a tray of non-blood drinks, and bought two shots of tequila. Rabbit didn't see where the money disappeared to, and didn't want to think about it. He and Jim Crowe toasted, the huge man saying "To evil," and drank.

Rabbit had to swallow a couple of times, his throat sliding up the way it always did whenever he drank tequila, and fought to keep it down. While he did, continuing to follow Jim Crowe and watching all of the people around him, seeing many in drag, he thought of the male prostitutes at El Zodiaco and the wiggers on the street the other night, and it occurred to him that when people pretend to be what they are not, like men pretending to be women, or white kids pretending to be black, they always overdo it to the degree where it becomes ridiculous. Look at a wigger standing alone in a club full of black guys, and he's the only one wearing a clock around his neck. Then it made him think about himself for a second, but he didn't like the way it made him feel, so he tried to forget it.

Finally, the Aborigine came to a stop and stepped aside with a wide sweep of his hand. Rabbit's eyes bulged. Before them was what must have been an extremely large wading pool, or something similar, with dozens—perhaps scores—of writhing naked bodies smeared with oil, squirming together with their skin glistening in the play of colored lights. Their groans and squelching could be heard over the music.

The pool was ringed with spectators, some helping shiny naked people out of the pool, some stripping down and rubbing themselves with glycerine from small poolside bottles, preparing to slip in and wriggle amongst perfect strangers.

Among all of the arms and legs and hands and feet Rabbit could see breasts, real ones, and dark triangles here and there were flashing into sight, and stiff…and many hands were stroking and pawing whoever was mashed up against who, all of them anonymous, none of them knowing or caring whose cock they guided into themselves or whom they allowed themselves to be guided into. The lubricant in which they squelched must have been edible because mouths were opening and clamping down on whatever passed by, sucking or gnawing on each other in what must have been communism in its ultimate degree.

"Humanity," Crowe said. "Quite literally, one big clusterfuck." Rabbit was speechless. "Every one of those people you see, every one of these around us, you've seen them all before. In the supermarket. On the street. They handle your money at the bank, they prepare the food you eat, they sit next to you at church…if you go. They move among us like werewolves, appearing perfectly normal until you catch them in the right place, at the right time. These are not necessarily homosexuals, and a great many homosexuals have no idea about this. What these are, these *things*, are perverted sick fucks, and they are everywhere."

"Why you showing me?" Rabbit whispered, barely audible.

"Because you *have to know* why some things happen. Why you have bad luck in some things. Why you get denied certain things while others are granted them. It's because these people stick together, they take care of their own, and if you offend one, you are blacklisted by all, and your life is made difficult in every way that they can manage…which is no small amount. Some of these people are police officers. Some manage restaurants and exclusive clubs. Some are government officials. And some are behind your luggage being lost at the airport, your credit rating slashed, your food contaminated. Your sudden losing streak is not plain ol' bad karma. It has nothing to do with luck."

"You son of a bitch."

"Pardon?"

"You're trying to make me paranoid. And it's working! I'll be wondering every time I look at even friends, or anyone! I'll never trust anyone again!"

"This isn't to drive you mad. This is a gift."

Rabbit glared at the giant man. "You think I *want* to know shit like this?"

"*Ha!* No, no. But you are a fool to not be beloved by those who can hurt you. It's not the same as being on the same side. Trust me, I hate these degenerates almost as much as I hate some of the other people I'm connected with. You see, I have my fingers dipped in many pies, all of them mutually exclusive. I have been brought into this enclave, that huddle, such-and-such cabal—"

"By whom?"

"None of your business."

"Then, why?"

"To contaminate. To use their networks ultimately against one another, and bring this whole diseased shithouse down in flames!"

"Are you serious?" Rabbit whispered.

"No, I've been deliberately wasting your time. Yes, I'm serious! Just like when the AIDS virus was released in Chicago almost twenty years ago, I have been released to do what it cannot. So many people have AIDS now, but still, nobody cares. No one has changed their ways out of fear for it. So I've been at work. I'm not Plan B. I'm more like Plan R. And every other plan is working in tandem, just like these people do. That's how my friends' friends have found out about you, and people like you."

Rabbit was taken by surprise, something he would have doubted possible after all the things he'd already heard. More surprises seemed unlikely. Now this.

"Yes, Nick. I know all about you."

Whew! He didn't know *all* about him. Not if he called him Nick.

"The internet is becoming a powerful tool. You can't fly all around Europe anymore at the same time your targets are being hit without attracting *some*body's attention. You've been in all the right places at all the right times. It was just a matter of time before someone put two and two."

"You saying Interpol's onto me? But how? I've taken every precaution! I've—"

"It's not Interpol I'm talking about."

"Then, who?"

"None of your business."

"Aw, fuck you."

"It's not important right now. You want me to tip my entire hand before we're even in bed together. Haven't you seen enough already to know that mine is the side to be on? Think about it, Nick. How do you fight an enemy you cannot see? It's not like they're organized. There isn't a list somewhere we can pinch and then systematically execute everyone on it. You cannot tell a single one of these people from another in a crowd. You have to become part of whatever they're a part of.

"You come to their parties, you schmooze, you meet people, maybe you form alliances. I know for a fact that one of these here is a pediatrician in Palm Beach, with a wife and two kids who are completely oblivious. Who could ever know something like that? I can't wait to know which one he is, because he has the opportunity every work day to really screw up some poor little child. And trust me Nick, you can't unfuck a child. I'm going to stop him before he does.

"But trying to get someone to reveal his deep, dark secrets, or even allude to them, even in an environment such as this, is a delicate art. How can you do something like that without arousing suspicion? Well, we think we've come up with the answer.

"I am a pastor of a church that condones this kind of thing, and many other things just as bad, or worse. Why? Because that way, we attract sickos looking for acceptance and company. We, and I mean myself and others like me, other pastors of similar churches all over the US, have managed to uncover this hideous underworld subculture. If we had not, it would continue to exist under our very noses, but because we have, we know about it. Before too long, we will be a part of it, and learn exactly how far-reaching it is, and then, like exterminators stamping out an infestation of cockroaches we will wipe the world clean of them.

"And this is where I—" he broke off, because a naked man had appeared at his side, his pallid skin glistening and his toupee askew.

"Jim? James? I thought that was you!"

For only an instant, Rabbit could see that Crowe was drawing a complete blank, so the forced flicker of recognition in his eyes and the smile that followed seemed so painfully obvious and patronizing that he almost winced, knowing that he could have done it a thousand times better.

The Aborigine made a comment about not recognizing the man at first because he normally was not such a snappy dresser.

Ha ha ha. Hey, do you know Nick here? Why no, I haven't had the pleasure.

"Well, look, whyn't you get acquainted while I find the little boys' room? Back in a jiffy."

"Jimbo, shouldn't you be looking for the *big* boys' room?" the naked man asked.

Ha ha ha. Crowe excused himself and made his escape, leaving Rabbit standing there with a naked man waiting on a handshake. Over the guy's greasy shoulder writhed a hundred-armed monster in a flesh pit, and pressing them from all sides was a tide of rococo nightmare shapes that leered and cackled with delight. Rabbit fought back the rising fear that welled up into his throat, put on his best smile, and leaned forward, grasping the man's hand in both of his.

"I didn't catch your name?"

"I can't believe I let you talk me into this," the small man said, wrinkling his nose and stroking his milkstain mustache that looked more like tennis ball fuzz than facial hair.

"I can't believe I bothered," snapped the other man. "After that fiasco of a party you tried to throw! I haven't seen Gwynn since!"

"Let's not talk about it."

"You're right, let's not. There'll probably be crack in here anyway, so it's no biggie. Hey, what's that crowd over there by the paintings? Might be worth investigating."

"Later. I want to see this fleshpit you keep telling me about. Doesn't seem too likely."

"It's around here somewhere. First, let's see what they're all gaga over."

The larger man pulled his nervous and reluctant friend along. They came to the art display, trying vainly to see past all of the gathered admirers, moving this way and that, but always having their views blocked. Pushing their way to one side, they came to the red velvet ropes and saw two young women on the other side, one gorgeous, and the other showing definite potential. Like one of those A-list actresses who goes off a diet before shooting begins, who puts on some glasses and doesn't wash her hair for a few days so she can play the ugly duckling, at least until the makeover, and she comes out a beautiful swan.

"I could layer it," the vixen was saying, toying with the other's hair. "Give it more body without you having to use chemicals, or…"

Megan was looking at the two men looking at her, and Enolah followed her gaze. The taller of the two men was looking at Megan skeptically, the smaller man looking with interest, the both of them laughable in their steampunk Beau Brummell outfits with the powdered wigs and buckled shoes. She might not have cared, but for the way Braswell was looking at her, the expression of "Ha! No, not happening. It's a waste of time trying to make that one over."

Megan read that in Braswell's sneer, and her eyes grew cold and grey as slate, her mouth tightening into a cruel slit.

Jim Crowe's towering figure appeared behind the two men, and sensing his presence, they looked up and shrank into themselves, cowering. He read Megan's expression and went along with it, glowering at these two men he'd never seen before.

"Enjoying yourself, Professor Braswell?" Megan asked. Edmund (call me Eddie) shot her a startled look. She was smiling, the wheels in her head audibly turning. "And I'll be damned, Professor Monga. I swear, you stand in one place long enough, the whole world'll pass you by."

Both professors were baffled, frantically trying to remember where they might have seen her before.

"Mr. Braswell—or should I call you Ed? How's your little friend Gwynnevere doing these days? The romance going well?" She relished the look of panic on their faces. She remembered something Blue Tick had told her while they were talking earlier. "I tell ya, that crack she makes sure packs a wallop, doesn't it? Which reminds me. You're of fairly high standing with the Board of Trustees, aren't you? Y'ever heard of something called an honorarium?"

"Uh…(ahem) In passing, yes. Why—"

"I've been meaning to talk to you about a few things," she said, bluffing, and succeeding.

"What's an honorarium?" Lloyd Monga asked.

Megan put on a very solemn face. "It is a nicer way of saying 'blackmail.'"

XXV

"So, you see now?"

"See what?"

"Why you shouldn't kill Vlad Bilowas."

"Uhhh…no."

Jim Crowe took on a patient tone. "Because with him, you could become part of this trading of women. Make friends with your enemies, and become one of them, and you'll know far more than just one screaming man strapped to a chair can ever tell you."

They stood outside, watching the Guavaween parade on Seventh Avenue in Ybor City. It was much like Mardi Gras, with the krewes of the parade floats throwing shit to the screaming, tumultuous crowd. It was the Saturday before Halloween. Everyone was already wearing masks, after the Carnivale fashion, but not because of any tradition.

Security cameras were mounted all over Ybor, surveilling the crowd, and at the other ends of their wires were policemen trying to pick out faces they recognized; nothing attracted fugitives and criminals quite like a good party. Surely, someone they had been looking for would show up and finally get apprehended. Because of this, street vendors at their little kiosks sold a wide variety of masks so that evil people could still come and spend their money without being seen and snatched out of the crowd by goon squads, and innocent civilians wouldn't see it and have it dampen their mood.

Crowe wore a Zulu shield over his face with eye holes cut into it, and Rabbit had chosen a Phantom of the Opera mask and a black Humphrey Bogart fedora that Professor Lloyd Monga had been happy to let him borrow.

Fireworks blossomed above them, brilliantly colored sprays that left orchids of purple smoke staining the sky. Rabbit watched a flurry of orange snakes sizzle upwards, intertwining like a quadruple helix, and looked back down to Earth at all the revelers. Revel without a cause, he thought to himself.

Since the blackout had only affected the range of that substation, and had only lasted until the next day, the public's interest in it fizzled out rather quickly.

Ditto with the explosion. Sure, people had died, but the only people who cared were the relatives of the bereaved because 1) hey, when you're rioting, shit happens, and 2) this was Florida in the 90s. Fast food news for microwave minds. Neve's unidentified body was the hot topic for a whole two days.

A five-petal lily of shimmering red light bloomed, and each of those petals burst also. Rabbit looked up again as a thread of light streaked through the purple tendrils, scattering snowflakes of glitter, and the rocket exploded into a dazzling spray of green and yellow and white. Fireworks made by child slaves in Chinese sweatshops. But no matter who he told, and no matter how loudly Rabbit told them, nobody would give a shit.

It was hard enough to get people's attention these days, let alone keep it.

Speaking of which, he wasn't getting it through Gwynn's thick skull (very thick, he'd discovered) what he was trying to tell her, that all her beauty—her fake hair and her skin and her beautiful face and her knockout body—was as fleeting as glory. Like one of these firecrackers. A bright flash and a lot of noise, then nothing.

Then a string of amber beads flung by a man on a float struck him on the plastic Phantom of the Opera side of his face, and he had an idea.

XXVI

Christmas had come and gone for Vlad Bilowas like any other day: in the company of a whore. He'd spent it with a beautiful American girl in the States, a gift from his friend Nick Coniglio. The girl had two-toned hair, a dyed blonde that had grown out dark brown, but that was okay because she was heart-breakingly gorgeous. She didn't really get into it, though, so it wasn't all that special. Just did her duty as many times as he wanted that whole day, and it was free of charge, except what he'd paid to fly over.

He and that crazy bastard he had hunted down and tried his damnedest to kill had become fairly close, after, of course, Coniglio had let him go. The time they spent together with that Smithsonian Institute Collector's Edition Torture Kit had been unpleasant to say the least, that time they euphemistically termed his "re-education" after the manner of the Chinese Communist Party. And it had worked, the name they gave it, because it made him somehow feel better about being tortured and brainwashed, It was all for his own good, anyway, and it certainly beat the hell out of being killed at the end of it.

They kept referring to something that they called Stockholm Syndrome, and were both happy when it seemed to have taken place. Now they were all bosom buddies, and he had played host to them when they came to visit Europe and tour it with him for a month, back in November. Coniglio and that big black man, the one they called Jubal Sig-wav, or something like that, had charmed the socks off of everyone Bilowas had introduced them to, and by the time they had returned to Florida to set up their reception facility for the smuggling of hot Ukrainian girls, they had made quite a few contacts that Vladimir had never even heard of.

Well, of course he'd never really been that popular —not like his good buddy Nick. Now, that guy was like a freaking *Jedi*, and Vlad's admiration for him was outshined by what a pal Nick had been to him. He even had a special little song that he'd sing whenever he saw him. Nick would smile that great big smile and croon "Mah mama done tole meeee!" and everyone would laugh.

No idea why, but if Nick thought it was funny, it couldn't be that bad.

And that girl that he had provided for yesterday's Christmas cheer, boy oh boy, she was something else. Now sitting in his hotel room at the Heather-Leigh, paid for by Coniglio, Bilowas could still smell her fragrance, even though he had been with her far from here, in a small house in the woods outside of Tampa, where even if she could escape, there was nowhere to go. Her scent was in his head, clouding his brain.

She had acted funny, though. A bit odd. Nick had warned him about that, saying that a few weeks ago—once she'd finally realized her begging and pleading and Milady Felton-esque feminine wiles weren't getting her anywhere—she'd told her captors about a storage facility with a strange brew she'd concocted inside it, offering it to them if they'd let her go. They had gone and gotten the stuff, not letting her go, of course (a laughable idea) and forced her to take some of it to make sure it wasn't poison.

They had squeezed it out of a medicine dropper over her mouth, but she managed to jerk her face away and it got on her cheek, and dribbled down the curve of her jaw to her chin. They squirted the rest of the juice in the dropper on her face and gave up.

The stuff soaked into her skin and she hadn't been right since. So, she didn't really get into the spirit of Christmas with Vlad, but it wasn't that bad. She was still appropriately submissive.

Abruptly, Vladimir sat up, frowning. Hurrying to the bathroom with his hands scrabbling at his pants, he felt it coming like diarrhea only towards the front instead of the back. He managed to get himself out of his fly in time to point in the general direction of the toilet, and cried out as he pissed what felt like barbed wire, a length of it that seemed to go on forever.

His eyes scrunched shut, squeezing out tears, and through the searing pain he heard the echo of Nick's voice reminding him of something he'd been told during his "re-education," that all glory is fleeting.

Rabbit still hadn't decided what to do with Gwynn.

He had had this idea of asking God to make up his mind for him. He would strike a deal. If Megan was interested in patching things up, he would settle down, buy that Big Beats place—since he imagined poor Mr. Coleman would want to retire—and convert it into Immortelles, the fine art and antiques shop. If she said no, God help the world, and Gwynn in particular.

The way he saw it, if Gwynn and her gang of two-bit hoods hadn't burglarized his house and killed his (at the time) true love, he would not have set upon this path of vengeance and murdered so many people unrelated to his vendetta along the way. Therefore, all of those deaths were on her head. She had to answer for them. But if it was in the cards for him to live a quiet life with this girl, he would cut Gwynn loose, let her go with a warning, and keep a close eye on her to make sure she never tried to come back an' git him like in the movies.

Well, after letting Megan blackmail those two college professors for a recommendation, and paying a large honorarium to the school so that she could have her dream come true, and fixing her up with a brand new identity so she could have the name she always wanted, and repairing all of the damage to her apartment, she couldn't possibly have any hard feelings.

This was the icing on the cake, though, the societal debut that would put her picture in all of the papers.

He stood in the audience at Kilgore n' Friends disguised as Chris Hammond, with his scruffy black goatee and his longish hair, his John Lennon sunglasses, his Che Guevara shirt and blue jeans torn at the knees a la The Ramones. The place was packed. The city had been buzzing for a month about the big unveiling, and the newspapers had saturated the people with Jubal Cigouaves' dramatic fight and triumph over AIDS and the Immigration people down at Krome.

Some of the people at the Royal Nonesuch had thought it delightful that Jubal Cigouaves wasn't real, wasn't a Haitian refugee, and wasn't really making fools of them with his underground art phenomenon. So delightful, in fact, that they were more than happy to pretend to grant him amnesty, especially since their friend Jim Crowe was going to pose as the artist at the inauguration of his groundbreaking show "Beyond the Pale." It showed their generosity and their appreciation for the arts and cost them nothing, and gave them something to laugh about together in secret as they crowded together in the gallery, smiling and glad-handing and raising their champagne flutes in toast to the flashing cameras of the paparazzi.

It was one of the few art show openings Rabbit had been to where the guests actually looked at the paintings, and that pleased him no end. Their oohing and ahhing made him wish he were dressed as himself and basking in his rightful place up there instead of Crowe, but he knew that he had doomed himself to a life outside of the spotlight because of the lifestyle he had chosen. He consoled himself with the knowledge that, as a chameleon hiding in the crowd, he had the greater pleasure of hearing people praise him amongst themselves instead of to his face, and that counted for so much more.

The ting-ting-tinging of a spoon against a champagne flute made all heads turn to the dais at the far end of the gallery, and the podium where Peaches Gilbert stood, immaculate in his pinstriped aubergine suit with French-elephant ivory shirt.

"*He-ey!* Hey everybody! Gather round now."

There was a sprinkling of murmurs around Rabbit, some saying Oh, look, it's Peaches! and some Oy vey, that guy gives me the creeps, with others shushing and admonishing. Rabbit was happy to hear sincere viewpoints spoken quietly, but because of them he couldn't hear everything Peaches was saying.

The house lights dimmed and a spotlight came on, bathing Peaches in white light that made him shine.

"Welcome all of you to this *very* special event! As you all know, Vincey and I have been honored for almost nine years to represent some of the best artists—" Part of what he said was garbled here, but Rabbit knew it was a bunch of fluff, so it didn't matter. He went Blah blah blippity blah for another two minutes, and then Rabbit's ears perked up.

"—A most remarkable young woman. She'll be challenging the minds of the students at our University this year with her revolutionary class History in Context. Please give a warm welcome to the beautiful Professor Ashley McLachlen!"

The people applauded as a very attractive young woman—too young to be a professor, but who knows?—stepped away from her little clique with her glass of red and came toward the dais, beaming. Peaches was clapping with his bony hands cupped so they made more noise, and the rings and bracelets he wore sparkled in the light as he backed up to give her room at the podium. She stepped up onto the soapbox they had stashed behind it so she could be seen, and people remarked on how adorable she was, being so petite and all.

Her auburn hair was shoulder-length and had been square-layered by a stylist who knew what she was doing. There was a passing resemblance to the model in that much-talked-about new painting by the featured artist, but not really enough to remark upon. She wore a stunning sauvignon-blanc Marchesa Grecian Goddess chiffon halter gown with chanterelle accents and next season's Manolo Blahniks, all of which had been duly noted by the reporters on the scene.

Enolah, who had toned down her own beauty to keep herself from stealing Professor McLachlen's thunder, stood off to one side listening to the peoples' comments, and was pleased. She had spent a lot of time with Megan on Worth Avenue in Palm Beach and at her salon in Coquina, coming up with the debut ensemble and hairstyle, and was now being paid back in praise the same way Rabbit was. Her protégé was a success.

"Thank you all very much, you're far too kind," Professor McLachlen said. She didn't appear nervous, but Rabbit could tell she was putting on a brave face. "Ladies and gentlemen, it is a pleasure and indeed, an honor to introduce the artist who has been a source of inspiration to us all. He left the abject poverty of his homeland on a flimsy raft made from trees he cut down with a machete, and some rope from a decorative life preserver he stole from the side of a yacht, and he braved the treacherous waters of the Caribbean with nothing but faith to guide him.

"When he landed in Miami, all odds were against him. He was unwashed, unfed, and unknown, but hope gave him courage. He got odd jobs to build up enough capital to invest in art supplies, and he gained fame painting portraits on the sidewalk in Coconut Grove. Because of his Undocumented Transient status, he had to keep himself under the radar, but in the underground of the art world, news travels fast. Kept in hiding to avoid deportation, he worked hard, and now his paintings hang in private collections in France, Japan, Lichtenstein, and all over the United States. He has become a beacon of hope for People of Color and Guest Immigrants, and an icon of the American Dream. This inauguration marks not just the newest series of paintings by an incredible artist, but his first public appearance, and the celebration of one man's triumph against both Nature and law to leave his humble origin and realize his dream of becoming an American citizen!"

The crowd hooted and clapped its approval, and Professor McLachlen had to wait politely for a moment. Her smile was radiant, basking in what she knew was going to be the first of many such moments to come, that performer's eon, when she would be looked upon and listened to by many and applauded.

"Ladies and gentlemen, it is with great pleasure that I give you…from Beyond the Pale…Jubal Cigouaves!"

The spotlight swept from her to Jim Crowe, towering over his entourage and looking to the crowd like the strongest and healthiest specimen ever to be dying of AIDS. He feigned a bashful smile and a little wave, and the thunder of the peoples' applause was deafening. He went to the podium, bent a little to kiss Megan on the cheek, and offered his hand to help her step down off of her soapbox.

They had been completely unprepared for the wild cheers of the crowd, expecting at most a polite moment of clapping, but in that moment Crowe represented the satisfaction of the guests' dearest wish: the triumph of the faithful against terrible odds, and that triumph happening in their presence on a gala night made them feel somehow part of it.

Megan left the spotlight feeling exhilarated, but also a bit relieved to have survived her first fifteen minutes of fame.

When the house lights came back on and the party resumed there'd be time enough to enjoy the peoples' attention, but right now she needed a moment of peace to rally herself.

Even though she felt a hundred pairs of eyes on her at that moment, she felt the pressure of one in particular, and turned to look at the crowd. There she saw him, the one face that did not turn to watch Cigouaves, looking at her with adoration. At first she didn't recognize him, with the longish black hair and the shabby outfit, but then it hit her.

There he was.

Somebody different every time, but always there.

And he was behind every change in her life, not her. Every new exciting step she took was on a road paved by him. And behind every pair of sunglasses for the rest of her life, his eyes would be watching her. She swallowed, and turned back to the guest of honor, clapping with her hands cupped like Peaches had and shouting "Woooooo!"

Behind the podium, Jim Crowe smiled down on the crowd and politely waited for them to settle down.

The next day, Rabbit went to her with a hundred thousand things to say in his head. Today would be the day that decided everything. Would he hang up his gloves and settle down, or take his revenge on the world? Would he let Gwynn go or torture her to death? Good or Evil? Back up, or dive off?

She couldn't possibly *not* take him back, he thought, not after last night.

He knocked on the door of her new place, watched her shadow darken the space underneath it, watched the tiny pin-point of light in the peephole get blotted out, and waited.

He waited what felt like eons, watching the peephole and then closing his eyes, willing the door to open. He saw that dancing glitter in the darkness and swayed on his feet, opened his eyes again, looking at that peephole, beseeching. Another long moment, and just as his heart began to break, the light reappeared in the peephole, her head moving away from it, and he heard the clicks of the locks coming undone. He came back to life, his back straightening, his spirits lifting. The door opened and bathed him in light from the windows inside.

She looked more beautiful than he'd ever seen her, more beautiful than that first night at the Heather's. Her hair was its natural color, and she'd gotten some more stylish glasses. She was dressing better, like a girl, for a change, and what's more, like an A-lister. Enolah had been coaching her well.

The look in her eyes froze him, though, and every possible thing he could have said to her evaporated into nothing. She folded her arms across her chest, leaned her shoulder against the door jamb, and raised her eyebrows at him.

He couldn't make his mouth work.

Come on, God, he thought.

Make it happen.

But he couldn't speak. Megan nodded, cleared her throat, and stood up straight.

"Word of advice. Next time you're about to shoot someone, just go ahead and shoot him. Don't let him piss you off into making a mistake, 'cause he might have a grenade to stuff in your pants."

He stared at her. She nodded again, looked down, backed up and closed the door.

XXVII

"So, moment of truth," Blue Tick said.

He and Rabbit stood in front of Gwynn in the small house out in the woods. Outside, the leaves of trees rattled against the house, and the ticking of the second hand on Rabbit's watch was very loud. There were no spectators this time, just the three of them. Wind howled in the forest. Minutes passed.

The Smithsonian Institute Collector's Edition Torture Kit was open on the table next to Gwynn, its instruments looking so elegant with their mahogany handles in their sunken niches of blue felt. She watched it from her dentist's chair.

A bird started twittering outside somewhere, and the great big hole inside Rabbit yawned even wider. His face twisted horribly and his hands grew into claws that ached to reach and tear out Gwynn's throat. A growl of frustration started in the back of his throat and rose until he lurched forward and doubled over, grasping both arms of the chair and screaming into Gwynn's face.

She was white with terror. It had been many months since she had been captured, and she was still tripping from the acid that had soaked into her skin. Her captors had felt that was torture enough for the time being—well, that and loaning her as a sex slave to Bilowas for Christmas—since it had been her intention to doom no small amount of people to the same fate for the rest of their lives. But now it was time to end it and move on. And Rabbit couldn't do it.

Tick frowned. This wasn't like Rabbit at all. He'd become despondent over the whole Megan thing, and this should have been his outlet, but he was just screaming, and now collapsing and sliding slowly down the dentist's chair, his knees touching the floor, now pounding on Gwynn with his fist, but weakly, like a crying man pounding on a door that won't open.

His scream had died back down to a growl, and suddenly Tick knew. He had seen a movie ten years before where a guy had spent his entire life training to be the best swordsman in the world, so he could get revenge on the man who'd killed his father. Then in the end, after he had killed the guy, he didn't know what to do with the rest of his life. Granted, he didn't act like *this*, but, of course he wouldn't. It was a comedy.

Tick nodded to himself, went over to the small table with the torture kit, wedged a finger into a niche to pop out the one that looked like a straight razor, and leaned over Gwynn with it. She started to scream, but he shushed her irritably. Cut the straps that held her to the chair and stood back to let her get up. She looked at him with wide eyes. He sighed. Gestured with a jerk of his head toward the door.

Gasping with relief, she shook off the straps and jumped off of the chair, careful not to touch Rabbit, and ran for the door, struggling to contain sobs of desperate laughter. Outside the house, the woods rang with her joy as she ran, stumbling and crashing through the branches of trees and bushes.

Tick put his hand on Rabbit's shoulder, gently shook him.

"She got away, boss. C'mon, let's go catch her."

Gwynn burst from the forest's embrace and collapsed onto the grass by the side of the highway. Scrambling to get up, she squinted at the glare of the sun's reflection on the pavement, staggered out onto the road and looked both ways. A car was coming. Still a long ways off, but coming. She'd heard the noise of something big crashing through the woods behind her, and that car wasn't coming fast enough.

She limped out into the middle of the road with her hands up high above her head, waving.

"Please," she whispered.

She was starving, having been kept alive with IVs for the past several months because she couldn't eat. LSD is like that. She stood there, wild-eyed and haggard, with a mop of brown hair and not much clothing, frantically waving her arms like a castaway with a plane passing by.

The crashing in the woods had stopped, and she could feel eyes on her from the darkness behind the swaying leaves.

"Please."

The approaching car slowed. She started clawing her fingers through her hair, trying to dig out all the twigs and leaves and make herself look presentable. She knew she stank, but it might not matter. She smacked her chapped lips and dreamed for a moment that they might have water in that car. Ahhh, a nice cool Coke, maybe.

The car pulled up alongside her. It had three people in it, and she couldn't understand why, but she was suddenly even more afraid. The driver had long brown hair, and the woman riding shotgun looked almost like an albino with a goofy hair-do. The guy in the back was shaven-headed with a chin beard, and they all were dressed like they were on their way to act in a Shakespeare play or something.

"Omigod, look at you! Are you okay?" the driver asked.

"Where's your car? Did you crash or...?" the albino woman started to ask, but stopped. Stared at her with big blue eyes. Blood red lips that split into a wide grin.

It took Gwynn a moment, but she recognized them.

The road fell out from under her. She fell and skinned her elbows on the pavement, scooted back from the car frantically and whimpered in fear when she saw the driver's door open. A foot with an embroidered slipper stepped out. She shut her eyes and rolled over, scrambling to get to her feet, but she was just too weak.

"Do you know who that is?" she heard Mistress Charlotte chirp from inside the car. The other door clicked open.

Gwynn stopped trying to get up, just stared at the swaying leaves of the forest.

"Remember from a couple months ago?"

There was something evil in that forest that she had only just escaped, and now she was going to charge right back into its jaws. This was her one chance to get away from it, but...

"Son. Of. A bitch," Lord Dave said. "I can't believe it."

"Whatcha doing all the way out here, Gwynnie?" Mistress Charlotte asked, mocking.

Rabbit and Blue Tick watched from the cover of the brush as the three strange people stood around the cowering girl and taunted her. One of them kept looking both ways down the lonely road to make sure no one was coming, and the others seemed to be calling each other Doctor, diagnosing the poor patient and discussing what to do with her.

"Oh, how the mighty have fallen," one laughed.

"We've been trying to get into that li'l storage unit you got there," the woman said. "Get some of that stuff you owe us. I think you ought to give us the key, li'l lady."

"Whatcha say?" the long-haired man said, and kicked her in the ribs. Gwynn cried out. He put one finger behind his ear to bend it forward. "Hmmm?"

Rabbit glanced at Blue Tick, and when the big man saw the look in his eye, he shook his head and chuckled quietly.

"Oh, Christ."

Rabbit handed over his gun and reached into his shirt-cuff where the Velcro-strapped sheaths were, slipped out his three little throwing knives that he'd never gotten to kill anyone with, yet. Toed his mark like a runner. Blue Tick stepped back to give the knight in shining armor some room, and watched him charge out of the forest to save the damsel in distress.

XXVIII

Professor Ashley McLachlen tried her hardest not to strut down the sidewalk toward campus, feeling a mixture of giddy pride and butterflies at the prospect of her first day of teaching. She was well-dressed, her knee-length burgundy dress and long auburn hair contrasting with the sapphire amulet at her throat that set off her deep blue eyes.

With one long-nailed hand, she smoked a cigarette the way her friend and mentor had shown her a lady should. Heels clicking on the concrete, she turned more than a few heads as she sauntered past the store windows she used to gaze longingly into.

Married men stared appreciatively at her bottom moving under the fabric of her burgundy skirt, at her legs, wondering if she was new around here.

Behind her eyes whirled her opening statement to her first body of students, beginning with a quote from a sixty-some-odd-year-old book called *Generation of Vipers*. "Since most colleges teach nothing, not even the first steps on how to think or the rudimentary facts on how to acquire information, the flat hat on the pate of the American graduate is a hallmark of philosophical treason—and there are enough of them to shingle hell."

She listened to the words in her mind, looking forward to how they'd sound when she finally got to speak them from behind her podium. Looking forward to dashing the fallacies in her students' thinking to smithereens and rebuilding their minds with realism.

She came to the intersection, swerving onto the crosswalk just as traffic stopped for her, and clicked her heels across the pavement. Drivers were watching her. She could feel their eyes, the pressure of their gaze on her face and ass and legs, skipping over her small breasts, but that was okay. They were looking at what she *did* have, and it felt nice.

Stepping onto the grass that bordered campus, she noticed a man in the shade of a tree, just as he noticed her. It took a moment to recognize him. Phil! Her old boss, Philip Coleman, only now he'd grown a beard...or, maybe not so much grown a beard as just stopped shaving. The smile of recognition that started to part her lips was arrested, cut off short by the glare in his eyes. The words caught in her throat when it hit her—there was nothing she could say.

His face twisted into a knot and he spat at her, the glob falling short into the grass, but a few flecks of mist starring her calf. She skipped sideways, farther out of range, her throat closing tightly.

She almost stopped. Almost stood there and faced him, to say something, *anything*. But she swallowed hard, then stood up straight again, mustering some dignity, and walked on.

Q & A with Maurice Aimee

MA. First off, I'd like to thank you for this opportunity to—

AF. No, thank *you*. It's flattering that you want to do this. I feel kind of stupid sitting here, but...

MA. Really? Because we can forget this whole thing.

AF. No, no, go ahead.

MA. Well, then, without further ado.

AF. Yes, please.

MA. I'm leaving all this in.

AF. You would.

MA. Okay. Tell us about Icarus.

AF. The series or the Greek kid who didn't listen to his dad?

MA. The series. If no one knows about the kid they have Wikipedia.

AF. Good point. Okay, you know how the Heresy series had many different main characters who came and went, appearing and then leaving the spotlight in the different books? The first one had Rabbit make a cameo appearance toward the end, and in the second book he was the bad guy. In the third, he was the good guy. In the fourth, they made a brief mention of him, and in the last one he was a good guy/bad guy, depending on your perspective.

MA. Yes, I started out thinking the series was about Evan, who disappeared until the last book.

AF. Well, Icarus is a series about Rabbit's early years. What drove him to become who he is, how he met Crowe. This one, and the one after it, were originally Volumes IV and V of a seven-part series, but they made the story a bit unwieldy, so I decided to cut them and make a spinoff series. I am hoping to also have spinoff series...serieses? I forget the plural of series. Whatever. Series. Spinoff series/serieses about the Satanists, and what Maya does in Europe after the end of Heresy, and maybe it'll turn into something like a crime version of Dragonlance, where they have all these books about that world written by different authors.

MA. Have you written anything for the others?

AF. I started writing the first one about Maya, but I have a restaurant to run, and an exotic ice cream company, and I paint as
well, and I am 200-something pages into "Memoirs of a Swine"
so I just don't have the time.

MA. Are you really plugging your other businesses?

AF. No! I'm just telling you! I'm swamped!

MA. When do you have time to sleep, by the way?

AF. You see these bags under my eyes?

MA. Really? Is that what those are from?

AF. There's time enough for sleep in the grave.

MA. Okay. So, about Neve electrocuting herself and causing a
blackout. Seems a little far-fetched, no?

AF. Actually, no. I read that Anna Karenina was written because
Tolstoy was at a train station and saw a well-dressed woman kill
herself by jumping in front of a train. He wondered what could
possibly have happened to drive her to that, and it led to him
writing the book. I'm not comparing myself to Tolstoy, and I'm
not saying that the reason I wrote TNW was because of this
happening, but when I heard about it from a friend, I decided to
use it as a pivotal part in the story.

MA. So, that really happened?

AF. I have not been able to find anything online to verify the
story, but my friend Jeff Ramsey told me once, while I was in the
early stages of writing this, that in 1997 he was living in Tampa,
and one night he was up late wondering where his life was going
and almost didn't notice it, but the power went out. After a few
minutes, he heard voices outside, and he went out to see what
was happening. There was a huge blackout and a spontaneous
darkness party. He wasn't feeling that sociable, so he didn't talk
to his neighbors, and instead walked down to the substation
nearby (that's his description of it, the way it's written? That's the
way he described it. I liked that better than using an accurate
technical description.) The same thing happened. He found the
brown-skinned girl, she managed to croak out "Kill me" (or
maybe that was his embellishment) and instead of mercy-killing
the poor thing, he ran and called 911. Told me he visited her
every day in the hospital, where she slowly died from being
cooked. For the record, I did tell him he was an asshole for

keeping her alive, but he said he never would have thought of killing her. He's just not a killer.

MA. What, and you are?

AF. Don't know, really. Never been in that situation.

MA. Would you have killed her, though?

AF. I think so. No. I don't know. Christ, that's a hard question.

MA. Okay, moving on, what's the story with this new series? Is it all going to be about Rabbit?

AF. You'll have to read it. I ain't telling.

MA. Ass. Are you continuing with the same three-word-title-that's-a-fragment-of-an-old-saying motif?

AF. I am, and I gotta tell ya, it's going to get tough after this trilogy, because I'm running out of names. "Gas Food Lodging" has already been taken. "Honor Among Thieves" and "All That Glitters" have been done so many times that, if I'm lucky, I may get to be in an omnibus of most popular books called "Honor Among Thieves" or "All That Glitters" and unless I change the theme, eventually I'll have nothing left to use but "Lather, Rinse, Repeat."

MA. (lol) Dork. One more question. Why is he called Rabbit?

AF. Long story. Short version: a bunch of black dudes used to call me that. Never was sure why.

MA. Oh, I thought maybe it was an homage to Eminem.

AF. Who?

Look for the next novel in the
Icarus series

A Mind
Diseased

Now in Paperback

"Canst thou not minister to a mind diseas'd,
Pluck from the memory a rooted sorrow,
Raze out the written troubles of the brain,
And with some sweet oblivious antidote
Cleanse the stuff'd bosom of that perilous stuff
Which weighs upon the heart?"
—William Shakespeare
MacBeth

In time with the music—pounding bass and tweaky noises like the sound effects of a video game—the muscles of Sucker's jaw were bunching under the skin of his cheek. The other men in the car were more calm. One of them ran a comb through his gelled red hair, blinking away the smoke that curled up from a hand-rolled cigarette dangling in the corner of his mouth; the other was absently drawing a pair of boobs with his black-gloved finger on the fogged glass of the driver's side window. Beads of rain on the outside of that window waxed the neon lights into large, soft glows, making him think of Christmastime.

"There he is," Sucker said quietly, and the other two looked in the direction he pointed. A balding, middle-aged man with glasses was crossing the street coming toward them.

"You sure?" the red-haired one asked.

"I'd know him anywhere. Gimme a gun."

"For the last time, kid, let the *pros* handle this."

"I wanna gun, dammit!" Sucker whined.

"Aww, let him have a gun," the driver said.

"Jesus. I said no."

"He said no," the driver said, looking over his shoulder and shrugging.

The middle-aged man walked right past the car and turned into a doorway that opened on a narrow flight of stairs. For an instant they had a clear view of his face and could see a peeling sunburn, and when his back was to them the bald spot on the back of his head looked like a scarlet yarmulke.

"There he goes, just like you said," the red-haired one muttered, and opened his door. "You sure you want to do this?"

"In the worst way."

They got out of the car into the drizzling rain and went to the doorway, all three of them casually glancing up and down the street and managing to look very, very suspicious as they entered. The stairway was dark and smelled like wet books. A fluorescent light was flickering nervously at the top of the stairs, and the three of them stared apprehensively at it while the older two drew snub-nosed .38s from the pockets of their long raincoats.

Their shoes squeaked loudly as they climbed the stairs, the sound blowing any chance they had of sneaking up on their prey. Sucker focused on that sound, the chorus of squeaks, and knew he'd remember it for the rest of his life.

At the top of the stairs was a long brown-carpeted hall with doors every ten feet on either side. Their quarry was jingling keys between the two fourth doors down, and looked their way, his face stern. The yellow light strobed above them, and clicked. The driver and the red-haired man stepped apart to give each other room, leaving Sucker behind them in the middle.

"We got a bone to pick with you," the driver started to say, but suddenly the hand that wasn't holding keys was thrust toward them, and light spat from it with three deafening cracks. The two men were flung backwards, falling past Sucker on either side, and rolled in a tangle of limbs down the stairs. The teenager winced and put a hand to one ear while the man rushed up beside him, firing a few more shots down the staircase.

"Jesus Christ, that's loud!" Sucker cried.

"I can barely hear you. Got earplugs in," the middle-aged man answered.

Sucker looked up at him and smiled. "Thanks, Dad."

"Any time. Now, mind telling me what's going on?"

"It's a long story."

"Well, make it quick. I've got a plane to catch."

I

Alabama

Once upon a time, there was a kid named Jared, who was passed out on the floor of the two-storey luxury apartment he shared in College Park with these three other guys: Todd Ferguson, Chris Stiles, and Nathan Wolske, who were at that moment out shroom-picking in the Alabama countryside, and having a grand old time while Jared lay where he'd fallen the night before. Curled up fetally on the gray carpet, twitching. Sprawled across the two couches, with blankets and pillows dutifully placed by the absent trio, were Amber, Mitzy, Lisa, and Brooke, from the apartment around the way.

Fall Quarter, Sophomore year in the mid-90s. They were eight friends about as platonic as you can get, still amused by the joys of living away from home and only just now knowing what it was like to share apartments instead of dorms.

Cuz, dude. Dorms, like, suck.

Well, out of the guys, Stiles was the only one who really talked like that, but he was nowhere *near* as bad as Amber and Mitzy, the strawberry-blonde and brunette wine cooler alcoholics, respectively. Now, *Mitzy* was like, totally, *hello*, yunno? Out there. And, according to Amber, Mitzy was, like, *so* whatever. But whatever.

How they'd met back in Freshman year, the other two girls were sitting behind Jared in orientation for Stuart England History class, at the start of Rush Week, going on and on and on with three other girls about what they had worn last night and what they would wear every day while rushing sororities. He'd tried to ignore them, the other three dominating the conversation, until one of them announced that she had, like, the *ultimate* accessory. She'd kept this from when she was a little girl, and she actually took it out with her in public.

To be seen with it. By guys.

A clear plastic umbrella—nay, *parasol*—with an adorable pink lining around the edges and Mickey with a bouquet of roses behind his back as he leaned in with his eyes closed to kiss Minnie on the check, and little pink valentines in the air around their heads.

"It is *the* accessory," she said for the eighth time. "It goes with *any*thing!"

Jared finally turned around.

"Hey, Trish, or whatever your name is. That isn't an accessory, okay? An accessory is the guy I get to hold you down."

Three of them—Trish, Trish, and Trish, by the looks of them—stared at him in stunned silence, while Lisa and Brooke bust a gut laughing. Their howls disrupted the professor's train of thought, and three hundred eighty-something faces turned to stare at the brunette and the redhead.

"Ahem," Professor Lohmann said. The howling continued, accentuated now and then by the thumping of desks by fists and the stamping of feet. "Er, ladies?"

Jared started to laugh a little, too. Not at his own joke, because he hadn't meant it to be funny, but at how obvious it was now that Brooke and Lisa had been only politely listening to Trish, Trish, and Trish, the whole time wishing they'd shut the fuck up.

"Ladies?"

Covering their mouths, they managed to choke their mirth down into maniacal giggles.

"I didn't know my joke was that funny," Professor Lohmann said. His joke was, of course, *not* funny, but he still told it during the first day of every quarter to each new batch of kids. Er, young adults. He told it five times every first day, and it never got funny. Ever.

"Now, class," he'd say. "If you are wondering who Stuart England was, you probably shouldn't even be here."

Usually, the only laughter was from sycophants and people embarrassed for him. Not today, though. Brooke and Lisa's eyes were shining with tears, their faces red.

The other three stared at Jared with horrified expressions, as if he were some kind of bug. Then, rallying herself, Trish made her rebuttal.

"What*ever.*"

And Brooke started shrieking again, Lisa putting her face in her hands and quaking all over. Their bodies were wracked by horrible convulsions that had them ramming their backs again and again into their seats, their feet stomping urgently. Paroxysms, they would be called by pseudo-intellectual gossipers later. As soon as they'd regained some semblance of composure, they made apologetic gestures to the professor and assembled classmates, gathered their books, and excused themselves.

The students stared at Jared accusingly for doing what they had all been too chickenshit to do themselves, and under that kind of attention, Jared folded. Even though he left the classroom calmly and with much dignity, he still fled.

This was the dawn of his Freshman year, when he was still in his James Dean phase with the hair and the outfit. Stonewashed jeans with the cuffs rolled up, white t-shirt, black leather jacket, and the Hair. Took forever to get the hair just right, considering it was kinky and frizzy as hell until Brooke introduced him to relaxer creams (but that's another story).

He'd been a gawky, gangly nerd until he hit seventeen and the last year of high school. The years before had not been kind, and his newfound confidence had no solid foundation. So, he fled.

Brooke and Lisa were on their way outside, to the stairways and flying buttresses linking the buildings and overlooking the Concourse. He followed them out, asking them for a cigarette when they took out theirs as an excuse to linger, and the rest is History.

Now, a year later, his eyes were invariably bloodshot, and swollen from passing out with his contacts in. His hair, though chemically straightened, was unkempt even on the good days, and his face was pale. Not yet marbleized by gin blossoms, but on its way, and bearing a constant stubble. He'd grown skinny from forgetting to eat, and was more often than not crashing early on whenever his clique gathered to smoke weed and drink, the rest of them shaking their heads at his alarming excess.

He'd come back from summer break like this, and no amount of talking to him would snap him out of it. The others assumed it was over his parents dying shortly after he'd turned eighteen. Murder-suicide during Spring Break, kept quiet for the most part. None of them really wanted to be the one to bring it up.

So, they carried on like this, all the way to midterm. Jared just barely hanging on in his classes, at least getting credit for attendance.

Though it was Autumn, Friday was a sweltering day, and that night the clouds burst open. It rained from dusk to about two, and our heroes took it upon themselves to go forth into the fields. Shaking their heads one last time at their fallen comrade, they left Apartment 51.

His eyes already reddening from the drag of his contacts against his blepharitis-pocked eyelids during REM sleep, Jared dreamed.

Bursting from the glare of the blazing sun, he swooped down over the cloud-floor, the downy carpeting under the immaculately bright blue of a noon sky. He hadn't dreamed he was flying since he was a kid, and the best he'd ever done back then was to rise up over the recess yard and dive-bomb the other kids until he remembered flying was impossible, lost his grip, became heavy, and fell. This time, he had actual *wings*. White feathers bound Icarus-style to homemade frames that were holding up pretty well.

This was a thrill he'd never felt before, laughing wildly as he executed a perfect split-S and a barrel-roll, skimming the tops of clouds and scattering wisps of them up in his wake. Twisting sideways, he turned and plunged downward, the billowing floor rushing up and past him, becoming a ceiling.

It was like parachuting over a calm, flat ocean, then crashing through the surface to see a completely separate, incredibly chaotic world, with confusion and danger unimaginable from above, now all about him. And, of course, he delighted in it.

Swirling walls of white and purplish-gray fell away beneath him to immense depths, and he slalomed between columns on his way down, the vistas constantly shifting as if built of melting wax. Arcs of lightning flashed across his path, narrowly missing him.

A bank parted and he plummeted through it, coming up shocked.

There she was.

Her long black hair billowed behind her, somehow growing even longer as she barrel-rolled, cascades of curly black stretching out to two long body-lengths past her pointed toes. Her hair and brown skin stood out sharply against the pale gloom and her own white wings, which didn't seem as DIY as his own. The joy of flight shrank away into nothing compared to the rapture of seeing her again.

Her naked skin was sprinkled with moisture from the clouds, setting off a haze about her. That face, so exquisitely sculpted that no one who laid eyes on it could remain agnostic; those black eyes flashing somehow brighter than any light ever could.

He made to dive after her, but something stopped him. His view changed to outside of himself, zooming out to encompass the entire scene, and further, the clouds darkening to gray, to black, to something somehow even darker, then to suddenly emerge from the crease in between two sections of the nuchal underside of a ram's horn. Farther, to see that spiralling horn set into one side of a helmet. Farther, to reveal a masked face, the helmet a nightmarish amalgamation of Medieval, Sadomasochistic, and Bestial, the eyeholes two slanting almond-shaped slits of glowing green.

Something flickered in those eyes, the being's attention caught, directed to some disturbance on such a miniscule level that it was bone-chilling to imagine.

Whatever it was, whatever Jared found himself horrified to be a part of, had taken notice of him. The view zoomed in at ungodly speeds back to the tableau among the clouds, finding him and his long-lost lover now no more than insignificant germs. Those clouds were somehow no longer clouds, though they had not changed in appearance. They had become tissue. Flesh. And what came out of them were not white blood cells, not the soldiers of an immune system, but they served essentially the same purpose. Shapes born out of lunacy and horror fell upon the woman from all sides. She did not scream, but Jared did.

The things clung to her first by the dozens, then the scores, until her thrashing figure was fully engulfed, and then a gust of wind blew them all apart, leaving no shred of her behind.

Shrieking now, the white feathers molting Icarus-style off of his cheap wooden frames, the pain inside of him and the cold of a world without her taking form and clawing its way up out of his guts, Jared Layton lost his grip and fell.

Jerking up and sideways, Jared found himself on the floor between the fireplace and TV, and the two couches that formed an L. It was still dark out. The sharp ache of loneliness was quickly supplanted by the searing pain of his chafed eyeballs. Dragging himself to his feet, he hurried up the stairs as quickly as his sluggish legs could take him, and he staggered to the long bathroom counter and mirror along one wall in the cul-de-sac formed by three closed doors: one to his room, one to Nate's, and one to the toilet the two of them shared. The counter with two sinks was immaculately clean on Nate's side and filthily cluttered on his.

Not even bothering to wash his hands, though sure he'd catch pink-eye for the umpteenth time, he clawed the flimsy plastic lenses out of his raw, irritated eyes. Not sure which cup he set them in, Left or Right, and not really caring, he hosed them down with disinfectant, then squeezed the saline bottle at his upturned face until it was wet from his forehead to the corners of his mouth, getting at least some of it into his eyes to sooth and relieve.

Gasping, he stumbled into his room and threw himself at his bed. His floor was littered with everything from laundry and broken shards of stepped-on CDs to empty bottles of whatever an under-aged drunk could get his hands on. Sometimes Vox, sometimes Thunderbird. His clothes still on, he writhed himself into a comfortable-enough position, reached behind him and fished his wallet out of his back pocket.

It flopped open, the translucent plastic ream of photograph sleeves tumbling out. Finding the four from the lovers' photo booth at the Palm Beach Mall, he browsed a moment.

The two of them laughing.

The two of them French-kissing, a little too obscenely.

Him blinking, her looking down. The one they'd screwed up but he would never throw away.

Then, finally, just them smiling together, cheek to cheek. He took that one out, throwing the wallet onto the floor. Stared at it, held it close enough to see without his glasses. He wouldn't cry. It wasn't possible. He just lay there and stared until he fell back asleep.

Florida, last Summer

Gwynn fell back on the waterbed, waves rolling out from beneath her and back again. She held the smoke as long as she could, gazing up at her reflection in the mirrored ceiling, watching her naked brown limbs tossed lazily on the rippling bed. She'd put those mirrors up not to watch some guy giving it to her from another angle, but out of sheer narcissism. She'd stare at herself, not Whomever, making her sexy little frowns, baring her teeth, licking her lips. Making faces at the camera she imagined herself in front of.

Her eyes closed, a slight frown creasing her forehead, and opened again halfway, seducing her reflection the way she suspected models did when they practiced. Her lips parted, letting tendrils of white smoke curl out. She brought a hand up to lay daintily on that arms shoulder. The other hand, holding the glass pipe her cherry of meth still smouldered inside, trembled.

Damn, she thought. The nightstand was too far away, and she certainly couldn't let go of the pipe before the cherry went out or it would tip over and set the sheets on fire. Like last time.

Her eyes went wide—sparkling blue surrounded by bloodshot whites—fixed on a lock of hair that draped across her face, erotically wayward. Brown! Her true color, that hideous, boring brown, was leaking out of her skull to mar the pristine blonde she'd worked so hard to get right. Weeks of painstaking experimenting with different tints to get that subtly varying effect *down the drain!*

Hurriedly, she swatted the lock away, hoping the exposed roots would be covered and not kill her buzz. Shit, too far that way. It became a battle, desperately rearranging her hair as quickly as she could, hoping she could be Perfect again before the moment passed.

There! Now, checking the cherry with a tilt of the pipe, shrugging when she saw it still burned, she set it down carefully within reach on the king-sized water bed, her coral-nailed fingers coming back to touch her hip suggestively. The other hand still held her hair bunched up above her, the elbow keeping her breast from flattening out in a spread. Her right knee rose to crook that leg and she pointed her toes gracefully...

And somebody knocked on the fucking door.

Bolting to her feet, the bed rocking and tipping the glass pipe over, she scrambled back to dry land. A dive at the nightstand knocked over the spray cans assembled atop it, making a racket she was sure the cops could hear. Fuck! Frantically scattering the cans, she found the air freshener but (shit!) it was Ozium first, to dispel the smoke, and *then* Lilac Dawn, or else it wouldn't work right. The hairsprays and keyboard dusters and whatevers clattered together as she looked for the Ozium.

The knock came again. Yeah, it was the secret knock, but you could never be too careful.

Armed now with both cans, she sprayed one here, then the other, then the first one over here, then the other, and a quick both-at-the-same-time for good measure. Dropped them both on the beige carpet, snatched her bathrobe from where it lay draped over the footboard, and tiptoed hurriedly into the living room.

Before answering, she went through the ritual, peeking out the window through the blinds (There was no squadcar out there in the parking lot, but that didn't really mean anything these days. The police came in all shapes and sizes.) then the eye-hole in the door. Her friend Mike stood outside. At least, it *looked* like her friend Mike. It could've been a pig disguised as Mike. Oh, what to do? Who could this person be, who was imitating Mike so perfectly he had even mastered the impatient sneer?

The cops that had pretended to be her friends before could never imitate their voices, even though many had come close. If it weren't for the sense-sharpening crank that howled through her, she might've fallen for their acts. She needed to hear "Mike's" voice, and called out as casually as she could.

"Whooooo is it?"

Her heart pounded as she watched the man shake his head. "It's Mike."

Yep, it was Mike all right. Slipping on the robe and tying the sash, pausing to part the revers just enough to show the right amount of cleavage, she opened the door. Shit, she realized. It hadn't even been locked.

"Damn, Mikey, you scared the hell outta me! *Please* don't do that again!"

"Gwynn, all I did was knock on the fucken door," he said, stepping in past her.

"Well, you know, these days—"

"Yeah, I know. They're even coming up through your plumbing."

She locked the door this time and turned to lean back against it, smiling demurely. "Sssso, what can do ya fer?"

"Oh, the usual. Got any lying around?"

"As a fatter of mact, I do. Have a seat."

Mike plopped down on the old threadbare sofa while she sauntered past. The sounds of haste and muffled curses as soon as she was out of sight made him frown and arch an eyebrow, but curiosity did not get the better of him. It sounded like a pillow fight in there, one that had stopped being friendly. The swishing and whumps and her panicked stage whispers of Oh-shit ohshit ohshitshitshit weren't really out of the ordinary. Neither was the acrid smell of something on fire.

He rolled his eyes. Gwynn Hutchinson was out of her cotton-pickin' mind. But damn, if she wasn't a hottie, though.

The frantic whumping subsided, followed by a long sigh of relief. A few wisps of smoke crept along the ceiling from around the corner, and the hiss of what sounded like spray paint made him shake his head and look around the Spartan apartment for something that might hold his interest. The place was barren, though. An old sofa. A beanbag seat, the seam torn with its innards spilling out.

In her kitchen, the microwave—chief culinary tool—had a glossy magazine page taped to the door, some young hunk posing in a lime green thong with his hands behind his head. When asked, she'd smile and say it was her television.

For the hell of it, Mike got up and moved quietly into the kitchenette. The refrigerator door opened with a low, drawn-out sucking noise, and he saw a half-full bottle of ketchup—no, *catsup*—and a full one of mustard, both of them squeeze bottles with dry overflow caked in dribbles down their necks. And a paper plate with a slice of pizza on it, the cheese coagulated and rubbery-looking. Aside from that, nada.

He closed the door gently and went back to the couch, plopping down again. A short while later, Gwynn reappeared with a Prince Albert can and sat down next to him.

"I can't get the lid off," she said sadly, holding it out for him and putting on her best doe-eyed expression. He tried to keep the sneer inside, but it was a struggle. Taking the can from her, he pulled the lid off with a loud pop and handed it back.

"Huh. I guess all that tugging loosened it enough."

"Yeah, I guess."

She pulled out one of the baggies and handed it to him. He held it up and wrinkled his nose at it.

"Dude, this isn't even close."

"Damn sure it! I measured it myself!"

"I don't care what it weighs," he said, tossing it into her lap. "You cut the shit out of it. I don't even have to open the bag to see it's almost pure talc."

"Mikey, you know I'd never do that to you. It must've been already stepped on when I got it. I guess those guys really saw me coming." She put on her pouty look and lowered her head so she could look up at him. "But you'll still buy it from me, won't you? I'll give you a discount on the next one. My phone bill is due and I don't have nearly enough to cover it. Hell, my rent's due next week and I don't think I can make that, either."

"That's not my problem, Gwynn," he tried to say, but he could see it *would* be his problem soon. His eyes flicked down to the nipple that had suddenly become exposed when her bathrobe's revers parted slightly. She pretended to blush and covered herself. Mike felt terrible about it, ashamed, and looked away.

They were quiet for a moment, then she pulled her left knee up to sit sideways, her ankle tucked underneath her, facing him. Her tone softened.

"You must've gotten a girlfriend, Mikey. Someone's been picking out what you should wear?"

"Huh? No...no, I'm still single."

"What then, did you hire somebody to dress you?"

He turned back to her, eyes wide, but frowning. "What're you talking about?"

"You're looking really good, Mike. That shirt really sets off your eyes." His shirt and eyes were brown, but that didn't really matter the way she said it. "And your *hair*. I always thought every guy should have a mullet."

"You uh, you really think so?" The smarter side of him knew she was lying, but he chose not to listen to it. God, she was pretty.

"Hell yeah, I do! I was pissed off when they said toughskin shirts were out of fashion. And really, how many guys can you say make corduroys look as good as you do? You need a great ass to pull off that outfit. Broad shoulders, too. It's a retro look, and you've nailed it, especially with those Keds. It gives you that homey feel. I like it."

She's fulla shit, he thought. No, she isn't. It's about time somebody agreed with my style. Christ, she looks so good. And oh shit, there's her nipple again! Don't look!

"You really think I'm going to fall for that?" he asked, trying to bluff his way through.

She put a hand to her chest, wounded. "I can't believe you just said that. Here I am, just—"

"Sorry. I'm sorry. Look, couldn't you just throw a little bit more in that baggie so I could at least get a buzz off it?"

"Mike. Michael. You know I can't do that. You don't want me to lose any money, do you?"

"Well, Christ, Gwynn! *I'm* losing money here."

"Well, don't look at it like that. Look at it like you're helping me out. I need this, Mikey. Bad."

"Shit…all right. Here." He paid her reluctantly. "And I hope you choke on it," he added, trying to make himself feel manlier about being a sucker. She reproached him for it with a look as she led him to the door and showed him out.

"Good-bye, Mikey. Thanks for all your help!" Gotta leave off on a friendly note. As soon as the door was locked, the bathrobe was back off. She hated dealing with these scummy types, wanted to steam-clean the couch after they'd sat on it. Comes with the territory, she reminded herself. Money's money, no matter how dirty the pocket you've got to reach into to get it.

In the bedroom, scowling at the burnt sheets, she sat on an undamaged spot and tugged open the nightstand drawer. The clutter inside was close to overflowing, and opening the drawer was always an ordeal because something was always falling over where it shouldn't and snagging. She wouldn't have it any other way, though. The nightstand's contents in one of her dresser drawers looked pitifully small, and if her little life clogged something up it felt so much better than it actually was.

She found her address book—also overflowing, for the same reason. There were pages falling out and folded up receipts with numbers scribbled on them, and business cards and scraps of cocktail napkin, and she leafed through these browsing through her regular customers. Picked up the phone and dialled a number at random. Fell back onto the bed and looked up at herself.

"Hello?"

"Hey, Pete."

"Gwynn! How you doing?"

"Oh, I'll live. What're you wearing?"

"Hmm? Jeans and a t-shirt. What're *you* wearing?"

"I got my Tommy jeans on, and a Tommy tee, with my white Nikes and no socks. And nothing else."

"Ooh, I'd like to see that," Pete said, but he sounded distracted.

"Well, you can, honey. Come on over. You need to get some stuff anyway, don't you?"

"Uh…yeah, come to think of it, I do. It'll be later, though. Charlie's on his way right now, bringing me some money. I've got to wait on him."

"Okay, sweetie, I'll see you when you get here. Bye-bye, now." Click. "Shit."

She tried another number, waited.

Answering machine.

"Shit!"

Another one. This time, someone more promising answered—Ian, that hunka hunka burnin' luhve.

"Lo?"

"Ian?"

"Hey, Gwynn. What's up?"

"I am. Whatcha wearing?"

Alexander Ferrar was born on a battlefield, and the first sounds he heard were the shots that killed his parents. He was reared by a cutthroat band of evil mercenaries, and he grew up hard, suckled as he was at the teats of war. He—okay, no, he wasn't.

He lives in Antigua Guatemala where he owns a restaurant-art gallery and a very popular exotic ice cream shop, and he has a beautiful wife. His grass is plenty green.

He's also the author of the *Heresy* series and *Icarus* trilogy of crime fiction novels, the sword-and-sorcery comedy *Saga of the Beverage Men*, the alternative history adventure *The Prince of Foxes*, and art collection *Variety is the Spice*.

But the other story sounded better, didn't it?

Made in the USA
Coppell, TX
11 December 2020